FAYE SNOWDEN

A KILLING RAIN

Book Two of the *Killing* Series,
Following *A Killing Fire*

This is a **FLAME TREE PRESS** book

Text copyright © 2022 Faye Snowden

FLAME TREE PRESS
6 Melbray Mews, London, SW6 3NS, UK
flametreepress.com

US sales, distribution and warehouse:
Simon & Schuster
simonandschuster.biz

UK distribution and warehouse:
Marston Book Services Ltd
marston.co.uk

Publisher's Note: This is a work of fiction. Names, characters, places, and incidents are a product of the author's imagination. Locales and public names are sometimes used for atmospheric purposes. Any resemblance to actual people, living or dead, or to businesses, companies, events, institutions, or locales is completely coincidental.

Thanks to the Flame Tree Press team, including:
Taylor Bentley, Frances Bodiam, Federica Ciaravella, Don D'Auria,
Chris Herbert, Josie Karani, Mike Spender, Cat Taylor,
Nick Wells, Gillian Whitaker.

The cover is created by Flame Tree Studio with
thanks to Nik Keevil and Shutterstock.com.
The font families used are Avenir and Bembo.

Flame Tree Press is an imprint of Flame Tree Publishing Ltd

flametreepublishing.com

A copy of the CIP data for this book is available from the British Library
and the Library of Congress.

HB ISBN: 978-1-78758-613-0
PB ISBN: 978-1-78758-611-6
ebook ISBN: 978-1-78758-614-7

Printed and bound in Great Britain by Clays Ltd, Elcograf S.p.A

FAYE SNOWDEN

A KILLING RAIN

Book Two of the *Killing* Series,
Following *A Killing Fire*

FLAME TREE PRESS
London & New York

To my boys, Khari and Zach –
you are loved beyond measure

PROLOGUE

Standing on a beach in northern California, Raven Burns wondered how killing a man could bring such peace. She bent and picked up a piece of dry wood and threw it as hard as she could toward the horizon now transformed into a ribbon of gold with the setting sun. The brown wood arced head over tail for a long time and a long way out. As she watched it travel she thought of Lamont Lovelle, the man who had driven her from her job as a homicide detective in Byrd's Landing, Louisiana by framing her for several brutal murders that he committed.

He began by killing a wealthy socialite who hated Raven. After he was done, Lovelle left the calling card of Raven's father, the notorious serial killer Floyd Burns. At the murder scene Raven found bright blue and fluorescent green glowing in the darkness beneath the bed. A peacock feather that said even though Floyd Burns was long gone, the daughter, Raven, was still here, the same daughter who had helped her serial killer father lure victims when she was a toddler, watched him kill again and again and was rewarded, Lovelle accused, with a job in law enforcement.

But Raven's career choice was no reward.

What Lovelle couldn't know was that the real so-called reward consisted of nightmares filled with screaming and blood and burning flesh, along with Floyd's voice in her head. The job was Raven's penance for the sins of her father, and frankly, what she thought of as her own sins for helping him. It was her one chance to make things right. Lovelle took that away from her. The very act of taking Lovelle out flooded her senses like a healing serum, made the rough edges of her mind smooth, the dark thoughts light. No wonder her father hadn't been able to stop.

But there was a difference.

Her father killed for pleasure. Raven killed out of necessity. Lovelle maimed her partner, killed the mentor who took her in after Floyd went to prison, and shredded her career as a homicide detective to ribbons. Like her father, Lovelle had a taste for killing. He ran when Raven exposed him as a killer, had almost gotten away with it. She had no choice but to go after him, and once again put things right.

Lovelle's death didn't trouble her. No. It was the peace that came after, warning her to stay as far as she could from her hometown of Byrd's Landing, Louisiana, the place whose soil grew killers like kudzu.

And then there was the voice of her long-dead father. After she hung up her detective badge, she hadn't heard him narrating her life in her head. But his cackle had returned the minute Lovelle fell with the double-tap to the chest from her sniper's rifle.

Can you stop after just one killing, Birdy Girl? Floyd asked her now. *Maybe you should dive into the ocean and keep swimming on out 'til you can pay your ole man a visit. Could save some lives.*

But there was no reason to swim out to sea until she couldn't anymore. She did nothing wrong. She squished a maggot. She did the world a favor. Turning away from the darkening water, she found the ball cap she had been wearing before rising from her beach chair to watch the sunset. She put the cap over her wet hair and pulled it over her eyes. She sat down and stuck both feet deep into the cool sand. Just another tourist watching the sunset. *As innocent as a brown baby rabbit,* Floyd said in her head.

She stayed that way for a long time, thinking. She missed Byrd's Landing. She missed the gumbo, the catfish, the bayou and, of course, her old partner, Billy Ray. She even missed the cruel humidity and the cloying smell of honeysuckle attacking her allergies. It was useless to resist. Byrd's Landing would reach out and claim her as one of its own regardless of how many miles she put between them or how many demons she slew.

But she wouldn't go back as a cop. She was done with the life. She would go as Jane Q. Citizen to prove that she had a right to peace just like everyone else. She would prove that she could be good, that she

was, in fact, a country mile different from her killer father. Besides, Billy
Ray was there, her friends, too, she thought as she drifted to sleep while
seagulls skimmed the folding waves.

"My decision," she mumbled, as if hearing the words out loud would
make them believable.

★   ★   ★

"Raven!"

In the fading sunlight was a boy atop a set of rickety steps that acted
as access from the resort to the beach down below. He was barefoot and
bare-chested, waving at her over the railing.

"Be careful!" she shouted back up at him.

His little head disappeared and she soon saw him bumping down the
steps while dragging a scooter behind him. He and that scooter were
never apart. He would spend hours on the sidewalks curving through
the resort's lawns while his mother slept off whatever her drink of
choice was the night before. What he planned to do with a scooter on
the beach was beyond Raven, but she knew that the thing was more of
a security blanket than anything.

He jumped from the last step and ran toward her, grunting with the
effort of maneuvering the scooter over the sand. He stopped cold when
he saw her face.

"What?" she said.

He edged closer. "For a minute you didn't look like yourself."

She cocked her head. "That's funny," she said. "I still feel like myself."

"I can come back if you don't feel like talking to anybody."

She bent over so she could see the brown freckles that draped over
his sunburned nose and cheeks. She tousled his thick, brown hair and
gave him her most inviting smile.

"I always feel like talking when it's talking to you. Where's
your mom?"

The smile forming on his face faltered.

"Sleeping."

Raven stood up and put her hands behind her back. "I see." She waited a few seconds before continuing, "You know what, Tommy? Your mama is missing out on a lot. I've had such a good time having you as my little buddy on my holiday."

The smile disappeared from his face. A shine of tears appeared in his blue eyes. "You leaving?"

"Yep."

"Oh."

She sensed he had more to say. She waited.

"Well," he said. "Will you? I mean, can you...?"

She wagged an index finger at him before he could finish, feeling only slightly guilty. "Now, now. Remember what we talked about."

"Vacation friends." He dropped the scooter and hung his head. He picked up a piece of driftwood lying on the sand. Just as Raven had done before, he threw it out to sea as far as he could. He wouldn't look at her.

"We only talk together when we're on vacation together, remember? No use trying to keep in touch when the vacation is over. You know why, right?"

"Because life will get in the way and we'll lose touch and we'll be sad eventually so it's best if we don't even try," he said.

"Exactly. If I come back and you happen to be here next year, we'll be buddies again. But not anywhere else."

"Are you coming back?"

"That depends," she said. "Are you coming back?"

"Don't know," he said. "We used to come every year when my dad was alive, but now that he's dead, I don't know if my mom is going to keep coming back here." He picked up another stick and started to draw patterns in the sand.

"Well, I don't know if I'm coming back, either."

"And friends don't lie to each other," he said.

"Nope, they don't lie."

He shaded his eyes and looked out to sea. "A whale," he said.

"I think those may be more like dolphins, buddy."

Three dolphins jumped cleanly from the water before twirling in the air and splashing back into the sea.

"Are you sad that you're leaving?" he asked.

"Sad that I won't see you anymore."

He rewarded her with the smile that she knew she could pull out of him. Tom Arthur craved attention and wanted to be liked. That's why she chose him. She had found the one person in the entire resort who would keep her secrets.

They watched the dolphins play for a while. And then she said, "Do you have something for me?"

"I wish I had my binoculars."

"Tom?"

"Oh, yeah," he said, as if just remembering.

He dropped the stick and stuck his hand deep down into the left pocket of his cargo shorts. The pointed tip of his tongue licked the corner of his mouth as he concentrated on getting the thing out of his pocket. He put it in her waiting palm, a look of pride on his face. She examined it for a moment or two, brushed sand from its screen, and peeled a Sour Patch gummy worm from its back case. Before she could say anything, he plucked the gummy worm from her fingers and popped it into his mouth.

"Tom," she scolded as a grin appeared on his face. And then, "Did you play with it?"

"Yeah, but only games. No calls, just like you said."

"Did it ring?"

"A couple of times but I didn't answer it. I let all the calls go to voicemail."

She waited for a moment, and said, "That's fine. That's real fine."

He squinted at the sparkling water before tilting his head at an odd angle. With one eye open and the other closed, he pointed his index finger and cocked thumb at the dolphins playing in the water.

"Did you keep track of where you took it like I asked you?" Raven said.

"Uh-huh," he said, and then, "Pow. Pow," punctuating each word with the recoil of his imaginary gun.

His actions unsettled Raven. If it were anybody else, she would say he knew what she had done. But that was impossible. Tom Arthur was barely nine.

"And where did you go when you had it?"

"To the pool," he said, now with his hands up to his eyes as if he were looking through the set of binoculars he had wished for earlier. "And then hiking with my mom down to the butterfly garden. She was sick, though. Couldn't keep up."

"Anywhere else?"

"To the restaurant with the pirate lady in front."

"And you wrote it all down, right?"

"Uh-huh." He reached down deep into his other pocket and came up with a piece of unlined paper. It was damp, the pencil marks smudged, the words misspelled as only a nine-year-old could misspell. He had written the day of the week she had been gone, the time of day, and where he had taken the phone during that time.

"Did anybody help you with this?"

He shook his head. "Nope. I did it all by myself. I'm pretty smart, you know."

She ran her fingers through his thick hair, smoothing it off his face.

"That's why I'm glad you're my friend. You are very smart, indeed."

"Did I do good?"

"You did real good," she agreed. "Real fine."

"Well, thank you for letting me play with it."

"You're welcome. Now there's just one more thing."

"What?"

"It's our secret, remember."

"Yes, our secret," he said emphatically.

She put the cell phone in the pocket of her loose jeans and turned back toward the water. She clasped her hands behind her back and contemplated the expanse of sea laid out before her. She didn't notice that Tom mimicked her stance.

Yes, she thought. Her father, the serial killer who had sown terror from California to Louisiana, was dead. And the man who carried on

Floyd's reign of terror – he was gone as well. She had made sure Lamont Lovelle would never walk this earth again. Even the ghost of Floyd had melted away back to hell where it belonged, only able to intrude from its depth with an occasional sentence or two. She was sure of it. She was completely and solely Raven Burns now. Not a cop trying to atone for her father's sins. The possibilities were endless. For the first time in her life she had the chance to chart her own path.

CHAPTER ONE

There was once this lawyer by the name of Ronnie True down in Byrd's Landing, Louisiana. He wasn't so much a good man as he was a human one. He had these good intentions, but he also had to deal with the needs of the flesh. He was a married man who took care of his family, but he was porn-addled and whore-addicted. He was charitable with his money but would lie in a lightning second to fill his pockets by one extra fifty-cent piece. And how he came by the money didn't matter much to him. He didn't give a hoot if he got it by honest work or defending some pervert against a scared, sixteen-year-old mama-to-be. His thinking was that there were a lot of honest, faithful folk in the homeless shelters.

Another thing about Ronnie was that he was a man who liked to hunt. He wasn't one of those hunters who couldn't bag more than a hangover on an overnight hunting trip. No. Ronnie was one serious man about killing animals. It was like he was born to it.

He mounted his kills on the oat-colored walls of his office. There was this shoulder mount black bear with teeth bared and claws out. The whole snarling face jutted so far out it looked like the thing was fixing to rip itself right out of the wall so it could get a taste of human flesh. Ronnie was able to face down what he would tell people was a monster and kill it, something that would have had a person of lesser determination fouling their underpants. Never mind that the black bear was the gentlest bear in the forest. His audience was still plenty impressed.

He had some pictures up on the wall, too, of course – Ronnie on a fishing boat in Florida with a big marlin swinging from the end of his line, his hair flying up like black wings on either side of his bald head. Then there was the picture with the dead elk and Ronnie standing beside it wearing fatigues in the middle of some tall yellow grass, grass so dry that it'd probably catch fire from an angry look.

But the bear was Ronnie's favorite. He'd tell all sorts of stories about the day he shot it – especially to new clients or other lawyers he was up against. *It thought it had ole Ronnie*, he would say, leaning way back in his big leather chair, *and you might've thought that too if you'd been there. But look*, and he would wave his hand, *now it's on my wall*. Ronnie fancied himself a tough son-of-a-sumpthin' like that politician who sent dead fish to people who riled him.

Ronnie was thinking about that bear now, about hunting, because for the first time since lifting a rifle when he was eight years old, he knew what the bear must have felt like, way deep down in his screaming insides, in that place that tried no matter what to hold on to this hell-bent earth. Because this time Ronnie wasn't the one doing the hunting. He was the one being hunted. And Ronnie wasn't running away or preparing to fight. Ronnie was just plain caught.

Another kick and he was sure his ribs cracked. The pain of that cracking spiraled along every single one of his nerve endings. He inch-wormed along the thick carpet of his office, trying to make it back to his desk, where he kept a loaded Smith & Wesson revolver in the bottom drawer.

For a blessed several long seconds the beating stopped. Ronnie thought it would finally be over. Maybe he wasn't worth it. A fish too small, or a doe not worth the bullet or the effort.

But no. It was just a change of weapons. He felt a whack across his back and knew it was the new 9-iron that he had been admiring while leaning back in his office chair that very morning. He screamed, arched his back. He begged, his words coming out wrapped in snot and blood. The only thing he got for his trouble was a return scream of rage. What he thought he heard was, "You were supposed to take care of him." And on each high note a slam of the 9-iron across his back, the pain so deep and long-lasting that he knew even if he survived, it would always be there lurking in his bones.

Even with the pain, the blood, the screams of rage, the Smith &

Wesson gave him hope. After all, it was a special edition with 'We the People' engraved all fancy on the barrel. He wouldn't let himself be prey. Not good ole Ronnie. He would reach the third desk drawer and then in a burst of energy he would pull from way down deep somewhere, he'd throw open the drawer, grab the gun and aim for the chest.

He did get there. But he wasn't near as fast as he needed to be.

Before he could bring the barrel up for the shot, he felt a barrel press against his own forehead. For a terrible instant he saw the light in the eyes of the person who wanted to erase him from earth. The third drawer, the Smith & Wesson, every dang bit of it was too late.

The bear that had been unmoving on the wall behind his desk all these years was now moving, its yellow teeth ready to tear out Ronnie's throat, the sharp claws going for his eyes. And he swore he heard it laughing. *At least you won't be killing anything else. At least more kids won't die, you witless piece of filth.* He started to say something, to beg some more, but then a jolt stunned all sound from his throat, scrambled his brains so that he couldn't catch a thought if it had walked up and slapped him in the face.

CHAPTER TWO

The first place Raven went when she returned to Byrd's Landing was a new restaurant that hadn't opened its doors yet. It wasn't the place she should've gone. She should've been visiting her foster brother, Cameron, who worked in the IT department of the Byrd's Landing Police Department. He told her he was dealing with something heavy and needed her support. But her first day back in town couldn't be the place that had caused so much misery.

The restaurant had a sign over the door. It was nothing fancy, just plain wood that spelled in red letters 'Chastain's Creole Heaven'. The restaurant was Billy Ray's way of making it clear that he wasn't going to let the town steal his joy. Not its love affair with crime, not the weather, and definitely not killers like Lamont Lovelle.

Billy Ray, her old homicide partner, finally had what he wanted, his own restaurant and a place for his father's recipes of gumbo, fried catfish, and shrimp and grits. For him it would now be coffee laced with chicory in the morning along with baskets of fried peach pies instead of dead bodies and the hunt for those who did the killing.

When Raven walked into the restaurant, he and Imogene Tucker were sitting at a card table on the otherwise empty hardwood floor. What had Lovelle called Imogene as he stood with a gun pressed to her head in the backyard of Billy Ray's shotgun house? That's right. He called her the 'bonus prize'. Before that, Imogene had been an investigative reporter for the Byrd's Landing local TV station. She dogged Raven's every step as Raven chased the town's latest serial killer. Imogene's singular ambition was to use the case as a stepping stone to a spot at one of the national networks. That was before Lovelle ditched the gun for a rope and proceeded to choke the ambition and life out of her. Raven saved her, but now, like Raven, Imogene was adrift. She still worked at the station as an on-camera reporter, but wouldn't do any more investigative work. Raven didn't have to wonder why. The trauma Lovelle inflicted side-lined Imogene.

Imogene and Billy Ray's heads were almost touching as they bent over a magazine. The tableau looked so intimate that Raven nearly walked out. It wasn't that she was jealous. This was Billy Ray, after all. He wasn't her lover and never would be. They had something more special. Every day they used to wake up, shower, clip their badges to their waistbands and have their first cup of coffee before willingly placing their lives into each other's hands.

That was enough for her.

She didn't want to interrupt him and Imogene because they looked so peaceful. And both of them deserved peace after what they'd endured.

"Hey there," Raven said in a soft voice.

They looked up. Billy Ray stared at her before saying, "Ain't you a sight for sore eyes."

"How sore?"

"I'd say going on about a year sore. Where you been?"

Raven pointed to an empty chair at the table. "Mind if I sit?"

"Nobody stopping you," he said. "I asked you a question. Where have you been?"

Stalling, she acknowledged Imogene with an incline of her head. Imogene returned her greeting with a nod of her own, but there was a wary look in her eyes. Billy Ray gazed at Raven for a moment longer before returning to the magazine. He flipped through a few pages with pictures of tables, chairs, and other restaurant equipment.

Breaking through the awkward silence, Raven asked, "Didn't you get my postcard?"

"I did."

"Didn't you see the picture of the beach on it?"

He nodded. "Saw that, too."

"Then why are you asking where I've been?"

He folded his arms and sat back. "Got a postcard three weeks ago. Where were you before then?"

"Rambling, roaming, getting right." She turned to Imogene. "How are you getting along?"

"I'm good. Welcome back."

"Thank you."

"You back for good?" Billy Ray asked.

She grinned at him. "Depends on what you mean by good."

He stopped flipping pages to study her face. "I mean good as in are you done chasing ghosts?"

"Or making ghosts?" Imogene countered.

Raven waited for Billy Ray to either rescue her or join in on Imogene's bad vibes. But instead he did nothing. He just gazed at her steadily. She draped the backpack she had been carrying over an empty chair.

"Nice place you've got here," she said.

He nodded without taking his eyes from her. "I'm thinking about how to furnish it. Thinking about getting most of the stuff second-hand. Chairs. Don't have to match. Dishes don't, either. But I want the tables to be the same." He held up the magazine.

"Interesting concept," Raven said.

"Not a concept," he said. "I don't like being wasteful."

"Some things need getting rid of," Raven said.

"Is this us talking in code about Lamont Lovelle?" Imogene said. "Is this how you do it when you shoot someone down in cold blood?"

"I don't know what you mean," Raven answered.

"Lamont Lovelle was killed about a week ago," Billy Ray said, his voice flat. "Shot down while crossing the street some place up in northern California."

"That's interesting."

"You telling me that you don't know?" Billy Ray asked.

"I'm telling you that I don't care."

"Did you do it?" Imogene challenged.

Raven tilted her chin at the scars around Imogene's neck.

"How are those healing up, Imogene? Did the doctor tell you that those marks will be permanent? Try cocoa butter. Maybe they'll fade."

Imogene touched the tips of her fingers to the scars around her neck. She shot Raven a dirty look and stood up, the chair scraping loudly against the dark floor. "I've got to go to work."

Raven watched as Imogene slammed out of the restaurant.

When she was gone Billy Ray said, "That wasn't necessary."

"She's got nerve being so judgmental," Raven breathed. "You two friends now?"

"She's been coming around since I got out of the hospital, checking on me."

"I bet."

"It ain't like that," he said.

"You mean she's trying to get a statement? An exclusive? Writing a feature article on the cop who was almost burned to death by a serial killer?"

He laughed roughly and touched the ridge of keloid scar that ran from the corner of his right eye and disappeared into his hairline. Compliments of Lamont Lovelle. "No, not that either. She's not up to anything, not my girlfriend, she's just a friend."

"Somebody better tell her that."

"Did you kill Lamont Lovelle?"

"Did you want me to?"

"I hate it when you do this."

He closed the magazine, pushed the pork pie hat he always wore back on his head and sighed.

"You really want to know?" she asked.

He looked at her for a long time. She held his eyes and thought about how she used to look deep into her own eyes every morning in the bathroom mirror. One green, one blue eye, just like her father's. And she thought now about what she used to see in them, her father beating and later stabbing her mother to death, and after that a trail of killings that still haunted her dreams.

What did Billy Ray see in her eyes? Did he see Lamont Lovelle through a rifle scope walking across the street to the Quiznos like he did every day for lunch? Did he see Lovelle come closer and closer before his shirt flowered red with blood? And did he see him collapse in the middle of the street, cars around him, horns howling in the bright afternoon sun? Billy Ray stared at her a few more seconds, and then finally, he grimaced.

"No," he said. "I really don't want to know."

She inclined her head to acknowledge the statement, picked up her backpack and placed it in her lap.

"So, what you up to next?" he asked.

"I'm not going back if that's what you mean. The chief can pound sand. I'm done with the job. I want a new life."

"Like what?"

"I don't know. Teaching, maybe, high school."

"You still at the apartment?"

"No," she said. "Lease ran out. Oral left me his place. I'm thinking about moving out there. In the meantime, I've got some rooms over at Mama Anna's."

"Oral's place doesn't sound like a new life to me," he said, his handsome face serious. "That sounds like you jumping both feet back into the old one."

She remembered Oral and his house with the purple wisteria winding around the porch posts and spilling over the pergola. She remembered the wide rooms, the hardwood floors of the warmest mahogany, and his garden, cherry tomatoes growing wild and untamed, and yellow cucumbers the shape of apples. Just thinking about the place made her smile. Oral was the man who supported her after her father was arrested. Her being in his house felt right.

"Do you think that's a good idea?" Billy Ray prompted.

"As long as I can get the blood off the walls."

"Why you always like this, Raven?"

She leaned toward him. "You don't understand, I'm not always like anything anymore. I've changed," she said. "And I'm serious. I'm going to clean up that place and get it livable again. It's not fair that Oral's place sits empty. Lovelle took Oral away from me, but I won't let him take his house away from me, too. Oral loved that place too much. In the meantime, I'm going to get my teaching credentials and start over."

"Here?"

"Here," she confirmed.

He grunted. "Must've spent a lot of money out there rambling. How are you going to make a living in the meantime, especially enough to get back to college?"

"I've got some savings," she said, before breaking out into a wide smile. "Besides, I'm hoping you can help me with that."

CHAPTER THREE

Raven's foster brother, Cameron, lived in a fourplex on Sugarloaf near to where Raven had her apartment before leaving town to chase Lovelle. The complex was new with clean lines that her linear-thinking brother would consider no-nonsense. He didn't think of home like most people. Home to him was anywhere he could park his gaming systems, have an occasional date sleep over, and change clothes.

She rapped on his door with their secret knock so Cameron would know it was her who had come a-calling. But the knock was unnecessary. He knew she was coming because he had called her as she left Chastain's. "Swing by tonight if you can, Sis," he had said. "We need to talk about *it*." She was just glad that *it* wasn't about Lamont Lovelle. Cameron wasn't the type to raise heavy subjects unless absolutely necessary. No, Cameron wanted to discuss a letter that he had received from an old high school flame.

In high school Georgia Height had been the love of Cameron's life. If it were physically possible he would have sunk right down into her warm brown skin just so he could experience life through her eyes. Raven had tried to tell him that this wish was more like possession than love. But he wouldn't listen. Maybe that was why Georgia turned tail and ran. Smart and going places, she had big plans. Those plans didn't involve a foster kid who had been passed from home to home like trash, and was still getting into trouble. She left high school without a backwards glance at the boy with the soulful eyes and tall hair.

"Raven!" Cameron said now from the doorway with both arms flung out from his tall, narrow frame. "How come you gone for so long?"

Instead of answering, she walked into the hug and held him tight, clapping his back loudly. She pulled back to look at him. The skin was tight around his big smile and his eyes held an anxious, worried look. Raven had the feeling that he was about to hurt more than he did when Georgia left him.

"Jeez," she said as she walked past him into the living room. "You still don't have any furniture?"

The place looked as if it were furnished by a teenager who had just won the lottery with the ticket his mama bought for him. Four armchairs resembling a row from a movie theatre faced an opposite wall with the biggest flat screen that Raven had ever seen. There were so many controllers and headphones on the coffee table that Raven couldn't tell if the table was wood, glass or made from two overturned milk crates.

"Don't hate. I got what I need," Cameron said. He pointed to a small table next to the kitchen that shared the living space with the sparse living room. "Rest your bones right over there. I'll grab something to drink."

Raven sat down while Cameron went to the refrigerator. He returned with two bottles of Fanta – grape for her, and orange for him. Raven took a long drink, not stopping until her throat burned.

Cameron laughed. "Same old Raven. Guzzle it up until you feel the fire."

"No other way to drink soda."

She knew it was a kid thing to do, but being around Cameron always made her feel that way. He wasn't always mature, but his ability to live from laugh to laugh made him a fun person to be around. Reaching past him to grab a stack of envelopes, she said, "What's this?"

"I dunno," he said. "Junk mostly. Keeps showing up in my box."

"You mean in your mailbox?" Raven confirmed, flipping through the unopened mail.

Sitting opposite Raven, one of his bony knees jittering to a rhythm playing in his head, he left the question unanswered. "You said on the phone that you staying at Mama Anna's?"

"Yes, indeedee," Raven said still perusing his mail.

"Well, if your rooms don't work for you, you welcome to stay here. No bed in the guest room but I could fix a pallet on the floor for you."

Raven shook her head. "Cameron, some of these look like bills. Postmarks are three months old."

His knee stopped jittering. He looked at her with a face as confused as a toddler's. "Who in the hell sending me bills through the mail? I pay my bills online."

She flipped a pink envelope over and showed him the return address. "This looks like your online bill pay didn't make the electric company happy."

She expected him to take it, but he didn't. Instead he said, "Is that why those mo-fos cut off my lights? Electric company needs to catch up with the times. Anyway, I fixed that when it went all dark and creepy up in here."

"You should open it."

"Why you busting my nuts? I told you I fixed it."

"Because I know you. You probably just slapped a Band-Aid over it. You fixed it just enough until it happens again."

"I ain't studying that, Raven," he said. "That's not why I asked if you could fit me into your busy schedule."

"Okay, then." She threw the pink envelope down on the table. "Where is it? This letter from Georgia."

"Damn," Cameron said. "Just like that? You got somewhere to be?"

"I'm surprised that you took time to open that one," she said.

"I had to," he said. "Her name was on it. Besides…" He stopped.

"Besides what?" Raven asked.

"It smelled like her, like I remember."

"You still remember how she smelled?" Raven said. "No wonder you can't stay in a relationship. Give it to me."

He reached into the pocket of his jeans and pulled out a crumpled envelope. He gave it to her. The stationery was light blue, heavy, and expensive-looking. She put it to her nose. Cameron was right. The envelope held the ghost of a faint, sweet smell, like cotton candy.

"Looks like Georgia had so much money that she didn't mind lighting dollar bills on fire," he said, motioning his now empty bottle of orange soda at the expensive stationery.

Raven ignored him, her eyes growing wider as she read.

Georgia was dead. Had been for several weeks, possibly more depending on when Cameron had finally decided to check his mail. Raven already knew that Georgia had become a civil rights lawyer, married well, and bought a house with a pool in the Point and a summer home in Florida. She built a reputation for community work, achieved all she dreamed of and more. What Raven didn't know and now read in the letter was that Georgia was living high off the hog right up until the time of her cancer diagnosis. Although she wasn't prepared for it, she handled it as she handled everything else in her life, with a courage so strong that she could've put out the fires of hell if the task had been on her to-do list.

Bottom line was that Cameron had a son. The boy was fourteen years old, and his name was Noe Cardova. Georgia and her husband had been having trouble, and he made it clear that after she died, he wanted nothing to do with Noe. Georgia ended the letter without drama and without apology. Since Noe now had nobody, he had become Cameron's responsibility. It was likely the most impractical thing she had ever wanted in her short life, but Georgia wanted Noe to be raised by blood.

"God, she sounds cold," Raven said.

"Well, she had to be if she left all this," Cameron said, waving his hands over his face and chest.

Raven shook the envelope until two pictures fluttered onto the table. They were of a boy with clear brown skin and only one dimple on the left side of his beautiful mouth, just like Cameron, who used to joke that the one dimple proved that everything about him was half-ass on purpose. Even God was in on it.

"Well," said Raven. "What are you going to do?"

He gave her a confused look. "A letter, Raven? Not an email or text? If she didn't have my number, the broad could have at least DMed me."

Raven didn't laugh. Instead she replaced the letter and pictures into the envelope. "You can't joke this away."

He took the letter from her and took out the pictures again. He stared at them for a long time. "Looks like my dad."

There was a wistful look on his face that Raven had never seen before. "Looks like you."

"I'm thinking that she's wrong about little dude's stepdad. They got married when that kid was four. I can't believe that the brother's gonna give him up like that."

Raven raised an eyebrow. "Your parents didn't mind giving you up."

She didn't mean to be cruel, but she wanted to make sure Cameron knew what he was getting into. He had a steady IT job down at the Byrd's Landing Police Department, but his lifestyle wouldn't accommodate a kid. Instead of a girlfriend of the month Cameron had a girlfriend of the week. Given the choice between a video game, a week's worth of groceries or a new pair of shoes, he'd laugh and say, "Who needs to eat anyway? Besides, if I get hungry I'll just wait for a potluck or until someone has cake in the breakroom."

"My dad was sick, Raven," he said. "And so was my mom. My dad may have walked away and left me, but as you like to forget, he came back. That man fought hard to get me back when he got better. He took care of me."

"Right up until the day he backslid and you watched him overdose."

"Do you have to be so damned mean all the time?"

Raven spread her hands. "I just call 'em like I see 'em. It's a big responsibility, Cameron. If you're going to do this, you have to be ready. You can't look at this through rose-colored glasses, or because you see it as a do-over for your father."

"It's not going to matter, anyway. If the stepdad doesn't want the boy for his sake, then he'll want him for whatever she left him. This ain't going to be a problem for me."

"So, why did you want to talk about it if it isn't going to be a problem?"

"You know how we always used to talk about what we wanted to be when we grew up?"

Raven said nothing.

"Well, you wanted to be a cop. I just wanted to be clean. And when you asked what I meant by that, I said that I didn't want to leave a mark on this world. Not one goddamn mark on the street corner where I had to hold a sign in raggedy-ass clothes begging for my parents' drug money, not on the foster homes that didn't want me, or the teachers who said I was no damn good, and I better get ready for the graveyard or a jail cell. I told you that when I grew up, I just wanted to have a job playing on computers and enough money to have fun until the day I died. I wanted to travel, try new things. And when this life was over all I wanted was to be a scent on the wind for a second, and then nothing."

"I remember that," Raven said. "No responsibilities."

"Yeah, right." He laid the photo on the table. He let out a long breath, reached out a finger and tapped Noe's face. "This makes me want to jettison that bullshit thinking. I want to fight for him like my dad fought for me, except I want to do right by the boy."

"This kid isn't one of your games, or one of your adventures, something you can try and say 'oh hell, oh well' if it doesn't work before moving on to the next bright shiny thing."

"I know that."

"I don't think you do."

"I just think it'll be fun having a little mini me running around here," he said. "Keep me company. I can teach him how to level up on *Call of Duty*, to sing all the words to every song Wu Tang ever wrote...."

"He's a fourteen-year-old boy who just lost his mother, and is about to be abandoned by the only father he's ever known. He isn't going to want to play video games."

"There ain't a teenager on this side of the Mississippi who don't like video games, especially the way I play them. The tournaments—"

"Everyone is not like you. You have a stack of bills that you don't even know if you paid or not. How are you going to raise a kid?"

"I got a lot of love."

Raven believed that Cameron indeed had a lot of love and compassion, but it was way deep down inside of him. He was willing to give it, too, as long as it didn't get in the way of what he wanted.

"You aren't ready to be a father. That boy will be a stranger to you. You'll have to help him navigate his new life without his mother.

You'll have to do some very grown-up things, things I've never seen you do voluntarily."

She stopped talking, and sat back. He waited for a beat or two, his face both wistful and serious.

"That's why I asked you here. I want you to help me."

"Help you? Help you, how?"

"Well, when you were running around in Cali, I talked to Georgia's lawyer. She told me that if I want Noe to live with me, I'll have to prove that I'm fit. Make sure my place is suitable and all, and I'm not after the money."

"Money?" Raven asked.

"Yeah, the boy has a trust fund. He's on her insurance policy, too. I guessed Georgia was living large. Like you always say about stuff like this, they gonna be up my ass with a microscope."

"That's smart. I'd do the same thing."

"That's why I need you to tell me what I need to do, what furniture and shit I need to buy. Help me get him in school and crap. I know I got a problem being a grown-up. So, help me. I mean, who sends bills in the mail anymore?"

"Don't let sentiment mess with your head, Cam. This is a bit more than you can chew on, I guarantee you that."

"I know that," he said. "But he ain't got nobody, Raven. I was like that, once. You, too. We can make a difference. I ain't perfect, I know, and I know I won't be a perfect daddy, but at least I can try. So, will you help me?"

"It's not like a new puppy."

"Well, thank God for that. At least he won't piss on my carpet."

She folded her arms across her chest.

"Okay, I'm kidding. I know he's not a puppy," he said.

"And you'll have to buy a couch."

"I can buy a couch, an armchair, hangers, whatever."

"And you can't run away when it gets hard."

"Ain't about to do that. You gonna help me or not?"

"Of course, I'm in. But, please, Cameron. Please don't let this child down."

CHAPTER FOUR

Several months later Buckwheat Zydeco's live version of 'Hot Tamale Baby' exploded from all four speakers tucked in the corners of Billy Ray's Creole restaurant. What was it that Billy Ray had always said – you weren't human if you can listen to zydeco without moving your feet? Raven was sure he didn't say it first, but he adopted the saying as his own. And hot damn if it wasn't true, she thought.

She tapped her foot as she waited for table five's order. Zydeco, Billy Ray, and her friends were home to her. Leaving California was the right decision. Like the song said, she was definitely, at this very moment, all right. The evenings were filled with the zydeco bands Billy Ray hired to play and the best shrimp gumbo this side of the Red River.

But his dream came at a high price that he paid with his nightmares. She knew he had them. She had them, too. Stealthy, evil little things that slunk into her skull while she slowly fell asleep, the images dragging her so far down that she couldn't even scream.

The bell jingling over the restaurant's door reminded Raven where she was. She didn't notice the tall man who walked in and sat in her section. But Imogene, who had come to stand beside Raven, did. She wasted no time calling Raven's attention to him.

"Oh my, my," Imogene said with one hand on her round hip and the other across the open collar of her silk, light blue shirt.

Raven glanced in the direction of Imogene's gaze. She chuckled. The man who had sat down was not only handsome, but sexy in such a dangerous way that Raven thought if Imogene were wearing pearls she would have clutched them.

He shrugged out of his jacket to reveal a broad, muscled chest covered by a tight button-up shirt. She couldn't tell the exact color of his eyes at this distance, but with the early afternoon light pouring through the tall windows, Raven wouldn't be afraid to bet that regardless of the color, his eyes were as attractive as his face. He saw them both staring at him and winked. Imogene responded with the thousand-watt smile she used on camera at her job as a local TV news reporter.

But now, she spent most of her time at the restaurant for what she called 'helping Billy Ray'. Raven suspected that it was the PTSD Imogene was running from, and a potential relationship with Billy Ray that she was running toward. Raven kept her face frozen in just the way Floyd taught her when coming into contact with something new and possibly dangerous. *Now, don't go smiling at no snakes, Birdy Girl*, he would say, *not until you sure a rattler ain't attached to the other end of its tail.*

"He's all yours," Raven told Imogene.

"As if he were yours to give away."

Raven balanced two plates on her right forearm and clasped another one in her right hand, a move she had been practicing for the past month. Since Billy Ray liked to serve his food steaming hot, she could feel the heat starting to burn a tattoo onto her forearm. Raven grabbed another steaming plate with her left hand.

"Yep, you're right about that," she said, looking with satisfaction at the plates. "Not mine to give away. But kind of disappointing if you ask me. Just what this place needs, another cop."

"Oh." Imogene turned to her. "Do you know him?"

"Nope," Raven said and started to walk away.

"Then how can you tell he's a cop?"

Any other time Raven wouldn't have been so indiscreet. But Billy Ray's was jumping. The imitable and now ubiquitous Buckwheat Zydeco at Chastain's Creole Heaven was pumping through the speaker. The music was accompanied by the happy but raucous hum of what was starting to be the restaurant regulars. She caught snatches of conversations around her and bursts of laughter. No one was paying attention to the help. And she certainly didn't think the object of their discussion could hear them from across the room.

"I can tell he's a cop because he has that predator look about him."

"Cops are predators?"

Raven grinned, not knowing how much like Floyd she looked at that moment.

"I know that's surprising, but cops and criminals both hunt. They just hunt for different things. And besides, his head is on a swivel. He's hyper-aware."

Raven could tell that Imogene was about to say something else, but Raven cut her off.

"These plates are hot. Gotta keep moving."

"Be my guest." Imogene stepped out of the way. "And I'm giving him back to you." She glanced toward the kitchen to where Billy Ray's back was visible. "My dance card is full."

Raven shook her head and took the plates to the corner of the restaurant that had been nicknamed the 'old folks' corner' because some of Byrd's Landing's oldest citizens claimed the live-edge slab of mahogany as their own. Raven teased Billy Ray about the expense, reminded him of his mantra to refuse new, to reuse and re-purpose. He just said he liked the idea of serving his shrimp and grits on a slice of Africa.

When there wasn't any eating going on in the old folks' corner, you could hear the slap of dominoes against the hardwood, or a cackle of victory as Mama Anna destroyed her spades opponents. And every once in a while, there was the musical roll of dice and a few dollars changing hands.

"Hey, hey," she said as several sets of brown hands reached for the plates. "Be careful. Hot. Hot."

"I can see," said an old man in a beret covered in Korean War patches. "Very hot."

"Now don't go abusing the help," Raven said. "Nowadays they call that sexual harassment, Mr. Joe."

"Well, the help shouldn't look so good," someone else said.

"Shut up, ole man." This came from Mama Anna, who was sitting at the very end of the mahogany live-edge slab. "You wouldn't know what to do with it if it fell on you."

"Probably gum it to death," the man sitting next to Mr. Joe said.

To this there was a lot of foot stamping and table slapping. Even Mr. Joe laughed before pulling out a handkerchief to wipe sweat from his face.

"Y'all some nasty old people," Raven said. She placed a fist on her slim waist. "Now I see you got water. Need anything else?"

"Sho' smells good," Mama Anna said.

"Smell better than yo' cooking," Mr. Joe said.

"You ain't never tasted my cooking, nor will you *ever*," Mama Anna responded.

Raven broke in the laughter that had erupted with, "Anything else?"

She pulled straws from the pocket of the white half-apron fitted snugly around her jeans.

Everyone turned their attention to the food. They inspected the plates of gumbo and shrimp creole as if in very serious contemplation of her question.

Then Mr. Joe said, "Yo' phone number?"

There was more laughter as Raven walked away. She heard Mama Anna say, "Joe, you crazy," before hollering after Raven, "Bring me some hot sauce, baby."

Raven walked to the sideboard chuckling to herself. She grabbed a bottle of Louisiana Hot and brought it back to the table. They were too busy with the food to notice her. She couldn't remember the last time she had a conversation like that – one that made her smile so much that she was sure that for the first time in a long time her eyes sparkled.

But she never felt so safe before, so peaceful. For one of the few times that she could remember, she was happy. Maybe that's what Billy Ray had brought to the town by opening this restaurant. It had become an oasis in a place otherwise beset by crime, corruption, and weather so uncomfortable that you would think the heavens were doing it as a punishment.

"Raven."

She looked up to see Billy Ray with a half-smile on his face. He jerked his head to the lone man sitting at the table near the door, the man she and Imogene had noticed earlier. Raven nodded and made her way over to him while saying hello to several people. She knew he watched her. She could feel his eyes on her as she drew near. *Cop*, she thought. *Definitely cop*. In her experience no one but a cop would look at a person that way, making what Floyd used to call 'them Sherlock Holmes conclusions', something about not only seeing but observing. That was the way Floyd chose his victims. He would stalk and observe. Wait for a vulnerability and then strike.

Or maybe, the happy side of Raven interrupted her thoughts, *the mysterious man sitting by himself just likes the way you look.* She shook that thought away, and she did it fast. She was just starting to get her life – a new life – together. She didn't need a man to complicate it. And there was no way that she would allow herself to be careless. She would always look for the rattler.

He glanced at her as she said hello and slid a menu in front of him. Brown. His eyes were dark brown and intense. She took the order pad from her back pocket and reached for the pencil behind her ear.

"You need a minute with the menu? I can get you something to drink first."

He picked up the single sheet of thick paper she had placed in front of him. "Not a lot to choose from."

"Some would say, but everything Billy Ray cooks is good, and quality."

"Billy Ray is the...."

"Owner." She had the feeling that he was trying to stall. She didn't like it. "What can I get you to drink?"

"I don't need a drink first," he said. "I think I can go ahead and order now."

"Okay." She waited with the pencil poised over the pad.

He sighed again. "I don't know what's good here."

"I just told you, everything."

She made herself smile to mask her frustration. It wouldn't do for her to ask another customer if they could read. Billy Ray's patience only stretched so far.

"Anything specific?"

"That depends," she said. "What do you like?"

A slow, lazy smile spread across his face. His teeth were straight and white. He was looking at her in a way that would give Imogene a heart attack. But she wasn't Imogene. She tapped the eraser end of her pencil against the pad and waited.

"Well," she prompted.

The smile faltered and was replaced by another. This second smile was more authentic. She could almost see the cogs spin behind his eyes as he considered another line of attack. Flirting, she realized. It had been so long since she flirted with anybody that she didn't recognize the beginnings of it. But she was in no mood to practice.

He rushed on. "I really don't know what I want. It's my first time here and I'm just looking for good food. The, what do you call it, the rooming house recommended it."

"So, you're staying at Mama Anna's rooming house, not the hotel?"

Mama Anna had a rooming house on the outskirts of town, not an Airbnb, but an old-fashioned rooming house where you inquired about rooms at the front door and dinner was served free every night. She started letting rooms to visitors and people down on their luck when she could no longer afford the upkeep or the property taxes. Her daughter ran it now, which was the reason Mama Anna could spend so much of her time at Billy Ray's.

"Yeah, I'm here on business but wanted to stay someplace local," he said. "You know, get the local flavor."

She waited but said nothing. It wasn't lost on her that she was also staying at Mama Anna's, and she needed to be careful. There was something about this man that made the hair stand up on the back of her neck.

"I just don't know what's good here," he said, giving her what Floyd would call a sorrowful puppy-dog look.

"The seafood gumbo is always on point," she said. "It's always hot, and we'll probably run out soon. If that's too spicy for your first time, Billy Ray makes a mean po'boy. How about we get you some po'boys?"

"That sounds fine," he said as the conversation hummed around them. "Does Billy Ray do all the cooking?"

"Yes, do you know him?"

He shook his head. "Why would I know him?"

"He used to be a cop."

He stared back at her blankly. "I didn't know that. The rooming house just said it was a good place to eat."

"Mama Anna's daughter isn't a bad cook," Raven countered.

"I know. But she doesn't cook every night. And sometimes, you know, she just phones it in. The other night she made some tamale pie out of a mix and a can of chili."

Raven knew but she kept her mouth shut. She wondered why she hadn't seen him around at the rooming house, but then again, she kept to herself there, ate in her room, used the back exit a lot. Most of her time was at Billy Ray's.

"You want something to drink with those po'boys?"

He leaned back and placed both arms along the booth. "Man, you're a tough crowd." He laughed.

She didn't respond.

"You got any IPA?" He said it like a challenge.

"Plenty. I'll bring you a couple of shrimp po'boys and the best IPA we have in the house. Ice cold. Will that do?" she said as she swept the menu away from him. She didn't care if it did 'do' or not, that was what he was going to get.

"I guess it'll have to," he answered.

She gave him another look before tucking the pencil behind her ear and walking away. She could feel him watching her as she weaved through the tables. Handsome, she thought. And funny probably. Raven liked funny. Her dad was funny.

Later, after she brought him his food, she leaned against the bar watching him as he destroyed the sandwiches Billy Ray had made for him. She thought about Jean Rinehart. Her dad had picked up her stepmother in a restaurant. Abe's Diner out in the country. Look how that turned out. Jean became just another one of ole Floyd's victims.

Raven chuckled before pushing the thought into a corner of her mind and turning the key to the closet where she now kept such morbid memories. When her mind was clear again, a voice said, *You don't have to marry him, but what about having a little fun?*

But Raven wasn't thinking fun. She was thinking cop in spite of that blank look that he gave her when she asked him if he knew Billy Ray. She should try a little harder to find out who he was and what he was doing in Byrd's Landing. She released her lean against the bar and went back to the table carrying a clutch of paper napkins.

"Thank you," he said through a mouthful of sandwich. And even though he was chewing as he spoke, he did it in an attractive way that Raven couldn't help but think was put on.

"This one is about gone." He displayed the greasy cloth napkin that Billy Ray insisted on using at the restaurant. "Who knew butter could taste so good?"

She smiled, not too warmly, and picked up the empty beer glass. "Another?"

"Just a minute."

He touched her wrist, and she gave him back the glass.

"Now I'll have another," he said after draining the glass of the foam that had been laced along the bottom.

As she took the empty glass from him, she said, "So, you said you were here on business? Where are you from?"

"California."

Raven felt her mask slip before she could right it into place again. It was only for a second, but she wondered if he noticed.

"Have you ever been there?" he asked.

She had the feeling that he was studying her very carefully. She picked up his now empty plate. Anyone else, maybe one of the regulars, Raven would have asked if he had licked it. She didn't have to wonder too long what he would do with that line.

"A few times," she said vaguely to forestall any more questions in that area.

"Business or pleasure?"

Raven's laugh was genuine. "Yeah," she said. "From the last waitressing convention. It was a blast. What brings you to Byrd's Landing?"

"You really want to know?"

"Did I really just ask?"

He looked around the restaurant in an exaggerated check to see if anybody was listening. He motioned for her to lean in closer. Only when she was close enough to smell him did he say, "I'm a scout."

She waited.

"I'm here on a secret mission."

"Let me guess," Raven said, straightening and laughing, "CIA agent?"

"Shhh!" he said, using the opportunity to grab her wrist. "You'll blow my cover."

"Cover?" Raven said, the laughter dying down a little.

"Yes."

So, she was right. Cop. But his playful manner confused her.

"Not CIA," he said. "I work for a company that makes movies. I'm a location scout."

"What's so secret about that?" Raven said, the amusement returning to her voice, the sparkle back in her eyes.

"I scout locations for a very large movie franchise. I can't tell you which one because, you know," he stopped and looked around. "The competition."

"Yeah, right."

"I'm serious. Why don't you believe me?"

"Because you got that look about you, walking into a room noticing everyone and everything that's there, one of those eager beaver cops who's never off the clock and can't stay away from the gym."

"You know a lot of cops?"

"I know a few," she said.

"Gyms aren't just for cops." He gave her a pointed look. "Sure you know that."

Raven didn't reply. He had her there. She spent almost every free hour at the gym or running the trails in Ronald Gold State Park. She'd also been learning jujitsu for both fitness and fun. Aside from Billy Ray's, the gym and the state park were her only two other happy places.

"So, location scout, huh?" she said finally.

"Yes, we don't advertise to keep the competition from knowing what we're up to."

"But you're telling me?"

"You're not the competition," he said.

"I see," she said, beginning to turn away.

He tugged at her sleeve. She looked down to see him handing her a business card.

"Give me a call if you ever want to go hunting with me."

★   ★   ★

Later, when the restaurant had calmed down, she took the business card from the back pocket of her jeans and studied it. Billy Ray came to stand beside her.

"Who was that, anyway?" he said, his eyes flicking toward the table where the man had sat.

"Mr. Wynn Bowen. Location scout."

"Locations for what?"

Raven shook her head. "Big movies. Franchises. Showbiz," she said and wiggled her fingers to show jazz hands.

Billy Ray gave a skeptical grunt. "I don't like him."

"You didn't even talk to him."

"Didn't have to. I saw him talking to you. I don't like his look. Be careful."

"Wow," she said. "Paranoid much?"

"I am," he said. "And if you know what's good for you, you would be, too."

CHAPTER FIVE

Wynn hadn't told her that the place she was supposedly helping him scout was at least an hour away, near the delta and almost out of Byrd's Landing proper. On top of that he gave her a paper map.

"Now I know you work for the CIA," she said from the passenger seat of his rental car, which was parked at Mama Anna's rooming house.

He turned to her and smiled a slow, easy smile with just the right amount of sexiness.

When he called her saying he needed a local to help him scout a location, she agreed despite her suspicions. She wanted to know more about him. Doing so under the guise of a date or helping him was far better than a background check. If he were undercover she would have learned nothing other than what he had already told her. Electronic files and databases would've been doctored to bolster his fake identity. At least this way she could read him, as Floyd would say. Or that's what she told herself anyway. The hopeful part of her craved the normalcy dating would bring to her new life.

He leaned over in a pretense of seeing the map closer. Their faces almost touched.

"I brought a map," he said, "because you can't really trust GPS so far off the beaten path."

"I thought that's why you brought me along, because I know the place? And yet you bring a map and don't tell me where we're going. Exactly why am I here?"

"For company. I hope that's okay," he said as he started the engine and slid the car onto Morning Glory Road.

Raven left that alone. Instead, she asked, "You ready to tell me what movie this is for?"

"No. I told you. Big secret."

"You sure you aren't CIA? A cop?"

"Damn," he said. "Can you cut me at least one break? I'm just a guy trying to get a girl to like me."

She knew she should have said something, but for some reason, and for some hopeful part of herself, she let it go. They were silent for quite a while, but that didn't bother Raven. She had long ago trained herself to be comfortable with long silences. Silences had a way of making people talk in an effort to fill the void, especially guilty people.

She turned her attention to the map. Raven didn't remember the last time she read a paper map. She used to do it with Floyd, though, her index finger lightly trailing the red and light blue lines that looked like the veins and arteries of California, Texas, New Mexico, and finally Byrd's Landing. GPS just wasn't the same.

"This is an interesting town," he said in the silence.

She smiled. "Does the turn in the conversation mean that you're all done with flirting?"

He turned a rueful face toward her. "I'm sorry about all that. But I do like you."

"You don't know me," she said. "It's your pants talking."

He laughed. "Are you this sure about everything?"

"I'm sure about nothing."

"If you think it's my pants talking then why did you agree to go with me?"

She looked out of the window at the trees of Byrd's Landing whipping by. Tall, thin white trunks clustered together.

"I agreed because I thought it would be fun," she said, deciding on the truth. "I needed a break."

They drove until they slipped the skin of the town proper and entered the sparser areas of Byrd's Landing. Water. So much water, wide and flat and glimmering in the sunlight. Further on lay the broad back of the Red River where a short time ago, but also in another lifetime, she had almost drowned. That water was thick and brown. She imagined the river and its banks swarming with diamondbacks. Beneath its surface were the hissing voices that almost undid her. The horror was as necessary to the town's beauty as the purple irises that sometimes grew wild in the fields.

"Great place for a movie," Wynn said.

"It's got a certain feel," she said. "That's why my dad and I moved here."

"Your dad still alive?"

"Nope. Died. In prison."

His grip tightened on the wheel as he glanced over at her. "Sorry to hear that."

"What about you? Your parents alive?"

"Yes, both of them. Retired. In Florida if you can believe that. They are two walking clichés."

"How long have you been divorced? Or are you separated?"

"How do you know I'm divorced?"

She laughed. "How could I *not* know? You obviously suck at flirting."

"I do?"

She was laughing fully now. "Yes, very obvious. And awkward."

"Okay, okay. I am divorced."

"How long?"

"Feels just like yesterday, but it's almost a year now," he said.

"Should I say I'm sorry?"

"It would be nice. As you might have guessed, I didn't want it. I travel a lot as you can see. And I'm a bit of a workaholic. I admit it, I am." He looked over at her. "I was raised that you put the job before anything, before your family, yourself, before everybody."

"Before God?"

"Now don't get like that. You a religious person?"

She thought of Floyd. "My dad was a preacher."

He didn't say anything for what seemed a long time. And then, "Not before God. God was first, your job was second, and your family was third because I was taught that you wouldn't have a family without a job. But my wife and I didn't see eye to eye on that."

"And now all you have is the job," she pointed out.

They drove for a few moments in silence before he spoke again. "That's one way to look at it. I still have my faith, though. That's what drives me."

"Faith in what?" she asked.

"What do you mean faith in what?" He laughed. "God. The Bible. You know, right and wrong. People who risk it all to set things right."

"Like cops?" she probed.

"Them, too. They don't have an easy job."

"So you like cops?" she asked.

"I like anybody who's willing to sacrifice in order to make sure people do right."

"Who decides what's right, Wynn?"

"Nobody decides. It's in the Bible, in our laws. Somebody decides for us."

"Wow," she said, meaning it. "You sound like a goody two shoes."

"Okay, I'm getting on my soapbox. Sometimes I'm too passionate about assholes who get away with things. I'll zip it for now."

Good, Raven thought, because he was becoming less appealing by the word. For a minute she thought he was going to ask her for an 'amen'.

"Kids?" she asked to make sure the subject about God and laws and right and wrong was good and changed.

He held up two fingers. "A boy and a girl, ten and twelve. Got some work to do there."

"I bet you do," she said. "You still have feelings for your wife?"

"No," he said, drawing out the word. "At least I try not to."

"Well, that's honest."

"Yeah." He laughed. "I may suck at flirting, but at least I'm honest. Can we not talk about this, please?"

"Suit yourself."

The peaceful silence that followed surprised Raven. She found herself enjoying the hum of the tires and the wind rushing past as she guided Wynn along Byrd's Landing's twisting roads. She enjoyed the smell of him, the light tang of his aftershave.

Shortly after, they were bumping along a dirt road that curved to the left. Raven could see birch trees outside her window, and a thin stand of eucalyptus. Barely visible among the trees was a ragged roof of an abandoned farmhouse surrounded by a broken-down fence. She noticed a shed, too, looking a little more solid than the farmhouse, but still old, unused.

He drove on for another three hundred yards or so until they were surrounded by land that stretched around them for miles. Some of it was covered by a thin layer of bright water with cypress trees rising from it, their branches hanging with red and gold leaves that flamed against a gray sky. Birds cawed, their cries sounding like grief as they dipped in and out of the water. Several white whooping cranes, bright against the steel blue of the wetlands, skimmed the surface of the glinting stillness.

Wynn parked and got out. Raven followed suit, still clutching the map.

"I don't think this is a part of Byrd's Landing," she said, looking alternately from the map to the land beyond her.

They stood with their shoulders touching. Raven didn't mind it too much.

He placed his finger on the map alongside hers. "It is, see. All of Kingfisher Road is still within the boundaries."

She looked where he tapped. "Barely. Just barely. What kind of movie are you shooting way out here?"

He was shaking his head before she got the words out. "Sorry, sworn to secrecy."

She looked back at the farmhouse and the abandoned farm. The occupants probably fled when they realized that the still water would soon swallow the place.

"Those wetlands could be protected habitats," she said. "Wouldn't that put a stake through the heart of your dastardly plans?"

He took the map from her and stared at it for a moment or two before saying pensively, "It's not. And this is a new map. It's not marked as protected."

"Well, it's going to get protected when you and your movie crew start tearing it up."

"We don't plan on tearing it up," he said. "Even if we do, it'll mean a lot of jobs for the natives."

"Natives? Is that how you see us?"

"I don't see you any kind of way," he said. "A movie here would be good for the town."

Raven grunted. "So you say."

"I need to take some pictures, and record some information about exactly where we are."

He went to the car and brought back a Canon camera. He began fiddling with the lens and controls. She heard the shutter as he started taking pictures of the area. After snapping a few, he went back to the car, and grabbed a laptop. After a few minutes he put the laptop down, started up with the pictures again. She whipped toward him.

"I'm sorry," he said. "I couldn't help myself. You mind?"

"Yes, I do."

"Sorry," he said. "They won't end up on Instagram."

"They better not."

"I'll delete them if it's a problem. You can watch me."

At first she was going to tell him he'd better, then decided against it. She'd have a lousy life if she went through it not trusting anyone. In homage to what she thought of as her new start, she caved. "Don't worry about it."

She twisted toward the abandoned farmhouse to the right of them. "What about that?" she said. "Somebody must still own this land, must have lived here once."

He pointed the Canon at the abandoned house.

"I'll talk to them first, get permission. Most people love being part of movies, especially filming locations. They can hang a sign, put it on Facebook. If they still have a problem with it, we'll buy them out."

"What if they won't sell?"

"Doesn't look like they want it. Besides, everybody sells, baby," he said. "Everybody's got a price."

★   ★   ★

Three weeks later they were officially dating. Wynn had decided the location he had scouted off Kingfisher Road was perfect for the production, and, as he told Raven, that meant a lot of work, including back and forth with the production team to convince them that Byrd's Landing was the place. After that there would be permits and permission, or as Wynn put it, a fair amount of ass-kissing with the town council.

But Raven hadn't actually said the word dating yet. She just wasn't ready. In the rooms she rented from Mama Anna, she brushed her curls out in the bathroom mirror and pulled her hair into a puff at the back of her neck. Wynn was waiting for her in the living room. They were going out to eat. She checked her face in the mirror one more time and returned to the living room. Wynn was nowhere in sight. A thread of suspicion, not the first one since they started dating, ran along the back of her neck.

"Hey, I'm in here," he said from the tiny kitchenette. "Getting a beer. Just didn't want to bother you. Hope you don't mind."

She did mind.

"What?" he said in response to her questioning look.

"I could've gotten that."

"No worries, I've got feet," he said as he walked toward her while taking a long swallow from the Blue Moon he had scavenged from her almost bare refrigerator. Raven radiated a mistrust so powerful, she knew he could feel it. But he pretended that he didn't. He bent down and kissed her on the lips. His mouth tasted like beer. His lips were ice cold.

CHAPTER SIX

Billy Ray was shaking a warped silver skillet over the restaurant's commercial stove. The place was loud, but Raven could have sworn that she heard the skillet scrape against the cast-iron burners as the yellow flames leapt around it.

"Table seven," Billy Ray said, sliding a steaming bowl of shrimp creole and hot rice toward her. "But Imogene will take it."

At the sound of her name Imogene came running over to grab the plate. "Which table again?" she said, turning her back to Billy Ray and pretending to search the restaurant.

Raven rolled her eyes. She'd bet every dollar stuffed in the back pocket of her new blue jeans that Imogene had turned around so Billy Ray could see her round bottom in the tight black pencil skirt she had worn over from the station. Raven was about to ask her why she just didn't bend over so he could have a better look, but she caught a warning look from Billy Ray and kept her mouth shut. He had been friendly enough when she returned, but Raven suspected that if she caused any more upset in his life he would excise her like a gangrenous limb.

"What?" Raven asked. "No news today, Imogene?"

"I've taken a leave of absence from the station. My last day was today."

"Why?" Raven asked.

Imogene said, "Girl, things just started getting to me."

"You mean Billy Ray started to get to you."

"Is that what you think? That I'd put my career on hold running after a man? Chile, no. I think it was that last big story I did. Claude DeWitt." Imogene shuddered.

"Claude DeWitt?"

"Yeah, back in the summer. You were gone. This kid got adopted by this rich couple. It went okay for a while, but when he got to be a teenager, they couldn't handle him." Imogene stopped, shook her head.

"What happened to him?"

"Those bastards locked him up, beat him. That boy ended up starving to death. The people in this town."

"Not only this town, but the world, Imogene. What about your career, though? I thought you wanted to be the next Robin Roberts?"

"My career will be there. It can wait for a little bit. Just like you, I need the time out. Besides, Billy Ray does need the help."

"Table seven," Billy Ray interrupted them. "You gone stand there all day? Food's getting cold."

"I can take it," Raven said.

"You got another customer."

He pointed his spatula at the old folks' corner, which she knew was empty because Mama Anna had finally let Mr. Joe and the others sample what she termed her fine cooking. Raven turned in surprise to see a man sitting at the huge table. He had picked up the deck of cards that was usually there and was now compulsively cutting the deck over and over again with one large hand. He always had to be doing something with his hands, she thought. If he didn't have a baseball to throw in the air, leave it to him to fixate on a deck of cards. On the table in front of him were a tightly rolled newspaper and a briefcase.

She looked at Billy Ray. "No."

"He said he ain't leaving until he talks to you."

"Kick him out."

Billy Ray leaned both hands on the counter. "I don't need to kick him out. He hasn't done anything to me or you."

"That's a bunch of crap."

"Nothing that he shouldn't be forgiven for, anyway. We all got something that we need to be forgiven for."

"Billy Ray," she breathed.

"I'm not in the mood, Raven."

With that he was back in the kitchen. Raven walked over to the man at the table who kept cutting the cards again and again, so fast that it almost made Raven dizzy. Billy Ray was right. She needed to do her business. Today her business was to take orders and bring the food without breaking the secondhand plates.

Raven thought about Jean Rinehart, her stepmother, who had died years ago. Jean used to be a waitress, and Raven was always struck by how professional she was. How neat and clean, and how generous. Jean had a way of making any customer feel like the broken-down Abe's Diner was the only place that could satisfy their stomachs. She was able to do so even if she thought the person was what she called a snake in the grass. Raven tried to channel Jean as she stared at the gray temples of the man who now regarded her levelly. She tried her hardest to channel the woman she saw her father kill with one red-heeled spiked shoe.

"What can I get you?" she said in a friendly voice.

"Don't, Raven."

"I don't know what you mean," she said.

"I don't want any food."

She sighed and put the small notepad in her pocket. She moved a whorl of curl out of her face with the pencil and stuck the pencil behind her ear.

"Then I'm afraid you made a mistake. This is a restaurant. We serve food."

"Don't play with me, Raven."

"Wouldn't dream of playing."

"Then sit down and talk to me," he said, his dark eyes boring into hers. "Please."

"And if I said no?"

It was his turn to sigh. He sat back. "I was hoping that you would be reasonable."

"I passed reason and went straight to go to hell when you stabbed me in the back and almost got Billy Ray killed, Chief Sawyer."

Just then Billy Ray passed the table carrying two plates and humming under his breath to the Buckwheat Zydeco's song 'Turning Point' playing on the speakers.

"He looks like he's getting along okay to me," the chief said.

"His face is scarred all to hell."

"Doesn't seem to bother him too much. Besides, he'll have a story to tell for the rest of his life."

"Along with a limp."

"Chief," Billy Ray said as he came back to their table, now empty-handed. "You want some whiskey? I managed to get my hands on some Pappy."

"How can I refuse that?" he said. As if reading her mind, the chief warned, "Don't walk away."

"And if I do?"

He held her gaze. "Then there's some nasty business in California that I may have to get involved in. There's been a couple of detectives down here questioning. I sent them on their way without much to lean on."

She drew back as if he had slapped her. She wasn't afraid. Raven had covered her tracks. Hadn't Floyd taught her that? It was just his nerve that got her. She was about to tell him to go to hell in a gasoline jacket when he held up a hand in a placating gesture.

"All I'm asking is that you hear me out," he said. "And if you want to walk away after hearing me out, by all means be my guest. But I'm going to bet that you won't be able to."

She folded her arms across her chest without saying anything.

"Please sit."

Curiosity got the better of her. She pulled out the chair at the head of the table and sat. He knocked the card deck against the table a few times before straightening the edges and slipping the cards back in the box. He set them aside.

"I'm guessing you haven't been reading the papers lately."

"Why would you guess that?"

She hadn't been reading them, but any piece of satisfaction she could keep from him suited her just fine.

"Because you're here hiding out at Billy Ray's. Wasting a lot of damn time, and a lot of good brain power."

"Are you saying that serving the public is a waste of time? That's new."

"Always a smart ass," he said.

He unrolled the paper and turned it over so the first page showed. He shoved it toward her. Raven read the headline. He was right. She hadn't been reading the newspapers, but she was aware of this. How could she not be with Imogene Tucker gum-popping and hip-shaking her way all over Billy Ray's hardwood floors these past few months?

Even though Raven told her to shut it every time she brought it up, she couldn't help but get a taste of what was going on in what Floyd used to describe as good ole Byrd's Landing. Another murder, and yes, another serial killer. Bodies were turning up all over the small town in places related to government business or where the wealthy gathered.

"Two weeks ago we found another body," the chief said.

"Where?" Raven asked before she could stop herself.

"At BLPD. The courtyard between the offices and the morgue."

Raven let out a small laugh.

"I don't see anything funny," the chief said.

"That's bold," she said. "Don't you have security cameras around that place?"

"We do. But they weren't working on that particular night. Cameron was upgrading the back-end systems so the cameras were offline."

Raven nodded. Convenient. She wondered if anybody saw anything, was about to ask, then remembered where she was and now who she was.

"What has this got to do with me?"

"That's the fifth body we've found in the last four months. All young boys. Between fifteen and nineteen. It's like the killer's on a mission."

She stared at him. She made sure to keep her face disinterested, but that didn't stop her brain teeming with questions. She kept silent, not because she wanted him to go away, but because she was afraid that if she opened her mouth the questions would tumble out. Chief Sawyer used to tell her once a cop always a cop. Raven desperately hoped that wasn't true.

"The body before that was found behind the courthouse. The perp made sure that they avoided the cameras in the area," the chief said as if she had asked the question. "One in the alley by the theater, another in the doorway of a bank – we have images from that camera, by the way, but it's useless – and this last one in the middle of the construction site of the new wing at Memorial. I don't think we have any camera footage, though I'm not sure yet."

Something about the chief's last statement bothered Raven, but she let it go. This wasn't her problem. Now was her chance for a new life. She wasn't going to let the chief foul it up. She ignored the cop questions niggling the back of her mind. The chief kept talking.

"All naked as the day they were born, and wrapped in blankets. Our CSI said the blankets are brand new, just out of the shrink wrap. All with damage to their foreheads, throats slit. Exsanguinated."

Raven's eyes flicked down to the newspaper and back up. She found herself looking into the chief's face. He was frowning.

"What has this got to do with me?" she said again. "My father certainly didn't do this one, and neither did I."

"Don't you care about these boys?"

"Yes," Raven said. "More than you know. But still, why are you telling me this?"

"Five dead bodies, Raven. Young boys who were most likely tortured and killed."

She let silence play between them. Billy Ray came over with a heavy glass of whiskey, neat. He sat the glass on the table and left.

The chief waited until he was across the restaurant before saying, "There are no connections between the victims. All different. Some poor, others wealthy, middle-class. But all white boys. Some blond, others brunette, one with blue hair. So, whoever is doing this isn't looking for a type."

"You sure the type isn't just white?"

He sat back, framed his face with an index finger and a thumb along his chin, what Raven used to call his Malcolm X pose. Him looking at her that way used to make her feel stupid; now it just annoyed her.

"What do you want?" Raven asked.

"We got nothing."

"No."

"The lead I have on this now is smart as hell. Used to work major crimes. Breaker. You remember him?"

"No."

"Tall guy, likes to dress nice. I know you didn't work with him a lot, but he's been with me from the start."

"Didn't you hear me?"

"And I can't get help from anybody else. Nobody wants this. They got their own problems. Since nothing is across state lines, it's Byrd's Landing's problem."

"I said no."

"It would just be for this case. We bring you back on a temporary basis."

He stopped talking and opened the briefcase on the table. He lifted her service weapon out first, and then her badge. He placed it on the table between them. Raven couldn't help but look at the badge, the way it gleamed beneath the recess lights in the ceiling above them. Chief Sawyer must have polished it before packing it into the briefcase, but hadn't bothered removing the black band acknowledging the death of Presley Holloway, one of Lovelle's unfortunate victims.

The picture in her mind of those boys, bled out, wrapped in blankets, left all over town, rubbed at her conscience. She could do something about this, but in the end she would have to relinquish her sanity.

"You have other people who can do this," she said. "Breaker for one."

"No, he's too close. He has kids, and he keeps personalizing it. When he's not personalizing it, he's running away from it, going down all sorts of rabbit holes. He could use some help. Your help. Besides, you were the best homicide detective I've ever had. That hasn't changed."

"That doesn't mean that I have to be the one to bring this guy down."

"You owe me."

Raven laughed so hard that bitter tears came to her eyes. She rubbed them away while still sighing and laughing.

"I know you don't think you do, but you do. The California cops were climbing all up my ass about you. I covered for you."

She leaned forward, her voice laced with both anger and pride. "I didn't ask you to cover for me," she said. "What do you think I am, Chief? Stupid? They can't put me at the scene. I was hundreds of miles away. An airtight alibi."

"I wonder how much digging they would have to do to blow that alibi all to hell."

She leaned back before saying, "They'd have to do an awful lot of digging."

The badge and holster made a grating sound on the table as he used both hands to slide them over to her. She slid them back.

"You have a responsibility."

"No, I don't," she answered. "I'm not a cop anymore. The responsibility's yours."

She had never seen him like this. He looked old, grayer than she last remembered. She knew he had a boy who would be these boys' ages soon. He had saved her life once. No, twice. At one point in her life, he had been the only person who believed in her.

"We have been through a lot together," he said. "And I tried to never throw that bullshit you went through with your father in your face."

"Are you saying that you're about to?"

"No, I'm saying don't make me do it." She saw in his eyes that he knew a protest was coming. He held up a palm to stave it off. "If you won't take the case, at least come with me."

"Where?"

"Crime scene," he said. "I told you, Memorial."

She sat back, flabbergasted. That's what bothered her about how he described the Memorial victim. They *thought* they had camera footage. And it wasn't like the chief to leave, as Floyd would say, whiskey sittin'. He was on duty.

"Why in all things holy would you tell Billy Ray to bring you an expensive glass of whiskey?"

"A prop. Distraction. It won't go to waste. Not Pappy Van Winkle. I'm sure Billy Ray will take care of it."

"Chief," Raven said. "You've got to be the only man I know who can lie without saying a word."

"I'll drive you," he said, ignoring her comment. "After you see this, if you still say you want out of it, I'll leave you alone."

"Promise?"

"On my children," he said. "But the Raven Burns I know wouldn't let shit like this stand."

CHAPTER SEVEN

Detective Breaker met the chief and Raven next to the recently poured foundation of the new obstetrics wing of Memorial Hospital. The chief introduced him before stepping away to placate Dr. Fabian Long. Long was CEO of the hospital, and wanted the crime scene wrapped up as soon as possible so the fellas, as he put it, could get back to work.

Detective Breaker was a handsome man with curly black hair and a haunted look in his eyes. He wore an expensive three-piece suit under a perfectly draped trench coat. Raven didn't know what annoyed her more – the gold watch chain or the diamond and onyx pinkie ring. But where was her empathy? She remembered how her stepmother dressed, mini-skirts, matching tops, and always the bright red heels. The more Floyd's crazy showed itself, the fancier Jean dressed, the higher and sharper the red heels. If she couldn't control her marriage, at least she could control the way she presented herself to the world. Perhaps Breaker felt the same way about this case.

"Where's the scene?" she asked him, wanting to get the entire thing finished so she could get back to the restaurant before closing.

"Down there," he said.

'Down there' meant the very foundation of the new Memorial Hospital wing. In the throes of construction, the imagined wing was a large, square hole rimmed by slanting walls of packed dirt, and floored by concrete. By the several people in orange vests and white jumpsuits walking all over the smooth surface, Raven concluded that the still clean and white concrete must be bone dry. The entire scene was lit by haloed circles of white light that pooled onto the concrete floor, making it gleam in places while leaving others in shadowed darkness. A crane on the edge of the hole stretched a long tentacle up toward an overcast sky, appearing to touch the pockmarked moon.

"You know who it is?" Raven asked.

"No idea. Chief called a halt to everything when he thought it'd be another Sleeping Boy case. Had to wait on Your Grace." Breaker said.

She cocked her head at him.

"That's you," he explained.

"Hey," Raven said. "Not trying to step all over your Gucci shoes, Detective. Chief asked me to take a look, that's all."

"What good is a look going to do except waste my time and everybody else's?"

"Fresh pair of eyes," Raven said. "And then you can have your serial killer all back to your little ole self."

He appraised her for a long moment before gesturing to a uniformed officer with a clipboard. She recognized the officer, a big man with a handlebar mustache named Newell Taylor. She didn't know why Taylor never liked her, but he didn't. He gave her wide berth when she worked for the department last year. When they were forced to work together, he provided one-word answers when speech was required, and grunts when it wasn't.

After Raven signed in, Taylor handed her a pair of booties and a jumpsuit. She pulled the booties on, but looked skeptically at the jumpsuit.

"Really?" she said.

"Chief's orders," Taylor said. "It's the way we do things around here now. No cowboys. Or cowgirls."

"How about cow woman? Or cow person?"

"Medical examiner here yet?" she asked Breaker.

"No, still waiting on her, too. Tonight's been an exercise in patience."

"But I see BLPD crime scene investigators," she said. "How did they beat Rita here?"

"She's finishing up at another scene. I hear she's on her way." He looked at his watch. "Should be here in about twenty or thirty minutes."

Raven saved that piece of information in her head. It's not that she didn't like Rita Sandbourne, the medical examiner, it was that she didn't want the questions she knew Rita would ask. And she didn't want the memories, or the pressure to return to the force.

"So we don't have time of death yet," Raven said. "What time did everybody leave work?"

"By five thirty p.m. this place was a ghost town," Breaker said. "Union."

"Who found him?"

"A supervisor wanted to make sure he set the alarm," Breaker answered. "You know, like when you leave home and think you left the iron on? Came back around eight thirty to check. So, it looks like the killer dropped the body between five thirty and eight thirty p.m."

"There was an alarm?" Raven asked.

"Now, that's wishful thinking," he said. "He did forget. No alarm. No camera."

"Convenient," Raven said. "I hate convenient. I'm sure you're detaining him."

"We're taking his statement, yes," Breaker said.

Raven tilted her head to the side and said, "Don't take this the wrong way, Breaker, but how long you been in homicide?"

His lips twisted into a smile. "First case, came from major crimes. I'm sure the chief already filled you in."

"Okay," she said. "Piece of advice. Don't just take his statement. Detain him, question him on even the smallest detail. And question him yourself. Don't turn it over to a uniform."

"You automatically think he had something to do with it?"

"I don't automatically think anything, that's why you need to question him."

She turned away from him and studied the foundation. More lights in the northeast corner, which had been cordoned off with police tape along with a set of white metal stairs leading to the concrete floor below.

"You think that's the entry?" she asked. "The stairs?"

"Yes, why wouldn't we?"

Raven studied the slanted dirt walls. "The killer walked daintily down the stairs carrying the dead weight of a body wrapped in a blanket, not knowing who might wander down here?"

"I don't know if the walk was dainty or not, but that's the only way down there. What else could he do, drop the body in from the sky?"

She said nothing, just gave him what Billy Ray called her 'Floyd', deadpan serial-killer stare.

"I see," Breaker said. "This is going to be a waste of my time."

She grinned, telling herself to lighten up a little. "More than likely," she said.

"Thought so."

He took his trench coat off and handed it to Officer Taylor, who was standing next to him like a valet. Taylor took the trench coat without delay, pressing down the neat folds, brushing off any imaginary dirt. The coat was followed by the jacket. Breaker put the jumpsuit over his slacks and the vest with the gold watch. After he was done, he slipped on the shoe covers and said, "And for the record, my shoes are Berluti, not Gucci."

★   ★   ★

As they passed the metal stairs, Raven didn't notice any evidence tags on the steps as they walked by, even though Breaker said the killer used them to enter the dump site. They both stopped at a metal ladder leading down from the slanted mud walls.

"After you," he said.

"Good thing I'm not afraid of heights," Raven said as she swung around and descended into the hole in the ground.

"You like homicide?" she asked Breaker when he was standing beside her on the ground below.

"I don't. Major crimes geek all the way," he said. "Do you?"

"Bit obvious, isn't it?" she said. "If you don't like it, why don't you fly away?"

"Because there's nobody else who will do this, is there? I see something needing to be done, I don't dick around. I do it."

"Whoa," Raven said with a little laugh. "Shots fired. Is that a jab?"

"Take it any way you want to."

"I will," she breathed.

It was cooler at the bottom than up top, with more of a damp earth smell mingled with the late November Louisiana chill. Two Byrd's Landing crime scene investigators concentrated on a long, swaddled bundle that must be the body. She recognized them both. A slim, short man named Tim who helped with the Lovelle case, and April, an older woman with curly graying hair who spent way too much money at the racetrack.

"Do you want to see the body?" Breaker asked.

"We'll get to the body in a bit. You got a flashlight?" Raven said.

"This not enough light for you?"

He was right in a way. The construction site lights made the area as bright as an operating room. But there were corners and dark shadows where the light failed to reach. Those were the places Raven wanted to go.

"I want to see exactly where I'm walking," she answered him absently. "And stay behind me, will you?"

"Your wish, Madam," he said.

"Another thing," she said. "Who are the orange vests walking around down here?"

"The foreman and a few of his team leads. They're showing us the lay of the land."

"Get rid of them."

"What?"

"Get rid of them. The entire place should be a crime scene, not just your precious little corner. They can tell us the lay of the land from photographs. They don't need to be down here."

Breaker motioned another uniformed officer over. He whispered to him, glanced at Raven and whispered some more. The uniform walked away toward the foreman and the other construction workers.

"I'd grid search this entire area in daylight," she told him as she pointed the flashlight in front of her feet.

"There," she said after a while. She pointed down and said, "See that?"

"Scuff marks, shoe prints," Breaker all but sneered. "They're all over the place. It's a construction site."

"That doesn't look like the other work boot prints, does it to you?"

Breaker didn't argue with her, just waved Tim over. "Get some adhesive and lift that print, and photograph it," he ordered.

Tim gave him a nasty look, but did it anyway. It looked like Breaker wasn't making nice with the team. He was in more trouble than he knew if he thought of them as just the help. It was always a good thing to keep the crime scene investigators on your side.

"When you're done, bag that over there, too, Tim. Please?" Raven said, pointing at a cache of empty soda cans and water bottles against the far wall. She whistled when she also noted a bottle of Perrier lying on its side.

"Expensive tastes over there," she said.

"Those are from the construction workers," Breaker said. "The foreman said they eat lunch down here."

"They don't clean up after? And they drink Perrier?"

"I don't know much about what they drink, but they're a messy bunch. You ever been on a working construction site?"

The bunch was indeed messy. Aside from the drink cans, there were food wrappers, and a couple of grease-spotted Burger King bags.

"Did you match the trash to the people who work here?"

Breaker folded his arms across his chest. "Haven't exactly had time yet. Besides, you're grasping at straws."

"From what the chief says all you have are straws right now."

"Tim, bag and tag all of it. You may want to map how you walked over here, and cordon it off so everyone will come this way. And lift all of the unique footprints you find. I know it's work, but they may come in handy."

"Sure. Welcome back, Raven."

"I'm not back," she corrected him.

"Not yet," he called without turning around.

"Why would the killer leave evidence opposite of where he placed the body?"

"Found any evidence on the stairs yet?" Raven pressed.

"How else would he get down?"

"Was there evidence on the stairs?" Raven asked, coming closer to the opposite wall. "Blood, pieces of clothing, footprints, anything? You did look at all that while waiting on me, right? You don't do everything Chief Sawyer tells you to, do you?"

Breaker pressed his lips together.

"If I were him," she said, "I wouldn't use the stairs. Too much can go wrong with carrying deadweight down a long flight of stairs."

"Then what would you do? He didn't roll them down the dirt walls. I did get a look at the blanket. It's clean."

"Ever occur to you that he wrapped the body in the blanket after rolling it down the embankment?"

"But then the body wouldn't be clean. This killer always leaves the body clean."

"Why?"

"What do you mean why? I don't know why. I'll ask the fucker when I find him if it makes you happy."

"You asked the FBI for a profile yet?"

"Yes. White male, private, mid-thirties, professional, organized. Probably a neat freak."

"White because the victims are white."

"Yes, and most serial killers are white."

"You mean the ones that are caught are white," Raven said. "Are they saying the crimes are sexual?"

"Isn't that what they always say? Like Freud, they have a one-track mind," Breaker said. "You don't believe these crimes are sexual?"

"I'm just along for the ride on this one. I don't know enough to believe anything. But if I were you, I would expand the crime scene like I told you, get some people out here to do a grid search tomorrow."

"Noted."

She turned back to him and smiled. "I wait tables now, you know that?"

"I heard."

"There's this old Korean War vet who comes into the restaurant all the time. I know what it means when you give somebody advice and they say, 'noted', Breaker."

Stepping carefully until she was close to the far wall, she ran the light over the dirt surface. Rivulets had formed in the slanting dirt wall at what seemed regular intervals – except in one notable area. The place was almost smooth, as if someone or something had used the wall to slide to the floor.

"Tim," she said as he was finishing tagging and bagging the trash on the floor. "You're going to want to photograph this, and get some measurements."

Breaker came over to stand beside her.

"One thing about this town, Detective Breaker," she said, "is that you can never take anything for granted. The killer may have used the stairs, but the body definitely came in this way."

★   ★   ★

A few minutes later Raven and Breaker were kneeling beside the blanket-wrapped body of the Byrd's Landing serial killer's latest victim. April, the curly-haired CSI who liked the racetrack, was tending the body as they waited for the medical examiner.

"Can we get a look underneath the blanket?" Raven asked April. "You get all the pictures you need?"

"Yes, finished a few minutes ago," she said. Raven didn't like the suspicious look on her face, and wasn't surprised when April continued. "You know that we aren't allowed to touch the body until Rita gets here, right?"

"I'm not asking you to touch the body," Raven said. "Just the blanket."

"That's splitting hairs."

"I promise," Raven said, looking April in her gray eyes while thinking about the thundering hooves at the racetrack, and the bets that April on her salary shouldn't have been making. "I won't tell."

April looked at Raven for a few more seconds before her thin lips tightened. With gloved hands she carefully started pushing the blanket aside, almost lovingly. Knowing April the way she did, Raven understood that she was doing it out of respect as much as necessity.

"You know how my father was, right?" Raven asked Breaker.

"Who doesn't?" he said, his tone both clipped and suspicious.

"I think he loved me somewhere in there, but he told me a lot of stories; some, I'm sure, just to scare the daylights out of me."

"I don't doubt," Breaker said.

"There was one story he told about how in the olden days they used to place living human sacrifices in the walls of new buildings, as offerings to the gods. He would describe in chilling detail how long it would take someone to die locked in the walls of the building, what would happen to their body, how they would go crazy first. I was very young. Never forgot that story. Gave me nightmares for days."

"Okay," he said. "But this isn't a wall, and this kid is dead."

"No, it's not and yes, he is," she said. "Quite dead."

April had managed to get the blanket open enough so the gash in the boy's throat was visible, and was pushing apart the folds to get to the face.

Raven went on. "But think about how these boys are killed. Throat slit, washed, and wrapped up, and then left at places that represent wealth and power."

"I don't understand."

"When you're looking at the crime scenes, think about what's most important to this particular killer," she said. "I think for this one it's each part of the ritual – cutting the throat, bleeding the body out, wrapping the bodies in blankets. He's organized, like you said. Everything has to be just right."

"The chief didn't tell me you liked to talk in riddles."

She turned and favored Breaker with a hard gaze. "You're a detective. You need to learn to love riddles."

The blanket was finally open, cradling the face of the dead boy. How ridiculous to call this murderer the Sleeping Boy Killer. The look on the victim's face was definitely not somnolent. His skin was pale, white as chalk, his eyes half-lidded and his blue lips parted in memory of his last breath.

April sucked in her breath.

"You know him?" Raven asked.

"That's what's crazy about working in a small town," April said. "I know most of 'em. And I know this boy. Don't you, Raven?"

"Not the crowd I hang with," Raven said.

"What about you, Breaker?" April asked.

"Remember I'm not from around here," Breaker said. "I barely know you."

"His name is Henri Toulouse. He's Judge Toulouse's boy. Goes to school with my son."

"Well, crap," Raven said. "I do know the judge."

Raven had made Judge Toulouse's acquaintance several times. He was a family court judge she had appeared before after getting into trouble at one of her numerous foster homes. She remembered him as an overly thin man with greedy eyes and a mean mouth.

Breaker covered his eyes with his hand, the pinky ring diamond glittering in the abundance of light on the crime scene. "And I thought there was no way that this case could be a bigger pain in the ass," he said.

"Looks like you hit the jackpot," Raven agreed.

She stood, and studied the pools of light on the floor. Her mind went to all the secrets the dump site was hiding in its shadows and crevices. There was more evidence here than Breaker could probably even dream. The killer had more to say. Now, with this new site, he was expanding his message.

"I don't think that the killer's motive is sexual," she said. "To me this feels like the ritual of sacrifice. But for some reason, for this particular victim, the perp's willing to subvert part of the ritual in favor of the location."

"You mean the cleaning part," Breaker said.

"Yes, I mean the cleaning."

"So?"

"So, this place and this particular victim mean a lot to the killer. Did the other victims have any connection to the dump sites?"

"No, not to the dump site itself. That looks random."

"Well, this one isn't random. Look hard for a connection between this site and the victim, or between this site and the other sites."

"That it?" Breaker said. "That's all Chief Sawyer's ace detective has, a grid search and a connection for something that doesn't even have walls yet?"

"What do you want from me, Detective Breaker?"

"For you to stay and help us with this." It wasn't Breaker who answered, but the chief, who had come to stand behind them unnoticed.

"You're breaking your own rules," Raven said when they were facing each other. "No jumpsuit."

"I wanted to get down here before you ran away," he said. "And it looks like I was just in time."

Raven didn't bother to say that she couldn't do it. He knew that. Her face said it all. Police work would destroy her. She barely managed her job when it was her father who was the killer. She couldn't imagine how it would be if she tried to go back with blood spilled by her own willful hands. Without saying a word, she brushed past him on her way to the ladder.

Before she could grab the cold metal to begin her climb, the chief said, "You're going to regret this, Raven."

She turned back to him, and said something that she would never forget as long as she lived. She said, "I don't see how that could be a possibility, Chief."

CHAPTER EIGHT

Raven used a ride share to get back to the restaurant instead of letting the chief drive her. The less he thought she owed him, the better. She walked back into the cheer of Chastain's Creole Heaven without a word of explanation to Billy Ray, and he, in his Billy Ray fashion, let her be.

She left the restaurant around one a.m. with Billy Ray walking beside her. They had been the only ones left as she stayed to help him deep clean the kitchen, including scrubbing every ounce of grease from the industrial Viking stove.

He was pensive, walking beside her with his uneven gait, his hands in the pockets of his loose, black slacks, his expensive, Hoodoo pork pie hat pushed back on his head. She could tell he had something on his mind.

He reached his '67 Buick Skylark first and sat with the engine idling while she made her way to her Mustang. She resented this act of chivalry. He should know by now that she could take care of herself. Maybe it was the chief's visit that spooked him even though he kept quiet about it. She rummaged through the pockets of her hoodie jacket for the keys to the Mustang. The pockets were empty.

Knowing that Billy Ray would wait until she got in the car, she placed her water bottle on the hood and dug into her backpack. When she found the keys snug in the bottom, she held them up so he could see them. She got into her car and flicked her lights several times so he'd get the message. She didn't need saving anymore. A few more seconds passed before he drove away.

She started the engine before realizing that the water bottle was still on top of the car. She opened the door and attempted to retrieve it from the hood. But she couldn't reach it. She stepped out of the car. It was then she realized why Billy Ray stuck around. Several of the parking lot lights had blown out in succession earlier that day. Aside from the Mustang's lights, the place was as dark as a crypt.

And the Byrd's Landing air was thick with mist. It just hung there, heavy and carrying the mildewed smell from the woods adjacent to the restaurant, a smell reminding her of decay. A mist she could almost taste glazed the parking lot, making the newly painted white stripes glow in the dark.

She thought she heard a long, low whistle. It sounded so real that Raven swiveled, trying to see where it came from. When Floyd spoke up in her head for the first time since forever, she reasoned that the whistle was simply a partner to the subsequent auditory hallucination.

Whew whee, Birdy Girl. Ain't this dark somethin'? During my time I'd call this a killin' dark.

Raven felt breathless, as if there was not enough air in the entire town to fill her lungs. She normally wasn't so easily spooked, but the dark parking lot, the memory of the streetlamps popping out one by one like firecrackers earlier that day, the Memorial crime scene and hearing Floyd so clearly in her head, all of that did the job.

Floyd agreed with her, saying, *Why that's enough to spook the piss from anybody.* And in her mind she could see him, the hard eyes, the greedy grin, his sparkling, white fedora.

No, not this. She balled her hands into fists and pressed them to the side of her head. *Not this again. You are over, old man.*

You mean you thought I was over. What did I tell you? Souls don't die, Birdy Girl. No, no, no.

She closed her eyes even tighter, so tight that she started to see bright lights behind her eyelids. She kept them shut, kept pressing them tighter and tighter until Floyd's grinning face disappeared, until she could no longer sense his presence.

She opened her eyes, gulped air. She did it. That had never happened before, not once in her life. She had never been able to wish him away so completely like that. She could push him to the back of her mind, but a remnant like a wisp of smoke always remained. She slowly brought her hands down and purposely turned toward the Mustang. She groped along the top of the car until she felt the water bottle.

"I wished you away," she said in a whisper full of amazement.

But then she heard footsteps in the mist. She looked up again to see a silhouette of a dark figure beneath the remaining working streetlamp. She knew it wasn't Floyd because Floyd was dead. But the figure had the shape of him, the same height, about five three or five four, the same wiry build and what looked like the same yellowish blond hair. A square of white floated by the man's throat. In the gray mist it appeared to be glowing. He was holding a book of some kind and staring intently at the restaurant.

No, not at the restaurant, but at her.

"What the hellfire," she mouthed, reaching for a weapon that was no longer there, hadn't been there since she left the force. "Not real," Raven breathed.

Floyd had jumped right out of her head and into the street. She was imagining him. She closed her eyes and opened them again. He was still there. *All right*, she thought, *let's see if you're real enough to take a beating.* She turned around to grab the baseball bat behind the driver's seat. She did it as fast as she could, or thought she did. But when she turned around, the figure was gone. Whatever had stepped momentarily into the light had faded back into the darkness.

CHAPTER NINE

A full week later Raven ushered the last customer out of the door of the restaurant around seven. It had been long enough to forget about the man in the mist. No, not forget exactly, but to lock him into that closed place in her mind so she didn't have to think about him.

Tonight was special. Billy Ray was closing the restaurant for a birthday party for Cameron's son. With her help, Cameron now had custody of Noe Cardova. Cameron's lifestyle really wasn't compatible with a fourteen-year-old boy, but Raven was proud that Cameron was making the best of it.

And today was Noe's fifteenth birthday. Both Raven and Cameron decided that since this was the first birthday Noe would be without his mother, and especially since it was in the middle of the holiday season, they'd make it special. That included closing the restaurant, hiring a zydeco band, and having a party so loud and huge that Noe might be able to forget why he was there in the first place. Maybe he could have a few moments where the grief from his mother's death wouldn't bend him double.

Raven and Imogene went about moving tables around as the band set up, a brief burst of the accordion or the rough stroke of the frottoir amid their laughter. Billy Ray was in the back making a fresh batch of seafood gumbo, and a towering red velvet cake. The bell above the door jingled and Raven looked up to see Edmée Crowley sweep in, with a tall, mousy-looking redhead trailing her.

"Raven, ma cherie, hello!" She walked up to Raven and kissed her on both cheeks French style. A cloud of perfume and scented lotion enveloped Raven. Being this close to Edmée was like stepping into a garden of magnolias. But the smell wasn't obnoxious – it was just

Edmée. She and Raven had spent their teenage years in the same foster system and in high school together. Spending several months in the same home cemented a close friendship that had become distant after they went their separate ways.

"Oh, is this how we do it now, Edna Mae?" Raven laughed. "With kisses?"

Edmée wagged an index finger at her. "Now, now," she said. "It's Edmée. Just push the Edna and Mae together. I haven't gone by that name in years. And yes, ever since my visit to Paris last year, I greet with both cheeks."

"That's too good of an opening, but I'll resist," Raven said, still laughing.

"Where's the birthday boy?"

"Not here yet," Imogene said, both unfriendly and unsmiling.

Edmée flung her long, silky hair over her shoulder.

"Oh, Imogene," she said. "I didn't see you standing there."

"That's weird," Imogene responded in a flat voice. "Because I'm right here. Standing here. Been standing here next to Raven the entire time."

"Oh, don't be like that," Edmée said. "I'll give you kisses, too."

Before Imogene could step out of the way, Edmée had grabbed Imogene's shoulders and kissed her soundly on both cheeks.

Imogene wasn't the only woman Edmée missed. Raven looked inquiringly at the redhead in black standing behind Edmée. The woman clutched at a sheer wrap embroidered with tiny pink flowers as if to keep it from slipping from her narrow shoulders. Red curls piled atop her head spilled around her narrow face.

"Oh forgive me," Edmée said, placing a hand at the small of the woman's back and moving her forward. "Isn't she beautiful? We had a girls' day – mani-pedis and Stella had an entire makeover for the party."

She introduced both Raven and Imogene, and the woman gave them a smile with thin lips covered in pink lip gloss. "Pleased to meet you. I hope I'm not intruding."

"Not at all," Raven said. "The more the merrier. How do you know Edmée?"

"How does she know me?" Edmée broke in. "Why, she gives me oodles of support for my boys' home. Without her, Heron House wouldn't be the same."

Edmée ran the house on Heron Street, a home for foster kids who were too old to place. She was also a rabid zydeco fan, almost as rabid as Billy Ray. She'd reconnected with Raven when she came by to check out one of the bands. Billy Ray was there, and they spent the entire night arguing about zydeco until Raven waved the white flag by letting them both know that she had had enough. She didn't care who invented the term, the music, whether it was Creole or Cajun, brown or white. She just wanted to go home and go to sleep.

Stella smiled. "Edmée is being Edmée. Always generous with the praise. I help with what I can. I also do business with Billy Ray."

Raven could feel the look of confusion that swept over her face.

"Meat," Stella explained.

"Oh, I love her. She is so modest," Edmée said. "Stella owns one of the best sheep farms in Byrd's Landing. Billy Ray orders his meat from her. Why do you think he has the best lamb this side of the Mississippi?"

"Careful, Stella," Imogene said. "Or you'll be blinded by Edmée's light."

"Billy Ray?" Edmée asked, ignoring Imogene's comment. She removed a long, white cashmere sweater and threw it carelessly on one of Billy Ray's mismatched chairs.

"Kitchen," Raven said.

"You can't go back there," Imogene warned.

"Why?"

"Health hazard."

"Don't be ridiculous," Edmée replied as she sauntered back to the kitchen, giving the band a 'hey boys' finger wiggle as she passed. Both Imogene and Raven watched as she made her way to Billy Ray.

"I hate her," Imogene said.

"Don't be like that," Raven said. "But I kind of hate her, too."

"For someone who runs a non-profit, she sure dresses like she gives zero fucks about keeping things toned down."

Raven had forgotten that Stella was standing there until she spoke. "She does a lot of good for Byrd's Landing. We have always been so very proud of her," Stella said.

"We?" Imogene prompted.

"I mean the town," Stella explained.

"I know," Raven said. "I lived with her for a few months, and then went to high school with her. She had it as tough as I did, but came through all that. And she's managed to do some good along the way."

"Come on, Stella," Imogene said. "Let's get you something to drink."

"I would love a white wine," Stella said.

The band continued to warm up. Raven stood watching them for a moment. Music notes would swell the room briefly before it became quiet again. After seating Stella at a table near the front with a glass of Chardonnay, Imogene came back and stood next to Raven. She stared toward the kitchen where Billy Ray's voice and Edmée's laughter, as musical as a song itself, floated back to them.

"Don't worry," Raven said. "She's married, remember?"

"When did that mean anything?"

"Forever, in my book," Raven said. "And the same in Billy Ray's. He's not going to mess around with a married woman."

Imogene turned to glare at her. "You think you know him."

"I do," Raven said.

"You weren't with him when he was going through the worst moments of his life. I was. He's vulnerable."

"Leave it alone, Imogene." She wanted to also tell her to leave *him* alone. Billy Ray wasn't interested in Imogene. The news reporter and ex-cop had nothing in common. But she was sure that Imogene wouldn't listen.

"You think I have the hots for him, don't you?" Imogene said.

"What I think is that you're barking up the wrong tree."

"It's not like that. I just don't want to see him jump from the frying pan and into the fire."

"Don't you mean jump from the fire back into the frying pan?"

"Not funny."

"I wasn't trying to be. I was trying to say that he's getting his life back together after that awful night with Lovelle. Let him."

The bell jingled again, signaling the end to the conversation, and Raven let out a sigh of relief. Cameron and Noe walked in with Noe's best friend, Clyde Darling, alongside him. Noe shrugged off his coat while Cameron started yelling, "Where it at, where it at, where the party at?"

"Over here, man," one of the band members yelled back. "All night."

"Look," Raven said. "My favorite person."

Cameron spread his arms out like he was waiting to be hugged. Raven ran past him and started poking at Noe because she had discovered how ticklish he was. She didn't stop until she had him laughing. Then she grabbed him in a bear hug and rocked him from side to side, before rubbing the sleeve of his friend Clyde's jacket in a less physical hello.

She pulled back to look at Noe. "How are you, boy?"

"I'm all right, Rave," he said.

He hadn't started calling her aunt yet, and she decided to let it go. With a boy like Noe, what she could sense anyway, he would do that when he was ready. She'd settle for Rave for the time being.

"Hanging in there?" she asked.

"Sure," he said.

"How are you, Clyde?" she asked the young man standing next to Noe. If she didn't know any better, she would say they were brothers. Both Clyde and Noe had the same light brown skin, and big brown eyes. They kept their black hair cut close to their heads, and dressed in a nerdy Lands' End sort of way in khaki pants and university hooded sweatshirts.

She thought about the boys who were being killed. She thought about Henri Toulouse. All white, naked and wrapped in a blanket. She felt a stab of guilt at the relief from the thought that Noe and Clyde didn't match the killer's profile. At least, from that, they were safe.

"Noe!" Imogene said. "Clyde!"

Cameron, standing there with a black power pick sticking from his high afro, watched Imogene hug Noe before placing her hands on either side of his face.

"Uh-huh," Cameron said. "So, I guess this is how it is. A brother with a kid can't get no love anymore?"

"Oh, I love you, Cameron!" It was Edmée coming from the kitchen, her large dark eyes full of sparkle and amusement, her coral-colored lips stretched into a wide smile. Just as she had done with Imogene and Raven, she kissed him on both cheeks. Stella was walking toward them, awkward in low heels, the wine glass clutched in her big hand.

"Now this is what I'm talking about," Cameron said, pulling Edmée into a hug.

"Let her go, Cameron," Noe said, laughing and slapping him on the back.

"And you, Noe," Edmée said. "Your friend, too. Two peas in a pod. How are you, Clyde Darling?"

The boy blushed beneath his light skin.

"I'm fine, ma'am," Clyde said politely.

"Oh don't ma'am me," Edmée said. "You make me sound like an old lady. Aren't you going to try and get me again today?"

Clyde's smile broadened and he relaxed. "Oh, yeah, I'm going to get you all right," he said.

"Okay, I am ready," Edmée responded. "Knock yourself out."

"April 10, 2008."

"April 10, 2008. A Thursday. I had just started my job at Memorial as a social worker. Exactly fourteen days before I met my wonderful—"

"…and rich husband," Imogene cut in.

"But this is not why I love my Dr. Long," Edmée said before winking at Clyde. "But it certainly is a nice advantage."

"Okay," Clyde said. "What about June 5, 2005? What was the day and who won the World Series that year?"

"June 5, 2005. A Thursday. How could anyone not remember that the White Sox won that year, especially since they hadn't won since Jesus was a baby?"

She started to turn away when Stella said, "What about July 12th?"

Edmée paused for a second and cocked her head. "Year, darling?"

"I don't know. This year," Stella said.

"What a softball," Clyde said, laughing.

"Before I forget, this is my Stella," she said, introducing her to the boys and Cameron. "She helps me at Heron House."

"Happy Birthday, Noe," Stella said. "I hope you don't mind that I crashed your party."

"Don't mind at all," Noe said, looking around at the band, the decorations. "Everybody sure went through a whole lotta trouble."

"You deserve it," Edmée said.

"What about July 12th?" Clyde asked. "You ain't going to lose to that softball question, right?"

"No more games," Edmée said, waving the question away. "Here, Clyde and Noe, get your two beautiful young faces together so we can take a selfie."

Raven shook her head as Edmée pressed her cheek against Clyde's and held her phone up so she could snap a picture of the three of them.

"Send me that, will you," Billy Ray said as he came out of the kitchen drying his hand on a white towel.

"Hey, man." Billy Ray clasped hands with Cameron before they went into a bro hug.

"Hi, Unc," Noe said to Billy Ray. He had grown very close to Billy Ray since living with Cameron. It was as if they could talk hurt to hurt.

"How you doing?" Billy Ray asked. "You ready for a party? How about you, Clyde?"

"Always ready, Mr. Chastain," Clyde said with a wide grin.

"Heard that," Noe said.

"Stella, I didn't know you were coming, but welcome," he said.

Stella blushed before taking a sip of her wine.

"What you making, Unc?" Noe asked.

"Your favorite. Both you and Clyde come on back."

"They can't go back there," Imogene shouted. "Health department."

"Lighten up, Sis," Cameron said. "Drinks? Shots? Stella, you coming?"

"No," Stella said. "I'm going over to watch the band warm up."

As the boys disappeared through the door, Raven asked Edmée, "Why do you do that? Play those memory games."

Edmée had an eidetic memory, and ever since she met Clyde, he'd been trying to stump her with random dates. When Edmée talked seriously about it, she referred to it as no more than a parlor trick. But Raven, who had spent half of her life running from her own memories, knew it was much more than that.

"Oh, don't be so serious," Edmée said. "It's fun for the boys. And it makes me look like a superhero."

"Being unable to forget anything is a huge price to pay in order to be a superhero," Raven said.

The band started playing. They didn't ease into the music; they announced it with frenetic guitars, the frottoir, or as Raven came to learn, the washboard, and the accordion. Raven cocked her head to listen. She was trying to get better at this but sucked. Edmée flew onto the dance floor. "Buckwheat Zydeco," Edmée shouted over the music. "'Throw Me Something, Mister!' The best song!"

And then she started to dance, twirling and jumping to the music with her long black hair whipping around her. She looked both wild and graceful.

Raven made her way behind the bar.

"Whew, Chile," Imogene said, sitting on one of the barstools. "Whiskey, straight. Lots and lots of whiskey."

"Coming up," Raven said. "You sure you can handle it?"

"Let me put it this way," she said. "If I don't have it, I couldn't handle it."

"Same here," Raven said.

Raven poured two fingers of whiskey each into two crystal glasses. She found a sharp knife behind the counter and began slicing the lime for the Corona she knew Cameron would want. She stuck the slice into the mouth of a beer and pushed it toward Cameron, who had come to sit by Imogene.

Edmée had started doing a swim-like motion with her arms, and now she was jumping around singing in French along with the song. The man on the guitar burst out with a *yeah, go, ma petit* every few seconds.

Imogene pushed the empty whiskey glass away from her and then asked for a tequila and lime. She poured salt on the soft place between her thumb and index finger and licked it with a perfect pink tongue. She then downed the tequila and slammed the empty shot glass back on the bar. She sucked the lime, slung some of Cameron's beer in her mouth and said, "What the hell, if you can't beat 'em, join 'em."

She removed her platform pumps and went out on the floor and started dancing with Edmée. Imogene's dancing looked more like jumping. Edmée laughed, grabbed Imogene's wrist and twirled her around. Imogene insisted Stella lose her low heels so she could dance with them.

How different they were from each other. Stella with those curls piled high and gazing at her huge, red feet as if telling them not to trip. She kept looking back at the band, trying to catch the beat. A fish out of water, Raven thought.

Imogene was short, round and brown, a description she gave to herself on more than one occasion. She had light brown skin that the old folk would call high yellow and wore a long red-blond weave.

Edmée on the other hand was almost as tall as Billy Ray, always graceful, and dressed to the nines. If needed she could walk into any photographer's studio day or night and be ready for a photo shoot. Raven didn't know if she had eyes for Billy Ray, but if she did, he wouldn't stand a chance.

But Raven didn't want to think about that right now. She didn't want that to ruin what should be a happy occasion. The boys emerged from the kitchen and were soon keeping a shy Stella company at one of the tables near the stage. Clyde, the more extroverted of two, grilled her about the farm, how it worked and if she made a lot of money. That night, everyone was feeling good. Even when Wynn showed up, Billy Ray didn't protest when Raven let him in.

Later on, she felt Cameron watching her. She turned to him and smiled in question. It was when he returned the smile that she knew what he was thinking. *This*, he was saying, *this is good*. All the hell they had both gone through, all the time she had spent trying to prove herself worthy, all of that was over. She, both of them, were finally being rewarded. She had good friends to support her, a boyfriend, and her plan for a new life all laid out. She wasn't the freak with the serial killer father anymore. The past was dead. The present was good, and the future was waiting.

All during that night, there was gumbo, presents to spoil Noe rotten, and the red velvet cake with cream cheese frosting. Edmée had brought sparklers and the cake was presented amid bright jets of sizzling lights while they all sang the Stevie Wonder version of 'Happy Birthday'.

Finally, Billy Ray said, "All right, all right," and started taking the sparklers off the cake and placing them in a bowl of water. "Y'all don't get too crazy and set my place on fire. There's already been enough of that," he finished under his breath.

CHAPTER TEN

Cameron and the boys were long gone by the time Raven walked out onto the back porch of the restaurant. The night was brilliant, the sky full of so much light Raven thought it was making her a promise. Wynn was helping Billy Ray clean up and they sounded like they were getting along. Their laughter floated from the kitchen out of the back porch's screen door. She could hear Imogene every now and then humming loudly before breaking out into song as she cleaned the dining room floor. She had a good voice, which surprised Raven. A church voice that Raven was finding a joy to hear. Imogene had gotten tipsy, but she knew how to handle her liquor. She stopped drinking more than an hour prior, and started pounding Advil with large amounts of Perrier.

Raven gazed at the stars for a long time, and leaned against a porch post, just thinking how lucky she was at this moment. At the end of the gravel pathway was the shotgun house Billy Ray had lifted from its foundations when he opened the restaurant, and transported from the abandoned neighborhood near Peabody. This one wasn't a duplex like he lived in before. It was a single with the three rooms set one behind the other. He had painted it red, and hung white Christmas lights around the doors and windows. And there was another bottle tree to drive away evil spirits, the dead limbs covered in red, blue, yellow and hot-pink glass.

"What's got you so pensive, my Rave girl?"

Raven startled. She turned to see Edmée sitting on the high porch rail with her legs dangling over the edge.

"I thought you left with Stella," Raven said.

"I put her in a Lyft," she said. "I did my duty for the night." She was drinking a glass of Chardonnay so full that she had to lap at its surface to keep from spilling it.

"Well, it looks like someone else is going to need a Lyft tonight," Raven said with a smile.

"No worries." Edmée waved a hand expansively. "Billy Ray will take me."

"Why does it have to be Billy Ray?" Raven said. "Wynn or I can take you. Or Imogene."

"Billy Ray smells better," Edmée responded. "He has a nicer ass."

"Did you forget that you're married, Edmée?"

"I forget nothing," Edmée said, bobbing her head.

Raven decided not to lecture. She didn't want to break the mood the cool night and bright stars were giving her by getting into heavy conversation with Edmée. Billy Ray could take care of himself.

Edmée's loud sigh intruded into Raven's thoughts. "I do miss our long talks, Raven, like we had in high school. They call Noe and Clyde two peas in the pod. We were together so much they used to call us Thing 1 and Thing 2."

"That wasn't a compliment, if you remember correctly."

"Why do you say that? I do, I do remember correctly," Edmée said, nodding emphatically. "I can't help but remember correctly. It's like having an extra limb, useless, dragging me down no matter what I do…." She lapped at her wine some more. "Sometimes it makes me want to burst out into big tears."

Raven laughed. "Okay, Edmée, I think you've had enough. You've gone from happily drunk to maudlin. I didn't think you drank this much."

"I usually don't. But tonight I need it. Go ahead, ask me a date, any date. I'll be able to tell you what was happening on the news, where I was, what I was wearing. The day of the week, anything your little heart desires to know."

"Edmée," Raven said mildly.

"I'm a parlor trick. At parties, my husband points his beautifully slender hand and says, 'Watch what my wife can do. Go ahead, roll over, Edmée.' Do I find it annoying? Wouldn't you? Here I am able to rise above the hell that was my childhood, build a successful non-profit business, keep a yard and grow my own vegetables, a garden so bomb that it was featured twice on the news, and all that man cares about is the fact that I can tell you if it was raining or sunny on a particular date, if it was a Tuesday or Wednesday."

Raven walked over and sat beside Edmée in the ensuing silence. She looked at her friend. "You want a hanky, Edmée?"

Edmée slung an arm around Raven's shoulder. "That's why I like you, Raven. You're truly a bitch. I know this is the world's smallest violin stuff, but I did so like talking to you when we were teenagers."

"I'm not getting out of this conversation, am I?"

"Not a chance in hell," Edmée said. "Now you may wonder why I stay with the great Dr. Long. I wish I can say 'late, great' but that man will probably outlive me by a thousand years."

Edmée now gulped the chilled Chardonnay. She savored it for so long that Raven could taste the tartness of the wine on her own tongue.

"Why do you look at me like that? Do you think I am a bad person? This is true."

"Okay, Edmée. It's time for you to go home. You're drunk."

"I am that. But I'm also happy sitting here under the stars with you. Let's not talk about my Fabian or about how the wine is killing my brain cells. You asked me a question that's bothered me all night. How I live with the affliction of memory."

"I did, but we don't have to talk about it now."

"Yes, we do," Edmée countered. "So, how shall I put this? You…" she said, jabbing Raven's chest with a manicured fingernail, "…came from hell. But I am still in hell. I live it every day. Every memory of what my cousin did to me, those men who raped me over and over again, every memory lives here. In my head. The sound, the smells, the fear. I feel it as if it's happening right this minute. At least your memories have soft edges. But no, no, no, not for Edmée."

"I'm sorry, Edmée."

"I know you are. But do you know how I cope? By dancing." Edmée suddenly stood and twirled. The wineglass she had been holding fell, the wine spilling into the soft earth below. "By buying expensive clothes, painting my face and curling my hair. By doing good for people who are less fortunate, that does help. Nothing makes you forget your problems like helping somebody else with theirs."

"Like you're helping Billy Ray?"

"Oh what, are you mad now? You think I'm going to steal your boyfriend again like I did in high school?"

"I didn't have any boyfriends in high school," Raven said, though she was aware Edmée knew darn well that Raven was going out with Wynn.

"You mean that you didn't have boyfriends for long, because I took them. Every single one. You know, I didn't even want them. But beating you was such a distraction."

"Is that what you thought you were doing, beating me? Sorry, I thought we were only in competition on the track field."

"And I beat you there, too." Edmée pointed at Raven. "Every time."

"Not every time. I almost had you once. You cheated."

"Be serious. It was only a garden snake. A little baby snake who still had his little round baby eyes, and you screamed for your mother like a three-year-old."

"It took me out of the race."

"Oh, don't give me that, you could have just hopped over it like I did, or told on me. But you didn't."

"Edmée," Raven said, "you are not right in the head."

"Yes," Edmée agreed cheerfully, "I am not right at all."

She sat back down, and once again slung her arm around Raven's neck, this time pressing her head close. "But you never got mad, did you? Because you knew inside what I was going through. You wanted to make sure that I stayed happy so my memories, my demons, wouldn't slice me to pieces. That's why I do love you, my Raven."

"Sounds like you and Dr. Long aren't getting along too well," Raven said, wanting to get Edmée's mind off high school.

Edmée sighed. "We don't. He just doesn't know about it, yet."

"Must be upsetting for the both of you with that boy's body being found at the construction site for Memorial's new wing."

Edmée shuddered. "Just unbelievable what some people will do."

"Did you happen to know him?"

"You mean Henri Toulouse?" Edmée said. "No. I think Fabian knows the father, though. A judge. Fabian hates that they found the dead boy there. He said he's not going to talk about it in the press. It'll ruin the opening."

"How are you going to have a successful opening of the new wing if you don't acknowledge that a body was found there? People might think you're callous."

Edmée touched her throat. "Me? Why, it has nothing to do with me. That wing is Fabian's pet project. I have my hands full with my own work. I told him when he started that I can't be involved in this at all."

"And he's okay with that?"

"My husband is a very understanding man."

"Must be," Raven said.

"Jealous?"

"Completely."

They sat for a while in companionable silence. Raven felt nice having Edmée close to her again. It brought back so many memories of them supporting each other through high school.

Suddenly, Edmée said, "Raven, the stuff we talked about in high school...what my cousin did to me, making me bed those men for money. I was so young. You do understand that, don't you?"

"It wasn't your fault, Edmée," Raven said. "Your cousin was evil. Someone should slow cook her in her own fat."

"It would have been easier to cope if there wasn't a baby," Edmée said, staring into the night.

"But you had an abortion. There was no baby."

Edmée touched her belly. "There was a child that lived here for a while. They took that away from me. All I ask is one thing from you."

"Anything, Edmée, you know that."

"I never told, Billy Ray, I mean. Only you, my husband and my cousin know about the sex stuff. No one else."

"It's not sex stuff, Edmée. It's rape stuff. You have nothing to be ashamed of."

"You're so kind, my friend," she said. "But please, I just ask that you not tell Billy Ray."

"Relax," Raven said, "I have no reason to tell him. Besides, Billy Ray and I don't talk about everything."

CHAPTER ELEVEN

Speaking of not telling Billy Ray everything, Raven didn't tell him that she was proceeding with her cleanup of Oral's house. She didn't want the argument. Except with Billy Ray, there wouldn't have been an argument so anyone would notice – no shouting or slammed doors. Instead, there would be her stating her position, his look of dark disapproval, and then, the most annoying of all, a dismissive grunt. She couldn't let his or Imogene's condemnation make her forgo her promise to Oral's memory. She'd erase the damage Lovelle had done while chasing Oral through its bright rooms with a scythe. Laughter would fill his house again.

The last time she was at the house was during a crime scene walk-through. Bloodstains jutted up the interior sun-yellow walls. Bits of brain clung to kitchen cabinets where Oral had taken his last breath. Lamont Lovelle had succeeded in not only ushering Oral's soul from this earth with his blasted scythe, but he left a picture so grotesque that it was all she saw when she thought of the man who had mentored her. That needed to change.

That was why about two weeks after Noe's birthday party, she found herself parking her red Mustang in an uneven dirt yard choked with weeds and pockmarked with pecan shells from the grove next door. Oral never was a fan of manicured front lawns. He preferred to let the wisteria and the wide wraparound porch speak for him. Now, this late in the year, the wisteria branches were thick, bare, twisted. They clung to the pergola in a snarling, determined grip of ownership.

At the front door she lifted the heavy combination lock and held it against her palm for a few seconds. She reached into her back pocket for the napkin she had scribbled the combination on after a call to the lawyer who handled Oral's last will and testament. She thumbed the combination into the lock, and was heartened when it popped open with one hard click.

The heavy door creaked unevenly in warning as she pushed it open. When she stepped into the house a smell with the force of a shrieking wraith almost knocked her backward. The house had been locked up for over a year. With no one to pay the bills, the electricity and water had been cut off long ago. She recognized in the odor, the smell of rot, old blood and, oddly enough, the hot, corrupted scent of burning feces.

Oral Justice was killed in the summer. The house was shut up in the summer. For one wild moment Raven thought that the entire hell of that July and August was escaping through the door to terrorize her anew. Her eyes watered. She didn't realize she had stopped breathing until she gulped and coughed low and hard in her throat in an effort to let in new air.

Holy demons of all things sinful, she thought. She only hesitated for a fraction of a second. She owed it to Oral. She took two steps inside with her knuckles pressed against her nose. All of the furniture was in the same position that it had been in on the day that Oral died – the overturned glass coffee table, the broken shards now covered in a thick layer of grime. The hardwood floor held none of the shine she remembered. Oral's blood telegraphed in dark patches in various places. Her eyes followed the blood splatter on the wall and the cast-off on the ceiling. She remembered it being a bright arterial red. Now it was oily, black.

Without realizing that she did so, she walked the house the same way she did when it was a crime scene. She finished in the kitchen, where most of the damage to Oral's big body had been inflicted.

She told herself not to do it, but she had to. She didn't know why but something beckoned her. Maybe it was her father's voice surfing the wave of frenzied whispers in her head. She opened the refrigerator door as if in a trance. Something caught up top and before she knew it, the freezer door came along for the ride. This time she did stagger backwards, and almost fell. Floyd's cackling laughter grew louder and louder in her head.

Roaches poured from the freezer, their black legs making scurrying sounds as they hurried out of the refrigerator and pattered in streams down to the tile floor. What would usually be wrapped cubes of frozen meat were now black squares of putrefaction.

Reminds you, don't it, Birdy Girl, Floyd's voice, the voice she thought was dead, said, *that animal flesh we be eating. Meat. Things alive at first and things that can decompose just like us humans when the good Lord puts us down.*

"Shut up," she gasped. "Shut up. You're dead."

The bottles in the refrigerator door jangled against each other as she slung it closed. The door bounced back, refusing to shut. She looked down at her sneaker-clad feet to see the roaches attempting to clamor up the legs of her jeans. She shook them off with a screaming sob.

She had seen horrific crime scenes, some in which the body lay for months. But she never gave much thought to cleaning up such a sight. Someone else scoured the blood from the walls, pried up the floor, removed the broken furniture, and, yes, even cleaned out the refrigerator.

Her entire body went rigid before it released again with a command to run.

As she ran, she imagined that the smell was not only clinging to her, but piercing through her flesh to settle in her bones so completely that she feared it would still be there when they dug her up a hundred years later.

CHAPTER TWELVE

Willie Lee Speck had told her to meet him at a rundown motel in the Bottoms. Painted a dirty yellow, the building was square, squat and solid in the way of motels for the poor. As she walked toward it, a boy in a neon-green shirt rode past her on a bicycle, white earbuds in his ears and an iPhone in one hand.

"Lay it down," he sang repeatedly in a melody too big for just those three small words. His intent gaze on the phone and the repetition told Raven that he didn't sing for pleasure but for practice. She heard the phrase two more times, first sweet and clear and then fading as he rode out of sight.

"Lay it down," he sang. "Lay it down."

She watched the boy for a few seconds before turning her attention toward the motel. A tall man with a broad chest and big hands walked out of one of the rooms on the first floor. He emanated an energy so strong that it was a wonder that his body just didn't fly apart from its constraining center. His glittery eyes were narrow, and his left hand jumpy. His mouth worked like a washing machine with what she knew to be a huge glob of red Bubble Yum to help mask the smell of whatever job he was working at the moment. Willie Lee Speck, one of the town's only two trauma scene cleaners, at your service.

She scanned the parking lot until she saw the familiar faded brown and white VW truck. The ancient VW was a fixture at Speck's cleanup scenes. The homeless man who owned the truck scavenged from Speck's jobs. His treasure hanging from the flatbed railings consisted of cracked belts, tinkling wind chimes, and several faded bath towels tied to the railing so they wouldn't fly away when the VW was in motion. The flatbed was filled with dishes, toasters, and anything that couldn't be slung over the railings. The VW's owner, a withered man in short pants and a straw cowboy hat too big for his peanut-sized head, came toward her. He held a length of ceramic onions strung along a frayed rope.

"I'm pretty sure that's a biohazard, Ozy," Raven said to him as she waved to Speck, who was making his way toward her with a merry glint in his tiny eyes.

The old man looked at the blood droplets spattered on the onions. His tongue worked in and out of his mouth as if his brain were trying to say something but his tongue was too slow to cooperate.

"Willie Lee said I can have it," he finally managed. "You reckon I can wipe it off?"

"Willie Lee's a son-of-a-robber," she said. "Wear gloves when you do it."

His gummy eyes wandered toward the VW, back to the onions and back to her.

She shook her head.

"Here," Willie Lee said, his voice jaunty.

He tossed her a box of latex gloves and she reached up reflexively to catch it. She gave it to Ozy, who took it and held it to his chest. As he shuffled to the VW with the rope of ceramic onions in one hand and the box of latex gloves clasped to his chest with the other, Raven stuffed her own hands in the back pockets of her jeans. They itched as she thought of what else might be clinging to that box.

"What's shaking, Detective?" Willie Lee said, still chewing.

"Don't call me that."

She headed toward the back of his van parked near the open door of the motel room. He fell into step beside her.

"Still hate my guts, huh?"

"I don't hate your guts," she said. "I just prefer it if you call me by my name. I'm not a detective anymore."

And she meant it. She didn't hate Speck's guts, but she sure didn't like him very much. Willie Lee Speck owned The Cleanup Man. He was usually hired by those who didn't have the money for a more caring and thorough cleaner to sanitize trauma scenes. The other service in town, the reputable one, was too busy to help her.

"And what would that name be since it's not Detective anymore?" he asked.

"Just Raven."

She jerked her head to the open door of the room from where he had emerged. She needed to think. Maybe there was another way of cleaning up Oral's house rather than hiring this slime bucket.

"What's it this time?" she asked him.

"Suicide," he said, smiling as wide as he could with a mouth much too small for his head and oversized body. "Shotgun. Gloriously bloody. Do you know what I thought when I saw it?"

"I can guess," Raven said dryly.

"I thought that's fresh, green money, baby."

"You're a prince among men, Willie Lee."

"Somebody's got to do it, right?"

"Who was it?" Raven asked, lightly probing for the humanity that she thought was there, that had to be there.

"Don't know and don't care."

She resisted the urge to call him a maggot. That would only make the smirk smeared across his face wider. She made sure that she didn't blink while she looked at him. She wanted to stare him down. She wanted to shame him.

"What?" he asked, his hands out. He rubbed the tips of his fingers together. "It's all about getting paid."

She said nothing.

"Okay, some teenager I think, an addict. Put Daddy's shotgun between her legs and under her chin, and ba-boom." He held his hands out to mimic an explosion.

"That's sad," Raven tried.

"Maybe sad for her, but good for me," he said. "I charge a lot more for a kiss from a bullet than an overdose. And anyway, she was a junkie. Who cares?"

"I don't know," Raven said. "Maybe her family?"

"I'm sure they don't give a shit. You should see these people. Pigs behave better."

"What people?" Raven challenged.

"Keep your pants on," Willie Lee said. "I'm not talking about 'people of color'. I'm talking about people, people who let their lives get like this." He gestured toward the hotel.

"You mean poor people? Hurt people?"

"Fucking losers."

"How are the kids, Willie Lee?"

"Good," he said. "Lucy just started kindergarten, got JoeJoe signed up for baseball. Life's good."

"I bet," she said. "Probably even better since you have a few more scenes to clean up with those boys turning up dead."

"Are you kidding me?" he said. "They won't let me anywhere near that. They think that their boys are too good for me and my guys to clean up. Like those poor fucks would care who swept the last of their leavings into a lawn and leaf bag. Anyway, those scenes are pristine. Not much to clean up."

Raven looked at him for a long moment. She wanted to punch him in his smirking face.

"Anyway, what can I do you for?" he asked.

Raven sucked in her breath. She couldn't imagine Speck in Oral's house with his flip attitude and bad jokes.

"Never mind."

"No, what?" he asked, following her back to her car. "You came here for a reason. What is it? You got a job for me?"

She turned to face him. "I might."

"I thought you were waitressing for that gimpy cop."

She said nothing. When he realized that he wouldn't get a rise out of her, he pressed. "No, what is it?"

"I need help cleaning up Oral Justice's house," she said.

"You mean that murder that happened last year? The man with the fucking scythe? That place has been shut for a long time." Another grin. "I'd love to do that house."

Raven strode over to him until she was close enough to smell his stale breath and sweet remnants of his bubble gum. When she spoke again, her voice was cold and frozen.

"You are not *doing* that house," she said. "And if I *allow* you to help me, there are some rules you'll need to follow. You don't go into the house without me there. I do as much work as you do. And you keep your nasty little rat-mouth shut. No sick jokes, no snarky remarks, and you do the job right. By the regs. You understand me?"

He smirked again. God, she thought. She'd love to see him when he didn't have that grin on his face.

"You got yourself a deal. But you better be ready to pay me."

She looked at him for a moment longer before turning away.

As she strode back toward the Mustang, he shouted, "When do we start?"

She said nothing.

"I may be too busy, you know."

She still didn't turn around. If he were too busy, he wouldn't have jumped on her offer so quickly.

"You know you gotta tell me something if you want me to help you."

"I'll call you."

Standing next to the driver's side door of the Mustang, she watched Ozy hang the ceramic onions next to the wind chimes. He then started rearranging the junk in the flatbed, probably to make room for whatever he could scavenge from that poor girl's motel room. Something moved in the sunlight and she swore that it was a bear's paw, the long sharp claws out as if it were in mid-lunge.

She shook her head. *Get with it, Raven. Get out of your head.*

Maybe Billy Ray was right. She should just sell the place. But no. Oral deserved better. And her work with Speck would be the last thing she would do that involved blood and murder. That's what this bright morning was telling her, the music in the air, the boy practicing for a band he was probably just starting to imagine. They were telling her to lay it down. Lay it all down.

As she watched Ozy a little longer, it started to rain again, a hot, uncomfortable rain even this late in the year that trickled down her face like tears, like the water dropping from the sky was really coming from inside her own body. Rain in this much sunlight, Floyd would tell her, means that the devil's beating his wife. She looked up as drops fell into her eyes. *Well,* she thought, *he must be beating the hell out of her.*

Back in the car she didn't bother wiping the rain away. Instead she leaned her head against the headrest and took one long breath. *I'm doing the right thing, I'm doing the right thing,* she told herself repeatedly until her phone rang.

Her heart froze.

Billy Ray. She could tell by the ringtone, no longer Buckwheat's 'Walking to New Orleans', but zydeco, nonetheless. Something cold moved in her heart when she heard it. Billy Ray never called her on her days off. *Don't answer it,* a voice said, her voice. And for some reason the vision of the man standing in the fog appeared to her, and she heard Floyd's voice, *I'm thinking that you don't have much of a choice, Birdy Girl.*

She pressed the answer button, "Yeah," she said, swallowing down the lump in her throat.

"You need to get down here," Billy Ray said without preamble.

"Where?"

"BLPD," he answered in a flat, disconnected voice.

"Why?"

"Noe's missing."

CHAPTER THIRTEEN

Raven was barely aware that she parked the Mustang in the same spot that she had used in her previous life as a homicide detective at the BLPD. Her heart hammered too loud in her chest for the recognition of ironies. It had been over a year since she had been in that parking lot. Yet her parking space sat there empty as if waiting for her return. The same fountain that had greeted her every day for years greeted her again, bright water clattering against the stone basin. To her frazzled mind it sounded like *we knew you'd be back, we knew you'd be back.* Even the desk sergeant was the same, a pudgy man named Spangler who had always been kind to her.

She greeted him, then asked, "Cameron, Billy Ray, where are they?"

"Interview Room D. But you can't go back without a visitor's...."

She continued down the hall while his voice faded, walking as fast as she could without running. Her thoughts came faster and faster now. Questions surged through her head in more of a prayer than a denial. How could it be Noe? He didn't fit the victim profile. The chief said white. Noe definitely was not white.

She stepped through time when she opened the door of the interview room. Nothing had changed, not the light blue walls, not the metal table and chairs, and not the smooth suppleness of the two-way. She searched the corners of the room for cameras that would make the glass unnecessary, but the chief hadn't gotten around to installing them in this room, not yet.

Cameron sat with both elbows on the table, his head cradled in his hands. He looked up at her with shock in his eyes. His mouth hung open in disbelief.

Tell him to close his mouth, Floyd's voice in her head again. *He'll catch flies.*

She tried to push Floyd away, but couldn't. The weight of his evil was too heavy now, even though he had been decomposing into dust for over a decade.

Edmée was there, too. She sat beside Cameron with one arm around his shoulders.

"What's happening?" Raven said. "Cam? Edmée?"

Edmée looked left, and Raven followed her gaze.

Well, well, the gang's all here, came Floyd's sing-song voice. *Just like in the olden days.*

Billy Ray was standing opposite the two-way, leaning against the wall with one hand in the pocket of his slacks, his ever-present pork pie hat pushed back on his head.

"What's happening?" she asked Cameron again. "Talk to me."

She knew it was the second time she asked the question, but she couldn't help it. Cameron's mouth worked, but not well enough to make sound. Raven turned back to Billy Ray. She told him with her eyes that he would have to be the grown-up in the room. My God, didn't he already know that? Cameron, at the moment, was useless, just as he himself feared he would be when he learned that he was now daddy to an almost grown boy. Billy Ray's silence frightened her more than words could. Noe was most likely dead.

"They don't have a body," Billy Ray said slowly as if reading her mind. "He's missing."

"How long?"

Billy Ray held Raven's gaze, waited a beat before saying, "Since Friday morning, before school."

"What? Since Friday? All weekend? How's that even possible?" Raven asked.

"I'm sorry," Cameron managed. "I thought he was spending the weekend with Clyde."

"And Clyde's parents probably thought Clyde was spending the weekend with Noe and Cameron," Billy Ray said.

Raven turned a disgusted look toward her foster brother. "Come on, Cameron. That's the oldest trick in the book. Where's Clyde? Did you talk to his parents?"

"I talked to his daddy," Cameron said. "He just said his kid ain't missing, and he hadn't seen Noe in a while."

"I don't believe this," Raven said.

"My fault, Raven," Cameron croaked. "You were right. I'm not cut out to be anybody's daddy. How can anybody expect me to know how to be a father to a fifteen-year-old kid I don't even know?"

"Now you got excuses?" Raven said.

Everything about Cameron at that moment irritated her – the black power pick stuck in his big afro, his vintage and very expensive Air Jordan tennis shoes, the long-sleeved Wu Tang Clan T-shirt he was wearing without a jacket in spite of the weather, and his tears. Especially his tears. She couldn't understand how he didn't know that Noe was missing a couple of days.

"Leave him alone," Edmée said. "He's having the worst day of his life. Why do you need to make him feel shittier than he already does? Raven. Please."

Edmée slid a long green scarf from her neck, and draped it around Cameron's shoulders.

"Because a fifteen-year-old kid is missing and probably dead," Raven said. "Because it's his responsibility to look after his son."

"That's enough, Raven," Billy Ray said. "No cause for all this snapping."

No, it's not enough, Raven wanted to scream. *Noe is missing and it's my fault.* She took a breath in and let it out slowly. It wasn't until she thought she could speak calmly that she said, "Missing person report?"

"Took it at the desk," Billy Ray said.

"Maybe I should go," Edmée said. "I don't want to cause any trouble."

Raven was preparing herself for what she would have to do to find Noe. Edmée was having a calming effect on Cameron. That was good. *Let her*, Raven thought. There would be more hard times and grief to come in the next few hours if what Raven suspected turned out to be true.

"No, don't go," Raven said. "Take care of Cameron. Who's working this, Billy Ray?"

"DeShawn Breaker," Billy Ray said. "You know him?"

"Not well," she said. "I met him over at the Memorial crime scene. I don't understand why he—"

"Yes, that's right," Billy Ray said, before mouthing, "Homicide's got it."

Holy flock, Raven thought as she pulled out the chair next to Edmée. She sat down so hard that she felt the sting all the way up her thighs.

"Where's Breaker?" Raven asked.

"Said he's getting some water and coffee for us," Billy Ray said.

Cameron snuffled, and ran the sleeve of his T-shirt across his nose. Edmée pulled a Kleenex from her purse and handed it to him. Raven stood up and motioned for Billy Ray to follow her outside.

Once in the hallway, she closed the door behind them and whispered, "How bad does this look?"

"I can't say," he said. "But I'm thinking it can't be connected to all these killings going on."

"Because Noe's black?"

"Yes, because Noe's black. This killer is only snatching white kids so far."

Raven tried to catch hold of the hopeful thread now running through her. Noe didn't fit the profile. He could still be alive. But she knew that there was no logic in these things, nothing to count on.

"Maybe Noe ran back to his stepfather? Grandparents? Cousins?" Raven asked.

"Cameron already made those calls. They haven't seen him," Billy Ray said.

"You think they're telling the truth?"

Billy Ray looked at her and said, "Why would they lie? They didn't want nothing to do with him once they were shut of his mother."

Raven nodded, her mind moving on to other things. "You think Breaker was watching all this behind the two-way?"

Billy Ray gave her a half-smile. "I would be. Wouldn't you?"

Just as she was about to answer his question, Breaker arrived with two bottles of water under one arm, and balancing a full-to-spilling cup of coffee with both hands.

"Whoa," he said in a friendly voice. "Can you open the door for me?"

Billy Ray opened the door and held it there while the man entered the room and put the drinks on the table.

"A full house, I see," he said. "Why don't you two stay out there and I'll be along directly."

Raven looked through the door to see Cameron's eyes, still red from tears. She wasn't sure if she should leave him.

"Go on and talk," Edmée said, looking over at Raven. "I'll stay with him."

Yeah, Raven thought, losing patience again. *Why don't you change his diaper while you're at it?* She loved her foster brother, but there was one thing about him she just couldn't abide. He had a way of making everything about him during tragic situations. Raven knew he didn't do it on purpose. He was an emotional man when it came to some things, but his sobbing and sniffling when someone else was dead or their life was on the line required that he be taken care of as well.

Once Breaker was back in the hallway, all of his faked friendliness was gone. He looked down at his feet. His leather shoes had a spit shine that any army recruit would envy.

"Your partner and I got reacquainted over at the Memorial crime scene," he said to Billy Ray. "I mean ex-partner. You used to work here, too, right?"

"Used to," Billy Ray agreed.

"So, you're Billy Ray Chastain? I don't think we've ever met but I've heard a lot of good things about you."

"And you're DeShawn Breaker," Billy Ray said.

Billy Ray waited. Raven waited. They all waited.

Finally Billy Ray smiled. All charm, he said, "I see you know a lot about me, but I know next to nothing about you."

"Sorry." Breaker smoothed back his curly black hair with the palm of his hand. "Chief pulled me over from major crimes about six months ago. I've got the Sleeping Boy case."

"I get all that, but why do you have Cameron's case, man?" Billy Ray asked.

Breaker blew out a breath. He looked down at the buffed linoleum before looking back at them.

"Because we have a body in the morgue."

Raven didn't feel the breath leave her body. Instead she felt air rushing in before landing in her gut like a punch. Billy Ray placed a hand on her shoulder and squeezed.

"Your guy?" Billy Ray asked.

Raven couldn't believe Billy Ray's voice was so calm. Noe might be dead and here he was as calm as still water.

"Is it Noe?" Raven asked.

"It's likely," Breaker said. "We don't know because, of course, he didn't have any identification on him, being, you know," he stopped before continuing on, "naked." Breaker pulled at his red tie as if it were choking him.

"These killings your first homicide case?" Billy Ray asked.

"Yeah," he admitted. "They are. Gotta be a first time for everything, right?"

"God bless it," Raven said. She put her hands on her hips and turned away from him.

"The chief should have asked for help," she said, turning around to face him.

"You know damn well he did," Breaker countered.

"I'm not talking about from me," Raven snapped.

"Couldn't get any other help. Who'd you think would want this case? Besides, the mayor doesn't want this going national."

"Yeah," Raven said. "Better to have another dead body than a three-minute segment on *Good Morning America*."

"Where is the chief, anyway?" Billy Ray asked.

"He's on his way in." Breaker flipped his wrist to check his watch. "A half hour or so. This was supposed to be his day off."

"Why are you talking to us and not Cameron?" Raven asked.

"We need your brother to identify the body. I thought that it would be better if the news came from one of you."

CHAPTER FOURTEEN

Once Floyd told her she would go to hell if she snitched on him. She was too young to know any better, so she believed him. The hell Floyd described was scarier than any hell she could imagine, filled with snakes that the devil would make her swallow. He said they'd eat out her throat on the way down to gnaw at the insides of her belly. He threatened that the devil would call her mother out of heaven to take care of her in hell. So she kept silent, and stayed silent until she had enough years on her to disbelieve that a hell like that existed.

Now she wasn't so sure. Maybe that same hell Floyd imagined bubbled up through the soil of Byrd's Landing and ate away at your soul with teeth of hatred and murder and grief.

Cameron wasn't crying anymore as he waited to identify the body. Raven stood on one side of him, Billy Ray on the other. Edmée was there, too, her heavy perfume emanating from her as if she were trying to cover the smell of death, her face white with fear. She was standing next to Billy Ray, too close in Raven's opinion, but calling Billy Ray on it was a battle for another day.

And there was Detective 'Shiny Shoes' Breaker standing off to the side next to a button by the window. His hands were clasped in front, his cufflinks flashing gold on his starched cuffs. He reminded Raven of those southern preachers twirling on stage in their five-thousand-dollar suits while passing the collection plate.

"Tell me when you're ready," he said.

Raven glanced at Cameron, now tearless. He had on what he called his chill face, the face that he used when other kids teased him in the foster home, a set mouth, unblinking eyes, and breath so slow it didn't look like his lungs were working. Raven could only detect the slight tremble to his mouth because she knew to look for it. Anyone else would think he didn't care.

Like Detective Breaker.

She pictured Breaker's notes in her head. He would say that the victim's father cried crocodile tears when he reported his son missing, and then dried up like a plugged pipe when it came to identifying the body. *'I need you to tell him'* my sweet behind, Raven thought. *You just wanted to observe without the distraction of having to tell him the news. Let the patsies, Raven and Billy Ray, tell the father. I'll just watch. Well,* Raven thought, *let's get this show on the road.*

"Cameron," Raven said softly. "You need to say when you're ready."

"Yeah, go ahead," Cameron said in a voice as bland as his face.

Detective Breaker pressed the button next to the glass. The drape moved aside with a low hum. Rita Sandbourne, the medical examiner, stood next to the body still in its black body bag. Rita nodded a brief greeting to Raven and Billy Ray before turning to Breaker. She was thinner than Raven remembered, but Raven was almost certain that Rita wore a Grateful Dead T-shirt under the white lab coat.

Breaker looked at Cameron and said, "Are you sure you're ready?"

"How can anybody ever be ready for shit like this?" Billy Ray said. "Stop dragging this motherfucker out. Get on with it, man."

Breaker motioned with two fingers to Rita. She carefully unzipped the body bag to expose the corpse's face. And waited. For a second or two, nobody moved. Raven finally blinked several times to chase away both astonishment and tears. She felt Cameron's arm slip from hers. He fell to his knees with one sob. He just stayed there, silent, on his knees, weaving like a drunk. Finally he made a sucking sound as if he were trying to suck up all the air in the room.

"Oh, God," Edmée said. "Couldn't they have at least cleaned him up?"

She slapped a hand over her mouth before running to the bathroom on the other side of the small identification room. Raven heard the toilet seat slam up before Edmée started dry heaving. Billy Ray went after her.

Cameron's lips started moving. He was praying, praying like Raven had never in all of her years of knowing him heard him pray. And Floyd was there again in her head, *Well, I guess there is something to that ole saying about atheists in foxholes.*

But Raven wasn't focused on Cameron. The boy's face on the table captivated her. The eyes were open, and though she knew them to be brown, they looked fogged over, erased. His skin had gone ash gray, and the familiar hair that she could see swirled over his head in caked coils of dried blood. More blood streaked his face, and there was a round, caved-in wound on his forehead.

"Like the rest?" Raven asked.

"Yes," Breaker said. "Throat slit, exsanguinated."

"But the body's not cleaned," Raven said.

"No."

"And that wound on his forehead? What's that?"

"Probably a skull fracture, but we don't know from what. That's the thing we're holding from the press, in case, you know...."

Yes, she knew all right. In case they had a crazy who wanted to confess. If they could tell them about that one strange wound on the forehead, then the cops would take them seriously.

"But, as I said, like the others. Naked, wrapped in a brand new blanket."

"Where?" Raven said. She turned to face him. "Where did they find him?"

She pretended that she didn't see Breaker flinch. She had her father's eyes. Sometimes she knew that they looked as cold as Floyd's.

"The mayor's front porch."

"You should have plenty of cameras there."

"No," Breaker said. "The mayor didn't want them. He's paranoid. Always afraid of being spied on. Has someone from crimes go over on a regular basis to sweep the place for bugs."

She held her gaze steady on Breaker's until he cleared his throat and turned away. If it were her, or maybe Billy Ray, she would have made sure that they had cameras installed everywhere that the killer might elect to display a body. The perp was making no secret of who he was taunting. The establishment, right? Or as Billy Ray would have said, The Man. The killer was sticking it to The Man. If it were her, she'd like to think that she would've placed a camera around the mayor's residence. She turned back to the body. Rita was zipping the body bag closed over those ghostly eyes.

"I'm sorry for your loss," Breaker said to Cameron, who was on his second round of Our Fathers. When it was the only prayer you knew, it was the prayer that would have to do.

She assessed Breaker; this man with the gold cufflinks made a lot of assumptions. No wonder a killer still roamed the streets of Byrd's Landing.

Breaker cleared his throat again. "I'll go get the paperwork."

"It isn't him," she said flatly.

The look of surprise on his face was comical. "I don't understand," he said, looking down at Cameron.

"Clyde Darling," she explained. "A friend of Noe's. You've got another murdered boy and now a missing one, Detective."

Raven bent down to help her brother stand, murmuring to him that they would find Noe and that it would be all right. She didn't know or care if she lied, but she would do everything in her power to bring Cameron's son back to him, Floyd's made-up hell and the very real one of the BLPD be damned.

CHAPTER FIFTEEN

After the chief deputized Raven, and gave her the badge and service weapon he so desperately wanted to give to her weeks ago, she drove with Billy Ray in a BLPD unmarked Dodge to her rooms at Mama Anna's. While Billy Ray waited outside, she raced up the wide staircase to change clothes. She didn't want to notify Clyde Darling's parents in the purple and gold LSU sweatshirt she had been wearing when she got the call about Noe. She had told Billy Ray that she would be no longer than ten minutes.

She wasn't in her rooms five before there was a knock on her door. She knew who it was. Wynn. She had been ignoring his repeated calls all through the conversation with Cameron and the identification of Clyde Darling's body. She opened the door and greeted him with an absentminded kiss on the cheek before striding back to the bedroom, stripping off her faded jeans as she went.

He followed her, saying, "Whoa, whoa, I just got here."

"Don't be an ass," she said without turning around. "Noe's missing."

Now back in the bedroom but in matching bra and panties, she withdrew a holstered six-inch hunting knife from beneath a stack of obsessively folded T-shirts in the last drawer of a tall antique chifforobe. Next came a .22 revolver in a holster fitted for the small of her back. She threw both on the bed. They landed with a thud next to the shoulder holster with the Smith & Wesson and the BLPD detective's badge the chief had given her at the station earlier.

"Wait, what do you mean 'missing'?" Wynn said, his eyes narrowing at the small arsenal on the bed.

"I mean missing. Maybe dead missing," she answered as she

pulled on a pair of tight black jeans and a white spotless T-shirt. "And Clyde's dead."

Wynn let out a breath and crossed both arms over his head. "Fuck," he whispered. "That poor boy. What happened?"

"Byrd's Landing happened."

She sat down on the bed to put on her socks before reaching back for the holstered hunting knife. She strapped it to her ankle, pulled on her boots and stood up. She removed the Smith & Wesson service weapon from the shoulder holster and swapped it with her own Glock that she kept in her nightstand drawer. She made sure both weapons were loaded before doing so. The shoulder holster went on so easily that it felt like reattaching a lost limb. Next she placed the backup weapon at the small of her back, then clipped the badge to her waistband. And finally, the suit jacket from way back in her closet, the one she thought she would never wear again. The weapons and the clothes she hadn't worn for over a year didn't feel alien to her. They felt like home. Just like that, she was back. Detective Raven Burns.

Wynn stared at her as if he'd never seen her before. His eyes moved fast and worried from the badge, to the Glock in the holster, to her ankle where the knife was.

"What?" she said. "I told you that I used to be a cop."

"You said used to be. You also said that it gutted you."

She went to the bathroom to throw water on her face, and shake out her curls in the mirror. She was probably imagining it, but the suit jacket smelled musty. In the medicine cabinet she found an old bottle of perfume left by a previous tenant. She sniffed and shrugged before spritzing a small amount around the cuffs.

"No choice. I've got to find Noe," she said as she walked back to the bedroom. "Chief's bringing me back on temporarily until we catch this creeper."

Wynn folded his arms across his chest. She stood on tiptoe and kissed him on the corner of his frowning mouth. It was like kissing stone. She pulled back so she could look into his face.

"You even smell different," he said.

"You can't be serious?"

"This isn't what I signed up for," he said.

"You had to sign something?"

"Not funny, Raven. I never thought I'd be dating a maniac who feels the need to carry three deadly weapons strapped to her body."

Her laugh was without humor. "Never took you for being deer skittish, Wynn. What are you? A scaredy cat?"

"That's insulting."

"Okay," she said, not wanting to talk about it anymore. She walked to the bedroom door, stood there waiting for him to follow.

"Are the rumors true, then?" he spat at her. "Did you kill Lamont Lovelle?"

She drew back at the question. "Where in the left field did that come from?"

"I think I have a right to know," he said. "It's all over town."

"How would you know what's all over town when you've only been here for about a minute and a half?"

"I have a right to know," he insisted.

Her laugh was filled with humor, a lot of Floyd humor. "That's the stupidest thing I've ever heard. You don't have a right to know anything."

"I thought we were having a relationship here? Was I wrong?"

"You do this now when my nephew is missing and his best friend is dead? You want me to sit down with you and cite chapter and verse about my career as a cop?"

"I think you owe it to me."

"I owe you nothing. Get real."

"Just tell me."

She looked at the door, the time on her Android and back at him. Almost fifteen minutes had passed. "Now?"

"I need to know if I'm wasting my time."

"You giving me an ultimatum?"

"I want to know the real you."

"Who the heck do you think you've been sleeping with these last few months? You got the real me."

"You keep me at arm's length."

"No time, Wynn."

He took a tiny step back from her, which led him further back in the bedroom. She wanted to scream.

"If we're going to have a serious relationship, I need to know everything about you," he said.

"And you'll tell me everything about you?"

"Yes."

"Even the times you skipped school, or stole a Snickers bar from the Fast Mart? Are you going to tell me about the first time you masturbated? The first time you banged a girl?"

"You don't have to be so crude."

"I'm just asking," she said.

"No, you're not. You're being combative."

"Combative? Try confused. Clyde Darling is lying on a slab in the morgue. My nephew is missing and maybe dead, and all of a sudden you want a dissertation about my life?"

"I just want to know who I'm dealing with."

"What do you think I'm going to do? Cut your throat with a straight razor while you sleep? Gut you while we're making love in the shower? You think I'm going to shoot you in the back of the head and dismember your body with a chainsaw?"

"That's sick."

"Sure it's sick. But that's what you're calling me, right, sick?"

"No, no, no," he said, backing off and, to her now immense impatience and irritation, backing up.

She took a deep breath to control her anger. This was why she dated infrequently when she was a cop. She had managed to find partners who wanted to know everything, or those who wanted to know nothing. She could never find someone who was content to walk the middle of the road in her life. She took several more deep breaths before counting up to ten and then back down again. She couldn't let this anger overtake her. Not with so much on the line. She scratched the side of her head in the silence, woke up her Android to check the time. It was getting late and the longer it took to find Noe, the grimmer his chances of survival became.

"Look," she said, "this isn't working. Get out."

His eyes widened and he started shaking his head. She could have sworn that his nostrils flared.

"Are you dumping me?"

"Yes," she answered. "And when you find your Girl Scout, have her call me to give me some pointers."

"Just like that."

"Yes. Just like that."

He gave her a look that she didn't care for, one that felt like a slap. For not the first time she wondered what she really knew about this man who wanted her life story along with the footnotes now that she was a cop again. A part of her, deep down, knew, had always known. But she would deal with that later. Right now, she needed to find Noe.

CHAPTER SIXTEEN

An hour later Raven and Billy Ray stood on a rundown cement porch of a red-brick house near the Bottoms. No lush green grass in the small front yard. Instead, a tangle of ankle-deep weeds blessed here and there with yellow wildflowers. Raven took a deep breath, and then looked at Billy Ray, who was eyeing her curiously.

"Are you going to knock or are we going to stand here just looking?"

He stood behind her with his pork pie hat on, and his Oakley sunglasses draped over the back of his neck. Raven wondered why he even bothered with sunglasses. Clouds had started moving in hours ago, turning the sky a washed-out gray. Billy Ray gazed back at her with a casualness that said he could step away as easy as whistling.

"What if I said stand here all day looking?"

"You'd be standing by yourself. Food's not going to cook itself. I have a restaurant to run."

"Is that more important than finding Noe?"

He sighed hard, and stuck his hands in the pockets. "You don't need me to do that. I mean finding Noe ain't no hill for a climber. You got this, Raven."

"That's where you're wrong," she said. "I need you to have my back."

"Like I told you when you asked me to come here with you, I'll do what I can, but that might not be much. I'm not a cop anymore. And I've got a business to take care of."

Lucky you, she thought, but didn't say out loud. She lifted the heavy brass knocker and let it fall against the door.

The man who answered was tall, his brown lips spotted pink from drink or maybe from disease. He had narrow shoulders, and a defeated caved-in chest. But his intense black eyes were spectacular. They were large and long-lashed – probably beautiful eyes once, probably made him look deep and mysterious when he was younger. But now they danced with a meanness that would frighten the devil.

"Y'all selling something?" he asked, his eyes swinging from Raven to Billy Ray.

"No," Raven said, showing him her badge. "I'm Detective Burns and this is Billy Ray Chastain. We're looking for the parents of Clyde Darling."

The man reared back as if he wanted to fight. Raven suddenly felt sorry for the boy who ran the streets of Byrd's Landing with Noe.

"He hurt?" he barked.

"May we come in?" Billy Ray asked, his voice mild and unthreatening.

The man's eyes narrowed knowingly. "He hurt someone?" It was barely a question, and there was a hint of glee in it.

"Please, Mr. Darling—" Raven started.

"I ain't no Mr. Darling," he said. "My name is Brown. Memphis Fields Brown. I'm the boy's stepfather. Y'all come in. I'll go find his mother."

His tone was such that Raven wouldn't have been surprised if he said *its* mother. They followed Brown inside. The house smelled of recent cooking. A plate of fried potatoes and fluffy yellow eggs sat on the coffee table.

"Sorry to interrupt your supper, Mr. Brown," Raven said.

"It just better be important," he huffed before leaving without any further comment.

While he was gone, Billy Ray made his way around the small room. He picked up a framed picture on a brick fireplace that looked like it hadn't been used in years.

"The man's into music," Billy Ray said as he turned the picture toward her.

The silver frame held a photo of a much younger Memphis Brown. He wore a gray slender suit and black pointed shoes. He was caressing an upright bass lying across one shoulder like a lover. His eyes were indeed striking, filled with both pain and ecstasy.

"Wonder if he was any good?" Raven asked.

Billy Ray put the picture back and gestured toward the upright bass on a stand in the corner. It was the only thing in the room polished to a high gloss. A careless layer of dust lay over everything else.

"Look like he still plays," Billy Ray said.

"I don't think so," Raven said. The bass Brown had cradled so lovingly years ago now had no strings.

Remnants of Clyde were all over the room. An English book on the coffee table, a sweatshirt draped over an armchair, a Spider-Man comic book claiming the edge of an end table. She was relieved when Brown came back in the room with Clyde's mother, a broad-shouldered woman as tall as her husband; but unlike him, there was a look of abject fear in her eyes. She wore an apron over a pair of sweatpants, and was wringing, literally wringing the tea towel she was holding into a tightrope. Brown plopped down on the couch, picked up the plate and began shoveling egg in his mouth. He hadn't even bothered to introduce his wife.

Raven introduced herself and Billy Ray, which made the fearful light in her eyes brighter.

"Is Clyde all right?" she asked.

"Can we sit down, Ms. Brown?" Raven asked.

"Call me June. Please," she said. "And I still go by Darling. June Darling."

June Darling wrung the tea towel so hard that Raven was surprised it didn't rip in half. She saw Raven's look and let go. June breathed deeply before smoothing her hands over her long braids.

"I'm sorry I'm not dressed," she said, tugging off her apron. "I didn't expect company. I was just cooking. We're eating early so we can go to the movies later."

"We sorry we have to interrupt you," Billy Ray said in a soft voice.

She looked at him as if he had just thrown her a lifeline. But it wasn't a lifeline that was nearly long enough.

"Is it about Clyde?"

"Yes," Billy Ray said.

"When was the last time you saw your son, Ms. Darling?" Raven asked.

June's eyes flashed on Raven. "I told you, June. Call me June."

"June, then," Raven agreed.

"Friday before he went to school. Said he was going to spend the weekend with a friend."

"Kid's spoiled," Brown snapped. "My mama never made me no hot breakfast every morning before I went to school. And she certainly didn't let me slap up out the house and go God knows where for an entire weekend."

"Mr. Brown," Raven said. "Didn't you get a call from Noe's father asking if you had seen Noe? Asking about Clyde?"

"Some mealy-mouthed man sounding like a teenager called me about Clyde. I told him I hadn't seen his boy, and mine wasn't missing. Told him he was spending the weekend with a friend."

"But he was supposed to be spending the weekend with Noe. Didn't Cameron tell you that?" Raven asked.

Brown waved his hand dismissively. "I didn't have time for all that. Man can't keep track of his boy."

"You mean Clyde wasn't with Noe?" June said, her eyes wide.

"You have other children?" Billy Ray asked. Raven knew it was to turn the subject from Clyde. They didn't want the grieving mother just yet. They needed June thinking clearly for a while longer.

"Two girls," she said. "But they went with their father after the divorce."

"Ain't no surprise about that," Brown said. "They went with the person with the most money."

June made no move to indicate that she even heard her husband. She was staring out of the big picture window to the spots of yellow in the yard.

"I got Clyde. He got the girls, and I got the boy. We still tease each other over that. My ex is okay. Divorce wasn't bitter. It was just time, you know?"

"Because you and that no account womanizer think y'all on a TV show or something. Ain't no real black folk gone be liking on their ex like that. But at least the brotha got some sense. Not you, though. The only reason that boy want to live with you is because you ain't got no rules," Brown said. "If that fool murdered someone you'd help him hide the body."

She favored Brown with a look, not an angry look, but one of sympathy. "Quit it, Memphis, I say. Don't let these detectives see how ugly you can be. Where is my boy, Detective Burns?"

"What kinds of things did Clyde get away with, Mr. Brown?" Raven asked.

He balanced the plate of food on his skinny lap. He leaned forward and counted on his fingers. "Truancy, shoplifting, staying out all night, stealing from his mama's purse, and all kinds of drugs."

"Those are lies, Memphis. So he skipped school a couple of times, fell asleep over a friend's house and forgot to call. He smoked a little weed. You did worse when you played, if I remember right. Why you so high and mighty now?"

"How about stealing from your purse? Shoplifting?"

"It's not stealing if he's welcome to it," she said. "And he didn't shoplift anything. The store made a mistake. He had nothing on him. You had it in for Clyde ever since we got together."

Brown eventually crossed one leg over the other and sat back. He muttered something loud enough for them to hear, but not loud enough for them to understand.

"What was that, Mr. Brown?" Raven pressed.

"I said what about the lying," he said. "You can't explain that away, now can you?"

June sighed and ran her hands over her face. "He does do that, you right. He has a little trouble with lying."

"How's that?" Billy Ray prompted.

"Clyde likes to make money...."

"You mean hustle. He likes to hustle."

"Shut up, Memphis!"

They sat in silence for a moment before June continued. "He likes money, you know, the feel of it, the smell. And so every chance he gets, he's mowing somebody's lawn, or cleaning somebody's gutters, or helping them with odd jobs."

"I don't understand how that's a bad thing," Billy Ray said.

"It's bad because he'll lie about it in a second. I didn't have a problem with a lot of it, but in spite of what my husband says, I do draw the line at some things."

"Like what?" Raven asked.

"We've talked enough and you've heard plenty. Where is my son, Detective?"

"Just one more question..." Raven tried. Once she did tell June where Clyde was, June wouldn't be in any shape to answer more questions. Not right away, anyway, and they had no time to waste.

"No," June said. "No more questions."

"Yeah," Brown said. "Get on with it so I can finish eating and we can go. We late already. Shoot."

This time June threw the tea towel she had been wringing. "Get out, Memphis. Get out. I can't stand the sight of your face right now."

Brown slowly removed the tea towel from his plate. He walked from the room in a put upon but dignified manner. When he was gone June sunk into an armchair and covered her face with her hands.

"Lord. Oh, my Lord. That man."

They waited through several sighs. Raven sensed that June knew what they were about to tell her. The woman with the braids and tea towel had gone from wanting to know to putting it off for just a bit longer.

"Brown's not a bad man, he's just scared is all," June said.

"How long you been married?" Billy Ray asked as he took Brown's place on the sofa.

"Going on ten years now," June answered. "He used to play bass in a jazz band at this club me and the girls used to go to after work."

"And what do you do, June?" Raven asked.

"I'm a paralegal. Between jobs now. I used to work at a firm downtown. Got laid off when the owner got put in the hospital."

"Put in the hospital?" Raven asked.

"Yes," June said. "Robbery or something. They beat him up pretty bad. He's not getting out anytime soon."

"Sorry to hear that. They catch the guy?" Billy Ray asked.

June shook her head. "Just life, you know?" she said. "Sometimes bad things come at you all bundled up." She looked them straight in the eye. Raven started to speak, but June cut her off.

"But Memphis? His bark is worse than his bite. He loved playing bass, the band, all that stuff. But he was scared of it, too. Always waiting for the other shoe to drop. Took to drinking. Pretty soon he was doing more drinking than playing and the band got sick of it. We were, you know, going out at that time, and he asked me to marry him. Said he'd help me take care of Clyde. But I just think he did it because it gave him an excuse not to play."

"Can we call anyone for you, June?" Billy Ray asked.

She continued as if he hadn't spoken. "I can't rehearse, he'd say, because you know I got to take care of you and Clyde. We were the perfect excuse. He just thought he wasn't good enough. He tortured himself all the time, now he's torturing us."

"Must be hard on Clyde," Raven said, not missing the way June's eyes brightened at the use of present tense.

Billy Ray reached over and covered June's trembling hands with his own. He looked into her eyes and said, "You said you saw Clyde on Friday before school?"

She nodded warily. "Yeah, that's right. I made him breakfast, we joked around for a few minutes, I helped him pack for the weekend and he left."

"When was the last time you heard from him?"

"He sent me a text Friday afternoon from Noe's phone saying he would be late coming home today. But you just said he wasn't with Noe."

Billy Ray and Raven exchanged a look.

"Why didn't he use his phone?" Raven asked.

June looked embarrassed. "Memphis took it. As punishment for breaking curfew."

"Did Clyde say why he would be late?" Billy Ray asked.

"Said he and Noe had a gig together, a way to score some cash."

"A legal way?" Raven asked.

"Of course, legal. My boy's not a hood rat. But I get worried because sometimes he can be careless, and like I said, he can be loose with the truth. He said he was going to do some yard work for somebody." June shuddered. "I was okay with that. As long as he wasn't going to work with that creepy blood and guts guy."

"Blood and guts guy?" Raven asked.

June nodded. "That's what I call him, anyway. He cleans up after dead bodies and stuff. I found out that Clyde had worked for him and I told him to cut it out. That he wasn't allowed to do that."

"Why?" Raven asked.

"Clyde had nightmares," June said. "That's how I found out. Those jobs followed him in his dreams and he'd wake up screaming. So, I put my foot down. No more. Besides, I met that Willie Lee Speck, and there's something wrong with him."

Willie Lee Speck, Raven thought. The same piece of excrement she was thinking about hiring to clean the crime scene at Oral's house.

"What made you think he was creepy?" Raven asked.

"Because he'd come around here begging me to let Clyde work for him. Kept spitting in my flowers and winking at me. Had some guy with him with all sorts of junk in the back of his VW truck. I asked who he was, and he told me just some homeless guy who helped out, too. All that stuff was dead people's stuff. Sick. Both of them grave robbers if you ask me."

"Do you think that's the gig that he was going to, to make him late coming home?" Raven asked.

"I already told you no. I ordered him to stay away from that guy. Where is my son, Detective Burns?"

Raven told her. And there was a wail so loud and long that Raven thought the sound would follow her to the grave. She looked up to see Billy Ray with his hands over his face. Brown stood in the entryway to the living room with a look of greedy elation in his luminous eyes.

CHAPTER SEVENTEEN

Billy Ray left her with a howling June and Memphis Brown half-heartedly patting his wife on a shoulder that was at the moment insensible to any touch except grief. Raven gave Brown her name and number scribbled on a piece of paper from her pocket memo tablet. She told him to call if they thought of anything, anything at all about what could have happened to Clyde. She told him that the coroner's office would be in touch for a formal identification.

When she got outside the sky had darkened considerably. Threads of lightning flashed in the clouds, followed by a low grumble of thunder. The air felt new and wet and dangerous. Billy Ray was kneeling on the sidewalk by the yard, sifting a handful of Byrd's Landing's dark soil from one hand to the other. He didn't acknowledge her when she squatted next to him. For some reason she felt it important to keep her mouth shut. A soft rain was falling. Billy Ray started to speak as if the rain had awakened him.

"You know these flowers here, the bright yellow ones?" he asked her. "Oral ever tell you what they were called when he taught you how to garden?"

"I think he told me that it was sneezeweed."

"Yeah," he said quietly. "Sneezeweed. There's superstition that breathing dried sneezeweed can actually *make* you sneeze. And you know what they say about sneezing, right?"

"Floyd used to say sneezing chased away the devil."

Billy Ray chuckled. "He would know." He waited for a long moment before saying, "Don't seem to be doing Memphis and June any good."

Raven said nothing. Billy Ray had something on his mind, and he had confided in her so rarely these days that she knew the best thing to do was to let him take his sweet time on getting whatever was bugging him out of his head.

"You think Breaker ever looked into these killings as a racial thing?" he said. His voice was soft, with an edge running underneath that she had never heard from him. She didn't like it.

"Because the victims are white?"

"Yeah," he said. "And where the killer is leaving the bodies – the police station, that bank, places that are usually run by rich, white people. People who benefited from black people's blood."

"The last time I checked, the mayor, Marcus I mean, he's black."

"Maybe that doesn't matter to the killer. The mayor is still at the doorway to power."

He started digging into the dirt as if he were looking for something. He said, "You know the whole time I was in there talking to Memphis and June, I was thinking to myself that's what all this could be. Black folk taking their revenge."

"By killing children?"

"You see this dirt, here." He opened his fingers and let the dirt fall through them. "It's evil, like this town. Did you know that this parish had more lynchings than anywhere in the entire country? There's the blood of black men, women and children running hot in the soil of this place. Maybe that's what your father smelled, what Lovelle tasted and liked. What this killer is loving on right now. Place got evil all through it. Attracts the devil like a piece of rancid meat attracts the buzzards."

"You saying Byrd's Landing is a rancid piece of meat? Then why stay? Why don't you leave?"

"Why do you think? Because I always knew that you'd be coming back, that you couldn't stay away."

"Okay, fine," she said, throwing up her hands. "If you hate it this much, let's go. Help me find Noe and let's get the hell out. We'll go back to New Orleans by your sister. We'll buy a house on the same block, raise our kids side by side, have cookouts every Sunday."

He bowed his head, and then turned toward her. "You will never,

ever leave this place."

"Yes, I…."

"No, you won't."

"I will."

"Raven."

He stood up, dusted his hands off and pointed toward the house. "I've grown up with uncles like Memphis Fields Brown so beaten down by racism that they can't breathe."

"If I heard correctly, June said that it was his taste for alcohol that beat him down."

"Maybe, but what drove him to it? That man's got trauma going generations back."

"I never heard you talk like this, Billy Ray."

"I never had reason to bring it up," he said. "But that doesn't mean I don't think about it now and again. You looked bothered." He said the last like he didn't give a damn.

"It bothers me that you think that these boys got what they deserved."

"I'm not saying that. I'm just saying that maybe the assholes who run this town are getting what they deserve."

"By using these boys? That's still sick."

"And if that's the case, why should I have to get involved in it?"

"Because you can."

"Doesn't mean I should."

"Clyde and Noe blow the crap out of your race angle. You know that, don't you?"

"I don't think Clyde is a victim of the Sleeping Boy killer. I think he's a copycat, and Noe got in the way. Or the other way around."

"What do you mean?"

"Maybe the killer was after Noe and Clyde got in the way. Or maybe our friend in there, Memphis, finally got up the nerve to take Clyde out and Noe got in the way. He couldn't stand that boy. Did you see the look in his eyes when he found out that he was dead? That was pure relief, Raven."

"He's not the type."

He didn't answer. Instead he turned his face up to the sky. The rain started falling harder now. Billy Ray closed his eyes as if he were enjoying the feel of it on his face.

"What are you trying to say to me?" Raven asked.

He brought his head down to look at her. He wasn't frowning, but his eyes weren't friendly.

"Noe's probably dead, you know that, don't you?"

He continued before she could say anything. "I don't like it, but he's probably not topside anymore. And I'd bet all the farms in Georgia that the serial didn't do him. It's a copycat."

"Then where's his body?" Raven spat.

"I don't know. I've told you before that I can't explain why crazy does what it does. But I'll tell you one thing. I can't, Raven. Not anymore. I don't owe this town a damn thing. I can't help you with this."

"You got to be kidding me?" she said. "You pull this now? I thought you cared about Noe."

"Not did, do. I do care about him. But I'm not putting my body on the line anymore for this town, or to find another dead body."

She turned away in disgust, but his voice stopped her.

"Now listen. I ain't saying that I won't help. I'm just saying that the help's going to have to come from the restaurant. I can be your sounding board, help you explore any theories you want, but it'll be from the front of my stove or behind my bar. I'm there for you, but no more knocking on doors, or interrogating suspects. No more of these fucking notifications. With that you're on your own."

His words felt like a punch. She was too hurt to say anything.

"Well?" he asked.

"Well, what?"

"Are my terms acceptable?" She could have sworn that he was smiling a little. For a second he looked like the old Billy Ray.

"I guess they'll have to be."

He nodded and started walking toward the unmarked Dodge. She watched his broad back before following him, wondering how easy it would be for her to fit a desk into his office. It was the small smile that spurred her on, that flash of the old Billy Ray she wasn't ready to give up on. Not to the bitterness he had finally allowed her to see, and certainly not to his bleeping Viking stove. He was going to help whether he liked it or not. He was going to know what it was like to catch bad guys again and enjoy himself while he did it.

CHAPTER EIGHTEEN

After talking to Clyde's parents, Raven felt as if she had awakened inside of a nightmare. She drove back to the station, dropped Billy Ray by his car and went inside to find out what conference room they were using as the case's command center. After getting her bearings, she planned to locate Willie Lee Speck to see if he had seen Noe or Clyde before they went missing. She would fast-track this entire investigation for both Noe's sake and her own. But the chief grabbed her arm before she could do anything.

"I need to talk to you for a minute."

He said it as if he were asking for a favor. Before she knew what was happening, she was in her second interview room of the day, this time waiting for the chief. The room was smaller than the one before, and had both a two-way along the wall and a camera tucked in one corner. Raven paced, reached the wall, turned on her heel, and paced again. She felt caged, restless.

Something wasn't right about the chief asking her to wait in an interview room. Why not his office? She could feel Floyd's ghost perking up in her head. She saw the blue and green peacock feather in the hatband of his blinding white fedora and him fixing his mouth to speak. She closed her eyes to send him away. *Oh, Daddy*, she thought, *how can you torture and love me at the same time?*

She was about to tell Floyd to get back in his grave when the door whipped open. When she saw who was behind it, a breath so sharp went through her that she felt as if she had been stabbed. For the first time in her life she was glad that she carried Floyd with her since he had died. *Breathe*, he said. *And steady it, don't let this son-of-a-biscuit-eater see that he's got you.* She didn't know if she could steady anything. Anger twisted along her veins like white-hot heat. She wanted to scream with all her being. But there was Floyd again saying, *Steady, Raven, steady,* all the while sitting on his wooden milk crate, cracking pecans, and then casually picking the nut meat from his teeth with a preternaturally long pinkie nail.

It was pride and Floyd's whispering voice that helped her find her way. And it took only a second. She stripped her face of feeling, not only her face but her innermost being. Floyd took over and for the first time in her life, she was grateful.

"Well," she said, a teasing smile at the corner of her lips, "I guess your name isn't really Wynn?"

She thought he was a big guy when they first met, but with the gold badge clipped to his hip, and the holster under a jacket that was already too tight for him – hadn't she already told him that? – he looked enormous.

"No," he said, his eyes raking her face.

She noticed that he was carrying a manila folder. It was its thinness that helped Raven understand why he had pushed her about Lamont Lovelle at her rooms earlier. She scanned his face for remorse, shame, something, but it was as blank as hers.

"So, baby's got secrets?" she said, laughing, a dangerous light in her eyes.

"Have a seat," he said.

She sat on the edge of the table and folded her arms across her chest. She could feel the pull of the shoulder holster. Like Floyd, it was a source of comfort.

"You know what I mean," he said. "In a chair."

"The table works for me."

"I really don't care what works for you. We've got at least one other person on the way. Maybe two. The room's too small for you to be posing on the table."

She didn't answer him. She just studied him in that assessing way she had seen in Floyd when he was thinking about killing again. Raven felt literally outside of her own head. She had heard people say that before, but for the good Lord's sake, that's what she felt. As if she was just watching ghosts from outside of her body. Finally, the boyfriend who had just become a phantom took a deep breath.

"If you're looking for an apology, you aren't going to get it."

"Does it look like I'm looking for a blooming thing from you?"

"Look," he responded, "I was just doing my job."

"You know, you're one cold sucker. Just one question, did you enjoy it?"

"I did what I had to do," he said.

Raven laughed softly. "You sound helpless, like a child."

She stood up and walked toward him until she was close, close enough to kiss him. He stepped back. She moved closer.

"You did...what you had to?" she mocked. "Every moment when you were with me? Every single moment? In the car? At Chastain's? In my bed? Was all that what you had to do? What about your precious integrity? Where did you lock that away while you were banging me?"

He took another step back. "I needed to get close to you. I was doing my job."

She wanted to kill him. She could see herself killing him. She'd use the knife, and she'd take a good long time.

The door opened, and a BLPD detective walked in.

"Hello there," he said in an incongruently cheerful voice. "I'm Liam Golden from BLPD Internal Affairs. I took Presley Holloway's place."

Raven slowly turned away from Wynn and faced the new voice full-on. He was a short man with a big belly and a bright smile. He held out a meaty, white hand. She left it there in the wind.

She turned back to the not-boyfriend. "What should I call you, anyway? What's your real name?"

"Detective Delbert Stevenson."

Raven tilted her head and smiled. "Well, I can't say that I'm pleased to meet you, Detective Stevenson."

Golden sat in the chair behind the table and leaned back until the chair touched the wall. He gestured to the chair on the other side.

"Have a seat."

"What's this about?" She knew but didn't want to make it easy.

"Detective Stevenson works for a police department in California," Golden said. "Homicide."

"I could tell that by his big shiny badge," Raven said. "What does it have to do with me?"

"They have a few questions about the murder of Lamont Lovelle," the chief said, now crowding into the small room.

"Well, I'll be," Raven said. "A party. What is it that Billy Ray says? If I'd knewed you were coming, I'd baked a cake?'

Raven finally sat down in order to get whatever was about to happen over as quickly as possible.

"So, this is your next trick to get me to incriminate myself since pillow talk didn't work?" She laughed and pointed a finger at Stevenson. "Look, Detective Golden, I think he's actually blushing."

"You can call me Goldie. I don't abide much by titles. And yes, I do think the big man is turning red under his genetic tan."

"Raven," the chief said. "Goldie, cut it out, please."

"Can we all just be professionals?" Stevenson said.

Silence swelled the room, and with it Stevenson's embarrassment.

"Look, I already know that the chief told you why you're here," Stevenson said, pulling at the collar of his jacket.

"I didn't tell her anything," the chief said, looking at him as if he were something foul-smelling that had crawled into the room. "I didn't need to. She was hundreds of miles away when Lovelle ate that bullet."

"You mean her phone was hundreds of miles away when Lovelle ate that bullet, don't you, Chief Sawyer?"

"Does your brass know just how deep undercover you were?" Raven asked. "You know by sleeping with me you jeopardized your whole case. When they find out, they're going to boil you alive. Say goodbye to that big shiny badge, Stevenson."

"What they don't know won't hurt them," he answered.

"What? You think I won't make sure they know?"

"Maybe you will," he said. "But I think you'll confess. The woman I know will take her medicine. She'll do the right thing and pay for her crimes. She's not going to want to live with this secret for the rest of her life. I don't care what happens to me as long as there's justice."

Raven laughed so hard it hurt. "You have sorely miscalculated."

"I don't appreciate this. Not one bit," the chief said from where he stood near the closed door.

"Yeah, you sound like a broken record. I don't like this any more than you do," Stevenson said. "But it's necessary. She murdered Lamont Lovelle."

"Why now?" Raven asked.

"Because you've been reinstated," Goldie answered for Stevenson. "Dirty cop and all that on the force. That's the only reason I'm here."

"Did you know, Chief Sawyer? Who he was?"

"He's not one of the ones who came knocking on my door about you several months ago. His department didn't coordinate any of this undercover operation with us. I found this out while y'all were talking to the Darlings."

"And now we're accused of not being professional. What a joke," Raven said.

"You ready for some questions, Raven?" the chief asked.

"I've been ready. I was ready twenty minutes ago. It's you lot that can't get on with it. We're wasting precious time. So ask me what you want to ask me, Stevenson, so I can find my nephew."

"Of course, you've already been questioned in California," he said.

"I was," Raven said.

"But there are some holes."

"Oh, I doubt that," Raven said, enjoying the calm feel of her voice, and the sweat dripping from Stevenson's bald head.

"Why?" Stevenson said. "Because you're so thorough? You know what happens when the perps start to think they're smarter than the cops, don't you? Your chief taught you that, right?"

How could she have not noticed what a pompous ass he was? Raven gave him her best innocent face, widened her eyes and said, "Because I didn't do anything wrong."

She inclined her chin toward the camera. "Who's watching?" Raven asked the chief.

"Nobody. I thought you'd want me in here."

"How many suspects do you offer moral support to, Chief?" Stevenson asked.

"Oh, you sound bitter. Shouldn't I be the one who sounds bitter?" Raven asked.

"Raven's family to this department. I'm not going to let an asshole from California come out here and mess with my family."

"Even if she's a murderer?"

"I don't deal in hypotheticals. It gives me gas," the chief said. "Give me some proof."

Stevenson opened the file folder. "Do you know a boy named Tom Arthur?"

Raven sat up straighter. "Yes. Why? Is he all right?"

"He's fine," he said. "But he's your alibi witness, right, this nine-year-old boy? This child?"

"He's a friend," she said.

"He's your vacation friend, right?" Stevenson asked.

"Vacation friend?"

"That's what he told us. You met him in Pismo while you were on vacation. How come you two got so chummy so fast?"

Raven couldn't answer him, not because she didn't know the answer, but because it reminded her too much of Floyd. She had seen Tom Arthur alone on a bench by the resort's lawn, his scooter propped next to him. His head was bent, and every now and then he would look up and squint, which told Raven two things. The first was that he was lonely, and the second was that he was trying not to cry.

"Or did you make the first move because you thought he needed someone? Profile him like your dad profiled his victims, just looking for someone who could provide a good alibi? I read Floyd Burns' casefiles. I know what he did, how he was. You made Tom complicit in your crimes just like your dad did to you. Didn't you?"

It was both the words and the sneer in Stevenson's voice that had her standing. The chief saw what was coming and placed himself between them.

"You disgusting piece of butt filth," Raven said.

"Enough of this," the chief said. "This isn't how we do things down here."

"What? You want to hit me?" Stevenson asked. "Take that knife out of your boot and gut me like you emotionally gutted that kid by using him, and then leaving him?"

"That's not what I did," Raven said.

"That's exactly what you did."

"Keep talking, Stevenson. Just know that no matter how long it takes, or how much you think you see it coming, you're going to pay for this."

"Is that a threat?"

"I don't make threats," Raven said. "I make promises."

"Look," the chief said, "I know that there's a lot of emotion going on in this room, but you both need to tamp it down. Stevenson, mind yourself. Raven?"

Raven blinked, remembering where she was, and why she was there. She needed to regain her cool if she was going to be able to leave without wearing handcuffs. She willed her beating heart to quiet before sitting down.

"I'm fine," she said. "So, you're saying that you talked to Tom?"

"We did," then a pause, "I did. Seems you made yourself quite a little friend."

"He's a good boy," Raven admitted, thinking of the little human who followed her all around Pismo on his scooter. "Lonely."

"You like kids?" Stevenson asked.

Raven remembered the conversation she had with Tom Arthur about kids. *I love kids*, she had told him, *as long as they belong to somebody else.*

"I like kids okay. Especially teenagers. But Tom was a special little boy. Smart, not boring. We spent a lot of time together because his mother spent a lot of time…."

"Drunk. Neglectful?"

"Let's just say she was enjoying her vacation," Raven said.

"He told us that you left Pismo Beach for an entire day. And that happened to be the day Lovelle was killed," Stevenson said.

Raven was ready for this question. "Don't try that on me. You suck at lying. Are you sure you aren't really a location scout?"

"Answer the question."

"I don't need to answer anything. You have my phone records."

"They do," Goldie answered for Stevenson, "and that's where we're struggling. You see, your phone records put you at several locations all over Pismo, but the video cameras...." He stopped.

She waited. She knew he wanted her to jump in but she didn't. She had seen this coming, too.

"We checked them," Stevenson said.

"Yikes. I feel sorry for you. I hate that duty."

"You aren't on any of them," Stevenson said.

"You mean all the video cameras in Pismo? You had to check them all? Wow, your life is rough."

"We checked the relevant ones. Why do you think that is, Raven?" Stevenson asked.

"I hate having my picture taken. Remember?"

"That's not funny."

"Well, it's funny to me," Raven said. "This entire thing is hilarious. You spend months pretending to be my boyfriend, and then presto-change-o, all of a sudden you're a detective trying to make me for Lovelle's murder. Don't you think that's funny?"

"Why weren't you on any of those video cameras?"

She eyed him for a few moments, and then she said, "You must be pretty desperate to blow your cover. I know Detective Golden thinks it's because I've been reinstated. But you tell me, why now?"

"People are dying."

"Darn straight people are dying, Jack, and the longer I sit here talking to you donkey butts the more people are going to die, not to mention that my nephew is *still* missing."

"Exactly."

The silence that seeped into the room brought with it an understanding. Raven started laughing in earnest now. "Are you flipping kidding me?" She laid her fingers across her chest. "You blew your cover because you think I have something to do with these murders? Did your department really let you come down here all by yourself? Seriously?"

He stared at her, saying nothing. She turned to the chief, who gave her a look that said, *no accounting for idiots.*

"You do have a past," Goldie said.

"You got that wrong. My father had a past, a past that he's paid for with his life. Not me."

She stood up, shrugged into her jacket.

"You're not leaving," Stevenson warned.

"Sure I am. Chief?"

"She's leaving," the chief said. "You got nothing. And you coming in here springing yourself on her failed to work her up into a confession. I did my part. You need to go home."

She watched blood suffuse Stevenson's face. He turned to her, furious.

"You came to my town..."

"I was nowhere near your town." She didn't even try to make her voice convincing.

"...parked yourself on top of a building three blocks down from where I work..."

"Did you find anything on that roof? Any hair, fibers? Proof I had been there, or do you just have a rich imagination? You ever think of bottling it up and selling it to the movies?"

"...and waited until you saw him, and then you shot him down like he was some kind of rabid animal."

"Not like, was," Raven contradicted. "He was a dangerous animal. And now he's dead."

"So you admit it?"

"That he was a rabid animal, yes, I admit that. That I killed him? No. You have a lot more work to do before I'd ever admit that. But there is one thing that I want you to never forget when you realize how badly you failed."

"What's that?"

She grinned at him then, a slow, dangerous grin with a tinge of blood in it. "I dumped you first."

He went rigid. There was anger in the hard-line body, along the angle of his jaw. He tried to stare her down, but Raven didn't look away. She just stood there with that maniacal grin on her face. He slammed the door so hard when he left that the chief jumped.

"What a tool," Goldie said, looking at the closed door.

"Goldie," the chief warned.

"I mean it. What a fucking tool."

Goldie stood up now and picked up the thin folder Stevenson had left behind. He opened it, sighed, and flipped it shut. "I'm telling you if you did kill that motherfucker Lovelle he motherfucking deserved it."

"Goldie, keep it family. PG," the chief said, pointing to the camera.

"Are you kidding me? I turned that son-of-a-bitch off before I fucking walked in here."

The chief hung his head and rubbed his face with his hands. "Goldie," he said. "You are Internal Affairs."

"That's right, IN-ternal Affairs, which means outside pricks should mind their own fucking business." He pointed at Raven. "Call me Goldie. No more of that Detective Golden shit."

He took a business card from his shirt pocket and flicked it over to her. "One more thing. I'm not a murder cop, but I ain't no math teacher turned cop like Holloway. If you need any help with this, give me a ring."

Raven stared at the door for a few moments after Goldie left. She turned to the chief. "Tell me, Chief, where in the blazes do you find these guys?"

"Old friend, from the old days." He stopped, looked at her carefully for several seconds. "I'm sorry. Are you going to be all right?"

"I have to be if I'm going to find Noe."

★   ★   ★

She walked through the double glass doors of the BLPD and past the water fountain. Her stomach heaved once, twice, but she stopped short of vomiting.

See what happens when you stick your head in the sand, Birdy Girl? Floyd's voice again inside her head.

Billy Ray waited for her at the end of the long sidewalk.

"What are you still doing here?" she asked him when she got close, her voice only a little thick.

"The chief asked me to stay, told me what was going down. I'm sorry."

"Should have known, right?" she said, her throat hurting from the emotion she was trying to suppress.

"I told you there was something weird about that fuck," he said.

"Thanks for not saying I told you so."

"I ain't saying that. I'm just saying that he smelled a little fishy."

They stood there looking at the setting sun falling across the cars in the parking lot.

Finally Billy Ray said, "Is there anything I can do?"

"I need to talk to Willie Lee Speck to see if he saw the boys over the weekend."

"You up for that tonight?"

"If you come with me? Can't Imogene handle the restaurant?"

She could tell by the look on his face that he was about to say no. "Billy Ray, my nephew is missing and probably hurt bad. You just asked if there was anything you can do. You can. Help me do this."

"And if I don't?"

"In one day I've lost my boyfriend, my nephew, and sure as you're standing there they are going to be looking at my brother as the perp. If you don't help me, I'm going to find the nearest rain puddle and drown myself."

He smiled. "Now that's something I'd want to see."

She smiled back. "I promise it won't be pretty."

For all their joking, he walked close to her as they made their way to the Mustang. She was almost smiling when she felt eyes on her back.

Expecting Stevenson, she turned, but it wasn't him. There was a man standing in the shadow of the fountain, his face obscured by the falling water. Even though she couldn't see him, she could feel his intense hunger as if it was something alive reaching for her.

"Who's that?" she asked.

"Who?" Billy Ray asked, turning around much too slowly.

She clutched at his sleeve. "That man, there, there," she said. She could have sworn she turned her face away from the man only for a split second. But, that couldn't be because....

"Raven," Billy Ray said, puzzled. "You all right? There's nobody there."

CHAPTER NINETEEN

Raven called Willie Lee Speck on the way out of the BLPD parking lot. He told her to meet him on Watercress Street. The house was a brick job not far from where Clyde's parents, the Darlings, lived, and just barely in better shape. At least the lawn was green, though full of cattails waving in the wind.

"Here?" Billy Ray asked as she parked the Mustang along the curb.

"That's what the man said," Raven grunted, putting the car in park.

She knew it was the right place because she could see Ozy in the driver's seat of his prehistoric VW truck. One wrinkled elbow hung out of the open window. He must have been fiddling with the radio because every now and then loud static punctuated the air. Adding to the discordant sounds were the wind chimes hanging from the truck's rails, silver bars clanking in the wind.

"What's that all about?" Billy Ray asked, pointing to the truck with its bed full of junk.

"You don't want to know."

Speck must have heard car doors slamming because he was walking out of the open front door to meet them. Raven wondered what Floyd would think about someone like Speck. He'd probably call him raw-boned, loose-jointed and ham-handed. He'd also say that there was more oddness to Speck than met the eye.

"Hey," Speck said, lifting one of his big hands in a wave. "What's up, Ray Ray? You ready to tell me about that job now?"

Billy Ray eyed him with a face filled with so much distaste that Raven almost wished that she had left him at the station.

"What job?" Billy Ray asked.

"Nothing you have to be worried about," Raven said.

"Hey, ain't you that gimpy cop Lovelle fucked up? You own a restaurant now, don't you? Chastain's Creole Heaven. I read it in the paper. Where's the gumbo? The catfish? I heard you guys do a lamb creole with homemade stock and butter beans that'd make you want to slap your mama for some more. You guys do DoorDash?"

"No, but tell me, is your ass jealous at the shit that's coming out of your mouth right now?"

"I don't hear that one a lot, but look, don't get your feelings all hurt," Speck said. "What's up with ex-cops anyway, Ray Ray? Y'all must wear your nerves on the outside of your skin."

"It's Detective," Raven corrected him.

Speck paused for a second while the wind blew his stringy black hair from his face. "Now you just confusing the shit out of me for the hell of it."

"Man, why do you stink so much," Billy Ray said while putting the back of his wrist over his nose.

Speck brought his branded polo shirt up to his nose. He sniffed it and then aired it out. Billy Ray was right. The smell coming from Speck was like....

"Death," Speck said. He hooked his thumb over his shoulder toward the house. "That's a decomp back there. Some old lady died in her sleep and her drug-addict granddaughter just found her. It's been weeks. They had to scoop her up with a soup ladle. Smell gets everywhere. Sometimes the wife don't even let me in the house until I hit the showers. Even makes me strip down to my uglies right there on the back porch before coming in."

No one said anything for a moment or two. Chimes from Ozy's traveling graveyard sideshow clanked again, this time loudly. Raven turned toward the sound to see Ozy now standing outside of the VW. He just stood there pushing the wind chimes hard as he glared at them, his chin jutting out. Speck looked in the direction of Raven's gaze. He lifted a hand and said, "How you doing, Oz my man?" He turned back to Raven and Billy Ray. "He thinks you're here for the old hag's junk."

"Do you always talk so much?" Billy Ray asked.

"Yes," Speck and Raven answered him at the same time.

"Though I am enjoying the break from the stench in there, I ain't got all day. Whatcha want?"

"Do you know a boy by the name of Clyde Darling?" Raven asked as she took out the small memo notebook and pencil from her inside jacket pocket.

"I do. He's done some work for me now and again. Why?" He looked back and forth between Raven and Billy Ray.

"What can you tell us about Clyde?" Raven asked.

Speck planted both hands on his hips and shrugged. "Not much, except he don't like gore, you know, cleaning the brains and bits of bone or flesh from the walls. You get that sometime with these jobs, but he don't want nothing to do with it. Wants the easy ones, and wants to work mostly at night or on the weekends. Scared of his mama. Don't say a lot."

"How can he say anything when he probably can't get a word in edgewise," Billy Ray said.

Raven leaned back and grazed Billy Ray's broad chest with her shoulder. It was her way of telling him to shut it. They didn't need to alienate Speck. "Why would you say he's scared of his mother?" Raven asked.

"Have you met his mother?" he asked. "Whew, Jesus. She spits so much fire she'd give a flamethrower a run for his money. Anyway, back to Clyde, he ain't never stood me up. Reliable, you know. Never gave me mouth. He's a good worker."

"How well do you know him?" Billy Ray said.

Speck rocked back on his heels. "Oh, you want to know how well I know him. But see, there's a problem with that. I only cared about what he did for me here. Me knowing him ain't no good at helping me clean out a hoarder's house or setting up the machines to get the smell out. I just need him to be on time and do what I tell him without whining about it. Why you asking me all these questions about Clyde?"

"When was the last time you saw him?" Raven asked.

Speck scratched his head, moved a chunk of black hair that was fighting with the wind behind his big ear. "Why, I don't know. Two weeks ago, maybe longer. He helped me with a job up there on Lakeshore. Not too bad, that one. Guy's heart gave out while he was taking a shit. Fell and banged his head. Didn't do too much damage, but there was blood to clean up. Head wounds bleed like a mother—"

"You didn't see him on Friday?" Raven broke in.

"You mean the Friday just past?"

"Yes, the one that came after Thursday, genius," Billy Ray clarified. This time Raven jabbed him in the ribs.

"No, why?" Speck asked.

"Were you expecting him to help you with this job today?" Raven asked.

Speck laughed and sighed. "Didn't I just tell you that the boy was a pussy? He wouldn't be wanting to work on no decomp. Why all these questions? Something happen to the little shit?"

"Yes," Raven confirmed. "Did he usually work by himself? Or did he bring any friends along?"

"By himself," Speck said. "I ain't running no welfare to work program."

"You sure about that?" Billy Ray asked.

"How would I not be sure? I need Clyde on standby when one of my regulars can't make a job. You know these types of gigs. Most of my workers are jailbirds or drug addicts. Not the most reliable group. Clyde's just the backup. Don't need any more help than that."

"So, you never met a boy by the name of Noe Cardova?" Billy Ray pressed.

"I told you, no. All these questions starting to piss me off, and Ray...I mean Detective Burns will tell you not a lot pisses me off, but once I get going...."

"I'm sorry," Raven lied. "Clyde ever talk to you about being in trouble, or threatened, or anything like that?"

"Nope," Speck said. "I told you he don't say much."

"Can you account for your whereabouts this weekend, Mr. Speck?" Billy Ray asked.

"If that's a fancy way of asking me if I know where the hell I was, hell yeah, I do. I ain't daft."

"So, where were you?" Raven asked.

"At home. Relaxing. I try not to work weekends if I can help it, which ain't often. I was soaking in the tub trying to get the smell of these animals off me."

"You think of your clients as animals," Billy Ray said before Raven could tell him not to bother.

"Why ain't they?" Speck challenged. "Always blowing their heads off, or beating each other to death, or overdosing, or dying on the toilet like they ain't got no home training, or leaving their grandma alone for so long that she turns into soup, calling me to clean up the ole gal's leaving when she goes four paws up."

"You really are a despicable human being, you know that, don't you?" Billy Ray said.

"At least I ain't like them." Speck jerked his head toward the house. "I'm alive and I intend to stay that way."

"So you were just relaxing at home with the wife and kids this past weekend, Willie Lee?" Raven asked in a gentle voice, hoping to get him off his soapbox.

Speck paused a beat too long. "No," he said. "Suze took the kids on a shopping trip in NOLA. Stayed the weekend with her sister there."

Raven waited. Billy Ray said, "You sure?"

Speck narrowed his eyes at him. The men were the same height, could probably touch forehead to forehead without moving an inch. And Speck did look angry to Raven, angrier than she had ever seen him. She thought for a minute that he was about to headbutt Billy Ray.

"Now, why wouldn't I be sure?" Speck said. "What happened to Clyde?"

"He's missing," Raven said.

"Well, that's not good," Speck said.

"He's dead," Billy Ray clarified.

"That was quick," Speck said, folding his arms across his chest.

"Can you come talk to us down at the station?" Raven asked.

"No, don't have time for that."

"Would you be willing to take a polygraph if we worked around your schedule?" Billy Ray asked.

"I'd be willing to do anything you want as long as I get paid. I make three hundred and thirty dollars an hour, plus mileage and per diem. That means you feed me dinner."

"We can't pay you to take a polygraph, Willie Lee," Raven said.

"Well, that means we ain't got nothing left to talk about."

"You've got my number. If you think of anything, could you call me?" Raven asked.

"Any more questions you can ask my l-a-w-y-e-r."

"Mr. Speck," Billy Ray tried.

"I hope you can spell," he said, turning away from them and moving up the walk to the front door of the house.

"Well, you did it," Raven said, looking at Speck's retreating back. "You actually succeeded in making Willie Lee Speck mad."

"I don't like him."

"Nobody likes him. But when he's happy he's talking. Something could've slipped."

"I think a helluva lot slipped," Billy Ray said as they walked back to the car.

"Like what?"

"You notice how he didn't ask how Clyde died?"

"I did. But this guy deals in death all day long. Maybe he just wasn't interested."

"And about where he was this weekend? His wife and kids away on the only weekend when he needed someone to vouch for his whereabouts?"

"Could just be a coincidence," Raven said as she opened the door of the Mustang and slid behind the wheel.

Billy Ray folded into the passenger seat and pulled the seatbelt across his chest. "I don't like coincidences, and last I checked you don't either. That motherfucker's hiding something."

Raven looked back at the house. Speck and Ozy were wrestling a mattress with a large, black stain out of the front door. Speck hadn't even bothered to wrap the mattress in biohazard materials. Ozy looked like he was trying to avoid the smell by filling both of his cheeks with air. In spite of his wrinkled face, he looked like a child trying to hold its breath.

She started the car and put it in gear. She did agree with Billy Ray about Speck. She didn't know if what he was hiding was about Clyde or Noe, but he definitely wasn't telling them everything.

CHAPTER TWENTY

That night Raven and Cameron spent time at his apartment frantically calling anyone with even a tangential knowledge of Noe. She searched Noe's room for some clue about where he could have been, but found nothing.

It was as if Noe never existed.

As for Cameron, he was losing his grip on reality, acting on impulse as ideas popped into his head. At one point he snatched his hoodie and ran out of the apartment without explanation, only to return deflated and sulky about an hour later carrying a six-pack of Fanta soda.

When it was clear that the night would bring no new leads, he parted and braided his hair from front to back in a tribal pattern that made him look young and immensely breakable. Raven's heart hurt for him but he was too angry with her to allow himself to be comforted. After all, she had blamed him for losing Noe.

The following morning Raven received a call from Goldie to bring her brother in as they had a few more questions for him. She did as she was told by collecting Cameron and driving him into BLPD.

Now, she sat next to him in an interview room, his right knee bobbing up and down. He still refused to look at her. Raven tried to apologize for her behavior when Noe first went missing, but Cameron didn't want any of it. She leaned across the table to try again, but the door opened, leaving her words unspoken. Liam Golden walked in, his shirt rumpled, his red, round face looking more tired than Raven felt.

"You find him, yet?" Cameron asked as Goldie sat down.

"Sorry, son, no," he said. "We wanted you to come down, though, because we have a couple of things we need to clear up."

"Okay," Cameron said, not a shred of hope in his voice. "I'll tell you anything you need to know. Just find my kid."

"I thought this was my case, Goldie," Raven said. "And Breaker's. Where is he?"

"Working on the Memorial case. Hard. Henri Toulouse, the kid before Clyde," Goldie said. "He's arguing with the chief about something or other. I told him I'd take this one. As far as this being your case, it is. But the chief wanted me to handle anything that has to do with Cameron. It's a conflict, you know that, don't you?"

"I'm just trying to find Noe," Raven said. "That's where both Cameron and I were last night, on the phone with his friends, seeing if we could find anything in his room about where he could be, checking out his computer, everything we could."

"Who was doing that?" Goldie asked. "The computer thing?"

"Who do you think was doing it?" Cameron said. "I was. That's my job."

"Not for this one," Goldie said. "You're too close."

"Don't tell me I'm too close," Cameron said. "He's my kid."

"Find anything?" Goldie asked.

"Just what he's into. Boring kid stuff," he said. "That's all."

"Erase anything?"

"Why you saying that?" Cameron turned to Raven, not quite catching her eye. "Why's he saying that?"

"Don't worry about it. It's routine," Raven said.

"Is it?" Goldie asked.

"Yes," Raven said.

Goldie laced his fingers together on the table. "So, you know how this works, Cameron. We're running your financials, your phone records, the boys', too, including social media, that sort of thing. Your sister is going to be doing the same for the Darlings."

"You've got Cameron's records yet?" Raven asked.

"Just the second day, Raven. You know the wheels don't turn that fast," Goldie said.

"Then why are we here?" Cameron asked.

"Like I told you, we just need to clarify a few things that were in the missing person's report."

"Like what?" Cameron said, his voice higher than it had been.

"Don't get so animated," Raven said. "Watch yourself."

Cameron said, astounded, "Don't tell me to watch myself. What, Goldie, you see a black man and automatically think he can't take care of his kid?"

"You know that we always look at family first," Raven said.

"Family first? Don't even talk to me. You already blaming me for him missing. You don't have far to travel in thinking I had something to do with it."

"I don't blame—"

"Don't lie!" Cameron said. "I hate it when you lie to me." Cameron batted away the tear that had appeared at the corner of his eye. "If you didn't think I had something to do with it, you wouldn't be wasting time here talking to me. You'd let Goldie do it, and you'd be out there trying to find him."

Raven stood up and pointed her finger at Cameron. "I told you when you wanted to play daddy that it would be a disaster. You need to wake up and focus. This isn't about you, it's about Noe."

"One-track mind," Cameron countered, now standing, himself. "Everybody else be fucked as long as you get what you want. You love throwing people away, Raven. Just was wondering when it was going to be my turn."

"That's some crazy crap you're talking. I don't throw people away."

He counted on his fingers. "Edmée after high school, and then me and Billy Ray last year."

"Billy Ray?"

"Man up in the hospital and you off on some—"

"Careful," Goldie said.

Cameron closed his mouth on what he was about to say.

"Both of you just need to cool it. Take a seat, Cameron. You too, Raven. I need a few things for you to clear up, Cam, and you can go back to doing whatever you think it'll take to find Noe, including braiding your hair, whatever."

"Fuck you, man."

"Get in line," Goldie said. "Now. You said that you saw Noe Friday morning, before school."

Cameron blinked two or three times, rubbed his face. "Did I say that?"

"Yes, you did."

Cameron started drawing patterns on the table with a long index finger. Raven thought he looked like a petulant child.

"Then that's when I saw him."

"You sure about that?" Goldie asked.

"Why wouldn't he be sure?" Raven asked.

"Because we got a report that Noe spent Friday night alone, that he spent a lot of time alone. You had a date Thursday night, right?"

Cameron looked up at the ceiling, thinking. "Who said that?"

"A woman named Benita Jeffries. This case hit the news last night. She saw and called into the station to say we should check you out because that kid was cramping your style in a major way. Says you let a lot of women take you away from your son."

"Aw, that skank. She just mad because we broke up. I dumped her ass a long time ago."

"But is the skank correct?" Goldie asked.

Cameron scratched his chin. "I don't know. I think so. Maybe. Does it matter when I last saw him? You know he got to school Friday, right?"

"You bet your sweet Aunt Harriet it matters," Raven said. "How many times did you leave him overnight alone?"

"He's fifteen, Raven!" Cameron shouted as if she were hard of hearing.

"That's fine," Goldie said. "Don't really want to question your parenting skills right now. So, the last time you saw him may have been Thursday evening?"

Cameron scrunched his shoulders. He was shutting down. "Could be."

"Morning?" Goldie tried.

"Maybe."

Raven hit the table with a flat hand. "We aren't just talking about Noe being in trouble. You know that, don't you?"

"Thursday morning, then," Cameron said. "I left for my date straight after work. Noe spent Thursday night alone."

"Score," Goldie said, his voice dry. "Do you have any insurance policies on your son?"

"*I* don't have any policies on him."

"What's that supposed to mean?" Goldie asked.

"I didn't take out any policies on my son," Cameron explained while looking at the red light blinking on the camera. "But his mama did before she died."

"Naming you as the beneficiary?"

Cameron nodded.

"That was nice of her," Goldie said.

"Noe's mother was a planner," Raven said. "If something happened to Noe, she wouldn't want Cameron scrambling around for money trying to bury him."

"How much did Noe's mother think it would cost to bury him?" Goldie asked.

"I don't know," Cameron said. "A few thousand. Maybe five. I didn't pay too much attention to it. All I wanted was my son."

"So a couple of thousand?" Goldie asked.

"Maybe."

"Five? Do I hear a ten?"

"Fine, ten. Happy now?"

"Ecstatic," Goldie said. "What about other financial benefits if Noe died?"

"Sure," Noe said. "He has a trust fund. I get a few extra dollars from it every month to keep the kid in khakis and sweater vests."

"You don't have a lot in common with him, do you?" Goldie asked.

"You got that right," Cameron breathed.

Goldie shuffled a few papers around.

"Cameron," Raven tried, "does Noe have any enemies? Or Clyde? Anybody they talk about at school who they've gotten into fights with?"

"All of that's in the missing person's report. And I told you when you wouldn't stop hassling me about it last night," Cameron said. "Not anybody who'd want to hurt him bad."

"Any idea where he might be?" Goldie asked.

Raven closed her eyes. That question, though it might have been a normal one that any cop would ask the parent of a missing child, it was the one that blew Cameron off the edge.

He stood up so fast that his chair fell over. "Y'all some crazy-ass mo-fos if you think I'm going to sit here and take this," he said. "I got my pride."

"Calm down, son," Goldie said.

"Don't you fucking 'son' me, Goldie. You've only got a few years on me anyway. Check your biases, brother."

Raven tried to touch Cameron's sleeve, but he jerked his arm away.

"What?" he said.

"You need to answer him," she said.

Raven didn't turn away from the hurt and betrayal in Cameron's eyes, even though he had done what she had been willing him to do since yesterday. He was finally looking at her. Fine, he could hate her. For now. She'd deal with it, but only after she found Noe safe. He bent down until he was no more than an inch from her face.

"No," he said. "I don't have any idea where he might be. Last time I checked, that was the job you signed up for."

CHAPTER TWENTY-ONE

After the interview with Goldie and Cameron, Raven made her way to the autopsy suite. She entered the door code and walked in to find Dr. Rita Sandbourne waiting for her to start the autopsy on Clyde Darling. Rita was there with a morgue assistant, a slender boy with horn-rimmed glasses who she introduced as LQ Buckner. Both he and Rita were wearing light blue scrubs in preparation for the autopsy.

Rita hugged her so tight that Raven felt as if her bones would break. When she finally let go, she held Raven at arm's length and gave her a good look. "I'm glad you're back."

"I've been back for a while," Raven said. "Just never thought I'd be back here."

"Sorry, but you're needed, sweetie," Rita said, gesturing to the body of Clyde Darling.

The body lay on a gurney wrapped in a white sheet knotted closed at both ends. The gurney was parked next to Rita's antique porcelain autopsy table, the one she used for special cases. Rita wasn't normally sentimental, and often irreverent, but she did have this one quirk that she seldom spoke of, and that was to be extra careful and respectful to those who left this world in a way she thought both painful and terrifying. They got the porcelain autopsy table.

"Let's get to it," Rita said. "I think I have a set of scrubs for you, Raven."

They left the autopsy suite and went into a small dressing room with several lockers. Raven shrugged out of her jacket and jeans, donned the scrubs, a disposable gown, and a hair bonnet along with a set of plastic sleeves. She ended her preparation by pulling on a set of latex gloves.

It wasn't like she was going to touch anything, but Rita liked to be thorough. Didn't want cop hairs ending up on her dead bodies.

"You haven't been around, Rita," Raven said as Rita adjusted a heavy plastic apron over her slim form before pulling on a pair of knee-high rubber boots for when the bodily fluids started to flow. Raven didn't plan to stick around for that part. She would hold on to her own boots, thank you very much.

"I was trying to give you and tall, dark and handsome some space," Rita said while looping the straps of her mask behind her ears. "Both you and Billy Ray went through a lot last year. I didn't want my face taking you back to somewhere neither one of you wanted to go."

"It would have been great to see you."

She felt pressured to lie because she and Rita had been close friends before Lovelle entered the picture. But Rita was right. Her face at Chastain's would have burst the illusion of Raven's new life like a soap bubble.

"Sure," Rita said. "That's why instead of waiting for me at the Toulouse scene, you bullied April into letting you take a peek under that blanket."

Raven kept her mouth shut.

Rita waited a moment or two then said, "Never mind. April's good people. I won't say anything, but please don't do it again."

"Don't worry about it," Raven said. "After this, there'll never be another chance to."

"So, you plan to leave us high and dry once you get what you want?" Rita asked.

"I'm out when I find Noe," Raven said, a stubborn note in her voice.

"Selfish much?" Rita replied, only half joking.

"You don't need me. You've got Breaker."

Rita looked at her as if she had just lost her mind. "Do you see him anywhere around here? Bodies showing up all over the place and Mr. High Fashion hasn't seen one autopsy. Says he can get what he needs from the reports."

And that's exactly what worried Raven. Breaker wasn't for homicide.

Some people were born to it, but not him. He may have been a good cop in major crimes, but Raven sensed that he didn't like to get his hands dirty. He would never stand for watching the ME crack open the chest of a child.

LQ was adjusting the lens on a Nikon camera when they returned to the autopsy suite.

"You didn't get pictures before the X-rays?" Raven asked.

"Yes, I did, but I just want to practice. I'm interning with Dr. Sandbourne."

"So, when you grow up you want to be just like Rita?"

He gave her a withering look. "I'm twenty-six."

"Hey," Rita said. "Don't get him riled. We need him. Come on, focus, LQ."

She walked over to him and together they grabbed the sheet and counted to three before lifting the body onto the autopsy table. They untied the sheet, going slow, rolling the body until it was free. Clyde was brown, lean and strong-looking except for the gaping wound at his throat.

"This one's different," Rita said.

"How so?" Raven asked.

"Not washed," Rita said. "Not even attempted. See all the blood?"

How could she not? His face looked like he had bathed in blood. Raven could not only see it, she could smell it. She had heard some describe the smell as iron, or steel. Maybe there was a scientific explanation for that. And sure, she smelled that, too. But the smell of blood reminded her of graves, gardens going to seed. She didn't smell iron, but decay, death and rot. For her, the scent of blood called to death like nothing else. Raven stepped closer to the gurney.

"Usually the Sleeping Boy victims come to me as clean as a newborn after its first bath. But this boy is different. Blood still on his face, soil on his hands, dirt under his nails. That's why I had them bagged at the scene."

"Enough for soil samples?"

"Yes. Before you ask, I also had LQ collect the dirt beneath the nails, the soil, too. Everything's already at the lab. Don't count on getting it back too soon. You know how long these things take."

"What about the kid they found at Memorial? He was dirty," Raven said.

"With dirt from the scene," Rita said. "But nothing else. He had been cleaned prior."

Raven stepped back to let LQ snap pictures of the full length of Clyde's body.

"Maybe he couldn't get Clyde clean because he had trouble dealing with him and Noe," Raven said.

"Let's hope it was enough for him to screw up and let Noe get away," Rita answered.

Rita tucked an earbud in her ear from a pair of Bluetooth headphones. She started a recording app on an iPad, said Clyde's name, age and case number.

"We're on now, Raven," she teased. "Watch your mouth."

"Any idea how long he'd been dead when they found him?" Raven asked.

"The mayor found the body when he was leaving for work, around seven thirty a.m.," Rita said. "By the fact that rigor was over and there's no bloat, I'd say maybe a couple of days."

"So that gives us a window of late Friday night or early Saturday morning?"

"Thereabouts," Rita said. "Goldie and the chief already been calling me asking about it. But you all know that I can't pin it down to the minute."

Rita had a clipboard in her hands and was examining Clyde's body. There were no bruises, marks, or anything on his torso or arms that indicated a struggle, just the blood spray from the stretched and gaping wound from ear to ear where the veins from Clyde's neck lay tangled and bulging.

Raven tore her eyes from Clyde's neck. "What's that wound on his forehead?"

"No clue," Rita said. "Maybe a hammer, but I'm not sure. This one looks like it came from one massive strike. A lot of damage."

"To the skull and the brain?" Raven asked.

"On some of the victims," Rita said. "Especially the smaller ones. And I've noticed that the amount of damage depends on where the wound was."

"What do you mean?"

"If the wound was right in the middle of the forehead, there was more skull damage. Off to the side, there seemed to be less."

"Couldn't that still be a hammer?"

"Maybe," Rita said. "But it just bugs the shit out of me because sometimes the blow appears so perfectly dead center, like one blow. I've already had an X-ray taken of this boy's head to get a better understanding of skull damage. I won't know about the brain until I can get it out of his head. Dissection will give me a better look."

Rita had moved to the head of the table and was massaging Clyde's scalp, feeling for more wounds. Later, as she slowly waved a UV light over Clyde's body, she said, "Doesn't hurt to double-check. Just like the other ones, no semen, though it looks like this poor soul pissed himself."

Raven's stomach knotted. She didn't need to hear that. "Anything else on the body that we could use?" she asked.

"You've got the blanket."

"I've already heard that the blankets aren't unusual. You can buy them anywhere. No foreign fibers or hairs on them in the other cases?"

"Not that I heard, but of course you're going to want to check the case files."

"You've seen a few of these, now, Rita. Have you any idea how this happened?"

"I have some. I tried to tell Detective Breaker, but he was so squeamish he wouldn't even hear me out. Told me to stick to my job and he'll stick to his."

"I've got a strong stomach. Spill it."

Rita looked over at her and said, "Remember the last time we traded theories?"

"I do," Raven said, smiling. "Almost got me thrown in jail. Talk to me."

Rita laughed. "Same old Raven. Fearless."

"Not fearless," Raven said. "These murders started without yours truly."

"Okay, you first," Rita said. "What are you thinking?"

"I think that whoever killed these boys hit them in the head first to stun them, probably a hammer, but maybe not. Which makes me think why not just cut their throats?"

"How would he get them to sit so still and wait patiently for a knock upside the head?"

"Maybe he tied them up?" Raven said.

"You're losing your touch, Burns," Rita said. "No ligature marks around the wrists. And there would have been bruising because they would have struggled like mad, especially with someone walking up on them with a hammer."

"Surprised them, maybe?"

"Had to be a hell of a surprise to make them sit still for this," Rita said.

"Then the victims knew the perp, trusted him. Anyway, he stuns them first, slits their throats and bleeds them out?"

"Probably by hanging them upside down. The other victims were completely exsanguinated. Now they had ligature marks around the ankles."

"Like an animal," Raven said. "Any idea what he used to cut their throats?"

"How about a big fucking knife?" Rita said with a dry chuckle.

"What happened to watching your mouth?" Raven said.

"I was just kidding, you know that. Besides, some things require the kind of cussing my pipe-smoking granny did."

She stepped away from Clyde's body, pulled off her gloves and threw them in a biohazard container. She picked up the iPad and started swiping through photos.

"The neck was pulled back, and the killer cut their throats starting at the left ear, most likely using a curved, flat blade. Something very sharp. Like this."

She showed Raven an image of a wickedly long knife that curved into an exquisitely sharp tip. It was beneath a heading that said slaughter knife.

"So the killer is slaughtering these boys," Raven said, confirming her worst fear.

"That's what I think."

"But why? Why the stunning? Why not just slit their throats?"

"Maybe he doesn't want to see them suffer," Rita said.

"Washing them, wrapping them in new blankets. Like he cares about them. But on the other hand, he's killing them. Some sort of sacrifice?" Raven said.

"To what?"

"I don't know," Raven said. "Anger? Revenge?"

"I thought you had to sacrifice to a person, or an entity, not to an emotion."

"I'm just grasping, Rita. I got nothing."

"Have a seat, sweetie," Rita said as she was grabbing a face shield.

"I wasn't planning on staying."

Rita turned around, found another face shield and handed it to Raven. "Oh come on," she said. "I've given you your space. Keep me company. Besides, your favorite parts are coming up. I'll catch you up on the cases for the next couple of hours, and maybe we can swap more theories just like old times."

Rita pulled on a fresh set of latex gloves. "I'll never understand these fuckers, which is why I'm glad that you're back. Do what you do, Raven. Find this bastard before he kills another kid. Find your nephew before he ends up on my table."

CHAPTER TWENTY-TWO

Raven removed her scrubs and threw the disposable apron and sleeves she had worn during the autopsy into a biohazard container. Dressed now in her jeans and jacket, she studied her reflection in the morgue's bathroom mirror. For a second Floyd's face flashed in the glass, the bright green and blue peacock feather in the fedora's hatband, his one green eye and one blue eye staring at her intently, a playful smile on his thin lips. It was as if any second he was going to wag his finger and say, *I know you, Birdy Girl, but do you know you?* The next second his bloody grin faded away.

And it was just her face.

Tired. Haunted by seeing Clyde cut up like that even though it was necessary and it wasn't her first autopsy.

"What have I done to deserve this?" she asked out loud, but in a whisper.

And though she asked no one in particular, Floyd was fast and ready with an answer. *Oh I don't know, Birdy Girl,* he said, *maybe shoot a man down in cold blood.* And then he was gone again.

She twisted open the faucet and threw cold water on her face.

It wasn't any surprise that she was going a little crazy with everything that had happened. It just wasn't fair. She pulled several paper towels from the holder to dry her face. When she looked in the mirror again, Floyd stood next to her. She would have sworn that she could feel his rough whiskers against her face.

Now, ain't we maudlin? Put your big-girl panties on and go out there and do what you do.

For once the old man was right.

She shoved down the feeling of helplessness and made her way to the conference room they were using as a command center for the case. The command center turned out to be just a rectangular room with cheap aluminum blinds covering the tall windows. She wasn't surprised to see the chief sitting at the oblong table. The case was too hot for him not to be all over it. What did surprise her was that Delbert Stevenson sat across from the chief. Stevenson looked so uncomfortable Raven wondered if he were sitting on a cactus.

"I thought you were on your way home," Raven said to him from the doorway. "Didn't your daddy call you back so you can take your punishment?"

"Don't start, Raven," Chief Sawyer said.

Stevenson turned to look at her. She could tell by the muscle jumping like a tadpole in his jaw that he was trying his best to keep his handsome face still and unbothered. He waved a hand at the chief. "Your boss asked me to sit in."

"Is this some kind of sick joke?" she asked.

Chief Sawyer shook his head. "I'm afraid not. Breaker's out."

"What?"

"Couldn't handle it. Quit the case."

"What do you mean quit the case?" Raven said. "You saying he went back to Major Crimes? You let him just walk out on you like that? Who runs things around here, Chief?"

"You don't understand," the chief clarified. "He quit the case and the force. On top of that he left town, got out of here so fast you'd think he stole something."

"Holy crap on a cracker," Raven breathed, coming into the room. She found a chair as far away from Stevenson as she could get. "There isn't anybody else in the entire BLPD except this bucket of guts?"

"Hey," Stevenson protested.

"You got Billy Ray?" the chief asked.

Raven ran her hands over her face. "No, I don't *got* Billy Ray. He thinks Noe's dead. He wants nothing to do with this." She glared at Stevenson. "What about someone else on the force? That IA guy, Goldie, he seems...."

Chief Sawyer raised an eyebrow. "Friendly?"

"Chief...." She stopped.

No, he didn't seem exactly friendly, but he did seem competent.

"We're tapped. If you want a partner, Stevenson's it. He says his boss agreed to let him help out for a while."

"His rogue cop? His troublesome, on-the-lam rogue cop who goes around sleeping with suspects on murder cases? Who's doing who a favor? I bet the minute Stevenson steps back into town his boss is going to send him to hell on scholarship. All they're doing over in California is damage control. Buying time."

"That's not what *she* told me, Raven."

"And on top of that, he sucks."

"Why?" Stevenson challenged. "Because I couldn't catch you? I'm not giving up on that one. You're going to pay for what you've done whether I'm still a cop or not."

"But I dated you," she said. "Isn't that payment enough?"

"Okay, okay," the chief said. "Can you two just put aside your differences and help us find this guy?"

Grief and desperation were plain on the chief's face. The hair at his temples looked even grayer than before. He ran a hand over his head. "They're killing children, for God sakes."

Raven looked at the man she had known as Wynn Bowen. "I don't even know what to call it."

The chief sighed tiredly. "For fuck's sake, Raven. Aren't you listening to me?"

"It's a problem," Raven said. "Do I call it Wynn? WynnDel? DelWynn? What?"

"You can call me Stevenson. Detective Stevenson."

She didn't turn his way. Instead she kept her eyes on the chief. "I like WynnDel. Has a certain ring to it."

"You saying you'll do this?" the chief asked.

"I'm saying I'll do anything to find Noe," she said. "Who else is on the team?"

"You're it," the chief said. "You've got Rita, of course, for a sounding board. You two always worked well together. There are rookies you are welcome to use to canvass, take statements, that kind of thing. You can have Officer Spangler, too."

"Fine," she conceded. "So, I gathered what I could from the autopsy. You want to give me what you're thinking so far?"

"I told you a lot of it already at the restaurant, and you saw the deal at Memorial," the chief said. "I can't tell you anything more than what you already know. All we've got is a pile of fucking bodies."

She opened a file folder from a stack on the table. "Still using paper," she said. "You'd think Billy Ray was here."

"I thought he would be, so I asked Spangler to make hard copies," the chief said.

She read the label on the folder. Henri Toulouse, the boy from Memorial. A picture with that name beneath it was fixed to a magnetic whiteboard at the end of the long table.

The chief saw her looking. "Judge Toulouse's kid."

Raven raised an eyebrow. "Got that much from the scene. What about a connection between Toulouse and the other victims. Or the site?"

"They couldn't find any. Victim number one was Michele Jean Baptiste," Stevenson said. "I was reading the files before you got here. As you can see, Toulouse is a redhead, Baptiste has dark hair – I mean the hair that's not dyed blue. Different builds. Tall, lanky. He's not from money, either. His mother is a dealer at the Four Leaf casino."

"Is Baptiste the one that was found in the doorway of the bank?" Raven said in a voice she hoped was all business.

"Yes," the chief said.

"Didn't you say you had video from that scene?"

"I also said it was useless. The killer busted it before stepping into the frame. All these boys, naked, throat slit, and bled. Wrapped in a blue and white blanket like all of them."

There was that word again – bled. Bled like he was being slaughtered for meat.

Raven stood up and walked to the whiteboard with the boys'

pictures on it, glossy eight-by-tens just like Billy Ray liked them. The chief was really expecting her old partner. She looked at each one of the photographs, paused to study them individually. She didn't want to think of these boys as victims or bodies. She wanted to think of them as living, laughing with their friends, going to high school, being obnoxious with their girlfriends and later regretting it, spending too much money on tennis shoes, not doing their homework, or sweating about upcoming college entrance exams if they were lucky enough to afford college. She wanted to remember them and catch the monster who stole their lives.

One of the victims, Elroy Malay, had a gap between his teeth that made him proud. His smile was just too big. If the ball cap pushed back on his head was any indication, he was fond of the LSU Tigers football team. Henri Toulouse was pictured in a light blue sweater with his arms folded. He looked like money and wanted everyone to know it.

Raven touched her fingertips to her throat, cleared it and turned back to the chief and Stevenson.

"No semen or saliva detected on the bodies?"

The chief shook his head. "You said you just came from the Darling autopsy. I'm sure Rita already told you no. Asking it again isn't going to get you a different answer. Clean as newborn babies. That is, until Toulouse and Darling. Until now, the only thing linking them was their race."

Raven nodded but didn't say anything. She could feel Wynn – no, Stevenson – looking at her, but she didn't acknowledge it. She thought about when Floyd killed. It didn't appear that he did, but he chose his victims very carefully. He stalked them, and sometimes would even get to know them. He said it made the surprise better, and whew boy, how he loved a surprise. There were a couple of deaths that weren't on his radar, usually people he killed because he believed that it was necessary, or because they pissed him off. Those killings looked different, no fires like he was also fond of doing when he had the chance. The deaths were quick. Clean, without flames or ashes.

"What do you think, Raven?" the chief said.

She was back at the table. She opened another file folder, flipped through a couple of pages before looking over at Stevenson, who still eyed her, his face baleful and accusing.

"What do you think, lover?"

Stevenson thrust his hands in the air and sat back.

"Raven," the chief said.

"Sorry, couldn't resist. Right now, I don't think anything. I need to take this in. You must have your theories."

"Nothing that's getting us closer to finding this guy."

"You pulled the finances on the families, right? The phone records of these boys, and checked their social media, just like we're doing for the Darlings, Cameron and Noe? Talked to their friends? Tried to find out if they knew each other?"

"All of that. Read the statements, and then read them again. Maybe something will stick out to you a second time around. Lord knows it didn't for Breaker. He wasted so much time that it made me sick," the chief said.

"I see," Raven said idly while flipping through one of the file folders. "And the video?"

"Aren't you listening?" Stevenson said. "Chief Sawyer just told you."

"What video are you talking about?" the chief asked.

Raven fixed the chief with a look, and then Stevenson. "All of it," she said.

"I don't understand—" Stevenson began.

"You mean surrounding businesses where the bodies were found?" the chief asked.

"Maybe that's what I mean."

"I'm sure Breaker did that," the chief said.

"Are you? The man who just ran home back to his mama?"

"You even sound like your father," Stevenson said, disgusted.

Raven walked over to Stevenson, her fingers lightly trailing the table. She leaned in when she got close to him. "Does that scare you?" she asked. "That I sound like my daddy? Why don't you go ahead and follow Breaker? Run along on home. Maybe your wife will take you back."

She felt a hand on her shoulder. She straightened to see the chief standing beside her.

"What do you mean all of it?" he asked, the question bringing her back to the room and the problem at hand.

"I mean all of it," she said, walking back to the stack of folders. "Every last bit of it from the surrounding businesses and maybe even within a five-to-ten-mile radius. I would start with the high school, the last place Noe and Clyde were seen. Check the city buses, too. Places they liked to go."

"We don't have enough people for that," the chief said.

"Find the people."

"How?"

"What about recruits from the academy?"

"We couldn't fill a class this year. There aren't any academy recruits in this hell hole."

"Besides, some of these murders are months old," Stevenson said. "Most of the videos are probably recorded over."

"Even if they aren't recorded over, that would take way too many resources. I'm not even sure it's necessary," the chief cut in.

Raven unzipped her backpack and stuck the file folders inside. "I'm getting kind of tired of you two telling me what you can't do," she said. "I thought you said you were desperate."

CHAPTER TWENTY-THREE

The next day, Wednesday, they still had little evidence. There was the footprint found at Memorial that didn't match the work boots on the construction site, and the soil evidence now making its way through a third-party lab. All too slow. Noe could be locked up somewhere hurt and dying or starving and dying. The key word was dying. She refused to entertain the thought that he was already dead.

Raven squeezed the red Mustang into a corner parking space in the lot of Chastain's Creole Heaven. The parking lot was full to bursting with the lunch rush. Several people left their cars while popping their umbrellas open to shield themselves from a pelting rain. Two women in spiked high heels and pencil skirts held the *Byrd's Landing Review* over their bone-straight hair.

She reached into the passenger seat and grabbed her Dell laptop and her backpack. She flicked the door handle up before kicking the door open with her booted foot. She ran through the parking lot hunched over the laptop, trying her best not to get it wet. She could have gone around the restaurant to Billy Ray's house, but she didn't want to get any more soaked than she already was. She'd have to use the restaurant's front door.

The scent of sautéed bell peppers, celery and onions overlaid with spicy cayenne, and sounds of zydeco greeted her like old friends when she opened the door of the restaurant. She heard someone slam down a domino on the mahogany live-edge table in the old folks' corner, followed by Mr. Joe's triumphant cackle. Raven looked up briefly before lowering her head and making a beeline for the kitchen.

She heard Imogene's questioning "hey" over the zydeco and the low roar of the lunch crowd. Ignoring Imogene, Raven walked through the kitchen and right into Billy Ray's follow-up to Imogene's question. "What? Wait," he shouted.

She made sure she didn't catch his eye. For a minute she thought he would throw the spatula he had been holding at her. In the end he didn't. He couldn't. It was the lunch hour. The place was packed, and people were hungry. The Billy Ray she knew wouldn't abandon his customers. That's why she planned noontime for her invasion. Besides, waiting until noon gave her the time she needed to contact the BLPD technology department and tell them what they needed to do regarding collecting the videos from surrounding businesses, and centralizing them in the Cloud.

She continued straight through the kitchen and out the back screen door, walking the gravel path that led to the shotgun Billy Ray used as both an office and a residence. For the season, he had set a pitiful-looking Charlie Brown Christmas tree in a black pot next to the front door.

In the old days, before Lamont Lovelle, his front door would have been unlocked. But not now. Though he hadn't bothered giving her a key, she had one anyway. She had swiped it and made a copy after seeing it hanging against the pegboard in the restaurant's kitchen. She rationalized that he would have given it to her eventually, but just hadn't gotten around to it. After all, Billy Ray was closer to her than any other human being on the planet with the exception of Cameron. She wouldn't let a little left-over trauma from a night with a serial killer mess that up. Raven unlocked the door and walked in like she owned the place.

Billy Ray used the first room of the shotgun as an office, the second room as his living quarters, and the third a private kitchen for him with a bathroom set off to the side.

She dumped her backpack and the laptop on the only bare spot on his desk, and then got busy removing the ceramic owls he collected, the recipes clipped from various magazines, the old *Jet* and *Ebony* magazines, stacks of books on everything from poetry to carpentry (which he would tell her with a laugh weren't that different), and a three-ring binder filled with stained recipes that he had collected from his father and other home cooks around the south. There was not a computer in sight, an absence that was so quintessential Billy Ray that Raven felt comforted. But there was a printer on the floor near the outlet, probably for printing recipes from his iPad or making copies of them from magazines.

Once the desk was cleared, she set up her Dell and turned it on. As it was booting up she pulled a rolling magnetic whiteboard filled with shift schedules and menus closer to the desk. She took a picture with her Android before erasing it. She then removed the various recipes Billy Ray had affixed to the board. He didn't need them anyway, she reasoned. He only had to look at a recipe once and in the end never really followed it. He added his own twist, and the food always turned out amazing. Still, she wasn't crazy. She smoothed the recipes on the now clean desk before placing them carefully between the pages of the three-ring binder.

She drew a line down the center of the board with a red expo marker. On one side she attached photos of the known victims, including poor Clyde. On the other she wrote the names of Cameron and Willie Lee in black marker. She had been so intent on what she was doing that she hadn't heard Billy Ray come in until he said in a soft voice, "What the fuck?"

Raven turned to him with a big Alice in Wonderland Cheshire cat smile. "I've accepted your terms."

"What are you talking about?"

"Your terms. You said you can't be at the station, but you'd help me from here."

"This isn't what I meant," he said.

"Isn't it?"

"You're crazier than a soup sandwich if you think you can come in and take over like this."

"Am I?"

"What about Breaker?"

She shrugged. "He quit. Turned tail and ran home, according to the chief."

"Surely the chief assigned someone else."

"He did," she said. "Stevenson."

"You gotta be fucking kidding me."

"Nope," Raven said. "I kid you not. That's why I'm here."

He opened his mouth to say something, and to forestall the stream of foul language that Raven knew was about to issue forth, she said, "Before you start yelling, this is about finding Noe. You don't get serious and help me, he's dead. You know that, don't you?"

Billy Ray placed his big hands lightly on his hips, bowed his head and then looked up at her again, his face somber. She could tell he wanted to say something, but she could also tell that he didn't want to hurt her.

He finally said, "Let me see if Imogene can handle the rest of the lunch crowd. I'll be back when I can. Don't touch anything else."

"You got it, partner."

"Don't call me partner," he called over his shoulder, the screen door slapping shut behind him.

$$\star \quad \star \quad \star$$

For someone who didn't want to be involved in police work, Billy Ray listened intently as Raven caught him up. She had spent the entire morning with Cameron and his coworkers making plans for the video evidence while two uniforms were out taking more statements from Noe and Clyde's teachers and friends. She told Billy Ray that Stevenson and the chief were treating Clyde's death as a copycat. Noe just happened to be caught up in it because they were together.

"You know that's what I think, too," Billy Ray said. "Taking both Clyde and Noe was way too sloppy. This killer is too organized to do something fool-headed like that if he didn't have to."

"How do you know they were taken together?" Raven asked.

"It's pretty obvious to me that's what happened," he said. "Who's talking to Clyde's parents? June and more importantly that cat Memphis? His name should be up there on that whiteboard with your list of suspects."

"Stevenson and the chief said they were going to swing by Clyde's parents and ask a few more questions. Try to get Memphis down to the station. One more question, Billy Ray."

"Don't let me stop you from asking it."

"For as long as you've known Cameron, you think he's capable of murder?"

"Why do you ask?"

"I think that's the direction the chief and Stevenson are going."

Billy Ray considered for a moment before holding up two fingers. "You forget," he said. "I've known him for only a little over two years. He's worth looking at."

"Well, I've known him for over fifteen."

"That's why you need to be careful," Billy Ray said.

"So, now you're questioning my judgment of character?"

"You let Stevenson put one over on you."

The room became so quiet that she could hear the rumble of engines and good-natured yells of goodbye as the last of the lunch crowd left the restaurant. She turned and looked out of the shotgun's front window to where Billy Ray had built his dream. When, she wondered, had he become so cruel?

Finally he said, "If Cameron wasn't your foster brother, wouldn't you be thinking that he's good for this?"

She turned her gaze back to him, making sure every bit of her face was as still as slate. "If I didn't know him, I'd want to check him out. But there is no way Cameron is good for this. Not in any universe. First of all, Cameron doesn't fit the profile. He's far from organized. And he doesn't have any place private for his kills."

"Remember what happened the last time you were so sure of something?"

"Another low blow. You're two for two."

"I'm just saying it needs exploring."

"Don't worry about it. We're looking at it. We've talked to him, pulled Cameron's financials and phone records."

"You? They let you talk to him?"

"After a fashion. Goldie questioned him. He let me sit in."

"Probably just to throw Cameron off," Billy Ray said. "There would be no other good reason for you to be in the room with him."

"I figured, but hey, I'll take what I can get."

"How did it go?"

"You saw him on Monday," she said. "He wasn't any good for actual facts, but if it was raw emotion Goldie was after, Cameron gave that to him in spades, and dug his grave a little deeper in the process."

"Stevenson or Chief Sawyer question him yet?"

"Nope," Raven said. "Cameron's not really talking to me right now, but I made it clear to him that he should lawyer up if they come calling again."

Billy Ray laughed. "That's reason double for the chief and Stevenson to put a target on his back. Your son's missing and you scream lawyer."

"Right now, the state Cameron's in, it's a smart move."

"You think that's the right thing to do?"

"For a black man in this system, it's the only thing to do."

"Okay. I'll give you that. But still."

"You really think he did this?" Raven asked.

"No, but you're doing more harm than good if you start out of the gate saying fuck you to the rules."

"I'm not saying screw you to the rules. I'm just trying to find Noe."

They sat for a few moments in a comfortable silence that made Raven loath to break it. After a while, she did by telling him about her theory of the boys being slaughtered and offered for sacrifice.

"Might be something else you want to check out," he said. "I could arrange for you to talk to Stella if you want to know how a righteous slaughter is done. You may want to take a ride out there. Could give you some insight."

She wrote down the address he gave her, but didn't make any move to leave.

"So, you want to camp out here?" he asked finally.

"Yes," she said. "When I need a break from Stevenson, and that snake pit called the Byrd's Landing Police Department."

"Okay, I know that look. What else am I in for?"

She told him.

CHAPTER TWENTY-FOUR

"This is insane," Stevenson said.

Raven told him to shut up without even bothering to turn in his direction. The son-of-a-biscuit-eater had finished with the questioning of Clyde's parents, and tracked her down at Chastain's. He was like gum on a shoe that she couldn't shake off.

Regardless, she stood looking at the elderly people in Chastain's old folks' corner thinking that maybe Stevenson was right. She could hear Billy Ray banging pots around in the kitchen even over the music. Billy Ray didn't like what she was about to ask them, but without any other prospects for help they really had no choice.

She stared at each one of the old folks in turn. The people at the mahogany live-edge table looked right back at her, some of them bemused, others wary. She knew that the reasons they hung around Chastain's were not because of the food – okay, maybe it was the food. But the primary reason was that the restaurant, with its loud music, constant laughter and raucous voices, was an escape. They had trouble in their lives just like everyone else, and maybe because they had been around longer than most, more of it.

But during the months Raven waited tables, they seldom talked about their troubles, and if they were careless to let any of it slip, it was always wrapped in laughter. Mama Anna had just turned eighty. Her family had a little money but she had outlived it, hence the rooming house, or according to what people say today, she had the place converted into a long-stay boutique hotel. Byrd's Landing gossip had it that Mama Anna used to be a hellraiser. She had run away from home at sixteen dressed as a boy, ran all the way to New Mexico, where she danced with the devil for a good long time before returning to Byrd's Landing.

Mama Anna's friend, Miss Vera, who usually sat opposite her, was a proper churchgoing lady who never entered Chastain's without her wig on, or as she would proudly say, her stockings rolled down. But Raven knew her husband had cleaned out their bank account and ran off with a church secretary almost forty years his junior. If Miss Vera, not a fool by any means, hadn't had a secret stash set by, she would have been up what Floyd would have called soupy poop creek without a paddle.

Mr. Joe was a Korean War vet and proud of it. His younger friend, Mr. Walter, was a Vietnam vet, and absolutely not. And then there was Mr. Bello, a college-educated computer operator for Standard Oil when they had stakes in town. The others teased him for being a draft dodger because he managed to avoid both wars.

"Now, you want us to do what, Chile?" Mama Anna said, looking at Raven as if she had left her brains on the porch of the restaurant.

"Help find Noe," Raven answered.

"How we gone to do that?" Mr. Walter said. "Joe could barely find himself last night. Joe!" he yelled to his friend. "Where you at?"

The whole table exploded in laughter, and Mr. Walter was so tickled with his joke that he pounded the floor with his cane. Stevenson gave Raven an *I-told-you-so* look.

"You can help us look through some videos," Raven said, unsmiling.

"Ain't gone do you no good," Mr. Walter said. "Vera blind. Anna's mean and impatient. The draft dodger, well, you know...."

"Walter," Mama Anna said, and Raven was grateful for the serious tone, the first time she had actually seen her so serious. "Shut your mouth before your brains fall out."

Her tablemates must have caught the tone, because the laughter stopped and nobody spoke. Raven nodded to Cameron, whom she had called to the restaurant, using her no-nonsense cop and sister voice, the one that could usually get him moving no matter how much she had pissed him off. He placed a box on the table and began pulling out Dell laptops.

She and Stevenson had argued earlier on a three-way call with the chief about having Cameron involved in any way in the investigation.

Raven was able to fast-talk both of them into it even though Cameron had been officially suspended pending the outcome of the case. Cameron's accounts had already been locked, she told them, and his access to any BLPD computer systems revoked. Besides, this way, they could both keep an eye on him and keep him busy. "Or keep him one step ahead of us," Stevenson had said.

But Raven responded that Billy Ray would be at the restaurant the entire time keeping an eye on Cameron. She further told them that Billy Ray shared their suspicion. If he did have anything to do with this, Cameron would get away with nothing.

Raven had her two assigned uniforms call bus stations, residences around Clyde's and Noe's homes, theaters, fast-food places they frequented, and anywhere the boys may have been during the past weekend. They had orders to sweet-talk those they called out of any video evidence they might have had. They came back with hundreds of hours of video that needed to be examined. Cameron's coworker in IT centralized the videos on a secure server, and provided log-ons and passwords for the people around the table now staring at her suspiciously.

Mr. Bello, the former computer operator, looked at the closed computers and back up at her. "You know these old people won't be able to work a laptop."

"I don't believe that for a minute," Raven said. "But if they need help, you can help them. I'm going to leave Cameron here so he can help troubleshoot any laptop problems, too." Raven put an arm around her foster brother's shoulder and gave him a tight squeeze. He stiffened. Stevenson muttered under his breath. She gave each one of the old folks yellow legal pads and two sharp pencils.

"We have no idea where Noe and Clyde went after school on Friday," Raven said. "Clyde didn't have a cell phone because he was on punishment. And unfortunately, the last ping on Noe's phone was Friday late in the school day. We checked their social media accounts, but couldn't find anything there, either. We're counting on you."

"Why the movie star here?" Miss Vera asked, glaring at Stevenson. She never liked him, told Raven there was something funny about him.

"I've been telling you for months that I'm not a movie star, Miss Vera," Stevenson said.

"Location scout," Mr. Joe said. "Boy a location scout for them movies up in Hollywood."

"He's not a location scout," Raven corrected.

"What?" Mr. Walter said. "You lose your job? Maybe Billy Ray can give you something that can tide you over."

"Never mind all that now," Raven said. "There are a lot of videos we're going to have you review. Some from the school and some from people's houses, and some from restaurants and such. I'm also going to have you review the videos from the city buses. And when you see Clyde or Noe, I want you to write it down, and tell Billy Ray."

"Write what down, exactly?" Mr. Joe said.

"The date and time stamp on the video if it has one, the place it came from, and what makes you think it's Noe and Cameron."

"What were they wearing in case we can't see their faces?" Miss Vera asked.

"What they usually wear," Raven said. "Noe had on a pair of khakis and a blue hoodie with Howard University across it. Clyde had on a LSU sweatshirt. He was wearing khakis, too. Both of them had on navy blue Chucks."

"This don't sound like a lot of fun," Mr. Joe said.

"Sometimes fun ain't possible," Mama Anna said. "Especially when the work is necessary."

"I'm sure you know how to make it fun," Raven said.

"Got that right," Mr. Joe answered.

"How do we get to the videos?" Mr. Bello asked.

As she left them, she heard Cameron telling them how to log on. His voice faded as she walked toward the front door with Stevenson behind her.

"You've got our prime suspect looking for evidence," he told her as they exited the restaurant.

"My brother has nothing to do with this," Raven said. "And he's not looking for evidence. He's just helping them get logged on, and showing them how to get to the videos. As soon as he gets everyone going, and it looks like Mr. Bello can handle any problems they might have, Billy Ray is going to put him to work in the restaurant. He'll keep Cameron out of the way."

"You don't know that for sure. What if Billy Ray gets too busy?" he said, frowning. "This isn't how things get done."

"Maybe in your town, Detective, it's not how things get done. But in my town? We take help where we can get it. If we didn't, your sorry butt wouldn't be here now, would it?"

CHAPTER TWENTY-FIVE

The one-story weathered house was small against the wide expanse of a flat gray sky. A fine mist rose from the muddy yard, and Raven could see patches of standing water from the recent rains.

"Hello, Raven," Stella said from the porch of the farmhouse, her voice high and lilting like music. Although she wore a pair of all-weather work boots over her gray sweatpants, she didn't venture into the wet yard to greet them. Raven smiled as she slammed the car door, and waved. Stevenson came from around the passenger's side to stand beside her.

"What in the hell are we doing way out here?" he said. He twisted around to get a good look at the country road, the muddy front yard, the surrounding marsh, and the woman waiting for them on the porch.

"You remember Stella, right? " Raven said. "From Noe's birthday party. She owns this place."

"I remember her, but I didn't get a chance to talk to her at all," Stevenson said. "Still doesn't tell me why we're out here, Raven."

The way he said her name bugged her. He said it like he knew her. The fact was that he did, but not all of her. She turned and contemplated him like he was a stranger who happened to wander into her field of vision. He flinched.

"I need to get a feel for where this killer is coming from," she said, making sure her voice was devoid of all emotion. "Billy Ray suggested I talk to her."

He still didn't understand. Raven wasn't about to waste time explaining. She started across the muddy yard, feeling the wet coolness through her boots. Stevenson muttered and swore behind her. She didn't have to turn around to know that he was hitching up his pants so the cuffs wouldn't get muddy. On the porch Raven pulled her boots off without waiting to be asked. Stevenson followed suit with his shoes.

"Thank you," Stella said, pulling her own boots off before holding the screen door open for them to walk inside.

"I appreciate you seeing me," Raven said as they entered a small open room.

"No problem at all. Any friend of Billy Ray's is a friend of mine. Plus I love the company." She smiled and turned to Stevenson. "Wynn, right?"

"Sure," Stevenson said with a quick look toward Raven, who was glad that he didn't confuse things with an explanation that wouldn't make any sense to Stella.

Once inside, Stella gestured to an old but perfectly maintained couch patterned in pink tea roses and told them to sit. Raven sat on the couch while Stevenson took a seat on a wooden ladder-back chair near a black pot-bellied stove.

"Would you like some tea?" Stella asked.

"No, thank you," Raven said, but Stella, as if she hadn't heard, kept walking, saying something about putting the kettle on.

Stevenson stared at Stella's retreating back. White pieces of scalp shone through the woman's wispy red hair. He swirled a big hand over his own bald head and gave Raven a questioning look.

"Hair extensions," Raven whispered, assuming that he was referring to the night of the party when Stella was a newly made-over woman rocking pink lip gloss and a head full of red curls.

Restlessly, Raven picked up one of the magazines that had been arranged alphabetically on the coffee table. She flipped through a couple of pages, not seeing anything, before replacing it. Stevenson rubbed his hands together as if he were freezing though the Louisiana weather was mild, especially after all the rain.

Stella returned a few minutes later with a tray of cups, saucers and a tea kettle. She began fussing with the tea, not looking at them as she did so. Without asking, she placed two lumps of raw sugar into each of their delicate china cups.

"It's nice to have company," she said, finally sitting back on the couch next to Raven. "Being way out here by myself sometimes has me making things up, you know, seeing things." She laughed brightly. "Sometimes I swear the sheep are talking to me." She brought the tea cup to her thin lips and took a delicate sip. "So, Billy Ray said that you were interested in my process?"

"Yes, for a case," Raven said.

"I didn't know you were also a detective?" Stella said, looking at Stevenson. "Are you with the BLPD as well?"

"This is just a friendly conversation," Raven said before Stevenson could answer. "I asked him to tag along for company. Long drive. I hope you don't mind."

"Of course not," Stella said. "The Sleeping Boy case, correct? A lot of buzz in the farming community about how those boys are being killed. It puts unnecessary attention on what we do, especially with animal rights activists. So you think these boys are being slaughtered?"

"That's right," Raven said. "Throats cut, exsanguinated."

"Except, that's *not* right." Stella took a deep breath. "I'm glad the police are trying to find out how slaughter really works. These murders have nothing to do with how we treat our animals. I'm happy to help any way I can."

"We appreciate that. It's just you on the farm?" Raven asked, blowing on the tea. She didn't know what kind it was, but it smelled strong and bitter. She took a sip.

"Yes, since my husband died. It's not that hard to care for this place. I grew up on a farm. The animals are a handful but I manage it."

"I'm sorry for your loss," Stevenson said.

"Thank you. Unfortunately, his loss wasn't my first. My parents died before he did. They left the place to both me and my sister, who was going to sell it, but I went to court to stop it. God arranged the stars in my favor, and I won. This farm is a piece of them, though. It brings me some comfort."

"Where is your sister now?" Stevenson asked.

"Dead, thank God. Good riddance to bad rubbish. She and my

no-good husband, who, I might add, she was fucking before they kicked the bucket."

Stella stopped when she saw the look of horror on Stevenson's face. "Sorry. Don't mean to offend. But it's the truth. If you had known her, you would have been glad to be shut of her, too."

"How did she die?" Stevenson said.

"*They* die," she answered. "They both died at the same time. Murder, suicide. Years ago. God," she shuddered, "what a mess."

Raven sipped the tea, enjoying the warmth of it, and laughing quietly inside, knowing the effect Stella's oddness was having on the usually straightlaced Stevenson.

"Don't you get lonely way out here by yourself?" Stevenson asked.

"Sometimes," she said. "Billy Ray has been a good friend. We hang out now and then when he's not too busy. Other than that I have my animals. They keep me company, and I'm pretty sure not one of them would ever run off with my husband...."

"But doesn't that make you sad when you have to...." Raven stopped and waved her fingers beneath her throat.

"Do you mean the slaughter?" Stella asked. She put the teacup back on the coffee table. "It's hard to say goodbye to them. But otherwise, it's all very peaceful."

"You must mean for you," Stevenson said.

Stella smiled, her eyes only on him for a brief second. "You sound like someone who doesn't know where his food comes from." She turned to Raven. "It's better if you see what I'm talking about. Would you like to meet them?"

Raven said that she would. She knew that the interview wouldn't be a question-and-answer session. The minute she saw Stella standing on the porch in her no-nonsense work boots, Raven knew that it would be better if she let Stella take the lead. She was far from the shy redhead they had met at Noe's party. They followed her back to the front porch, where they reclaimed their boots and shoes.

The air was wet, earthy. Stella led them around the house. Stevenson, more worried about the mud on his pants than paying attention to where he was going, tripped over an old weathered storage box beneath what was most likely the kitchen window. He cursed.

Raven laughed. "You all right, there?" she asked, not caring if he was.

"I'm going to have to buy some new pants," he said, righting himself again.

"Sorry about that," Stella said. "I need to get rid of that old thing, but I never seem to be able to get around to it."

She led them into a huge clearing that held a sheep pen and a large barn. The colors of the sheep amazed Raven. She had expected white like in the movies and storybooks. But Stella's sheep were brown with legs the color of deep russet. Several smaller, white sheep were scattered among them. Stella indicated two bales of hay for Raven and Stevenson to sit. Raven sat but Stevenson stood with his arms folded across his chest, examining the mud on his pants and caked on his dress shoes.

Stella opened the gate to the pen. "Come here, Tatiana, come on, beautiful," she called.

"You name them?" Stevenson said in a disgusted voice.

"Of course," Stella said mildly. "I number them, too. But feels kind of odd to call Tatiana number 26."

She sat on the bale of hay next to Raven, rubbing the sheep's neck and scratching its head.

"Would you like to give her a pet?"

Raven got up from the bale and squatted. She offered both hands for the sheep to sniff as if she would have done with a strange dog.

"You have to be very still," Stella said in a low voice, gently pushing Raven's hands down. "She's very friendly, but you're a stranger to her. Show that you aren't a threat. Look like you don't care."

Raven did as she was told and soon felt Tatiana's wet nose touch her forehead. She touched the sheep's neck and stroked until the animal buried its face in her curls. She laughed.

"Isn't that cool? She likes you," Stella said.

"What's that building over there?" Stevenson asked abruptly.

"That's for the slaughter," Stella said. She turned back to Raven. "Come on, I'll show you."

Stella returned Tatiana to her pen and began quickly walking to the abattoir, a long wooden building with a slanted roof and no windows.

Raven lifted an eyebrow at Stevenson, who was lingering a little too long at the sheep's pen. "Coming?" she asked.

"No," he said, without looking at her.

"What a scaredy cat."

"Okay, fine, fine."

When they reached the building, Stella pushed open the double wooden doors, which opened onto a room without a back wall. Where the wall should have been were two thick columns with rolled-up metal doors that could be pulled down when privacy was necessary. Beyond appeared to be miles and miles of wet fields with mist hovering like smoke, and cypress trees rising from the water.

Several thick chains along with hooks hung down from the ceiling. On Raven's right was a pegboard of tools attached to the wall, beneath which was a low wooden cabinet. The top of the cabinet held a host of knives. Raven slowly walked over to them. The deadliest knife of them all lay next to a sharpening stone.

For some reason Raven's hands twitched. She itched to test for herself how sharp the knife really was. When she noticed Stevenson staring at her, she stuffed her hands in her back pockets and walked away. Soon she was next to a sign on the wall that read, 'The place where an animal dies is a sacred one'.

"So, how does it work?" Raven asked, sitting on a stool and hooking her feet behind the lower rung.

"Efficiently. I follow the teachings of Temple Grandin in my treatment of these animals," Stella said. "I pick the day of slaughter in advance, and I do give thanks for what they are about to provide."

"Like a sacrifice," Raven said, thinking about the Sleeping Boy victims.

"No, not like that at all. It's more like a trade. I give them a good life, and I don't stress them. In return, they provide sustenance for you, me, for all of us. That's why I was so eager to talk to you when you called. People are really misinterpreting what happens here."

"You slaughter all these sheep alone?" Stevenson questioned.

Stella smiled. "No. I'd like to think I'm a badass, but I need help just like everybody else. I hire locals from other farms, people from town. Not too many to choose from these days. Everyone seems to be moving away from here, especially with the encroaching marshes and the powers that be wanting to declare them as protected places. They don't care that they're killing small farms like mine."

Stevenson looked at the marshes surrounding the farm. "Seems it would be a little hard to grow anything out here, anyway. Maybe its best if they use this land to protect endangered species."

"Not everyone grows crops," Stella said. "Except they don't ask us any questions. They just make assumptions before deciding to ruin people's lives."

"You sound bitter," Stevenson said.

"I'm not bitter," she said. "Just sad. I've given up a lot to stay here, but when it goes, it goes. It's not about the place. Home is in your heart. I'm going to fight like hell to keep it, but if I lose, I'll find another place for my animals. It'll just take a little time, and unfortunately, a lot of money."

"What happens on the day of slaughter?" Raven asked.

"I tell my helpers when to show up. Before they arrive and just before sunrise I go down to the pen. I thank my animals, and I walk my favorite to the shed."

"So for the next slaughter it'll be Tatiana who goes first?" Raven asked.

"Yes, because I just want to get it over with, you know. Like I said earlier, sometimes it's hard to say goodbye." She stopped, stood up and touched the chains hanging from the ceiling. They rattled in the quiet shed. "I'll stick her, use the chains to hoist her up, and bleed her into the buckets."

"Stick her?" Raven said. "You don't cut her throat?"

"Of course," Stella said. "But I start with a stick so I'm deep enough to slide the knife across her throat. I don't want her to suffer."

"How long will it take her to die?" Raven asked.

Stella considered. "For her it'll be about ten, fifteen seconds. And I always make sure I do it right."

Raven stood up and joined Stella, who was making her way back to the wooden cabinet.

"May I?" Raven asked.

"Of course. Just be careful."

Raven picked up the largest knife she had been itching to pick up earlier. She flicked it through the air once or twice, amazed. She felt like a god.

"So you bleed the sheep?" Raven asked, admiring the way the late evening light slid down the blade.

"Yes. And you have to be careful. You don't want the blood to contaminate any of the flesh or other edible parts – heart, liver…."

"Where does the blood go?" Raven asked.

"Into these buckets," Stella said. "I sell it. Some people use it for things like blood sausage. It's a pain because you have to be so careful not to contaminate it, but it's good for me because I'm able to make a little extra money. I need every penny I can get to keep my business going."

"But I thought you were a patron of Heron House?" Stevenson said. "That must be expensive."

"I don't give money," Stella laughed. "I give time. I work there once or twice a month to help out, and to be with other people."

Raven ran a finger along the blade. It was so sharp that it cut her with only the thinnest of cuts. The pain was almost pleasurable. She put the drop of blood to her lips, tasted the iron in it.

"Put the knife down, Burns," Stevenson said. "You're creeping me out."

Raven returned the knife. Her OCD kicking in, she carefully lined it up with the others.

"Men," Stella said. "You're all so squeamish, just like my husband. He couldn't bear the slaughter. Except for Billy Ray."

"Billy Ray?" Raven asked.

"Yes," Stella said. "When he first started buying meat from me, he wanted to watch the slaughter. Unlike your bald friend, he likes knowing where his meat comes from."

That troubled Raven. Billy Ray never mentioned that he knew how the slaughter worked. Why not just tell her instead of pointing her toward Stella?

"Why do you do the first sheep without help?" Stevenson asked.

"It's just something I want to do for myself before all the stamping boots and men shouting. In the quiet I can see the animal doesn't feel any pain. Just a little reminder for me."

"How do you know they don't feel any pain?" Stevenson said. "Do you ask them after you cut their throats?"

Stella picked up a long, slender black instrument from the top of the cabinet.

"This," she says. "It's called a non-penetrating captive bolt gun." She touched her forehead and rubbed a circle there with her index finger. "I'll place it against Tatiana's forehead right here to stun her. I like the non-penetrating kind because the bolt doesn't penetrate the brain. No contamination. I can sell it with the rest of the meat. After she's unconscious, I hoist her, stick her and cut her throat. She'll die quickly. She won't feel any of it. But those boys? I bet they suffer, right, Detective?"

Raven didn't answer. There were things they kept out of the press on purpose, and one was the wound on the boys' foreheads. Stella didn't know about that.

Stella continued, "So, please, tell the press to stop comparing the murders to a slaughter. We have enough trouble trying to hang on to our farms without adding the wrath of animal right activists to the mix."

★　　★　　★

Back in the Mustang, Stevenson turned to her. "What was the point of all that? To get back at me?"

"It's not all about you," Raven said. "I'll worry about getting back at you when we find Noe."

"Then why are we here?"

"You're my partner, aren't you?" Raven countered.

"Not so you notice with you picking and choosing how you let me participate in this case."

"Look, you may think this trip is a waste of time, but at least we have a lead on what the killer may be using to incapacitate his victims."

"The bolt gun?"

"Right. Not as dumb as you look."

"I'll let that one slide."

"Don't do it on my account. But sure as crapping, the bolt gun is how our perp is incapacitating his victims."

"That's what you think?"

"No, baby," she said. "That's what I know."

"How?"

She looked over to the house, the mist rising off the yard, and the figure of Stella standing motionless on the porch watching them drive away. She thought about how sharp that knife was, the taste of her own blood in her mouth.

"Because if you haven't figured it out by now," she said, "it's what I was born to do."

CHAPTER TWENTY-SIX

Raven ended the night with an idea of how the Sleeping Boy killer went about his killings, in spite of what Stella thought, and the old folks still searching through videos. Other than that, they had nothing. She felt no closer to finding Noe. She had started seeing things on the drive back to town, the bright yellow line of the paved two-way road lifting up and wrapping around her and Stevenson cocooned in the Mustang's dark cabin. As much as she hated it, she had to get a couple of hours sleep.

But when she arrived back home, her bedroom felt too warm for sleep in spite of the time of year. She noticed that she had accidentally left the heat turned up to roasting temperatures all day. She opened the window, pushed back the thin curtains to reveal the rim of a silver moon in the Louisiana sky. She changed into her pajamas and lay down on her bed. Maybe she was wrong in thinking that sleep would find her. There was no way the whirlpool of her thoughts would let her rest. But when her head hit the pillow, REM clawed her down the instant she closed her eyes. Her world of lost boys was instantly replaced with dreams of Floyd.

*   *   *

One of the reasons Floyd Burns stayed married to Raven's stepmother for so long was that Jean Rinehart had this thing for order that pleased Floyd and rubbed off on Raven. All of their possessions were tucked neatly away in boxes or drawers, the faucets remained a shiny silver, the baseboards wiped clean of any dust or grime. Broken things, no matter how sentimental, were immediately discarded without tear or regret.

And since being married to Jean, Floyd almost became the father

Raven had always wanted. He still had those bad spells, though, but Raven had the ability to talk him down sometimes without him even knowing it. She had gotten so good at it that she actually allowed herself to believe that he had released the good angel lurking deep in his soul. To her, he had finally become what she believed to be normal. For a while there, Raven lived a fairy tale.

But during the latter half of his marriage to Jean, Floyd took to driving around, commenting on the passing scenery while Raven sat beside him. He would pick her up after school or daycare in Jean's two-toned purple and cream Chevy truck and thread his way through the streets as if he were on a mission known not even to him.

If Raven swallowed the lump of fear resting in her throat to ask him where they were going or what they were doing or what they were about to do, he wouldn't answer. Not because he didn't want to, but because he couldn't. She'd bet her favorite canned Campbell's tomato soup that even Floyd didn't know what he was up to when he got in a killing mood.

On the day that she knew he had changed back for the worse, he picked her up in what he called his Sunday best – a short-sleeved plaid shirt perfectly pressed by Jean and buttoned all the way to his chin. Atop his wiry blond-haired head was a white fedora with a blue peacock feather resting in the black hatband. His black pants were creased, his belt a liquid black circle of leather around his compact waist, the gig line straight as a purpose.

The truck too was so clean that the high purple and creamy white sparkled in the afternoon heat of Byrd's Landing. He stared straight ahead when he came to pick Raven up from daycare, didn't look at her as she climbed into the truck with an unladylike grunt. She shrugged out of the backpack that almost matched her own weight and wedged it between them on the bench seat in such a way that she wouldn't have to touch him. But she could still smell him and he smelled of Stetson cologne and Jack Daniels whiskey and several slices of Wrigley's mint gum, which told her that after all these years living with Jean, he finally had a mood going.

She watched him for a while, not saying anything at all. Then he turned to her, his face serious as a grave. He then used the several pieces of gum to blow a bubble, the belly of which touched the tip of his nose. To this day, Floyd Burns was the only person she knew who could blow such a bubble from Wrigley's chewing gum. His pink tongue snaked into the translucent bubble and it popped with a loud crack. Raven jumped, turned away from him and stared soldier-like out of the gleaming front window.

"Why, my little bird," Floyd said. "I am so glad that you can join me in this here journey through the pagan streets of a town so in love with death that they leave their animals in the street until their fur turns to gum and their bones melt in the heat."

Raven looked at him sideways without turning her head. She barely understood what he had said, but she didn't really need to. She didn't know the exact meaning of the words, but she knew that they told of something bad coming, something she would have to push into her nightmares.

"On the way over here, I passed two dogs lying in the street. One was in the middle lane near the center divider and the other was on the side of the road with its belly laid open."

She continued to stare out the front window.

"And do you know that I've passed those selfsame dogs for four mornings and four afternoons in a row. I never pointed them out to you because I didn't want to upset you. But they've been there for four days with the good folks of Byrd's Landing just driving around them like it was as normal as apple pie and cheese slices."

Raven knew this. She had seen them, too, knowing that they were probably running buddies who had died crossing the street together. She had asked Jean about them on that first day, and Jean told her not to worry about it. She told her to close her eyes the next time they passed. Later, she heard Jean on the phone asking someone to please at least remove the carcasses from the road so that her little girl, or any child for that matter, didn't have to pass dead dogs every darn day.

He was too busy staring out the front window at the stoplight for any more comment. A young ponytailed woman pushing an enormous baby carriage was crossing the street in front of them. She had a tired, put-out look on her face while a little boy, about four or so, swung from her arm as she tried to hurry him across the street and maneuver the baby carriage at the same time. He was having a fit trying to twist away from his mother while snot flew from his screwed-up pug nose.

"What do you think, Raven?" Floyd asked. "How many points? Might be doing both her and her old man a favor. Look at those balls of snot."

He revved the engine impatiently as the woman reached the shiny chrome bumper. She gave them a dirty look.

"Oh, she's a feisty one," he said.

"Daddy, please."

"There's three of 'em. With the little one there's three. Quick. How many points before they get away?"

She looked him over carefully. His fancy clothes meant that today would probably be a day that they didn't just drive around. She remembered what they did in daycare, red, white and blue windmills made from construction paper and glued to long silver straws. It was Fourth of July weekend, and Floyd Burns had a peacock feather in his hatband. She looked down at her hands, smaller but the same shape as Floyd's. He gripped the wheel and revved the engine in glee as if he were a child about to eat the last box of red hots.

Raven knew in both blood and bone that she had to answer. He revved the engine again, this time lifting his foot from the break so that the chrome bumper moved forward slightly to bump the carriage. The woman froze in fear. The boy swinging from her arm froze with her in such a way that it seemed the very snot running from his nose stopped in midair. For a moment they looked as if they were pictures in a painting. The woman's eyes locked with Floyd in a dance that seemed to go on forever, though it lasted no longer than a microsecond.

"How many points, Raven?" he asked, his voice as soft as the peacock feather in his hatband.

Raven sucked in her breath. She calculated the number in her head before answering him in a soft, fast voice. "Seven," she said. "Seven.

Three for the baby."

He laughed then and smiled big. He waved a friendly palm at the woman, rolled down the window and leaned out. "My mistake, darlin'. Wouldn't hurt you for the world. My foot just slipped, that's all. I was someplace else."

She brought her fist down on the hood of the Chevy and said, "Be careful. You scared the holy shit out of me."

"Sorry," he said again, still grinning. The woman gave him a disgusted look before flinging her ponytail over her shoulder. The miraculous thing was that Raven could see that the woman didn't quite believe him, but later, perhaps when she reached the other side of the street, she would convince herself that it was indeed an accident.

"Do you think," Floyd said, his gaze still following the woman as she cleared the front bumper. "Do you think that if I hit her and her rodent droppings that the good people of Byrd's Landing would leave them lying in the road for four entire days, four long cool, sweet mornings and four steaming, hot afternoons?"

Her shoulders relaxed and her young lungs welcomed the expulsion of the breath that she didn't know she held. She said nothing.

"No, I don't think they would," he said. "Not in normal circumstances, mind you. Something'll have to happen 'fore they start doing that with humans. A bomb maybe. Or a nuclear explosion. Lots of cracked buildings and burnt-up bodies. Even then, if there wasn't too many bodies, and if they was still thinking straight, maybe they'd stack 'em like cordwood on the street corners, maybe roll them up onto the sidewalk, throw some sheets or tarps over 'em. It'll probably take a little bit before they'd just let folks rot in the street." He said this all pensively as if it were a real problem that he thought about a lot but just couldn't figure out.

He turned onto Main while looking over his shoulder at a couple of teenagers carrying Burger King bags, and a drink carrier that leaked soda as they trudged along the sidewalk.

"But if they still had the fear, mind you." He slowed down a little, watched them for a while, then sped up. "If they still had the fear, they wouldn't bother with even that. They'd just let 'em lay. They'd let 'em lay like dead dogs in the street while they took care of their own selves."

He turned to look at her then. To Raven's horror, his face morphed into the head of a rattlesnake. Both the little girl Raven and the grown woman Raven screamed as it struck.

CHAPTER TWENTY-SEVEN

And thus Floyd announced himself, not just a voice or an image in a mirror but his full, evil, logical, illogical self. He had inserted himself right back into her life and her dreams. Somewhere beneath the graveyard soil he was making himself known and laughing with delight.

She was awake, her eyes open, the dark pressing in all around her as if it were alive. After a couple of seconds her eyes adjusted to the absence of light. She was aware that her heart beat like a jackhammer. She could feel each breath, scraping and tearing at her throat as it entered her body. It was as if her breath had sharp, serrated edges. She could have sworn it wasn't the dream that had awakened her, but someone whispering hot in her ear, "Repent."

As her breathing calmed, she heard a soft hiss that sounded like a rattle. She realized that it was not only the dark pressing all around her, but something heavy pressing against her side. She could feel its coldness through her pajamas. She lifted the thin covers from her body.

In the moonlight from the open window, snuggled up next to her side, was a coiled snake with a hooked snout like a pig's. She screamed, slapped on the lamp next to the nightstand, grabbing her Glock. She scrambled out of bed and crashed to the floor so fast that her flailing arms knocked the lamp off the nightstand. The bedcovers tangled around her kicking feet. Glass shattered as the lamp's light bulb broke. She heard another thump as the snake fell to the floor, and let out one prolonged hiss.

She was in total darkness except for the teasing sliver of light coming through the window. It was just her, the dark, and a snake. The snake hissed again. She screamed. Something told her to stay still, to be calm, that there were almost fifty species of snakes in Louisiana, and only a small handful could send you running to the emergency room. *That dang ole snake is probably more scared than you are.* The problem was that the voice belonged to Floyd. Her father could lie up a streak of blue lightning when it suited his purposes. The snake hissed again as if in agreement.

There wasn't a chance in red Hades that she was going to stay still waiting for the snake to slither over her bare legs. She felt for her Android on the nightstand, found it, and backed out of the room on her butt, kicking the door shut behind her.

Once in the living room she hit the speed dial for Billy Ray before she was fully standing. She didn't even think of calling the police, or animal control. After all, she was the police, and she had a good idea who placed the snake in her bed in the first place. She would deal with him later.

She flicked on every light she owned in the living room and kitchen. She was downing her second glass of ice water and still shaking when there was a knock at the door. Relieved beyond what she had the right to be, after all the snake was still in her bedroom, she threw open the door. The words she was about to say died on her lips.

Billy Ray was not alone. Edmée, wearing sequins and dangling earrings, stood beside him. Raven would bet her paycheck that those weren't rhinestones sparkling in the bright living room lights.

"Really, a tux?" Raven said to Billy Ray.

"I have a life too, Raven."

"Apparently so." She turned to Edmée. "Does your husband know that you're single?"

"Oh, don't be like that," she said, stooping to kiss Raven, her loud perfume announcing the dry feel of her lips on Raven's cheek. "Charity event that Fabian wanted nothing to do with. Billy Ray's filling in for him. My husband appreciates the night off."

"You party while Noe is missing?" Raven accused.

"Life doesn't stop, Raven," Billy Ray said. "Noe will turn up one way or another. Besides, this has been months in the planning and it's going to help a lot of people. Now you said something about a snake in your bed? You sure you weren't dreaming?"

"Yes, I'm sure I wasn't dreaming," Raven said, pulling them both into her apartment and shutting the door.

"How did it get there?" Edmée asked.

"Heck if I know," Raven said.

"What kind of snake was it?" Billy Ray asked.

"Big."

"Big?"

"Yes."

Billy Ray took a deep breath in. "Anything aside from big?"

"Look, I wasn't trying to paint its portrait. All I remember is that it was big and had a face like a fist."

"I see," he said. "Color?"

"I don't know. Dirt colored? Black?" she said. "And it rattled like a baby rattle."

Billy Ray hung his head. He looked back up at her and said, "You're telling me that while you were sleeping, someone slipped a rattlesnake in your bed and you didn't wake up."

"Why are you here if you don't believe me?"

"Because he's your friend, darling, and that's what friends do, right, Billy Ray?" Edmée said.

"Show me."

Both of Raven's eyebrows shot up. "Now who's losing their mind?"

"Okay, fair enough."

As he strode to her bedroom door, Raven started to doubt. Maybe she had been dreaming. The fears she had hidden deep in her soul were no longer confined to inside her head. They were starting to escape, like the man in black at the restaurant, Floyd beside her in the bathroom after Clyde's autopsy, and Floyd in her dreams as clear as the sky on a bright, blue day. Maybe she was starting to go insane.

Before she could tell Billy Ray not to bother, he already had the bedroom open.

"Overhead light?"

"Right side."

She heard his long-suffering sigh from the bedroom doorway. "Raven, did you shoot the snake?"

"No?" she answered, hearing the question in her own voice. Did she? She smelled the tip of the Glock.

"Knock it on the head with something?"

"No!"

"Come over here, please."

She did, with Edmée tapping behind in her stilettos. There on the bedroom floor was the snake entirely on its back, white belly showing, its mouth open and forked tongue lolling.

Raven shuddered at the sight of the thing. She gazed up curiously at Billy Ray. "I didn't do that. I swear that I didn't kill that snake."

"Oh, how delightful," Edmée said from behind them. "Billy Ray, Raven, don't you see? It's a zombie snake. Raven scared the shit out of it, so now it's playing dead."

"Wait, *I* scared the shit out of it?" Raven said, forgetting herself for a moment.

"Of course, I'm sure you did with all of your screaming and flailing around. No one is trying to hurt you, my dear. It's just a harmless joke. And that poor little snake is scared shitless right now."

"How do you know so much about snakes?" Raven said.

"Because I garden. See them all the time. Plus, I'm a country girl at heart. Grew up on a farm. Snakes get a bad rap but they aren't so bad, except the cottonmouths. I cannot abide by cottonmouths."

Raven gave her the side-eye. "Edmée, did you put—"

"No. Now how could I have done that? I was with Billy Ray. How do I have time to slip away from this handsome man, find a hognose snake to put into your bed to play some sort of trick on you when everybody is already so upset by Clyde and Noe? I would not think to do such a thing."

"Well, can we just kill it now?" Raven asked.

"No," Edmée said. "Not the poor darling. When he plays dead, you meanies are supposed to go away."

"It's my bedroom, Edmée. I'm not going to live with the thing like a new pet."

"Of course you're not. Go get me a big bowl with a plastic lid."

"Wait, what if it's somebody's pet that got out?" Billy Ray asked.

"If it was I think it would not have been so frightened when Raven started all the blubbering."

"Nice one, Edmée."

"Just bring me the bowl so we can get him out, and we can all finish our night."

Raven stood looking at her. Edmée clapped two times to get her attention. Raven said, "Edmée, I'm single. I don't have a big bowl."

"A pot?"

Raven said nothing. "A pitcher for water or mixing drinks? A big one?"

In the end Raven found a small gym bag. Black strappy heels and all, Edmée walked into the room and gave the snake a small nudge with her foot. The snake didn't move. She then bent down and touched its nose with the bright red nail of her index finger. Still nothing. She put her finger inside his mouth, looked at them and laughed.

"You're two bricks short of a full load, Edmée," Billy Ray said, his face troubled.

Edmée removed her finger. "It's just a little scared darling."

Then she started scratching the snake's head, petting it, and talking in soothing tones. Maybe Edmée had it wrong. Maybe Raven had scared the poor thing to death. But then they heard the hiss, not the big one that Raven had heard when she first became aware of it in the bed, but a little one. Then the entire coil begin revolving in opposite directions in a circle of tan and black like patterns in a spinning top. Edmée started laughing, calling the snake little baby, and little piggy nose. Surprisingly fast, she grabbed it by the back of its head with one hand, the middle of its back with the other, and looped the long body into the gym bag. She zipped the bag almost closed, saying to the snake, not to Billy Ray or Raven, that she would leave it a little open so he could get the air.

Billy Ray sent Raven a half-smiling look. "See," he said. "Aren't you glad I brought her along?"

CHAPTER TWENTY-EIGHT

After Edmée secured the snake, she and Billy Ray stayed long enough to go through the apartment to make sure that there weren't any more surprises. When she was alone, Raven stood in the doorway of her bedroom examining the bed, the lamp now put right with a new bulb burning brightly along with the overhead light, and the now locked window. Raven knew she would be sleeping under the light if not for the coming weeks, then at least for the next few days.

Billy Ray and Edmée didn't think someone had targeted Raven. Probably just a curious snake that climbed into her open window. She thought about the mysterious man who had been stalking her. There had always been a measured distance between them, as if he wanted to be, what Floyd would call, polite in his torture.

Now all that had changed, that is, if he were real. He had been in her apartment. She had felt his wet breath in her ear. And that word. *Repent. Repent.* What did he want her to repent for? The killing of Lovelle? Being her father's child? That's what Stevenson wanted her to do. Except he didn't want her on her knees asking for forgiveness. He wanted her in handcuffs.

Suddenly, she was sure it was Stevenson who had slipped into her apartment. The thought, both the words and the surety of it, hit her so hard that for a moment all the breath left her body. Stevenson. She put a robe over her pajamas and dropped the Glock into one of its deep pockets before heading for his rooms. As she rounded the corner, she almost knocked over an end table. She managed to catch it before the frosted glass lamp atop of it crashed to the floor. After she righted the table, she continued her journey with a speed and a purpose, weaving past the small tables and curios Mama Anna collected and placed throughout the large house.

His door flew open before she could bang on it, which she had intended on doing. He stood there, wary and confused but awake, which provided more proof for his being the culprit.

Raven had been going full throttle on only a few hours' of sleep since Monday. When she did close her eyes, all she saw was Noe hanging upside down somewhere while his blood flowed in sheets from his cut throat, and now Floyd, in her dreams. She was in no mood to play games with Stevenson.

"You walking abortion," Raven told him now. "You freak."

The confusion left his face. It was replaced not by fury, but understanding, as if he knew that this was a conversation that they would eventually have. "Look, I understand that you're angry with me...."

"Angry with you," she said. "I couldn't care less about your lying butt. I'm just here to deliver a message."

"Message? In the middle of the fucking night?"

"It wouldn't be the middle of the night if you had kept your crusty feet out of my apartment."

"What?" he asked. "What the hell you talking about?"

"Don't give me that," she said. "Whispering in my ear, telling me to repent. Leaving a snake in my bed. You are one sick, wasted piece of semen."

His face cleared, and now there was another emotion. For a minute she thought it was concern. "I wasn't in your—"

"That's a load of crap."

"I swear to you I wasn't. I don't have a key. You never gave me one, remember?"

"Then why are you wide awake? Why did you open the door?"

"I'm awake because I haven't been sleeping. I opened the door because of all the ruckus in the hall."

She was about to tell him that he was a lying piece of excrement when she heard someone clear their throat. They both looked down the hall to see Mama Anna standing there in a thick orange robe, her long gray hair parted down the middle and braided into two thick plaits falling on either side of her wide shoulders.

"What in Sadie's hell is going on around here with all this hollering and banging?" she said. "Quiet down, and keep your drama behind closed doors. I got a place to run."

Stevenson apologized like the good little boy he had always tried to be and started to close the door. But Raven stopped it with one flat hand and pushed her way inside. This was the first time she had been in Stevenson's rooms since she found out that he was undercover. How could she have missed it? Everything was just too neat, even for someone staying in temporary quarters. She picked up a silver frame with two kids in it. She had seen it before; they had even talked about it. Now she turned the frame toward him.

"They even yours?"

"Yes," he said, watching her warily. "I never lied to you about any of that."

"Such a good boy," she said as if she were talking to a dog. "How does it feel to be such a good little boy?"

She walked around the room, aware of the weapon bumping against her thigh.

"Say what you have to say and get out," Stevenson said.

But, of course, she didn't. She felt evil, a mean evil that started the moment she heard that whispered word, *repent*, in her ear, the instant she felt the snake in her bed. Something substantially uglier was replacing her anger. An unadulterated and exhilarating enmity that made her feel like her veins were filled with an electric current. She both loved and loathed the feeling. She looked at Stevenson. He no longer appeared human to her.

"Tell me," she said. "Do you bang all your suspects? Or just me?"

Stevenson looked at the floor, took a couple of steps back. Raven moved around him, circling like a predator.

"That wasn't the ideal way," he said. "But the only way that I could get you to talk to me."

"Of course when that didn't work," she said, "you decided that the only way to get me to break was by messing with my head? First by blowing my mind by telling me you were really a cop, and then by breaking into my apartment and leaving a snake in my bed?"

"I told you that wasn't me."

"I know what you told me. You told me a lot of things."

His cheeks filled with air as if he didn't want the words he was about to speak to escape. He let out a big sigh. "It wasn't all just pretend."

Raven started laughing.

"It wasn't," he said. "It did start because I had a job to do. But I did grow to care about you."

"Be for real."

"I'm being for real. Why do you think I'm still here?"

"You're still here because you think I'm going to slip up so you can cart my sorry behind back to California for killing that maggot."

A curious light slipped into his brown eyes. For a moment, it looked like compassion.

"You can't kill a man in cold blood and not pay some kind of price, Raven. Nothing good comes from killing, even what you think of as righteous killing."

"And it's up to you to decide what the price is?"

"No, not up to me. It's up to society. Believe it or not, it's for your own good. You won't be able to live with yourself. Whatever satisfaction you felt when you killed is going to turn into a poison that will eventually eat away at you until it claims your soul. The only thing that's going to bring you true peace is your confession."

"And go to jail for the rest of my life?"

"At least you'll have taken responsibility. There's honor in that."

"I'm not looking for honor, Stevenson. The only responsibility I have is to myself, my friends and finding Noe. I owe you nothing. I owe Lovelle nothing. I owe society nothing."

"Don't lump what's good in this world in with Lovelle. That's where you've messed up."

"When do you pay for what you've done?" she said. "What does your boss say about your methods?"

She wasn't surprised that she didn't get an answer. She walked to him, the weapon heavy in her pocket. "Oh, not so ready with the pretty words now, are we?" she said, tracking his eyes with her own as he tried to move away. "You don't think I checked you out after you pulled your jack-in-the-box stunt at BLPD? They fired you months ago, WynnDel. You weren't even a real cop when you followed me out here. How'd you keep hold of your badge? Did you run away so fast they didn't have time to ask for it back? Huh, WynnDel?"

"Don't call me that."

"They fired you because you became obsessed with someone who had the audacity to shoot someone down in your town, your house." She laughed. "Your town, like someone gave it to you."

The weapon was out of her pocket and in her hand now, not pointing at him, but gripped lightly and pointed at the floor like a whispered threat.

"You threw away your family, your entire career. You went psycho."

"I'm not crazy," he said, in a quiet, dignified way. "You, you are. Look at yourself."

"And when the chief didn't believe you, you had some friend of yours call in, didn't you? Pretending to be your supervisor, telling the chief you could work on loan. You aren't even a rogue cop, you're a pretend one."

"Look at yourself!" he said again, shaking a hand at a mirror over the small fireplace. "You don't even look like you. Your eyes are crazy. You're threatening me with a weapon. Me, I'm just trying to make sure justice is done."

"Don't you understand that the world doesn't need or want your justice?"

"What are you going to do? Shoot me?"

Raven felt cold and powerful. "Maybe."

He said, almost whispered, "This isn't you."

"How would you know who is and isn't me?"

"Shoot me or put the weapon away. It's pissing me off."

"Let me tell you something, WynnDel. I would love nothing more than blowing your brains all over the stock photo of your so-called kids. But I like Mama Anna. It would be too much for her to clean up. I know she would do it herself because she's too stubborn to hire anyone."

She had to give him credit. If he was afraid, he did a good job hiding it.

"Make your point."

"So, not tonight," she said, lightly touching his chest with the barrel of the gun. "But you call off your boy, the Floyd look-a-like your crazy behind hired to stalk me. No more snakes in my bed, and that includes you."

His eyes narrowed. "I have no idea what you're talking about."

"Don't lie. The best thing you can do is to shut up and listen. If I ever catch you in my rooms again, if I even get a whiff of your aftershave through the air vents, I'll kill you where you stand and swear that you had a heart attack."

"You'll never get away with it."

"Oh, I will," she said. "I will get away with it because you, son, are a rogue, psycho, stalker, pissant, waste of human flesh. They'll think you've finally snapped and I'll do everything I can to make them believe it's true. You get me?"

"Yes," he said, his voice hard.

"Good." She walked around him and out the front door.

Back in her apartment, she fell against the door and slid to the floor, the gun thudding next to her.

You done all right, Birdy Girl, Floyd said in her head. *Sounded just like your ole man. Just like how I told you when you had to face the bullies at school. Act like you crazy. Make 'em think it. Then them no-accounts will leave you alone.*

"The problem is, old man," she whispered out loud, "I'm not sure I was acting."

CHAPTER TWENTY-NINE

The next morning Raven felt so bad about her behavior that she showered, dressed, poured two cups of coffee and knocked on Stevenson's door. When he opened it, she willed her face blank, handed him one of the coffees and said, "You ready?"

He hadn't finished dressing, was still buttoning his shirt, his face covered in suspicion. "Is this your way of apologizing for last night?"

She kept her face Floyd blank. It was her way of apologizing. But she wasn't going to admit that. It wasn't the threat, because, as Billy Ray would have said, she meant that shit. If he was the one torturing her, she'd make him pay one way or the other. What she was most ashamed of was the thrill that had gone through her at the thought of killing him, and calling him a walking abortion. Instead of answering his question, she raised an eyebrow.

"I didn't break into your apartment," he continued. "I hate snakes as much as you do, and I may have done some things I'm not proud of over these past few months, but I'm not a complete asshole."

His words sounded so sincere that she almost believed him.

"Coffee's getting cold," Raven said. "Billy Ray called a few minutes ago. We're heading straight to Chastain's. Looks like Mama Anna and them found something."

"Why? When you know I'm not a cop?"

"Because you did something I thought you'd never make me do," she said. "Feel sorry for your no-sleeping, little pissant self. Besides, the chief doesn't know it yet, and I don't want it distracting him. And I'll take all the help I can get to find Noe."

"I swear I wasn't in your apartment last night," he said again.

Raven stayed silent. When he realized that there was no use

smoothing over old ground she refused to walk over, he smelled the coffee. "Is this poison?"

"Not this time."

"Okay, apology accepted. But I'm not too sure about getting into a car with you right now. I'll use my own ride and meet you over there."

★   ★   ★

The excitement along Billy Ray's slice of Africa in Chastain's Creole Heaven was like a living thing. The energy buzzed from Mr. Joe to Mama Anna and even to the usually soft-spoken Miss Vera. Mr. Walter was trying to tell all of them to keep it quiet, but no one was listening. When Raven, sitting shoulder to shoulder with Mama Anna at the head of the table, saw him reach for a spoon to bang on the table, she tried on Floyd's preaching voice.

"Hey now. Come on. It's all right. Quiet down for a minute. This is important. We need to hear each other."

The talking didn't stop all at once, but voices trailed off and pretty soon each old head was turned toward her. Raven didn't break the silence for a long moment. Finally, Mr. Joe said, "Well, come on, Rev. If you gone preach, you better get on with it."

"I don't plan to preach, Mr. Joe," Raven said. "Detective Stevenson and I just want to hear what you all found on the videos. We can't do that if everybody's talking at once."

"Okay," Mr. Joe said. "Mama Anna, you first."

"Why should she go first when I'm the one who found it?" Miss Vera said.

"You found the first one, but Mama Anna found the second," Mr. Joe said.

"Y'all forget that I found the best of all," Mr. Walter said.

"Oh God," Stevenson said.

Raven ignored him and told Miss Vera to go first. Miss Vera set an index finger on the yellow legal pad and read the time, date, and place she had written there, three forty-five p.m. Friday afternoon, bus number twelve going out to Lakeshore. Noe and Clyde had gotten off the bus on Magnolia.

"I showed her how to get some screenshots," Mr. Bello said. "Billy Ray let us print them on the restaurant's printer."

"Let me see, Miss Vera," Raven said, her hand out.

The photos showed Noe and Clyde getting off the bus. After Raven passed them to Stevenson, Mama Anna said, "So, I got to thinking. Maybe they didn't get to where they were going from that one bus. So I checked all the cameras on the connecting buses."

"Go on," Raven said.

"I don't like looking at itty bitty screens, either, so I got pictures, too."

Raven took the photos from Mama Anna. The boys had connected with bus number 21 and gotten off on the corner of Lakeshore and Cypress.

"Now, for the best," Mr. Walter said. "But y'all have to look at this on video. We found this one about twenty minutes ago, and asked Billy Ray to give you a call right away. You ready for it?"

Raven nodded. Mr. Walter scooted his chair closer to Raven. She could feel Stevenson behind her as he bent down so he could see better, so close that his breath was on her neck. It irritated her, but she kept her mouth shut. As her stepmother would have said, she had acted fool enough with him last night.

"This one has a lot of rain in it, so some stuff you can't see. Raining like the devil was emptying out his chamber pot. Plus it's dark," Mr. Walter said.

Mama Anna said, "Raining so hard even the ducks drowning. In my family, we call that a killing rain."

Mr. Walter pushed play. The video opened on what looked like a light-colored sedan stopping at a light on one of the few roads that led to the bridge out of town, the same one that Stevenson had taken Raven to on their first date. As was happening lately, Raven couldn't believe her eyes or her senses. She looked at the road they were on, pointed at the screen, and then she looked at Stevenson, who was now standing a bit straighter and watching with his hands placed lightly on his hips.

The sedan's hazard lights were on. Raven couldn't tell the exact make, model or color because with the streaming rain, it looked like she was viewing the entire scene from behind fogged glass. As she watched, the passenger door of the sedan opened. A boy bolted into the rain. The driver's door opened and another figure in a hooded trench coat raced after the fleeing boy. Soon, they were out of frame, and for a few minutes, the sedan just sat there with rain pounding its roof and both the driver's side and the passenger's side door open. If another person, maybe Clyde, was inside the car, Raven couldn't tell.

Video evidence made Raven feel helpless, frustrated. It should be so simple to step into the scene and stop the pending horror. She thought about that now as she watched. The first fleeing figure could be Noe. It had the shape and build of her nephew. There was not a snowball's chance in Hades that anyone could have recognized the trench-coated figure. She could see nothing of the face, couldn't even tell if the person was a man or a woman. Something must have slowed Noe down because after a minute or two the driver came back with a hand on Noe's shoulder, and one of his arms twisted behind his back.

This was it, Raven thought. The break they needed. She couldn't keep the exhilaration off her face.

"So," Mama Anna said. "Good thing we came in early so you'd be ready for this. Did we do good by you young folks?"

Raven yanked the power cord out of the laptop. It had enough battery life for another hour or two.

"Are you kidding me?" Raven said. "Yes, you did spectacular."

When Raven walked to the kitchen with Stevenson in tow, Imogene was already donning the chef's apron to relieve Billy Ray. For once on this loser case, they finally had something to talk about.

CHAPTER THIRTY

"Dude seems pretty tall," Billy Ray said as they watched the video evidence the old folks' corner had found.

"Not taller than you, or Stevenson, or Willie Lee for that matter. What makes you think it's a dude? Edmée's probably that tall in heels," Raven said.

"So if we were using height as a way to identify this suspect, so is your brother," Billy Ray countered.

"Brothers and girlfriends. They put the 'D' in dysfunctional," Raven said, trying to keep the mood light.

"She's not my girlfriend, just a friend," Billy Ray emphasized. "But I'm glad that we know something about the motherfucker now. I bet you he's taking Noe to the kill spot."

Raven felt something happening between her, Billy Ray and Stevenson as they grappled with this new evidence. Maybe it was their shared interest. Each one of them, no matter what stage they were at in their career or lives, had a job that could stop evil people from doing evil things.

She got up and started rummaging through Billy Ray's desk.

"You know," he said mildly, "if you're looking for a map you could've just asked."

"Never mind, got one."

She walked with the map spread out toward the whiteboard. She placed it over the pictures, and placed magnets at each corner. After the map of Byrd's Landing was displayed on the whiteboard, she found the coordinates for the street names of the bus stop where the boys were last seen on camera. Using a Sharpie, she drew a red star. With her finger, she drew a line between the bus stop and the place where they saw Noe, or thought they saw Noe, attempt to escape his kidnapper. She didn't need to look that up. Kingfisher, the same road she and Stevenson took to scout the fictional movie location when he was still masquerading as Wynn Bowen.

"That's pretty far away," Stevenson said, coming to stand beside her.

"Yeah," Billy Ray agreed. "About fifteen or twenty miles."

Raven's heart was beating so fast that her throat hurt. Wait until she told Cameron that she had this lead. They were so close. She could feel Noe with a sense she couldn't explain calling for her. Maybe it wasn't too late. Maybe he was still alive.

"So, whoever they met up with on Friday was driving them out of town," Raven reasoned.

"Whoa, now," Billy Ray said. "Don't let's get ahead of ourselves. We need to figure out where they caught that ride."

Billy Ray drew a big circle around the bus stop with a purple Sharpie. "How far do you think those boys could walk without getting tired?"

"Dunno," Stevenson said. "Nowadays, lazy as kids are, maybe three or four miles."

"Noe and Clyde loved running the streets together," Raven said. "My brother left Noe on his own a few times, and Clyde wasn't exactly having a dance party in the house with his stepdad. I'd say they had a little practice walking around, especially being too young to drive."

"Okay, give it five or six," Billy Ray said, drawing another ring around the circle to extend it. "Where does your ghoul live?"

"My ghoul? You mean Willie Lee Speck?" Raven responded.

Stevenson was already back at Billy Ray's desk rifling through a folder. He read out Speck's address. Raven quickly found it and drew a red star next to the location.

"He's in the circle. Right inside it, too," Raven said. "Close to the bus stop. Should we pull him in for questioning, this time not so nicely?"

"Might not be the worst idea you ever had," Billy Ray said. "But he'll just lawyer up."

"Wait a minute," Raven said. "Doesn't Edmée live somewhere up on Lakeshore?"

"I think so," Billy Ray said. "What about it?"

"Maybe they stopped by there?" Raven said. "She was really fond of Clyde, and him of her. Maybe he went there to whine about his stepdad?"

"She would've said something about it by now," Billy Ray said.

"Maybe she wasn't home?" Raven responded. "But that's a fancy neighborhood. I'm sure she has help around the place. Could they have talked to a housekeeper or gardener?"

"That could be," Billy Ray said.

"You think we should swing by there?"

"Sure. I'll go with you."

"I don't know, Billy Ray. Her husband might be home."

"I don't give a rat's ass who's at home," Billy Ray said.

"Detective Stevenson," Raven said. "Do you mind updating the chief and getting the uniforms to canvass the neighborhood to see if someone saw these boys?"

"Already on it. What about Cameron?"

"Let's not say anything just yet," Raven said. "I want to make sure we have something solid first."

After Stevenson left, Billy Ray asked, "You happy?"

"Happier than I've been since Monday night," Raven said. "We're going to find him, Billy Ray. I just hope he's alive."

Just then, Raven's phone rang. It was Rita telling her to get over to the morgue. She hung up before Raven had a chance to argue.

"You want to come with me?" she asked Billy Ray.

"Watch Rita cut up a body?" he said. "Hell no. What about talking to Edmée?"

"That's not important. Rita sounded pretty insistent. We can swing by Edmée's house after I talk to Rita. You want to meet me over there?" He gave her a two-finger salute in an answer that she took as an affirmative. She left Chastain's feeling hopeful. She was going to restore their nascent family, and reboot her stalled new life.

CHAPTER THIRTY-ONE

"Rita, things are popping. This better be good," Raven said as she walked into the autopsy suite.

"Believe me," Rita said, "you're going to want to tongue kiss me after this."

Raven looked skeptically at Rita. "Why am I here?"

Rita gestured at a body on the autopsy table, a full-grown man with lots of black hair on either side of his bald spot. A blue blanket was neatly folded down to reveal Rita's baseball stitching closing the Y incision on his chest.

"I don't have time for another case," Raven said.

"You need to make time for this. Sit."

Raven sat. Rita wheeled over to her and shoved the folder of the unfortunate man at her.

"Yours truly over there is Ronnie True, no pun intended. I finished an autopsy on him about an hour ago."

"Okay," Raven said. "But I must say that the cogs haven't quite clicked into place, yet."

"Someone beat the shit out of him, and left him for dead in his office months ago."

Raven glanced at the body. "He still looks pretty fresh."

"Pay attention, sweetie," Rita said. "A cleaning crew called 911 when they found him. He's been in a coma ever since. The family just took him off life support yesterday, which is how he finally ended up in my fine establishment."

"I don't get it."

"Just wait, you will." She tapped the file folder in Raven's hands. Raven opened it to find a diagram of a male figure. Rita had marked various areas on the arms, legs, torso to note scars and healing injuries. But Rita's notation of blunt force trauma on True's forehead claimed all of her attention.

"Are you telling me that a bolt gun made that wound?"

"I'm pretty sure that it did," Rita said. "Breaker, he had this case, took photos of True's injuries before they tried to patch him up."

Rita picked up the iPad on her desk. "Haven't got a chance to print these yet for the file, but look." She turned the screen to Raven so she could see it.

"Holy crap on a cracker."

"That's not exactly what I said, but it was close."

"But his throat wasn't cut," Raven said, looking back at the body on the table.

"Probably the only thing on him that the perp didn't beat the shit out of."

"But I don't understand," Raven said.

But the fact was, she understood all too well. The beatdown on Ronnie True indicated that he had made a dangerous enemy, but the injury to his forehead looked eerily similar to the non-penetrating captive bolt gun on the victims in the Sleeping Boy case. She remembered how Stella described the instrument when Raven asked about her process. The weapon she used to stun her animals didn't penetrate the brain. She preferred it so she could later sell the brain with the other meat. After all, Stella had said, she needed every penny she could get to keep her farm going. If she used anything that would penetrate the brain – a .22 or a penetrating captive bolt gun – the brain would be contaminated, and she could kiss any revenue she might get by selling it goodbye.

"But the boys weren't beaten like this guy was," Raven said.

"Nope."

"And this guy is much older."

"Yep."

"But why?"

"I don't know," Rita said. "But this is your first case. Not Baptiste."

"Did you...."

"Who are you talking to, Raven? Of course I did."

She handed Raven a fat three-ring binder stuffed with documents. On the spine was the name Ronnie True. Underneath that name was Detective DeShawn Breaker.

"This is the casefile Breaker put together," Rita said. "Likes everything printed out, like Billy Ray. Very tactile fellow. But here's the flash drive for everything in the binder."

"Thank you, Rita," Raven said, standing up. "You're a lifesaver."

Rita cocked her head, a crooked smile on her face. "I don't get that a lot in my line of work, but there is one more thing."

"What's that?"

"Where's my tongue kiss?"

CHAPTER THIRTY-TWO

Raven had time before meeting Billy Ray at Edmée's, so she took the True casefile to the makeshift BLPD command center. She had underestimated Breaker. He was meticulous, even documenting True's clients and cases. He also marked the cases that could have made someone target True for revenge. Breaker himself interviewed everyone who worked with True, including Clyde Darling's mother, June. It turned out that June was True's paralegal.

True mostly did family law cases, handled adoptions, property disputes, and a smorgasbord of other cases befitting a small-town lawyer. She flipped back to the page of his client list. Raven knew those names, including Stella Morning and Edmée Crowley. He represented Morning on the case against her sister for ownership of the family farm. For Edmée, he had done some contract work, and helped place some of the boys from Edmée's foster program. Judge Toulouse was also listed, but nothing about the case True had helped him on was mentioned. And then there was that rodent, Willie Lee Speck, on True's client list. It appeared to Raven that True wasn't particular who his clients were as long as they paid the retainer on time.

Raven didn't know what it all meant, but thinking about the judge, she wondered if Breaker had really quit or if the chief unceremoniously moved him out of the way. The chief would have had no patience if Breaker started poking at the hornet's nest of Byrd's Landing's powerful. She snapped the casefile closed and made her way to the chief's office.

"Come on in, Raven," Chief Sawyer said. "Stevenson was just catching me up. Great job on the video evidence. Already got things in motion with canvassing those neighborhoods."

She stayed by the door and leaned against the frame.

"Tell me something, Chief," she said. "Did Breaker really quit?"

Chief Sawyer folded his arms above his head and sighed.

Stevenson started to say something, but the chief said, "Let it go, Stevenson. It'll get you nowhere plus a migraine. Raven and me go way back. We family. Ain't that right, Raven?"

"I asked you a question," Raven said.

"You know I saved her life," he said, looking at Stevenson. "Or that's what she thinks, anyway. I was really just doing my job. But she credits me for the fact that she's walking around on this earth. Her old man was about to cut her heart out, but I stopped him. Took her under my wing, introduced her to Oral Justice, got her help. You ever say thank you, Burns?"

"I believe I've said thank you plenty of times."

"Come on in here and sit down."

Raven walked into the office and took a seat next to Stevenson.

"Breaker was burned out," the chief answered. "You saw him. He was off his game. You know how you can tell when Breaker's about to lose it?"

Raven didn't think for a moment about answering him, not with so much bitterness and mockery in his voice.

"His shoes get shinier, and his ties straighter. Everybody knows that when he starts wearing three-piece suits and the gold watch chain he needs a vacation."

There was an uncomfortable note in Stevenson's laughter.

"Careful, Stevenson," Raven said in quiet warning. "It bites."

The laughter stopped abruptly. She let the silence in the room play. Then she said, "Did you get rid of Breaker because he was following the Ronnie True angle?"

"How did you find out about True?"

"He died. Rita did the autopsy. You know what she found?"

"Not interested in what she found. Breaker was wasting his time. When I strongly urged him to follow the evidence, he decided BLPD wasn't for him."

"Did you also strongly urge him to keep True and Toulouse out of it?" Raven asked.

"He was wasting time."

"Wasting time or making Judge Toulouse uncomfortable?"

"That was a coincidence, Raven," the chief said. "Breaker was chasing unicorns when he should've been looking for horses."

"I see," Raven said.

"What do you want, anyway? You're not here just to bust my balls."

"I need a favor."

"What's that?"

"I need to find out what case True helped Toulouse on."

"Look it up," the chief said. "It's public knowledge."

"Breaker's notes say the case is sealed."

"Why do you need that information?"

"To solve this case. Find Noe, and to find out who's killing those boys. Isn't that what you wanted?"

"None of this True stuff is germane to your case. Besides, we already have a suspect for Clyde's murder and Noe's disappearance. That would be your brother, if you don't know it by now. I've got Goldie following that up."

"Cameron didn't do this."

"You don't know that," the chief said. "Or perhaps you do and that's the reason you want to ride out on wild goose chases."

"Then just tell me what the Toulouse case was about. Save me some time."

"No," he said. "You forget. I don't work for you. You work for me. Is there anything else?"

"There is."

She waited until he was forced to break the silence. "Well?" he said.

"Did Breaker decide that BLPD wasn't for him, or that the entire town of Byrd's Landing wasn't for him?"

"I'll let you figure that one out for yourself," he said, a challenge in his eyes.

CHAPTER THIRTY-THREE

The house Edmée Crowley and Dr. Fabian Long lived in was large and painted a blinding white. It was set back from the street amid a full to bursting fall garden that poured from the back yard to flow along both sides of a wide, circular front lawn. A maid in khakis and a polo shirt answered the door. She led Billy Ray and Raven into what she referred to as the parlor, a small room near the front of the house filled with an oversized fireplace surrounded by white marble.

The maid left them sitting on a soft, white leather sofa. Billy Ray removed one of the many mustard-colored pillows so he could sit comfortably. Raven sat beside him, not saying anything, just looking around. She thought she knew Edmée, but boy was she mistaken. The woman who lived in this house, who decorated this room with odds and ends like the glass trout riding a Schwinn, was a stranger. Billy Ray sat with his hands on his knees, bent forward as if he couldn't wait to finish with what Raven was sure he thought of as a routine chore. He wasn't intimidated at all by his surroundings. He even kept his pork pie hat on.

"Friends," Edmée said as she came sweeping into the room, the hem of her wide-leg slacks billowing around her.

Raven and Billy Ray stood and Edmée kissed them on both cheeks.

"No fair," she said. "If you told me you were coming sooner I would have had Karen make us a late lunch. How are you after your adventures last night, Raven?"

"Better today," Raven answered.

"And how is Cameron doing with all of this?"

"Oh, he's hanging in there," Raven said. "Frantic, kind of a pain in the butt. You understand."

"I can," she said, sitting in an armchair and crossing her legs. "That is the problem, isn't it? Oh the dreams, the nightmares of where that boy could be right now. It makes my head ache. To what do I owe this pleasure?"

"We wanted to ask you and your husband a few questions about Clyde and Noe," Raven said.

Edmée frowned. "I don't know if I'll have any answers."

"Well, maybe your husband does?" Raven said. "Is he home?"

"Why, of course, but I have to admit that I'm all over curious." She stood up and strode to the door. "Darling, Fabian, there are some detectives here to talk to you," she said in that ever-expansive way she had before turning to them with a wink. "Ah, here he is."

Dr. Fabian Long entered the room dressed much differently than he had the first time Raven and Billy Ray met him. He was as tall and lanky as ever, but instead of being dressed in a three-piece suit, he wore a pair of washed denims and a light blue cashmere sweater. He shook Raven's and then Billy Ray's hand.

"Yes," he said, smiling as he sat in the armchair next to Edmée's. "I can't say I'm happy to see you two. The last time we met was at the hospital, and I can't help but recall that the conversation was about murder."

"Yes, the Lamont Lovelle case," Raven said.

"Unfortunate," Fabian said. "The good part is that we won't have to waste money on a trial."

"Can I get you two something to drink?" Edmée abruptly stood and moved toward the door. "Coffee? A drink?"

"No," Billy Ray said. "Sit yourself down. I need to get back to the restaurant, so we don't have a lot of time."

Long caught the familiarity in Billy Ray's voice. He gave Billy Ray a look as sharp as razor blades before hiding it under a mask of friendliness.

Edmée sat down and crossed her legs again. She looked at them with polite inquiry.

"What's this all about?" Long asked.

"We're here about Clyde Darling...." Raven began.

"Yes, yes, I know," Long said, waving his fingers. "My wife told me about that unfortunate boy, and the chief and I have talked. What a tragedy. But I don't see what this has to do with us."

"They found a body at your construction site, Dr. Long," Raven said.

"But that was from the Sleeping Boy killer," Long responded. "Your chief said that they already have a suspect in Clyde's case."

"It may be nothing," Raven said. "We're just talking to all of Clyde's friends. They may know something important and not even realize it."

"It's certainly tragic," Long said. "My wife cried all night when she found out what had happened." He reached over the end table between them and grabbed Edmée's bejeweled hand. He squeezed it, never taking his eyes from Billy Ray.

"There's also Noe," Raven said.

"Noe?" Long said.

"Yes," Edmée broke in. "I told you about Noe, darling. He was Clyde's best friend. He was missing."

"Is," Raven said before she could help herself. "He is missing. And he's also my nephew."

"I'm sorry for your loss," Long murmured automatically, inclining his head respectfully.

"He's not dead," Raven insisted.

"Leave it, Raven," Billy Ray said. "Edmée, it seems the boys lied to their parents about where they were supposed to be last weekend as you already know. We've got some new evidence and are just looking at some possibilities."

"Like what?" Edmée asked. "I mean, I'll tell you what I can. I care for those two boys very much."

"That's why we're here," Raven said. "We believe the boys may have come your way before they went missing."

Edmée cocked her head and blinked. "I don't understand."

"We have video evidence of the boys getting off a city bus near your house."

Long laughed. "Why, the only bus stop is miles away from here. I know because sometimes I give Karen a lift after her shift."

"We're thinking that it was a distance the boys would've walked," Billy Ray said.

"That's just ridiculous," Edmée said. "Billy Ray. Really. When is this supposed to be?"

"Between four thirty and five on Friday," Raven said.

"But why would they come here?" Edmée asked.

"That's what we want to know. Could you have hired them to help out? Clyde was always looking for ways to make extra money," Raven said.

"Why would I do that?" Edmée said. "I loved those boys, but I only saw them at the restaurant or when I was with one of you. I would never have a reason to see them alone."

"Look," Billy Ray said. "We aren't accusing you of anything. We just need to know what they were doing in this part of town."

"When you say this part of town, do you mean white?" Long cut in.

"If you want to see it that way maybe that's what I mean. I think Clyde had a crush on you, Edmée. Could he have convinced Noe to come over here just for a visit? He had trouble at home and was pretty upset. Maybe he needed a sympathetic ear."

"If he needed a sympathetic ear, then he would have talked to one of you. You know him better than my wife does," Long said.

"But Edmée is good with kids," Raven said. "She runs the home and all. Maybe Clyde thought she would be a better listener, no judgment, you know. You were always playing that memory game with him, Edmée. He really liked you."

Edmée was about to say something, but before she could say a word, Long said, "My wife just said that they weren't here on Friday. Take that as your answer."

Billy Ray smiled without teeth. "Maybe they came over when you weren't home?"

"Karen," Long called while still looking at Billy Ray. In the time it takes a butterfly to close its wings, the maid was standing there. "Did you see two boys come over here on Friday, around four thirty or five p.m. in the afternoon? Two black boys?"

"No, Dr. Long," she said almost before he had the words out of his mouth.

"Thank you," he said. He waved her away.

"You still haven't said if you were home, Edmée," Raven pressed.

"I was home," she said. "I had a hell of a migraine, so I was lying down."

"Anything else, Detectives?" Long asked.

"Yes," Raven said. "Edmée, do you know a man by the name of Ronnie True?"

"Oh, yes," she said. "But of course. He did some work for the foster home. What a nice man."

"Do you know that he recently died?" Raven asked.

Edmée ran her hands through her long black hair. "I had heard that he was attacked. I knew he was in the hospital, but didn't know that he had passed. How awful."

Raven believed that she meant it. Edmée was looking quite flushed.

"My wife knew Ronnie True quite well. She sat by his bedside on more than one occasion. Didn't you, my dear."

"Yes, I did," she said.

"Did you know that Clyde Darling's mother worked for Ronnie True?"

"Yes, I did. You know, it's such a small world. But what has this to do with poor Clyde and Noe?" Edmée asked.

"I don't know," Raven said. "We're just...."

"Poking every place you can to see if you hit water?" Long said.

Billy Ray smiled again. "Something like that. But we certainly don't want to upset you or your wife."

"It's all right. I know you only do this for your job, but I saw that poor man in the hospital, and it makes me sick thinking about it. If there aren't any more questions...."

"No," Raven said. "But if you think of anything, you'll call me, right?"

"You know I will. Just thinking about this is giving me a big migraine."

Edmée made her apologies and left the room. Raven turned back to Long. "I never knew her to be so fragile. She wrangled a snake in my apartment last night."

"That's right. She told me about that, and I know y'all knew each other in high school. Snakes never bothered Edmée. As far as her being tough, people change in the space of a decade and more, Detective. One thing I know about my wife is that she hates it when people get hurt, especially young people. It takes her back to how she grew up."

"She just seems a lot tougher than that," Billy Ray said.

"Oh, she is," Long responded. "But not with everything."

Long stood up to walk them outside himself. Raven wondered if he did so to show Billy Ray that there were no hard feelings. On the massive front porch, the two men shook hands, and Raven watched Billy Ray get into his Skylark for the drive down Lakeshore back to Chastain's.

Raven and Long stood in silence for a few moments. She didn't make a move to leave because she was sure he hadn't finished talking.

Finally he said, "Yes, she's a regular trooper, but sometimes her over-grieving concerns me, especially about people she doesn't know."

"What do you mean by over-grieving?" she asked.

"Well, did you hear about that boy who was tortured by his parents?"

"Yeah," Raven said offhandedly. "I know the reporter who broke the story. The DeWitts, right? Claude DeWitt. His parents adopted and abused him. Ended up killing him, right?"

"Yes. That would be upsetting to anybody. But Edmée took it hard like it was her fault for only working with older kids. She cried so much that I had to give her a sedative."

CHAPTER THIRTY-FOUR

Stevenson called her as she was leaving the Long-Crowley residence to tell her that the video evidence was turning out to be a disappointment. Any evidence aside from the general direction the boys may have been taken was camouflaged behind a gray curtain of rain and obscured by the night. While BLPD worked to enhance the evidence, Raven decided to take up the chief's challenge. She would see for herself if Breaker had indeed left town.

She called him using the cell number listed in the True files. He answered on the first ring. When Raven arrived at Breaker's home, which was still in Byrd's Landing, his wife led her to the backyard. He was sitting on a paint bucket while his daughters played Double Dutch. Even at home he was dressed like he was going out, in a green paisley button-up silk shirt and a pair of black slacks. He had a beer in one hand and a Newport in the other, but he smelled strongly of soap and expensive cologne. By the number of beer bottles lining the glass patio table, it looked like he had been at it for a while.

"If that motherfucker said that I left because I was scared, he's a damn liar," Breaker said once they had been sitting for a few moments.

Raven glanced at the girls. They didn't appear to be paying attention to their father, and gave no indication that they heard him. They were too involved in their game. The two girls spinning the ropes in opposite directions looked to be maybe nine or ten. The jumper, tapping one foot in time with the ropes whipping against the concrete patio, looked younger but not by much.

"He said you were pretty burned out, that you ran."

Breaker reared back as if she had smacked him.

Raven went on. "He said the case got to you because you had kids."

"He's a liar. You see that now, don't you?"

"Then tell me why you quit."

"That's what I'm telling you. I didn't quit. The chief put me on leave. Told Goldie that I was cracking up, right after he brought you in." He narrowed his eyes at her. "Now, you tell me. Why do you want to talk to me?"

"Ronnie True is dead."

"Not surprised. Everybody knew he was headed that way."

"You handled that case, right?"

"I did."

"So, I'm sure you connected the dots between Judge Toulouse and Ronnie True?"

"That's a bingo right there," he said, holding his beer hand out to her.

"You follow up?" she asked.

"I tried to follow up, but the chief lost his mind. Didn't want me going anywhere near Judge T."

"I don't understand," Raven said. "Toulouse is just a family court judge. Where does he get that sort of pull from?"

"The mayor," he said. "They're friends, and as you know, any friend of the mayor is…"

"…a friend of the chief's," Raven finished for him.

Breaker knitted his brows as he examined the girls' Double Dutch. "The chief knows that if he loses the mayor's support, he might as well pack it in. He's not ready to do that no matter how big he talks about not caring about the job."

"I've known the chief for years," Raven said. "He may be a son-of-a-robber, but I don't think he would interfere in an investigation if he thought it was leading him to the perp. If he said you were wasting your time, he thought you were wasting your time."

"Well, if he wanted to run the case, then he should've run it. He told me under no circumstances to continue going down the road I was on."

"Did you?"

He gave her a bitter laugh. "Why you think I'm sitting here watching my daughters play jump rope?"

"Looks like a lot more than jump rope."

"Competition Double Dutch," he said. "Wife's got them on a team. She competed when she was a kid growing up in Pittsburgh."

"Why aren't they in school?"

He took a long drag of his cigarette and looked at her through the smoke.

"You don't think it's safe."

"I do not. Not until you catch the bastard."

They sat in silence for a few moments listening to the soft, rhythmic tapping of the oldest girls' tennis shoes on the concrete patio, the ropes whipping in the air.

"I see you brought the True casefile with you. You mind?" He set the beer on the table, put the cigarette in the ashtray. She handed the three-ring binder over to him, and he started going through pages.

"You want to know when he really flipped out?" he said conversationally. "When I found out why True represented Judge Toulouse."

"You found out?"

"You bet your ass I did. It was a child porn charge. Can you imagine that? From a sitting family court judge."

"Why wasn't that splashed all over the news?"

"Because it was hushed up."

"How did you find out?"

"June Darling," he said. "She used to do some paralegal work for True, but you probably know that. Do you think that Toulouse is connected to her son's death?"

"I don't like coincidences," Raven said.

"Yeah, I'm not too fond of them myself. You want to know what I think?"

"That's why I'm here."

"I think that's when the chief decided, really decided, that I needed to take time off for stress. The son-of-a-bitch didn't even give me time to update the files before he kicked me to the curb."

"You mean there's more?"

"There is. I did some more digging on Judge T. Man doesn't only like porn, he likes money. He and True had this shady adoption thing going on. If you had the money, you'd get the kid."

Raven looked at him like he had lost his mind. Maybe the chief was right, maybe Breaker had wandered too far off the beaten path to be effective. Toulouse selling children appeared to be one big rabbit hole.

"Now you looking at me like he did. But I'm telling you that somebody needs to follow that lead until it runs out. If it's not connected, fine, it's not. But it needs looking into."

Raven kept silent. She didn't know about that, but didn't want to upset him. She needed him talking.

"Did you find connections to any of the other boys' families?" she asked.

He didn't say anything. The Double Dutch ropes beat steadily against the concrete.

"No," he said. It sounded like an admission.

"Anything from the Memorial site?" she asked.

"No. As you know, the boot print looks interesting. Did a grid search like you suggested, but that's it. We were able to match the garbage that was left to the workers. Even that bottle of Perrier."

He was handing the casefile back to her, his eyes lingering on his girls. The look on his face said that he would do everything in his power to keep them safe. Next to the beer bottles was a .45 automatic.

★　　★　　★

Sitting in the car, Raven watched the girls through the chain-link fence surrounding the Breaker residence. They made jumping between the two ropes fast as cyclones spinning in the opposite direction look as easy as breathing. They did it while chanting, no less, in time with the ropes while their father watched over them with a .45 on the patio table. Perhaps the man had gone crazy.

Before she left, she had a conversation with Breaker's wife, who told her not to worry. The beer was lite, and the firearm wasn't loaded. His wife unloaded the weapon when he went to the bathroom. He would sit there drinking until six or seven. She'd cajole him into dinner, and then to bed. And after, she'd retrieve the unloaded weapon, load it and put it in the gun safe. And then the same scenario would play out the following day. She told Raven to catch the killer soon so she could have her husband back.

Raven picked up the True binder from the passenger seat. Breaker had included the True crime scene photos. True's office looked as if someone had driven a wrecking ball through it. Blood was everywhere. Even some of the pictures had been knocked off the walls. The meticulous Breaker had also included pictures of True's office before the crime took place. There was True standing in front of his big desk with his arm around the mayor's shoulder. She was about to flip the page when something caught her eye. She stared at it, scanning up and down and left and right before comparing it with pictures from the crime scene.

The half shoulder mount bear taxidermy in the office's before picture was nowhere to be found in the crime scene photos. She took her cell phone out and dialed Breaker's number. It was a long shot but she was hoping that Breaker was as detailed as she thought he was.

He answered before she heard the ring back. "Yeah. What else you need?"

He didn't sound like the relatively young man that he was. Relocations to Byrd's Landing came with caveats. Houses were cheap, jobs were plenty if you weren't picky, but you better be ready to protect your soul.

"Who cleaned up the True crime scene? Do you know?"

"Yeah," he said. "TSC. Trauma Scene Cleaners. Good people. They do good work."

"Not The Clean-up Man?"

"Hell no. That guy's a dick. True's family had enough money to make sure they did the cleanup right."

"Do you know if anything was stolen from True's office?"

Silence, and then, "Why do you ask?"

"There's a half shoulder mount bear missing from the crime scene photos."

"My head hurts too bad to ask why you care about that, but if it's missing, maybe he got rid of it before he was assaulted."

Raven ran her hand over the crime scene photo. "The area where it hung is still pretty light. If he got rid of it, it was recent. But I don't see a man like True giving something like that away. The thing was hanging right behind his desk."

"What are you saying?"

"Maybe the perp took it."

Breaker laughed harshly. "Careful. You'll catch my disease. Rabbit holes are contagious. Just ask the chief."

He hung up before she could reply. She sat in the car with the Android pressed to her chin, thinking. Something about the taxidermy looked familiar. Then she remembered. She thought she saw a bear claw in the back of Ozy's VW truck when she went to meet Speck about helping her clean up Oral's place. The same Ozy who followed Speck around in search of treasure from the dead. She needed to know if one of those treasures was from the half shoulder mount of a snarling bear with its claws out. If the gift did come from Willie Lee, he had risen to the top of Raven's suspect list. She wasn't worried about motive, not yet, but Speck needed another look.

She hadn't eaten. The only thing she had put into her body was that cup of black coffee in the early morning hours. And with waking up every minute fearing the sound of a soft rattle and cold scales slithering over her bare legs, sleep had been elusive as a cloud last night. Still, she drove the streets of Byrd's Landing, looking for that raggedy VW truck, her tired mind imagining the Floyd stalker look-alike in every darkened doorway, watching, waiting. It was late when her Android rang, and Buckwheat Zydeco filled the cabin of her car.

"Yeah, Billy Ray."

"You better go get your boy."

"What are you talking about?"

"Cameron," he said. "He's at a memorial service for the victims. At Gold's Park. Imogene also told me that he's going around telling everybody that Noe's dead, and all he wants is his body so he can bury him. I'm thinking that him giving up on Noe, and then going to a memorial service before they find the body is like a cat licking himself at a dog festival."

CHAPTER THIRTY-FIVE

Raven took the exit for the park where there was to be a candlelight vigil for the dead boys. And for Noe. She had run the trails of the state park many times, had been frightened by its isolation, the hiss of owls, and the dangers lurking there. But the park was one fear she could face. She parked the car and opened the driver's-side door to the respectful murmuring of the hundreds of people in attendance. Those who didn't have their cell phone flashlights on held lit candles in Dixie cups.

Cameron stood in a clutch of parents and other relatives of the victims at the very front of the crowd. When she reached him, she grabbed him by his skinny wrists. She dragged him behind her off to the side.

"Have you gone completely crazy?" she asked him.

"What are you talking about?" he said. "I'm here for my son."

"Are you sure you aren't here for you?"

"What's that supposed to mean?"

"You never wanted a son before you found out you had one. Now that he's missing, you can get on with your life. Not caring about anything but yourself. You sure you're not here celebrating instead of mourning?"

"You ain't right, Raven. All you doing since he went missing is telling me how much I'm fucking up."

She stuck her finger in his face. He knocked her hand away like he used to do when they were kids.

"Get your fucking finger out of my face."

"You did screw up. Your son missing three days and you don't even know it. And you're still screwing up. Running around here like you know he's dead...."

"He is dead."

"He is not!" Raven shouted.

Several heads turned their way. Raven waited until they looked away. She said in a lower voice, "Do you think I would be out here busting my ass if I thought he was already dead?"

"So you chasing fairy tales like you always do," Cameron said. "I'm just trying to be realistic."

Raven let out a nasty laugh. "So this is the one time in your life that you choose to be realistic? That's some sorry-ass timing, Cameron."

He turned his face away from her. She thought she saw shame on it. She grabbed his chin. He hadn't shaved since Noe went missing, and his face felt scratchy. She turned him toward her.

"You have done some dumb things in your life. But this has got to be the dumbest."

"Why?" he said. "Everybody saying he's dead. The chief, Breaker, even your boyfriend."

"He's not my blasted boyfriend," she said. "You're declaring Noe dead in your mind because you want to get on with things. Being a daddy is too hard on you, and now that there's a chance you don't have to do it anymore, you're jumping right in."

"You've always been one mean ole bitch."

"I'm just trying to keep your skinny behind out of jail, while at the same time trying to find your son!"

She marveled at the look on his face, the surprised Cameron look as if he had just touched something unexpectedly hot. Then the look changed to one of total resignation. "Ain't nothing going to keep me out of jail."

"You're unbelievable."

"Look, one thing I know, if someone wants me in jail, I'll be in jail. Ain't no helping that."

"There is certainly no help if you keep doing things that signal that you did have something to do with Clyde's murder and Noe's disappearance."

"How am I doing that?"

"By attending this memorial service without a doggone body, you moron. Like insisting he's already dead. Geez Louise."

"I don't have anything to do with Noe being gone!"

"I'm not the one you have to convince. For someone who didn't want to leave a mark on this world you sure are making one big godawful stain."

"You really think they're coming for me?"

"It's what I would do if you weren't my brother, especially now," she said.

"What should I do?"

"You drive here with someone, or did you take your own car?"

"I drove here with one of the other parents."

"Go tell them you have a ride back. I'll take you to my place."

"Your place, why?"

"To buy time. If they show up at your place tonight to take you in, you won't be there."

★   ★   ★

Cameron sullenly insisted they stop at the Chicken Shack on the way to her rooms at Mama Anna's. He ordered a chicken sandwich and fries, but Raven ordered nothing. She couldn't imagine eating. But not Cameron. The grease-stained paper bag rattled noisily as he stuffed Cajun fries into his mouth. She looked over at him to see if the man she claimed for a brother had the face of a murderer. He just sat there, calmly licking season salt from his fingers. To Raven he looked as if he didn't have one care in this whole wide world. What missing son? What threat of arrest? It wouldn't have been the first time that she was this close to a killer.

"I ain't done nothing to Noe," he said in the quiet enclosure of the Mustang. "Or Clyde."

"I know you didn't," she answered.

"I just know how to compartmentalize things better than you. If Noe's missing, my being hungry and eating something doesn't mean that I don't want him home. If the police think I killed my son because I'm eating a chicken sandwich, they're more fucked up than they already are."

They were silent the rest of the drive to her rooms. But Raven eventually stuck her fingers into Cameron's bag and stuffed two fries into her mouth.

She fixed a place for him on the couch. They were asleep for only a few hours before there was a pounding at the door. Raven's Android read three a.m. Not so much bewitching hour as the perfect time to serve a warrant hour. She pulled a thin robe around her and walked into the living room. Cameron was already sitting up. He had left a table lamp on, and was now staring at the door with that look of resignation on his face. Thank God he had slept in his clothes.

"Not a word," she warned. "Keep your mouth shut, Cameron. You hear me?"

He didn't agree or disagree, just sat there with his eyes fastened on the door. She opened it without asking. They both knew who it was. But she was somewhat surprised that aside from Officer Spangler and Delbert Stevenson, the chief was standing there, the look on his face grave.

"He here?" Chief Sawyer asked her.

"What are you doing here?" she said, blocking the doorway.

"You need to move out of the way. I'm sorry. We have a warrant for his arrest," Stevenson said.

"For what?" Raven asked, ignoring the apology.

"Don't make this difficult," Office Spangler said.

"Since you asked so nicely," Raven responded with acid in her voice.

She stepped aside. At the sight of Cameron standing there looking like he didn't know what to do with his hands, Stevenson drew his weapon.

"Put your hands where I can see them."

"Don't be an ass," Raven said. "You can already see them."

"Can I put my shoes on?" Cameron asked.

"Go on and do that, Cam," Spangler said. "But I'm going to have to cuff you."

"I understand," Cameron said, his voice low and defeated. The loud, smack-talking Cameron had disappeared at the sight of the handcuffs.

Raven went into the bedroom. She changed so quickly that she was still zipping her jeans when she walked back into the living room.

"Where do you think you're going?" Stevenson asked.

"I'm going with my brother."

"Look, Raven," the chief said. "He's just going to central booking, that's all."

"You really don't think I'm that stupid, do you?"

"He's already lawyered up. Remember the advice you gave him?" Stevenson said.

"I did," Cameron said, his hands now cuffed. "But I'll change my mind if you let Raven come with me. I don't care about a lawyer. I just want to find Noe."

CHAPTER THIRTY-SIX

Cameron sat opposite her, Goldie on one side of him, and Stevenson on the other. The record button on the camera tucked in the corner was blinking like mad, but Raven was sure that the chief was watching from behind the two-way. He'd want to see what the camera's eye might miss.

"We have a problem, Cameron," Goldie was saying. "You don't have an alibi. None. And you weren't straight with us."

"What do you mean he wasn't straight with you?" Raven challenged.

Stevenson gave her a look, not an unfriendly look, and held up a finger. She sat back. He was right. She shouldn't start this interview by launching an immediate defense.

"I told you that I had a date on Thursday," Cameron said. "That I went to work on Friday."

"I know what you told me," Goldie said. "And if I remember correctly, I almost had to pull it out of you. But I'm not talking about your date or your workday on Friday. I'm talking about late Friday, early Saturday when Clyde was most likely killed."

Cameron sighed, a big sigh as if this was the most annoying thing he had ever encountered in his life. "I told you. I played video games, watched some TV and fell asleep. Check my computer."

"We have it, and you can best believe that we'll check it," Goldie said.

"What?" Raven said.

"Search warrant. Served it last night," Goldie said.

"But I'm sure you could rig your computer up to make it look like you were playing. You had plenty of time to set up an alibi," Stevenson said.

"I don't know what you're talking about, man." Cameron said.

"Okay," Goldie said, and shuffled around the papers he had in front of him. "Tell me about the insurance policies again. The trust fund."

"What?" Cameron said. "We already covered this. Georgia and her lawyer set up an insurance policy on Noe in case something happened to him."

"And how much was that for?" Goldie asked.

"I told you when we first talked. A few thousand. Maybe ten. Enough for a funeral."

"Come on, Cameron," Stevenson said. "We aren't as stupid as we look."

Raven raised both eyebrows. He ignored her. "We did some checking, and we found an insurance policy for a hundred thousand on Noe. That's way more than a few thousand."

"That's bullshit," Cameron waved his hand at Stevenson. "I may not be a cop, but I know how this stuff works. Y'all will lie like crazy to scare up some shit."

Goldie pushed a paper toward Raven. She looked down at it. It was what they said, a State Farm insurance policy on Noe with Cameron listed as the beneficiary. Twenty bucks a month and a dead kid would get him one hundred thousand. Raven slid the policy over to Cameron.

"Found it in a shoebox marked with Noe's name in the bottom of your closet next to a pair of Air Jordans," Goldie said.

"So what? I got the number wrong. That doesn't mean anything."

"How could you get the number wrong?" Raven asked, already knowing the answer, her heart sinking. He didn't read the papers before signing, not the man who rarely opened his snail mail.

"There were a lot of papers, Sis," he said.

"I bet you're also going to tell us that you didn't call the insurance company to make the claim after Noe went missing?" Goldie said.

"That's bullshit!" Now Cameron was standing. "I didn't make any phone calls."

"That's funny." Goldie offered another piece of paper, this time to Cameron. "The call came from your cell phone, and they had all the information needed to make the claim."

"What number?" Cameron asked. "I have a couple of cell phones, one I lent to an old girlfriend and don't have back yet. One of the reasons I let her go was she was too far up in my business. Maybe she knew about the insurance and made the claim to get back at me."

"You let your old girlfriend keep your cell phone?" Stevenson asked.

"She was hurting for money. We made a deal that she would get it back to me once she was working again. I'd already hurt her enough. I figured that was the least I could do."

"How princely of you," Goldie said. "This the same woman you called a skank in our first interview? Benita Jeffers? The one who said Noe was cramping your style?"

"Yes, her. The only reason I called her a skank was because she was trying to set me up."

"Was that voice on the call to State Farm male or female?" Raven asked.

Goldie didn't answer the question. Raven stared at Goldie's grim face. She could tell that he didn't like what he was doing, but she couldn't tell if he believed that Cameron was a serious suspect. She looked at the two-way. She could feel the chief behind the glass, watching.

"Another thing we are looking at is the trust fund," Stevenson said.

Raven whipped her head around to face Stevenson. "Cameron told you about the trust fund. That shouldn't be a surprise." She looked back at her brother, who was nodding. He was as confused as she was.

"The insurance policy wasn't the only thing we found in that shoebox," Goldie said. "We also found papers that laid out the details of Noe's trust fund. Cameron gets a little bit of money out of it monthly to take care of Noe like he said, but Noe gets the rest after he turns twenty-five. There's a half-million dollars in it."

"And if Noe dies," Stevenson said, "Cameron gets that money."

"You forgot to tell us that, Sport," Goldie said.

"Fucking don't call me Sport."

"Well, what can I call you? You won't let me call you son?"

"How about my fucking name?" Cameron said. "Put a mister in front of it while you're at it, motherfucker."

"Your son is worth over a half-million dollars dead," Goldie continued. "Plus, with him gone you could get on with living your player lifestyle."

"I don't have a player lifestyle," Cameron said. "You think I paid any attention to that shit when I was trying to get my son? I was worried about having furniture, and a place for him to sleep. I was too busy trying to show everybody that I could be a good father to worry about this bullshit."

"Speaking of a place to sleep, we also found the blankets in your closet," Stevenson said.

Cameron opened his mouth to say something else, but Raven had had enough. She put her hand over his mouth like she used to do when they were kids and he tried to sing. "Don't say another word," she said. "It's time to rethink that lawyer."

He twisted his head away from beneath her hand. "Fuck that. I didn't do anything to my son. Why don't you believe me?"

Goldie picked up the iPad sitting beside him. He scrolled through the pictures so both Cameron and Raven could see. "These look familiar to you, Detective Burns?"

They did indeed look familiar, baby blue with white, fluffy clouds, the same blankets the serial killer used to shroud his victims.

"That doesn't mean a damn thing," Raven said before Cameron could respond. "Those blankets are common as dirt. It's a coincidence."

"I thought you said you hated coincidences?" Stevenson said.

"And we found a receipt still stuck to the unopened blanket," Goldie continued. "You bought two. What happened to the other blanket, Mr. Armand?"

Cameron's laugh was edged with bitterness. "First time someone calls me Mister, they're accusing me of murder."

"Don't talk, Cameron," Raven warned again, giving both Goldie and Stevenson a dangerous look. "It means nothing."

"Where is Noe?" Stevenson said, his voice soft. "You know, I get it. The boys were supposed to spend the weekend with you, and Noe got mouthy. I know how teenagers can be. Maybe you were doing something, had a hammer, lost your temper. Clyde tried to defend him and things just got a little complicated. Nobody believes that you meant to kill him, man."

"That didn't happen," Cameron said, his hands covering his face.

"You may not have had a choice with Clyde," Goldie said. "But there was Noe hollering at you, and you realized that if you didn't take care of him your life would be over, so you did him, too. Just an accident."

"No," Cameron said.

"What were the dates on those receipts?" Raven asked. "I bet my paycheck that you won't find any transfer evidence from Cameron's closet on the blanket Clyde was wrapped in."

Both Goldie and Stevenson acted as if they hadn't heard her question.

"And you know, you're a young man, didn't want to go to prison for the rest of your life for an accident, so you copied the Sleeping Boy killer," Stevenson said. "I mean, come on, why would a man buy two of the same kind of blanket?"

"I bought two because Noe…" Cameron said, his voice muffled. Then he stopped, brought his hands down from his face. "I can't tell you, man. All I can say is that I bought two in case one got so dirty I'd have to throw it out."

Suddenly Raven understood. Noe had lost his mother, and his life had changed drastically. He was going through some things that were so traumatizing that they probably sent him back to his six-year-old self. Knowing Cameron, he would rather throw the blankets away rather than wash them.

"I bet you also found two of the same sheet sets as well, right? You can't send a man to jail because he bought two of the same blanket," Raven said. "Tell them, Cam."

"Leave it alone, Raven," Cameron said. "I don't want Noe's business out in the streets. They won't believe anything I say anyway. It'd be a waste of time."

Cameron's eyes were teary, but he wasn't crying. He had spent his entire life battling demons, and he was suddenly very tired. He tried to send a smile Raven's way, but failed miserably. He sank back in his chair before putting his face back into his hands. "Okay, you got me," he said.

Goldie nodded sadly. "You ready to make a statement, son?"

"Hell no, you don't got him, and he's not making any statement," Raven said, knocking the iPad out of Goldie's hand. "He wants a flocking lawyer, Goldie! Chief, give me more time," she said, striding over to the two-way and pounding it with her fist. "You owe him that. You at least owe me that."

CHAPTER THIRTY-SEVEN

Raven couldn't get Cameron's face out of her mind when he gave up in the interview room. He was picturing the rest of his life in jail branded as a child killer. The Cameron she knew wouldn't stand for that, but the thought of losing Noe broke him. She had to do something. They had already talked to Edmée, and there was no evidence that the boys were at her home on Friday. Willie Lee was next on the suspect list. His house was in the circle after all, a distance the boys could have walked from the bus stop. She needed to talk to him, but he had lawyered up, even spelling it out for them.

Now standing in front of Speck's residence, she had decided to take the investigation to his front door but come at it, as that famed poet would say, slant. Her plan was to knock on Speck's door under the pretense of just wanting to talk about cleaning Oral's house. She would casually steer the conversation around to the case, wander around in search of any traces of Noe, or for evidence that Willie Lee Speck was indeed the Sleeping Boy killer. Maybe she'd find the hoodie Noe was wearing the day he went missing, or blood spatters on the drywall.

Of course, she knew how it would play in court if she did find something, but right now, she didn't give a rat's toenail. Her goal was to find her nephew. Alive. If Speck were the killer, they could work backwards later to find the evidence they would need to put him under the jail where he belonged. Besides, what were they going to do? Fire her?

The house was as Speck had described to her many times: sprawling, neat, and made of brick scrubbed so clean that it looked pink. A blue bicycle with a white seat lay on a field of thick grass. A tall bush of yellow angel's trumpet stood against the right side of the porch. On the front porch in the shade of the angel's trumpet lay an old-fashioned Raggedy Ann with bright, black button eyes folded over the armrest of a wicker rocking chair.

Raven studied the front door. It was made of a heavy, dark wood that gleamed from polish. Speck, she thought, did have it good. There was no camera on the front porch, so no Ring doorbell. The angel's trumpet effectively hid the view of the front door from the street. She was surprised that a man who cared about his lawn so much would let the bush with its thick leaves and trumpet-shaped flowers grow so wild.

A low, sweet whistle pierced her thoughts. It was so Floyd that she wouldn't have been surprised to find him standing right next to her. That should have been her first warning. Floyd rarely appeared unless there was a chance he'd be able to play. *We ready for some fun, Birdy Girl,* he said, not in a mean, killing mood, but in a mischievous way like he couldn't wait to see what would happen next.

She didn't let herself dwell on Floyd's antics or the fact that she could smell him ever since her return to BLPD. She rang the doorbell, expecting wind chimes to go along with the fairy-tale lawn and porch. What she got instead was a hard buzz that played for a good five seconds before abruptly shutting off. She waited. Nothing. She rocked back on her heels, a thought sidling along the edge of her consciousness.

Raven pressed the doorbell once more. No answer. She jiggled the handle, pushed the door inward a fraction. No deadbolt, either.

We gone do this? Floyd asked in her head.

Her answer to him was, *Yes, indeed we are.* She reached inside her jacket pocket for her pick set. She had the door open in less than fifteen seconds. That had to be a new world record. When all this was over she'd have to tell Cameron about it.

She began to slowly push the door open, calling out for Willie Lee. Not only was there no answer, she could only push it open a few inches before it stopped, refusing to go any further. She called Speck's name again, all the while thinking that something wasn't quite right. There was this smell, too, a sugary, rotten smell that reminded her of the inside of a dumpster.

The smell on the porch only hinted at what was to come. It grew as she forced open the door a few inches more. She sidled through the narrow opening to get inside. Her eyes watered in protest. She rubbed her nose with her knuckles as if she could erase the scent. She tried to close the door behind her but no joy. It had caught on something and wouldn't budge. She looked down to see a box she didn't realize had fallen blocking the way.

Looks like good ole Willie Lee never used the front door, Floyd piped up in her head again. *Maybe it's time for you to do, what do you police say? Call for backup*. But her backup would be Stevenson. There was no way that was going to happen. And no, she would have never thought that Speck and his family didn't use the front door. Everything on the outside appeared so perfect.

But Floyd was ready to set her straight on that topic. *Now that ain't quite right, is it? That bike was rusty as sin, didn't have no chain on it. And that doll with them black button eyes? Mildew running all up and down them white arms and legs. Playing cops and robbers with no sleep is making you blind, Birdy Girl.*

She knew Floyd was right. Her exhausted mind was seeing what she had expected, and that was Speck's perfect house representing his perfect life. She had been careless, stupid. She considered turning back. But she couldn't. She had to find Noe.

She turned toward what must be the living room. No choice but to look straight up. That was the only direction the piles of trash bags and junk filling the room would allow her eyes to go. Some of the garbage bags had burst open. They oozed a black, viscous blend of what must have been discarded scraps of food and God knew what all. Junk was stacked so high that Raven speculated that she could topple it with a breath. An overturned loveseat with a blue child's dresser in its gutted belly. On top of the loveseat, a toaster oven; beside the toaster oven, a broken espresso coffee machine. On top of the toaster oven and espresso machine, stacks of clothes, more bags, stuffed animals including what looked like a Tickle Me Elmo, its mouth wide as if screaming in fright from being buried alive. On top of that were clothes, more bags, and more toys – was that a red tricycle? – in a teetering tower that stretched all the way to the ceiling. The smells were changing. She'd see something, like a dead rat amid the junk, and the new scent of decomposition would mingle with the fetid, sweet smell of the dumpster.

Anything but this, her frantic mind thought.

She turned intending to bolt out the front door and call for backup, but she dislodged one of the towers. It fell with a crash into the foyer, further blocking her path to fresh air, to sanity. The little light that was coming through the front door window was now gone. She was trapped.

She covered her nose with the sleeve of her jacket, and fished out the mini flashlight from her jacket pocket. She flicked it on and noticed that she was probably only a few feet into the foyer. After that, the massive hoard went up and up. There was a trail between the bags, a walking trail in the putrid jungle.

Raven's mind screamed for her to get out. And for once, Floyd, who hated disorder as much as she did, was silent. *Not talking so big now, are you, old man?* Raven asked, knowing that even by asking it she had stepped over the line of sanity. She considered her options. Try to make her way through the trash and out the front door, or follow the trail through the hoard. She flashed her light over the blockage. Breaking her way through that was impossible. She had no choice but to follow the trail. *Pretend like you're on a hike, or a particularly steep, but nasty trail run,* she told herself before quickly amending, *a trail run in hell.*

She started carefully up through the mounds of junk, holding her arms out for balance, clutching the flashlight so hard her hand ached. Two times she had to stop because the smell made her gag so bad that she almost fell. Once she actually vomited a clear line of bile. After she was done, she wiped her mouth with the sleeve of her jacket and continued upward. A few carefully placed steps later, she was able to use the ceiling for balance. The scratching sounds her flashlight made against the ceiling sent her imagination in unwanted directions. She thought she heard movement in the trash heap, more rats, or cats that may have somehow gotten trapped. No telling what might be hidden in there.

When she thought that she couldn't take it anymore, the trail led downward into what must be the kitchen. The stove had been ripped out of the wall, the gas pipe reaching for nothing. The refrigerator's door hung open with various packages falling out of its gaping mouth. It wasn't as bad as Oral's refrigerator; at least it worked. There was a light, but from what she could see a good portion of the food had rotted.

The kitchen wasn't as full to bursting as the room she just made her way through. Thank God there was a relative clear path to the back door, and there was more morning light sliding through the kitchen window. She started toward it when something caught her eye. A fast movement, no more than a flicker, coming from the dining room.

Raven dropped the flashlight into her pocket. She unhooked her holster and removed the Glock. Careful not to topple any of the smaller hoards, she started toward the movement. Something brushed against her leg, soft as a kiss.

"Jesus," she said.

She looked down. A scrawny yellow, one-eyed cat hissed at her, showing every one of its tiny, sharp teeth. Raven gave it a gentle nudge with her boot to make it go away. But it wasn't having any of it. A paw fast as lightning scratched her so hard that Raven could feel the claws through her jeans. She yelped as the cat skittered away.

"Crap," Raven breathed, forgetting about the movement in the dining room. The thing had drawn blood. But she didn't have the luxury of forgetting for long. A blow to the back of her head drove her to her knees. Before she could regroup, there was another blow on her back, this one knocking her face down on the top layer of trash on the filthy floor. Instinct took over. Raven flipped on her back and fired two quick shots.

The two soft thuds that followed made her sure that she hit something. She would swear later, even if only to herself, that she saw stiff, blond hair, and a flash of black moving fast. She leapt to her feet, maneuvered through the trash, calling out "police." The only thing that returned her greeting was smoke from her own weapon.

Further in, she saw what she had shot. Not the man she was sure had been stalking her, but a black garbage bag. She felt the top of her head, and her fingers came away with blood. She made her way back to the kitchen. The cat had carved a place for himself on top of the crowded refrigerator. He had a very smug look on his face. Near where she had been lying was a marble rolling pin with blood on it. Next to it was a lead crystal iced tea pitcher, the rim almost a half-inch thick. The cat must have pawed the rolling pin off the refrigerator, and next the pitcher. There was no man chasing her, just a pissed-off cat. Raven wanted to lean against something. To take a breath. Except there was nothing to lean against. There was no good air to breathe.

Noe wasn't here, she thought. Any evidence of Speck being a serial killer, if that evidence existed, was buried in ceiling-high filth. She made her way to the back door and pushed it open. She thought that the fresh air was the sweetest thing she ever tasted. She walked down two cement steps into a diamond-shaped yard covered in pea gravel. On her right, stepping-stones led to a long shed with black windows.

On surer footing now, she thought, maybe, just maybe. With her weapon pointed to the sky, she rapped on the shed door. Just as with the front door, nothing. She called Speck's name and still didn't hear anyone answer in return. She gripped the Glock tighter and opened the door.

The air was cooler than the outside air, but ranker. The morning sun fought its way through the scraps and scratches in the black paint covering the window, casting jagged beams of light inside the shed. There was enough light to give her a suggestion of what was going on but not the detail she needed. She holstered her weapon and retrieved her flashlight.

"Noe," she called experimentally, as well as wishfully. She didn't expect anyone to respond. She wasn't disappointed.

What Raven saw in the flashlight's beam made her gag. Her stomach rushed to her throat. If it weren't for years of training by both Floyd and the academy, she would have been outside to puke more bile into the pea gravel. Several dead dogs were stacked in one corner. Some must have died fast and snarling because that's how they looked in death. The same thing that happened in the house happened here. She would see something first, and then smell it.

As she moved the light around, it flashed on dead possums and squirrels. There was a work table in the middle of the room. Raven told herself not to move toward it, but she couldn't help herself. She did so, slowly, her boots moving heavily over the hard floor, the circle of light leading her way.

On the square wooden table were more animals. A possum was stretched out with a nail in each five-fingered paw. She looked a day or two dead, the corpses of her children still poking their little heads from the pouch in which she carried them.

No time for screaming.

Something out of the corner of her eye made her spin around. She thought she heard a whisper, a voice that said *don't turn away yet, look again*. So she did. There on the table next to the possum was a non-penetrating captive bolt gun. This one wasn't like the one Stella had shown her, but an old-fashioned-looking one with a handgrip and a barrel with a mushroom-shaped tip. Enough to stun, to concuss, but not penetrate the skull. *So I can sell the brain with the other meat*, Raven heard Stella's voice in her head. She was going to take a photo with her Android, but stopped, reconsidered. Noe obviously wasn't here. No need to continue to contaminate this evidence by being inside the shed. Let the uniforms find it, and CSI deal with it. She dropped the flashlight into her pocket along with the cell phone, and started making her way out of the shed.

She would make the call from her vehicle so no one would think for a minute that she had been in that shed. She was already making up in her head what she would say. She went to question Speck, and noticed that his front door was open. When she realized that something was blocking the door, she stepped back to advise dispatch that she was going in, and to send backup. She'd just have to hope that CSI didn't find the bullet holes in the garbage bags or shell casings in the filth. *Just flows from the tongue like honey, them lies do, don't they, Birdy Girl?*

"Shut up, ole man," Raven whispered. "You've done worse. I'm trying to get some good done here."

Raven was so into her story that she didn't see Speck before she heard him. An angry roar ripped the lie she had been making up in her head to pieces.

CHAPTER THIRTY-EIGHT

This was not the mild-mannered, goofy, irreverent Speck she had known for almost five years. This was a monster who was not only protecting his hoard but the illusion of his sanity, the wholesomeness he portrayed to the world while disparaging the fallen. This was the thing that had stunned and carved up the neighborhood pets. He moved toward her in a blur.

"You piece of invading, slimy shit!" he growled. "You must have balls bigger than coconuts."

"Now just a minute, Willie Lee. I thought you were in trouble when you didn't come to the door," she tried.

"You lie like a rug," he said. "You may have gotten an eyeful, but you ain't leaving here upright."

It all happened so fast. Before she knew it they were toe-to-toe. She pushed him hard, trying to put as much distance between them as possible. In spite of the strength from her daily bench presses, he staggered back only a few feet. He laughed, roared and charged again.

Before he could touch her, she kicked him as hard as she could in the knee with the point of her boot, thinking, *This is going to be bad.*

Floyd, now enjoying himself, responded immediately in her head with, *Well, it ain't gonna be good.*

The kick stopped Speck only for an instant. She hoped it wasn't just from surprise that she was going to put up a fight. Two more swift, hard kicks to the legs, the knees, but he kept coming.

He curled his big hand into a fist and reached out with the punch. He was big and slow and sure of his advantage. She ducked the punch and delivered a series of combinations to his face. But Speck, crouching now, brushed her punches off as if they were tickles from a moth's wing.

He grabbed her by the shoulders with his huge dinner-plate hands. She countered with two swift forearms to his face. The impact made the bones of her arm feel like they had caught fire. She didn't know how he was able to hang on to her, but he was. She kneed him in the groin twice.

He let go and bent over in pain. But the big man didn't drop. Both adrenaline and anger kept him up.

Well, Birdy, Floyd said, *if you can't stop a man by kneeing him in the nuts, you might want to grab your ankles and kiss your ass goodbye.*

Before she could tell Floyd to shut his pie hole, Speck punched her so hard in the face that for a minute she didn't know where she was or how she got there. The blow knocked her flat. She skidded backward on the gravel, the palms of her hands feeling like they were going through a cheese grater.

She was hoping that by seeing her on the ground Speck would come to his senses.

But no such luck. Speck didn't have any senses, not at the moment anyway.

He charged her as she was starting to stand, his arms windmilling down, the blows catching her in the head and back. She ducked lower to avoid the punches, grabbed him by both of his legs. She hoped she had enough strength to bring him down. He still managed to land some punches, and she felt as well as heard the thuds on her back. One part of her wanted to let go and run away, but no way would she do that. This piece of filth was going down, or she would die trying.

Speck howled in rage long and loud as he continued to hit. Raven grunted. She pulled his thick legs forward with all her strength, trying to throw him off balance. She felt so much pain from the pounding fists that she would have sworn her insides were turning to jelly. Controlling her wrists as she learned in training, she kept pulling his legs forward while driving him backwards, hoping that he would slip on the pea gravel.

It took a second or two for her to believe that she had finally gotten the monster down, on his back like she wanted him to be. She could see that he was disoriented, but not enough. She scrambled on top of his chest and threw a couple of hard elbows to his face, telling him to calm down between blows. His answer was that he would calm down when he killed her. He turned to his side in an effort to shield his face from the blows. She snaked a forearm beneath his neck and grabbed her opposite bicep. He squirmed, but she kept squeezing and squeezing until she felt the squirming stop. He reared up one final time trying to buck her off, but she didn't let go. She pulled and pulled, pain and blood ringing loud in her ears. She didn't let go until she felt him go limp.

"And that's why," she said breathlessly as she slid from him, "we have the babies, you big, useless bag of guts."

That was all the celebration she allowed herself. He would only be out for a few seconds, if that. She placed two fingers on his neck. His pulse beat strong and steady. She tugged his arm from under his belly and the other from over his head. She felt a sense of deep satisfaction at the click of the handcuffs.

Raven's nose was bleeding. Her ears rang with a steady, shrill whistle. Pain rolled over her back like a deep wave, leaving what would become lasting purple bruises in its wake. Her conscious mind was replaced by the fear and confusion of the hoard, the hissing cat, the figure in the house moving with the shadows, and the carnage in the shed. So when she heard her name, clear and real in the harsh light of day, she whipped out her Glock and pointed it at the sound.

"Raven," the voice said again.

But she didn't respond. There wasn't anybody behind her eyes, and somehow she knew that. Floyd was in her place. A part of her was frightened. A part of her was pleased.

"Raven, it's me."

She kept the Glock trained on the voice.

"Stevenson, your partner," the voice said. The man stepped back with his hands up.

She took aim, her finger caressing the trigger. She waited for that God-like power to flow through her like it did when she shot Lovelle, but the voice came again, desperate.

"No," it said. "It's me. Wynn."

That stopped her. She blinked. Let up on the trigger.

"Wynn?" she said, confused, the blood still roaring in her ears.

"Yes, Wynn."

She was standing close to him now. He had her face in his hands. "Yes, Wynn."

It was his breath on her face that brought her back to her senses. She yanked his wrists away from her.

"You okay?" he asked. "What happened here?"

She spat a red blob of blood on the pea gravel. She pushed him away, giving him a long, measuring look. Speck was waking up now, groaning and twisting his body around. Raven looked over at the struggling man, and then back at Stevenson.

"Why, don't just shoot while you watch me get my ass kicked, stand there," Raven said.

As if she had dreamed him up, she turned her back on him. Using her now cracked Android, she called for real backup.

CHAPTER THIRTY-NINE

The chief wouldn't let Raven within a country mile of Speck. He considered her extrajudicial foray onto Speck's property reckless and illegal. She was officially off the case, but he hadn't asked for her badge back. Raven knew that despite all the trouble she brought him, the chief was hoping she'd stay. After all, he needed her. At least he let her watch Speck's questioning via the two-way. But she was stuck prowling behind the glass while Goldie and Stevenson fumbled through the interview.

Stevenson was out of his depth. He didn't want to insult Speck, make him lawyer up, not the man who had killed the neighborhood's Rovers and Whiskers, and probably Clyde Darling and countless other young boys. Not the man who probably this very minute was hiding her nephew somewhere in the belly of Byrd's Landing. Raven wanted to shout at Stevenson, but knew that the idiot wouldn't hear her. Banging once on the window would have to suffice, so she did that. At least all three of them jumped.

As for himself, Speck was content to play them, using the flat of his big and now dirty hand to push his stringy hair out of his face. She recognized the gleam of amusement in his eyes when he glanced at the two-way after she banged on it. The chief, who was standing beside her behind the glass, gave her a warning look. He knew as well as she that Stevenson and Goldie were being played, but for some reason, the chief was letting Stevenson take the lead.

Finally, she couldn't take it anymore. She stalked away from the viewing area and made her way to intake. That's where Speck would land after Stevenson finished whispering sweet nothings into Speck's disgusting ear and getting nothing in return.

Raven stopped at the door of the office used for processing prisoners into the jail just one door beyond. The room hadn't changed much since she left; it was a tidy square with a file cabinet in one corner, a plastic fern sweaty with dust in the other, and a metal desk above which were framed photos of the current president, the governor of Louisiana, the mayor of Byrd's Landing, and the chief, in that particular order. The officer behind the desk was also familiar, a woman with a head of pressed curls. Marna Williamson gazed at Raven with all the suspicion borne from the trouble Raven helped her find during their junior high school days.

"Hello, Marna."

"No. Nope. Nopity. Nope. Nope," Marna said. She snapped the manual she had been reading shut as if adding a last bit of finality in response to the favor she knew Raven was about to ask. She sat up straighter to get ready for the battle.

"Oh come on, Marna," Raven said, "I haven't even said what I wanted yet."

"Girl, you don't have to open your mouth for me to know that ain't nothing but trouble gone come out of it."

"Marna...."

Raven stopped as another officer in the room cleared his throat.

"That's Officer Williamson to you," he said.

The officer hooked his thumbs into his gun belt. This was no small feat for him because he had to clear a gut as wide as the Red River in order to do it.

"Officer Taylor," she said, smiling but not meaning one inch of it. "Twice since I've been back is a little too much even after a year of not having to lay eyes on you. The last time we met you were brushing the lint from Detective Breaker's overcoat."

"You can go now," Marna said. "We're expecting someone."

"I heard," Raven answered. "That's why I'm here."

"Nope."

"Is that the only word you know?"

"When it comes to you, yep."

"I think what Officer Williamson is trying to say is that you don't belong here."

"This conversation is between me and Marna, Officer," Raven said, resisting the urge to call him a big, slew-footed, red-faced, bald-headed waste of space.

Marna made a big production of lining up the top edge of the manual she had been reading with the stapler and Scotch Tape on her desk. "I would appreciate you not calling my husband names," she said.

"I didn't call him any...wait, what?"

"I know you, Raven. I know the look on your face when you're about to go off on a name-calling rant. And yes, Newell and I were married six months ago. If you'd stuck around, you would have known that."

Raven glanced at Newell Taylor, who was now smirking at her mercilessly.

Pointing at him, she said, "But he doesn't like black people."

"I like black people just fine," he said. "I just don't like you."

"I need a favor, Marna," Raven said.

"I don't have one to give," Marna answered. "But if it makes you feel better and go away faster, tell me what you got."

"Willie Lee Speck is going to come through here in about the next fifteen minutes or so."

"So they tell me."

"I need you to give me about ten minutes alone with him," Raven said.

"No," Marna and Taylor said in unison.

"I'll make it worth your while."

"How?" Taylor asked.

"You, big guy, fifty bucks?" Raven said. She ran the tips of her fingers over the cover of the manual Marna had been reading. "You, Marna. I'll help you study for the sergeant's exam."

"What good would an exam be without my job?"

"Nobody has to know," Raven answered.

"Speck would know," Taylor said. "How are you going to make sure he keeps his mouth shut?"

Raven shrugged. "I have a hunting knife in my boot," she said. "I can gut him."

"People are right about you. You're a freak. And the price just went up to a hundred bucks."

"I'm joking," Raven said. "Look, just think of it as a conversation between friends. Off the record."

"Yeah," Taylor said. "I could tell by your face that you're old friends."

Raven touched the bruises on the right side of her face. The places where Speck smacked her throbbed and were probably turning a nice shade of purple by now. She laughed a little. "I see news travels fast."

"Why do you need to talk to him?" Taylor asked.

Sensing that she would probably get further with him than with Marna, she turned to him. "Okay, cards on the table," she said. "He may know where my nephew is. You know he's missing, right? As soon as I find him and bring him home, I'm off the force and out of your lives. But every minute that passes decreases my chances of doing that."

"Newell, you can't seriously be thinking about letting her—" Marna began.

"He's fifteen." Raven meant to say the words with bravado, but they emerged laced with a quiet desperation.

Officer Taylor's mustache worked. He cleared his throat and looked down at the floor.

"Babe, you can't be serious," Marna said. "Besides, I heard that Stevenson is in there talking to him right now. If Speck is hiding her nephew, he'll get it out of him."

Raven looked at Marna. She said, "Have you met Stevenson? Marna?"

"Oh, hell."

"Give me ten minutes," Raven said. "I just need him to tell me where Noe is."

"How do we keep him from wiping the linoleum with your face?" Taylor asked.

"He won't," Raven said. "I don't think he has any fight left in him. And if you're so worried about that, cuff him to the table." She pointed to the hook in the metal table where the prisoners sat.

The room was silent a couple of moments. Raven felt something in Marna yield.

"Cameras?" she asked.

"I'll take care of them," Raven said, not knowing how she was going to keep that promise, hoping that the chief would be so thrilled when she found Noe that he would overlook them.

"You better make sure," Taylor said.

"I will."

CHAPTER FORTY

Speck sat cuffed to the ring on the metal desk when Raven returned to intake. He smiled when he saw her, smiled wider when he noticed the mess that was the right side of her face.

"Looks like you got a hurtin' on you, Rave Girl."

She stood with her back and one foot against the door as she regarded Speck. One of the last times she saw Noe, he was surrounded by people who loved him and by people who were beginning to love him, like Edmée, Imogene and Billy Ray. She remembered his birthday party being the first time she had ever seen him smile without trying since he had come to live with Cameron. She remembered poking instead of hugging him because he didn't like to be touched, not yet. She remembered rubbing Clyde's shoulder and that silly memory game he played with Edmée.

And then she thought about how she last saw Clyde. She tried not to imagine seeing Noe that way. With every ounce of will in her body that her exhausted mind could control, she resisted the urge to fly at Speck, to beat out of him what he had done to Noe. Instead, she walked over, squatted on her heels so she could look up into his face.

"What happened, Willie Lee? To the house, to the wife, to the two-point-five kids? Where are they?"

He spat in her face. She took a Kleenex from the box on Marna's desk and wiped it away. She crumpled the Kleenex in her hands dangling between her knees. She wondered how fast she could get to her weapon if she had to use it.

"It was a secret, wasn't it? The hoard? The filth? Is that why the wife left you? Or did you make her up?"

"Hell no," he said. "I ain't that crazy."

"Can you tell me how crazy? Because what I saw was that you're crazy enough to kill animals. Does that crazy extend to boys?"

"I ain't had nothing to do with that. I ain't no fucking animal," he said.

"There were corpses everywhere, Willie Lee."

"You invaded my space," he said. "Besides, you didn't find corpses, only carcasses."

"What will they find in that hoard? Your son, JoJo? Lucy, your daughter? Are they going to find Suzy?"

He went to spit again. But suddenly she was pressing her hand so hard over his mouth that he couldn't part his lips to bite her, like he was trying like hell to do. He swiveled his head from side to side, his lank hair swinging with each movement, brushing the back of her hand. Raven had one foster parent who used to press her knuckles into the side of Raven's head. To make the pain as deep as she could make it, the woman would hold the middle knuckle higher than the others, digging until Raven cried for her to stop.

That was what Raven was thinking when she pressed her hand over his mouth, how easy it would be to increase the pain by squeezing as hard as she could with just her forefinger and thumb. She didn't like the way the pain in Speck's eyes made her feel. His discomfort flooded her with good feelings. Speck pressed his big body against the back of the chair. He tried to speak but couldn't get his mouth open beneath her hand.

"I don't like being spit on," she said, her voice soft, unhurried, devoid of emotion.

His movements stopped at the sound of her voice. She could see the fear in his eyes.

"I want to remind you that it's just you and me here," she said.

He nodded slowly.

"Now, are you going to keep your bodily fluids to yourself?"

He nodded again. She took her hand down. His eyes glittered with pain. Spittle frothed white at the corners of his trembling mouth.

He took a few deep breaths before answering. "I done told that

Stevenson guy that I ain't touched none of them boys, and I ain't done nothing to my family."

Raven said nothing. She waited for him to continue.

He told her that at first the job didn't get to him, cleaning up after the dead, most from violent or horrific deaths, some from old age, filling dumpster after dumpster with the things they loved, photographs no one cared to look at again, books with writing in the margins and forget-me-nots pressed between the pages. He didn't mind heaving a favorite chair into the trash or throwing out magazines they liked so much that they had kept them years after the publication date. Not a lot of sentimental things survived. He was fine with that.

What got to him was how the relatives would only hang around until they could get their hands on the belongings that could be worth money, and Ozy waiting there all the while in his cowboy hat like a greedy ghoul.

"It got so that I couldn't throw anything of my own away. I didn't have no trouble with anybody else's stuff, but mine, I just couldn't do it. I just saw myself disappearing tiny piece by tiny piece every time I put something in the trash can. And I had to have more. I kept buying stuff. The wife put up with it for a bit, but next thing I know I come home to a note saying she was leaving and filing for divorce."

"Is that when you started killing those boys?"

"I ain't killed nobody!" he said. "I just got a few head problems, that's all. You would, too, if you saw what I saw."

"I understand that, Willie Lee. Just tell me where Noe is," Raven said, hoping that where violence failed pleading would work. "Just tell me and I swear I'm gone from your life."

He jerked at the chain. "I ain't killed nobody!"

"Come on, Willie Lee!" she shouted over the rattling chain.

She whipped out her phone and started swiping through the crime scene photos of the victims, ending with Clyde lying on the autopsy table, and Noe, smiling and alive, in the last picture. She tapped the screen.

"I can't do anything for those other boys," she said. "But I promised my brother that I would bring this one home."

He didn't even look at Noe's picture. "Then maybe you done gone and lied because I ain't got no idea where he is." He shouted it so loud that he was out of breath. He wiped his mouth with his free hand.

Raven tried another tactic. "Why did you kill all those animals? Were you practicing, trying to figure out how to move up to human beings?"

Speck threw his head back. "Fuck, you just don't listen, do you?" he said. "I ain't killed no boys!"

"Then why the animals?"

"Ain't no crime to study animals. That's what I was doing. Studying how to stuff 'em. Just another way to make money. Taxidermy."

They both knew he was lying. Raven didn't challenge him. He did his best to try to cross his arms without much success because of the chain. Raven hung her head.

"Let me see the picture again," he said.

Raven showed him the picture of Noe.

"I ain't got no use for the live one," he said. "Show me the other one. The one of Clyde."

"Why. So you can get off?"

"You know, you're a sick fuck. You might not like me but I'm a human being just like everyone else. I know I got some problems, but I don't like it that somebody did Clyde like that." *That's why you were so willing to talk to us earlier,* she thought. But instead of challenging him more, she showed him the picture.

"Huh," he said. "That's why y'all think I did it? Because I have a bolt gun?"

"Not a lot of people run around with bolt guns, Willie Lee," Raven said.

"Maybe not," he said. "But farmers do. And it looks like whoever did this used a bolt gun. But I can guarantee you that it wasn't mine."

"Then whose was it?"

"That I don't know. All I did was kill a dog or two, feral dogs, tormenting the kids in the neighborhood...."

Raven snorted. "So you say. Does that make you feel better?"

"As a matter of fact, it sure does. And I'm telling you sure as shittin' that I ain't done no human being that way."

"Well, you better do something to convince me of that, because that's what the chief and Stevenson are looking to take you down for."

He chewed his lips. "That thing hurt what you did with my mouth."

Raven waited.

"And you looked crazy while you did it, so if you're calling me that, I guess I'm in good company."

"You got anything for me?"

"You need to talk to Ozy," he said. "He the one gave me that bolt gun."

"Ozy?"

"Yep, just like us, he's crazier than a bag of cats."

"You're telling me that you don't know where he got it?"

"He said it was in a box of stuff he took while we were cleaning the office of that lawyer that got beat. Ronnie True."

"Ronnie True?" Raven said. "Breaker said you didn't clean up that scene."

"Aw, what does he know?" Speck said. "Who do you think Mr. Goody Two Shoes Trauma Cleaning Service comes running to when he gets too busy for a job but still wants his money? He contracts with me, throws the job my way. He don't care as long as he gets his cut."

"So you telling me you cleaned the True scene?"

"Yep," he said. "I remember I had two jobs that day, so I had Ozy helping me box stuff up. I told him he could take anything he wanted for helping me."

"Real free with other people's belongings, aren't you, Willie Lee?"

"The family said they didn't want anything in that office. Blood was everywhere. I mean everywhere. They told me to get rid of it all. What did you want me to do? Burn it?"

"If that bolt gun was at the scene Breaker would have had it bagged for evidence," Raven said.

"Well, maybe he was in a hurry. I heard the police hurting for people."

"So why would Ozy give you the bolt gun?"

"He was thanking me for all the other stuff I gave him that day. He knew I was studying taxidermy, and told me I might be able to use it."

"Did you let him take the bear shoulder mount taxidermy, too?"

"What bear taxidermy?"

"Are you playing with me now? There was a mounted bear in True's office. I saw a piece of it, a claw, in Ozy's truck with a whole bunch of other junk."

"No," he said. "I ain't let him take no taxidermy from that office. Why, if I saw anything like that, I would have kept it for myself."

"Where is Ozy?" she asked him.

"What's in it for me?"

"I don't really have to answer that, now do I? You're about to go down for being a serial killer. I'm trying to find the man who killed Clyde and kidnapped Noe. I believe the man who's been going around killing these boys has him stowed away somewhere. I find him, you walk. We're not working at cross purposes, Willie Lee. So where is he?"

"Ozy usually hangs around the abandoned bridge out of town," he said. "But all ain't right with him upstairs. You might not get much out of him."

She stood up and walked to the door. Before she could turn the handle, Willie Lee said, "Raven, when I get out of here, are you still going to let me do that Oral Justice job for you?"

Raven felt sorry for him. He didn't know it yet, but his life had changed. Once the news about his hoard hit the paper, and the *Byrd's Landing Review* got their hands on that house of horrors in the shed, especially after what he did to those dogs, he wouldn't ever work in this town again. She gave him a wan smile, and said, "Sure, Willie Lee. I'd appreciate you helping me out on that."

CHAPTER FORTY-ONE

Raven found Ozy exactly where Willie Lee told her she would. He was beneath a long-abandoned bridge leading out of town. The place he called home was a blue tarp held up by sticks, and his kitchen a Weber grill pressed up against the bridge's crumbling wing wall.

Raven could smell the sizzling meat as she got out of her car. Ozy looked up from the Weber and waved. He didn't seem surprised at all to see her.

"Hi, Ozy," Raven said, looking around. "This looks comfy."

"It's all right for me." Pointing to the blue tarp behind him, he said, "This here is for when it ain't raining. I use the truck when the water come down, especially like it's been lately."

Raven gave Ozy an appraising look. Of all the times she had seen him, she had never really talked to him. She had thought of him as just Speck's shadow, someone who followed him around waiting for Speck to throw him treasure from the dead.

"You got something for me?" he said, a hopeful spark in his eyes.

Raven chuckled. "What do you do with all the stuff you collect anyway?"

He pointed toward the mouth of the bridge. "Back there," he said. "Behind where I park my VW. I'm building me another junkyard. I could use some new stuff now that there ain't no more Willie Lee. I heard that y'all took him to jail. You sure you ain't got nothing for me?"

"Only a few questions, Ozy," Raven said, holding out her empty hands.

"Is it about Willie Lee?" he asked.

"Somewhat," Raven said, knowing that she would have to be careful. She didn't know how close Ozy and Speck were. Raven knew that

Ozy came from a long line of junkmen. It started off as a legitimate business. His family owned the junkyard on the outskirts of town, but when Byrd's Landing started growing his family's property fell victim to eminent domain. They gave them fair market value for the property. It was just enough money for Ozy's father to drink himself to death. After the father died, Ozy took the old VW, and as if he were acting on brainstem instinct, started collecting junk around town mostly by going door-to-door. She didn't know how he ended up with Speck, but now Ozy no longer depended on the living for their cast-offs. He took from the dead. Not exactly legal, but for the most part no one challenged him or Speck.

"That man ain't kilt nobody," Ozy said.

"That's not what the police think," Raven said. "Looks like he was bragging about one kind of life, and living another."

"Ah, he was just kind of sick in the head from cleaning up after dead folk," Ozy said, pushing three hot links around on the grill. "His wife left him because he liked the stuff more than I did. Took the kids. He went a lil' crazy after that. Lost both his first and second mind." He paused for a second. "I think it was dealing with all them dead people's leavings. Oh, he tried to be tough and all that, but it got to him. He kept wanting to find the secret. Started cutting things up to see how they go together. Went cuckoo bird."

"He said you gave him a bolt gun for stunning animals?"

"That I did. From that lawyer's office. Thought he could use it more than me with what he was doing."

He stretched his neck to look beyond her shoulder where the Mustang was parked. "You sure you ain't got nothing in your trunk you don't want? Lots of people keep things in the trunk that they stop using. They forget about it. I can help take some of that stuff off your hands."

"No, Ozy. I don't have anything in my trunk."

"Backseats?" he said.

"Nothing."

"Well." He watched her. "Since you helped me with the onions I guess it's all right."

"That's what I'm here about."

"You can't have 'em back. They mine now."

"I know that," Raven said. "I don't want them, but I wanted to ask you about something else I thought I saw that day you and Willie Lee were at the motel."

"You mean that shotgun place?"

"Yeah, sure. The motel where the young woman killed herself with a shotgun. The day when I told you that you needed to clean the blood off those ceramic onions."

"Come on over here."

Raven came closer. She stood next to him while he attended to the hot links on the grill.

"Interest you in something to eat? Looks like you could use regeneration."

"Sure. I feel like I haven't eaten in days."

He reached into a cooler and used a bottled water to wash his hands, and then sanitized them with Purell. They sat on the sidewalk eating the hot links and washing them down with bottles of cold water. Raven let the chilly night cool the bruises on her face, and the fresh air dislodge the images of Speck's hoard in her head. Even though she knew there was work ahead, sitting and eating with Ozy was a welcome break.

"Lots of folks think I'm crazy."

Raven barked a laugh. "Fill out a membership card and join the club," she said, then asked, "Are you?"

"A little bit," he said. "But not dangerous crazy. Not like those folk going around killing people. I'm just crazy because I got a dream."

"Rebuilding your daddy's junkyard?" Raven asked, wiping the grease from her mouth with her jacket sleeve.

"Sure do, and it's a dream worth having. I can show those assholes who run us out something. We Andersons keep coming back. They ain't gone keep us down for long."

Raven almost said that they kept him down for the last two decades, but decided to keep her mouth shut.

"Ozy," she said after a polite interval. "I'm looking for something."

"What's that? I ain't ready to sell anything yet."

"I just want to see it for now."

"Yeah?"

"The other day at the shotgun place, I could have sworn that I saw a bear's paw in the back of your truck."

"An ole black bear paw with its claws out?"

Raven nodded, and showed him a photo from her Android of the bear mount from True's office. "This. I think I saw a piece of this."

She was losing him. He scooted away from her with suspicion in his bright blue eyes.

"I don't want it," she said quickly. "Not now anyway. And if I did, I'll pay you for it."

"No pay," he said. "Trade me for it."

"Okay, I'll trade something for it."

"Something in your trunk?"

She let that go.

"I just need to know, did Willie Lee give that to you?"

"Why would Willie Lee give it to me?"

"Well, you follow...I mean he's the one you work with the most, right?"

"I do. But he ain't the one who give it to me."

"Where did you get it?"

He sat for a moment looking down at his hands. He took a deep breath, and sighed. "Well, you gone have to arrest me if I tell you."

"Why would I arrest you?"

"Because I took it, that's all. It was in the garbage, sticking up, I swear. But I still took it without asking. Knew it wasn't right when I did it."

"Whose garbage was it in?" Raven asked him.

He thought for a while. Raven could see him searching his memory. Then he said, "Sometimes I do work in those fancy houses on Lakeshore. They have me clean up and cart away junk. I got this at one of those houses. A fancy white house."

"Do you know whose house it was?"

"Not directly. I was tootling my van up and down the roads over there and knocking on doors, and I knocked on hers. Didn't really keep track of where I was."

"Hers?"

"That's right. White house. She said she had some old stuff in the backyard I might like, so I went round back. I didn't see anything, excepting for the bear paw sticking up out of the garbage, so I just took it." He stopped. "I thought if I asked her for it she'd realize that it was worth something and say no."

"Ozy," Raven prompted. "Who was it?"

"Don't know her name, but I stopped by there on Friday past to tell her that I was sorry about taking the bear paw, and asked her if she wanted it back. She pretended like she didn't know what I was talking about, but I knew she did because she went all white. So, I figured that she wasn't supposed to throw it away. I was trying to apologize and said I'd go get it right that minute and she could have it back but she kept saying, no, it was fine. And then I heard snickering and Clyde was there all dirty, so I told her that I'd help them in the garden to make up for what I done but she sent me away."

"Wait," Raven said. "Are you telling me you saw Clyde Friday evening?"

"Sure did. He and another boy was helping the woman who had the bear paw in the garbage."

"Do you know Clyde was killed, and another boy is missing?" Raven said. "Did you tell the police?"

"Well, now I'm right sorry about Clyde. I don't know nothing about another boy missing. I don't have no TV and the radio in the VW's busted. The only reason I know y'all took Willie Lee to jail is because them other boys what work for him told me."

"Willie Lee didn't tell you about Clyde?" Raven asked.

"Willie Lee and me don't talk unless it's about stuff we find."

"What about the people who work with Willie Lee? They didn't tell you Clyde was murdered?"

"Why would they tell me? They don't like me or Clyde no how. They think Clyde's taking jobs away, and that I'm touched in the head.

But they did tell me that they done arrested Willie Lee for killing all them boys."

"You sure it was Clyde you saw. Clyde Darling?" Raven asked.

"He was there. But I tell you, nobody should've thrown that bear paw in the garbage. It looked all beat to hell, but somebody could fix that up."

"And you don't know her name? Could you describe her?"

"I don't take no names, and don't study no faces that don't mean nothing to me. I just pay attention to the junk."

"Can you take me back there? Tonight?"

"I can't, they'll take me to jail for stealing the bear paw. And that crazy lady may go and say I tried to do something to her. I don't remember no how. We'd have to go up and down all those side streets until we hit on the one, and I don't pay a lot of attention, so we might even miss it."

"This is important," Raven said.

"I'm afraid, Miss Raven, you'd be wasting a lot of time because I don't know where it's at. Besides, you know what else is important?"

She took a deep, defeated breath. "No. What, Ozy?"

"Me breathing fresh air. Now kindly say thank you for the dinner and leave me be."

Raven looked at him for a moment. He had removed his cowboy hat before he sat down to eat. His peanut head was shaved so haphazardly that only a fuzz of uneven gray remained. His bright eyes, as alert as a bird's, appeared to be the only thing left alive in a face that had become a nest of wrinkles.

"I don't believe you," she said.

"Believe what?"

"That you forgot where you got the bear's paw."

He stood up when she did, wiping his greasy hands on his denim shorts.

"So, is this where you do your cop thing and make me? You gone knock me around some? I told you that you'd be wasting your time."

Raven smiled. "I'm not going to make you. But I'll trade you for your time. You can have anything in my trunk, anything I left on my backseats if you take a ride on over to Lakeshore with me."

"You just said you didn't have anything," he said.

"I know what I said. But how do you know I was telling the truth?"

"How do I know you telling the truth now?"

"Suit yourself."

She thanked him for the food, and turned to go. She hadn't taken two steps before he was running to catch up. After he got into the passenger's seat and clicked the seatbelt across his thin body, he craned his neck so he could look into the backseat to see what kind of a deal he made.

*   *   *

They drove for hours, until the evening darkness flowed through the streets of Byrd's Landing along with them. They drove up and down Lakeshore, along the side streets feeding into it, and several times through the adjoining neighborhoods, when Ozy, in a sudden flash of inspiration, exclaimed that maybe it wasn't Lakeshore where he found the bear paw after all. At one point she thought he was playing with her, but when she saw him with an index finger pressed to his chin, his face set in concentration, she backed away from that thought. It looked like he was really trying.

As they parked in front of Edmée's house for a second time, Raven asked him again, "Are you sure this isn't the place?"

He studied the late vegetable garden flanking the wide lawn, the stark, looming whiteness of the house.

"I would've remembered those vegetables, those beets and things." He stopped and turned to her. "Who puts greens in they front yard? I'm old and don't pay too much attention sometimes, but I hope I would have remembered that."

"But the house is white," Raven said. "Like you said."

"Lots of white houses around here," he said, his bottom lip poked out. "I'm getting pretty tired driving up and down these streets."

Raven sighed and started to open the car door. He grabbed her arm. "What you doing?"

"Maybe if we walk up to the front door it'll jog your memory."

"It won't."

"Well, maybe if you saw the woman again? The backyard?"

"The house dark. Ain't nobody home," he said. "All I remember is the stuff I get. I don't study in particular how no house looks."

"Then how did you find it when you went back to apologize?"

"I was driving my truck. I remember better when I drive on my own."

"Then let's go back and get your truck. You drive."

"It ain't no use," he said, close to tears. "I just don't remember. I ain't as crazy as Willie Lee, but I can only keep track of one thing at a time, and that's the stuff for my junkyard. Now can you take me back so we can finish this trade?"

Raven let her forehead fall against the steering wheel. Ozy was right. Edmée's house looked dark and empty. Even if she did have something to do with Clyde's death, and Noe's disappearance, she wouldn't have used her house as the place for her crimes. Besides, the video evidence showed Noe being driven in a direction going out of Byrd's Landing. She put the car in gear and drove back to the abandoned bridge.

When she opened her trunk, he clapped his hands like an excited child. She didn't protest when he grabbed a jack, and her first-aid kit. From her backseat, he took a fleece car blanket and a six-pack of bottled water. As he happily walked away from her car with his arms full of his new treasures, Raven thought bitterly, *You have a nice night, too, old man. I hope all that crap you collect doesn't wear out before you do.*

264 • FAYE SNOWDEN

CHAPTER FORTY-TWO

Raven called Stevenson from the car. To his credit, he picked up on the first ring.

"I got something," Raven said without preamble, the adrenaline pumping so hard she felt as if she were about to jump out of her skin.

"I can't talk to you," Stevenson responded.

"Why?"

"You're off the case."

"Well, at least I'm not fired like you, you idiot."

"Yeah, about that. The chief found out. Giving me a pass because he needs my help right now. I can't piss him off any more than I already have. I'm on thin ice."

"And here I was thinking we were getting along so well."

He hung up. She fished Goldie's card out of her jacket pocket.

"Whatever you want," he said when he answered his cell, "no can do."

"Didn't you hand me this very same card I'm holding right now saying you'd help me when we first met?" she asked him.

"That was before I found out that you were covering up for your brother, the serial murderer."

"He didn't do it!" Raven shouted.

"So I've heard. Neither did your father." And then silence on the other end of the line.

Raven beat the already cracked Android against the dashboard. The chief? Now that would be a laugh riot. Billy Ray would have been an option in any other case, but if what she was thinking were true, she couldn't go to him without proof.

She had it wrong. She had been running around thinking that by doing things her way she would find Noe, and save her brother from himself. During the entire time, Floyd sat right beside her in the shotgun seat, grinning his maniacal, happy grin, egging her on. She'd never be able to escape him or the ghosts of his kills. Now that she needed help, there was no one willing to give it.

With these thoughts running wild in her head, she didn't realize how fast the Mustang was hurtling down the deserted two-lane. When her headlights caught a man standing in the middle of the road, she slammed on her brakes with both feet. The man didn't move. He just stood there as if waiting for the Mustang to smash him out of existence. And that scrap of white floating at his throat? It was there because he was dressed like a priest.

Raven swerved with her feet smashing down on the brakes. The Mustang squealed like a pig at slaughter. The back end flew to the right. She jerked the wheel into the slide to straighten the front end. By the time the car stopped, she found herself with the front wheels in the mud on the shoulder, the bumper just kissing the deeper water of the bayou.

Her flashlight was already in her hand when she jumped out of the car. She searched the road. All around was deserted, the only sound breaking the silence the low hum of insects and soft caws of birds in the marsh. Above her a velvet darkness shrouded the sky, with a few bright stars struggling to break through.

She leaned against the back bumper and put her hands on her knees. She panted into the waving grasses on the shoulder. She knew the truth now. She hadn't gained peace from Lovelle's death. In fact, no one could gain peace from killing. By becoming a judge, jury and executioner, she became one with her father. The only thing different between them was the body count. She was paying a price. Her sanity was slowly slipping away.

No one was stalking her. There was no man beneath the light in the parking lot of Chastain's, there was no one in her apartment whispering *repent* in her ear, or leaving a snake in her bed. Billy Ray was right. It was probably someone's pet that had climbed into the open window. And the figure she thought she saw at Speck's house? She laughed a bit now, roughly. She had just been knocked in the head. There was even blood, the wound on her scalp still tender.

She straightened, took what she thought was a deep, cleansing breath. When she let it out, her soul still felt stained around the edges. If Noe wasn't out there, she would have given up at that moment. But instead of swimming out to sea as Floyd had teased her about a lifetime ago, she could have simply walked out into the bayou until the murky water replaced the air in her lungs. But she had a promise to keep.

Lack of sleep and eating catch-can had become as much of an enemy as the killer terrorizing Byrd's Landing. She stood, swallowed, and got back into the driver's seat. She cranked the ignition, put the car in reverse. The tires sputtered in the mud for a few seconds, but then they caught solid road and she guided the Mustang bumpily backwards.

Pointing toward town, she sat there with the engine running for a few moments. Her mind was going in eighty different directions, what she had learned in the last few days swirling like loose paper in a strong wind. There was Claude DeWitt and his murderous adopted parents. Ronnie True's beat down and his client list and his shady adoption ring. Then there was the piece of bear taxidermy found in the trashcan at a house near Lakeshore, the same place where Ozy swears he saw Clyde. Raven didn't want to believe that it could be true. But sometimes the evidence pointed in a direction that you had no choice but to go.

A glimpse of her face in the rearview showed a determined woman, but a woman who looked older than her years, and frightened beyond reason. She called Imogene, and then Breaker. After she hung up, she said to the dark night all around her, "Hold on, Noe, honey. I'm coming. One more day."

CHAPTER FORTY-THREE

Raven told Breaker that she had something that would see this thing over in a few days. The trick was that she needed him in order to make it vanish like a bad dream. She had told Imogene the same thing, and lucky for her, Imogene didn't hang up. They both agreed to meet her at Imogene's place the following morning.

The three of them were now sitting at Imogene's heavy kitchen table which was cleared of its vase of silk magnolias and matching place settings. Breaker had removed the pages from the casefile on True. They were spread all out on the table so they could absorb the full picture. Imogene had added her banker's box of notes on the Claude DeWitt case, the unfortunate boy whose adopted parents had tortured him to death.

"I'm still not convinced on how the Sleeping Boy killer is connected to the DeWitt case," Breaker said.

"Because he's the one that started it all, the one that brought it all down on this town's head."

"How did he do that?" Imogene said.

The way she sat there with her hair wrapped, her arms folded across her fuzzy robe, reminded Raven of one of the old people when they got tired of talking to you. *Too much wisdom and exhaustion to argue with a fool*, her face said, *but I'll ask you a question just to make you happy*. Even though it was going on one o'clock in the afternoon, Imogene had told both of them that she wasn't changing. It was her day off and she wasn't putting on clothes or makeup for anybody.

"I know you have a hard time believing me right now, Imogene. But trust me, this story is the key. You broke this story on a Friday. Ronnie True got his butt beat that Sunday."

"What door do you think that key's going to open?" Imogene asked.

"Cameron's prison door, and the door to the place where the killer hides his victims."

"Tell it to me again," Breaker said.

"The motive for the killing is revenge. The killer's trying to settle the score for Claude DeWitt's death."

"Still don't see how you're figuring that," Breaker said.

She placed a hand over his wrist. God, it hurt to move, but she would have had her pain magnified by ninety times if she could get him to understand. "It's in your notes, DeShawn. You found the first connection. Ronnie True and his adoption ring placed this child. I'm sure of it."

"You mean you're guessing that's why True got his ass kicked?" Imogene said.

"Yes, it's a hunch, and I think it's the first link in the chain."

Imogene stood up and dug into the banker's box on the table. "Funny how I got all this shit on computer, but I find things faster by going to paper files. You're right, Toulouse was the judge on the adoption case."

"His son was Henri, the one at Memorial," Breaker said.

"Right. And he was found at the construction site of the new obstetrics wing where all the babies are born. That's like the icing on the cake for this perp," Raven said.

"With a cherry on top," Imogene said. "Maybe he's satisfied."

Her fingers dug into the collar of her robe, closing and twisting it so the scars Lovelle left were covered. Those scars would be there for life. They said quite plainly what they were. Someone had tried to strangle Imogene to death. Raven knew that Imogene wanted the Sleeping Boy killer to be finished. She wanted him to sink back into the soil of Byrd's Landing so she didn't have to be reminded of how Lovelle cursed this town with his brand of terror.

Raven thought about letting her think that the Sleeping Boy killer was done. But Floyd was right. *Souls don't die.* Well, neither did evil, especially in places like Byrd's Landing. If she learned anything in these last few days, she couldn't live the rest of her life doing bad things for good reasons. She had to face that she didn't know what good was, not for anybody. Not even herself.

In a voice that she would use with a hurt child, Raven said, "This person will never be satisfied. Revenge was this killer's excuse for killing, that's all. The person doing this just needs to destroy. After they're done with this, they'll find another excuse. The killing won't stop until we stop them."

Imogene listened without comment. When Raven was done, Imogene looked down at her twisting fingers and let the robe go.

"What about the other boys?" Breaker said.

"It's all here," Raven said, hands held above the pages of the notebook spread all over the table. "The first boy, Michael Jean Baptiste? He was related to the couple who starved DeWitt to death. Elroy Maloy? Son of the social worker who cleared the parents for the adoption. You already know about Toulouse. Everyone involved in the case has had a young male family member killed by our perp."

"He's not my perp," Imogene said. "I'm not laying claim to him."

"And the dump sites?" Breaker said.

"All places of power. The bank, BLPD courtyard, the mayor's porch. It's as if they're giving the town a dressing down, like they're saying this is your fault for not taking care of your babies."

"How in the natural fuck did I miss all this?" Breaker said.

"Because when you started to figure it out with Toulouse, the chief shut you down. Not your fault."

"We could have saved lives," he said.

"Welcome to BLPD homicide, where politics is the first order of business."

"Could have saved lives," Imogene mocked. "Put regret in one hand, and shit in the other. See which one fills up faster. Now that you got what you want, Raven, walk your ass on down to the chief so I can get on with my day."

"Now, you know I can't do that," Raven said. "I don't have a bridge left to burn down there."

"Day ain't over yet," Imogene said.

"So, you think one of DeWitt's birth parents is the killer? Or someone close like that?" Breaker asked.

Raven turned to gaze at Breaker. She looked at him a long time, thinking. Well, they already thought she was crazy. Might as well keep talking and remove all doubt.

"I think it's the birth mother, or someone doing the bidding of the birth mother."

She told them about Ozy and the piece of bear claw he had in the back of his VW truck.

"How in the hell can those guys get away with just taking people's stuff?" Breaker asked.

"Where did he say he got it?" Imogene asked.

"White house on Lakeshore. It was in the outside garbage."

Imogene started laughing. She stood up laughing, punctuating it with a 'Lord, Lord' on the end. Shaking her head, she went into the kitchen and came back with a pitcher of Bloody Marys she had been trying to pawn off on them all morning.

"Raven, I always thought you were crazy, but whew, chile, I never thought you were as crazy as you really are. White house on Lakeshore. You sure you don't want some of this? That and two aspirins from the beating you took might make you come to your senses."

"Who else could it be?" Raven asked her.

"Well, if Ozy is telling the truth, and not making it up, it could be anybody up or down that street," Imogene said.

"Everybody up and down the street don't know Clyde and Noe. Edmée Crowley does," Raven said.

"Wait? You mean Dr. Fabian Long's wife? The CEO at Memorial?" Breaker said.

"The one and only," Imogene said dryly.

"That's a stretch," Breaker said. "But hell, I'm willing to play. Sure it ain't him?"

"Yes, I'm sure. It's her," Raven said.

"But she loves kids," Imogene said. "She's done so much for kids in Byrd's Landing it ain't even funny."

"That's why she slaughtered them like animals so they wouldn't suffer, washed them, wrapped them in blankets," Raven said. "Because she still cares."

"Why Clyde and Noe?" Imogene said.

"Because Clyde's mother worked for Ronnie True. His mother said that Clyde liked money, liked to work for it. But his stepfather said he liked to hustle for it. What if Clyde tried to blackmail Edmée?"

"Please, a young kid like that? Blackmail?" Imogene said. "What has she got to hide? And why Noe?"

"I think Noe was unexpected. She lured Clyde over and he asked Noe to go with him. Maybe Clyde was scared, I don't know. As far as what she's got to hide is concerned, she may seem like she's open about her childhood, but she's real careful about sharing the details. Copycat, maybe," Raven said. "Or she could also be the Sleeping Boy killer."

"Edmée doesn't have it in her. She'd be too afraid of breaking a nail," Imogene said.

"The other night she told me she was a country girl. She and her cousin lived on a farm."

"Girl, that evidence is as weak as a wet cracker."

"Maybe, but not when you put it all together with what Ozy said. And take a look again at Claude DeWitt's death, the day he died. July 12th."

"What has that got to do with anything?" Imogene said.

"Remember Noe's birthday party, and that memory game she's always playing with Clyde? That was the only date Edmée didn't want to comment on. I think she was too upset to answer the question."

"How can you remember the date from a game?" Breaker asked.

"That was my stepmother's birthday," Raven said. "That's how I remembered it."

"Still pretty thin," Breaker said.

A frustration so strong welled up in Raven that she found her hands moving before her thoughts commanded them. The next thing she knew the papers Breaker had laid out on the table were in the air and fluttering to the floor.

"I know it's circumstantial. But it's all I got," she said.

"What about the boot print from Memorial? The soil samples. Get anything from that yet?" Breaker asked.

"The bootprint is from an Ariat all-weather work boot, but that doesn't tell us anything unless we want to knock on every door of Byrd's Landing like we were in a blooming Cinderella movie. It's way too soon for the soil sample," Raven said. "If only we could prove that Claude DeWitt was Edmee's kid. The timing's right, but she had an abortion."

"What?" Imogene said. "That girl didn't have an abortion. She gave that baby up for adoption."

"How do you know that?" Breaker said.

"Because the floozy was trying to take my man," Imogene said.

"He's not your man," Raven said.

"He is, he just doesn't know it yet. I did a little checking to see if she had some skeletons in her closet aside from being married. I needed to know what I was up against. I found out that she had a kid that she gave up for adoption."

"You mean you sitting here the whole time with that info and you decide to keep it to yourself?" Breaker said.

"I'm sure those records are sealed. How do you know all of this?" Raven asked.

"Honey, people's mouths aren't sealed."

No one said anything for a few seconds. "Okay," Imogene said. "Let me put it this way. June Darling, Ronnie True's paralegal? She's not an Edmée fan."

"Why didn't you say something earlier?" Raven asked.

"Because it doesn't mean anything."

"Don't you see?" Raven said. "It means everything."

CHAPTER FORTY-FOUR

Breaker wanted her to take the evidence to the chief. He told both Imogene and Raven that Chief Sawyer would have no choice but to follow up. But Raven wasn't so sure about that, and neither was Imogene. They talked Breaker down, but Raven didn't know how long he would keep quiet. He wanted to be a normal dad again, maybe even go back to the BLPD to pick up his old job in major crimes. His girls could go to school, and the town could get back to the business of pretending as if it cared for its children, that is, until the next walking disaster decided they had an axe to grind.

Raven needed her old partner, Billy Ray, to help her pull the threads that would untie the knot of this crime. But he was nowhere she looked. It was as if the sour Byrd's Landing wind had whispered to him that he was about to be pulled down into a nightmare, urged him to run. She found him in the last place she expected.

The shotgun where Billy Ray battled Lovelle didn't look like it did last year, no bottle tree fighting off evil spirits. Someone had long ago stolen away the twinkle lights that Billy Ray draped around the windows and front door. The door itself had been ripped off its hinges, carried away. Beyond the threshold stood a maw of darkness.

With a flashlight she walked through the front door, half expecting the overturned furniture and a blue flame still burning on Billy Ray's Viking stove. The memories of that night followed her through the house and out the back door. But there was one thing that made her proud. She didn't run. She walked.

From the high porch she could see Billy Ray in the barren yard looking up at the frosted moon. His hands were knotted into fists at his sides. No oh-shucks pork pie hat pushed back on his head this time, no friendly bowling shirt to put people, especially white people, at their ease. Without these affectations of amiability, she could see the pain and frustration that he had been trying to hide since she had returned to Byrd's Landing. He stood next to a scarred stump that used to be a fully grown weeping willow before Lovelle tried to burn him alive beneath it.

He didn't turn toward her, though he had to know that she was standing there. She wasn't making any attempt at stealth.

"What in all things holy are you doing here, Billy Ray?" she asked him. "How in the hell did you get down there?"

The porch was at least six feet off the ground, bolstered by two-by-fours. After the first landing the only thing left were the supports, the porch so rickety that it was no small thing that it hadn't already collapsed. She figured he must have jumped, so in spite of the pain in her own body, that's what she did, swearing she heard bells jangling in approval as she stuck the landing.

He turned to her then, his eyes glittering with moonlight. His smile was amused. "I didn't come that way. But leave it to you to show off."

"What are you doing here?" Raven repeated. "I've been looking all over for you. This isn't healthy."

"I don't come here because it's healthy. I come here to remember, to remind myself that it was real, not a bad dream. The question is how did you find me?"

"After I eliminated all of the places you could be, I thought I'd find you at the only place you shouldn't," Raven said. "You'd think the scars and the medical bills would be enough to let you know that it was real."

Billy Ray laughed softly. "That's why I love you, Raven. You can always be counted on to say exactly the wrong thing at the wrong time. So, why you so hot on finding me?"

"We've got to talk about Edmée."

"No."

"Not your relationship with her. I'm talking about the Sleeping Boy killer."

"I know what you want to talk about. Imogene called me.

All you've got is a wish and an obsession, and that'll make it a dangerous conversation."

"Well, that ought to match your blind spot."

"Why? Because you think I'm sleeping with her?"

"Are you?" she challenged.

"Is that any of your business?"

"Are we really going to fight about the least important thing right now?"

"You appear to be willing."

"Okay," she breathed. "It's my business when it comes to finding Noe, which you don't seem to give a hollering hoot of a wet dream about."

"I care about that boy more than you know."

"Then why don't you listen to me?"

"Because you're talking out of your ass. Edmée wouldn't hurt a fly if it was shitting in her gumbo."

He turned, walked up the hill and through the alley leading out of the backyard.

"She grew up on a farm. Did you know that?" she called to him.

He shook his head without turning around.

"They had pigs and goats. Chickens. She told me stories when we were in school together about having to kill them. How bad she felt about it. I didn't think too much about it until she was handling that snake in my rooms at Mama Anna's like a pro, talking about how she used to be a country girl."

He stopped at the mouth of the alley and turned to her. "So?"

"These boys are being slaughtered out of revenge. The killer feels bad about doing it. That explains the method, the blankets, washing the body after. Don't you get it? They're sacrifices paying for the sins of their families."

"I hear you. But why Edmée?"

It took everything she had to maintain eye contact with him. For some reason, she saw Edmée in her mind's eye, all soft, asking that she not reveal her past to Billy Ray. When she finally decided to speak, it was too late. He had lost patience.

"Oh, I see," he said. "You haven't gotten around to making that part up yet."

"Come on, Billy Ray."

"You ever think it could be your boyfriend?"

"Stevenson? What in the hell are you talking about?"

"Stevenson. Did you check him out as possibly being a part of this?"

"Why would I do that?"

"Well, he used the same road that the killer took Noe and Clyde on," he said. "For his fake location for his fake movie."

"Lots of people use that road out of town. You want to arrest half of Byrd's Landing?"

"Rogue cop. Obsessed with putting you away. Lied to you about everything he is. How do you know he didn't take Clyde and Noe to get back at you? And here you are having no problem partnering with him."

"I have plenty of problems partnering with him. I don't have a choice. Besides, Stevenson being good for this is stupid."

"Man shows up out of nowhere and all of a sudden Noe and Clyde are gone," he said. "Why is that stupid?"

"Is this how we're going to be toward each other now that you have a girlfriend? A married girlfriend, I might add? Suspicious? Cruel?"

"You forgot jealous."

"You're jealous of Stevenson?" she asked.

He laughed. "Not even as a joke. But you sure are jealous of Edmée."

"You think I want to take the place of Edmée in your bed?"

"Of course not," he said. "But you do everything you can just to tear her down. She told me how competitive the two of you were in high school."

"So, what are we competing for now? Your attention? I'm jealous because you can't spit or take a piss without that perfumed succubus at your side?"

He looked at her for a long time. She didn't like that look. He said, "I rest my case."

"Don't you walk away from me, you fool," she yelled to his

retreating back, his T-shirt now a square of white in the darkness. "I have a lot to tell you."

"Stevenson, Raven," he said over his shoulder.

She chased him up the hill leading to the alley, but was no match for his quick, long strides even with his limp. She shouted every invective she knew for what she thought was just short of the jugular, but he rewarded her efforts with not one of his Billy Ray comebacks. She got only an accusing silence. The fear that she was about to lose him made her want to cry, but of course she wouldn't. It wasn't out of pride, but the fear that he wouldn't care.

She was standing on the run-down sidewalk as she watched him get into his Skylark parked on the opposite side of Peabody. He veered the little car across the street straight toward where she stood. Anybody other than Billy Ray, Raven would have been sure the Skylark was trying to mow her down.

On the wrong side of the street now, he stopped the car next to her, rolled down the window. He stared at her for so long that Raven thought he was going to say something profound. What he did say was, "You ain't going to want to stand out here too long. It's late, dark. No telling what this neighborhood is crawling with now that nobody lives down here anymore."

With that he rolled the window back up and drove away, the wheels rustling along the road in the dark. Raven stood there stunned. But then rage galvanized her. She scooped up a handful of dirt and threw it at his car, satisfied to see the dirt clod bounce off his trunk, not caring that the flashlight dropped and rolled as she did so.

She called him a demented pussy-whipped son-of-a-robber. She called him an adulterer, a hypocrite and ended with, "Your mother wasn't married to your father, you dumb piece of butt filth." That last bit made her a bit ashamed. It didn't matter that he hadn't heard her, had long since turned the corner out of sight. But, she asked herself, was he really sleeping with Edmée? Did he not care if she were killing kids? Did she really not know him?

Better question, Lovey, Floyd's voice broke in. *Did he really just leave you here in the dark?*

"Yes, he did," she answered back bitterly. "And you're right, Daddy. No telling what a man will do when there's tail involved."

She picked up the flashlight. The casing was cracked, the light flickering, but it still worked. She was ready to get the hell out of there. She reached in her pocket for her keys and froze. Her pocket was empty. Maybe in the car, she thought.

But no.

For Raven, there was a place for everything. Besides, she distinctly remembered getting the big flashlight because it was so dark out, and dropping the keys in her jacket pocket. And she remembered jumping from the porch steps to the ground in what might have been a more graceful somersault if her body wasn't in so much pain. She thought she heard something jangle, and then the argument. She forgot all about the keys.

The flashlight flickered and buzzed. Raven pointed it back at the house, then through the alley leading to the backyard. *Father of all things holy, please don't make me have to go back through that alley.*

But she knew she had no choice.

She pointed the struggling light in front of her and began walking, making as much noise as she could as she went. She knew that wasn't the smartest thing in the world given that she was probably alerting every crackhead in a five-mile radius holed up in these abandoned houses, but Raven knew that she could at least talk to a junkie. If they wouldn't listen to reason, she could very well defend herself. But a snake? Maybe a cottonmouth this time?

That would drive her over the edge.

She walked on, stepping carefully over the uneven ground in the alley. She talked to God as she kept walking, asked him to not carry out Floyd's wish for punishment for little girls who told on their daddies. She removed the Glock from its holster. If she saw one snake in the light of the flashlight, she didn't care if it was harmless or not, she was going to blow it to bits before it had a chance to play dead.

She walked a few more steps, stopped when a possum froze in the beam of the flashlight. When she finally made it to the backyard, the light sputtered completely out. She really did want to cry then, big gut-wrenching sobs like she did when she was a little girl. She started the flashlight app on her cell phone. It didn't provide much light but there was enough to guide her to the hulk of the damaged back porch.

It turned out that the drama wasn't necessary. Her keys were lying on the edge of the weed patch as if they were patiently waiting for her to come back. *Can't go anywhere without me*, they taunted. She bent to scoop them up. In that instant light flooded the yard, and then her name, as clear as crystal.

"Raven."

★　　★　　★

Raven whipped toward the light source. There at the edge of the fenceless yard was a small man with yellow hair dressed in black. Odd shadows made his eyes appear as black holes in his pale face.

The fact that she believed that this man was from her own imagination made it worse for Raven. She was dancing on the cliff of sanity and madness and was horrified at how close she was coming to falling over the edge.

With putting distance between the man and herself the only thing on her mind, she caught the porch's lip and pulled herself up. It crashed into a pile of broken sticks the minute she made it through the back door. She sprinted through the house, imagining the Floyd thing on the other side of the wall, running both unreal and unseen alongside her.

She exited the shotgun, pressed the button to open her car door, fumbled the key into the ignition — oh what she wouldn't give for a start button now — and drove out of there like a soul escaping hell.

He was there in her rearview, a hand reaching out to her, one long finger pointing.

She knew he wasn't real. She knew that she was only running away from her own madness. But the light. It was hard to believe that the light came from her twisted imagination.

CHAPTER FORTY-FIVE

Back at the rooming house, Raven knew that finding Noe would not only save his life, but would also preserve her sanity. The light felt so real when she was in the backyard of the abandoned shotgun, her name sounded so clear. She knew that the longer the case lingered, the more broken her mind would become. She tried Cameron's trick of compartmentalizing. She pushed her stalker in a corner of her mind so she could concentrate on what needed to be done.

Edmée had Noe. Raven was sure of it. But Billy Ray didn't believe her. The chief would think that she was trying to find a scapegoat for Cameron, and Stevenson, well, who cared what Stevenson thought? He was no longer her problem.

She had to somehow smoke Edmée out. Raven knew how dangerous that could be. Edmée could come after her, and that would be just fine. Raven could handle it. But worse, Edmée could spook so bad that she could kill Noe, if, that is, Noe was even still alive. That was something she had to face now.

She sat down on the couch and put her hands to the sides of her head. Clyde had come too close. Edmée didn't want to kill him. She had to do it. He taunted her with that day her son was killed. He knew about the baby, probably learned of it from his mother. That's why Edmée went ahead with the plan after Clyde had arrived with Noe. She smelled imminent danger, humiliation, especially now that she had Billy Ray in her sights.

Raven dragged her hands through her hair. She wondered if Edmée knew how much evidence Raven had. She immediately dismissed the thought that Billy Ray tipped Edmée off. Her old partner wouldn't betray her like that, no matter how pissed off he happened to be.

There was only one thing she could do. Confronting Edmée would never work. She was too competitive, she would never admit defeat. Yes, smoking her out was the right thing to do.

Raven hit the speed dial on her Android for Edmée.

She answered with an expansive, "Raven, darling, have you called to torture your old friend some more about poor Clyde?"

Raven pictured her flinging her long, black hair over her shoulder, could smell the expensive perfume sliding through the cellular circuits. Her rooms at Mama Anna's filled with Edmée's presence. How perfectly clear the connection was. She could even hear Edmée's breathing. She didn't know if she was signing Noe's death warrant if Noe was even still alive, but she couldn't wait any longer. This was the chance she had to take.

Raven said, "July 12th, Edmée. Of this year."

Edmée's sharp intake of breath sounded painful. Then nothing, silence again. Finally, Edmée said, "You wound me, Raven," and hung up.

CHAPTER FORTY-SIX

Edmée carried on as if nothing rocked her world. She never let on that she knew anything about Raven following her in a rented Hyundai sedan. Raven tailed her to the gym the morning after the supposed wounding. This after spending the night watching Edmée's house. She then tailed her to the hair salon, the nail salon, and finally to Edmée's foster home on Heron Street where her quarry stayed for several hours. It was well into the evening when Raven followed Edmée on foot as she Christmas shopped amid the jewelry, art and boutique clothing vendor stalls beneath a colorfully lit Texas Street Bridge.

Edmée was about thirty yards ahead, her tall, graceful figure easily distinguished in the crowd when Raven's Android rang.

"Raven, Rita."

"Yeah, Rita. What is it?"

"You know that dirt we took from beneath Clyde's nails?"

Raven stopped, unaware of the crowd of Christmas shoppers slowing to flow all around her still figure.

"Some of it was potting soil," Rita said.

Raven sighed. That did her zero good. She already knew that Clyde spent Friday after school helping Edmée in her garden. Just another piece of evidence Billy Ray could bat away, and another piece of the puzzle that no one but Raven thought fit.

"You sound disappointed."

"That's because I am," she said as she was putting her free hand back into the pocket of her hoodie and slowly walking on.

"Fine. Let's see if I can do better. The soil on Clyde's *body*? It's indicative to wetlands, swamps. Got me to thinking about the ones on the edge of town they're talking about protecting. That's got a lot of people riled. Maybe that's what this is all about. At least that's what I'm thinking."

Raven was suddenly aware of her surroundings, the lights on the bridge, the laughter and conversation all around her, shoppers laden with bags and boxes, middle-aged women in bright red Santa hats, the bark of the vendor stall owners, their gentle jokes and teasing cajoling their more-than-willing customers into one more buy. *It's Christmas.* Raven thought. *Or it will be soon. How could I have missed it?*

"Raven, sweetie? Do you think I'm right about the motive?"

"No," Raven whispered, wonder in her voice. "I don't think you're right at all."

Rita laughed lightly. "Way to burst a girl's bubble. And here I am working my heart out for you on a Sunday. Sorry I couldn't help."

"Oh no," Raven said. "You helped me more than you know."

She hung up while Rita was still talking. Yes, it was almost Christmas, and Rita just gave her the best present she'd ever had in the entirety of her whole troubled life. She was about to turn and make her way back through the crowd to the Hyundai. But then she felt something press against her back, smelled a cloud of expensive perfume.

"Raven," Edmée said lovingly in her ear. "If you wanted to talk to me, all you had to do was say so."

CHAPTER FORTY-SEVEN

"Edmée," Raven said. "Don't."

"Oh, don't 'don't' me, darling. I am so tired with the following around. Besides, my heart has been breaking. I simply must talk to you."

"You put a gun in my back because you simply want to talk to me?" Raven said in a low voice.

"Because you've always been stubborn, my Rave girl. And I am sick of you wasting your time when you should be out trying to find Noe. Walk with me. People are starting to stare."

Edmée walked Raven down Texas Street before turning down one of the smaller side streets. She made several more turns until they were in a narrow alley. Raven instinctively put her hands in the air.

"Don't be foolish. Put your hands down."

"I would, Edmée, but you holding on to my hoodie isn't exactly making me comfortable."

"I'm not stupid. If I let you go you'll put some move on me." Edmée kicked an empty soda can with her high-heeled shoe. "I don't want to get the dirt on me. This is a new skirt and it's so hard to get stains out of the white."

They exited the alley onto a street that ran behind the restaurants and stores. Beyond them lay the back of the Red River, the unmoving water the color of powdered rust.

Edmée sat Raven down on a tattered picnic bench behind one of the boarded-up restaurants.

Raven could see the gun at this point, a Smith & Wesson limited edition with 'We the People' written in calligraphy on the barrel.

"That's a fancy gun, Edmée."

"Yes, very fancy, pretentious for something meant to shoot people. I don't like it."

"Where did you get it?"

"Oh, don't be stupid, I know you know everything. Do you know that bastard tried to shoot me with this very gun? Serves him right that I have it now."

"You mean Ronnie True?" Raven asked. "You killed him?"

"Not on purpose. It was an accident."

"Accident?"

"I lost my temper."

"I'll say. Is that why you went there with a bolt gun? To help you with your temper?"

"Oh, Raven, please. Put your silly hands down. They're making me distracted. I didn't know how he would react, so I just slipped the bolt gun in my purse before I went to see him. I had no intention of using it on him. But he was just standing there with all of his stupid excuses. Not even the Virgin Mother would have been able to help herself."

"Where did you get the bolt gun, anyway?" Raven asked. "That's not something people usually have lying around."

"I had it with me ever since I left the farm I lived on with my cousin. She used to wave it around at me, threaten me with it. Terrified the shit out of me. When Child Protective Services finally came and got me, I took the bolt gun with me. I kept it. I knew she was going to jail, but in my mind back then I thought if I had it, she could never hurt or threaten me with it again."

"How did you even know who Claude DeWitt was? That it was your son who had died?"

"Are you kidding me, Raven? I made it my mission to find him. When I found out who had my son, all I could think of was that poem I studied in high school about the mother who aborted her babies, how she would never be able to return for a snack of them with one gobbling mother-eye. I thought, my baby is not dead. I would always be able to keep one eye on him. And I did."

"But why did you tell everyone that you aborted him?"

"They made me say it, the lawyers. I was so young, Raven. Scared. When it was time for the truth it was too late. All the explanations would have given me a big headache."

Edmée had lain the weapon down on the table in front of her. Dark rain clouds were rolling across the sky with a low rumble of thunder. Raven reached for the gun, but with the injuries to her body, she wasn't fast enough. Edmée got there before her and was now pointing the Smith & Wesson at her chest.

"Haven't you learned by now that you will never win, Raven?"

"Go ahead and shoot me if that's what you want to do. But don't let Noe die."

"Noe?" Edmée said, sounding genuinely confused. "What are you talking about? How could I let Noe die?"

"No games, Edmée."

Edmée's eyes widened. "You think I am this Sleeping Boy killer? Raven? You? After all we've been through?"

"You've got a gun on me, Edmée."

"The only reason I'm holding a gun is I could tell when I looked back that you were about to do something crazy," Edmée said. "I have nothing to do with these killings. I did kill Ronnie True. I confess it to you, but you will not tackle and roll around on the ground with me in a big spectacle. I will not go into custody covered in dirt and filth. Who was on the phone anyway?"

"Rita," Raven said. "She wanted to tell me that they traced the soil samples back to the farm you grew up on."

"You lie," Edmée said. "The state took that place long ago from my cousin. Turned it into protected wetlands. I'd be surprised if it were even there anymore."

"And where is there, Edmée?" Raven asked.

"A hateful place. Near where Kingfisher Road starts to run out, just on the edge of town. Nothing there now but a crumbling farm house and that hateful shed where my cousin whored me out."

Raven remembered the place Stevenson had taken her when he was pretending to be a location scout all those weeks ago. While gazing at the wide and flat water all around the abandoned farm, the new life Raven was trying to build was as near as her own breath. And now with this, Edmée's revelation, Raven realized that all along she was living in a mirage of her own making.

"What is wrong with you?" Edmée said. "You've gone all quiet."

Hearing Edmée's voice brought her back. She looked into Edmée's dark eyes, tried to find the connection between them that was once there. "It's no use," Raven said. "We have other evidence."

"By we, you mean you," Edmée said. "But tell me, please. I could use entertaining right now."

"For some reason, you took the bear taxidermy from True's office. Was that a souvenir?"

"Who would want such a souvenir? No, the stupid thing fell on his head, so I picked it up and smacked him with it again. The thing smashed all up. My fingerprints were all over it, so I threw it in the first dumpster I found. I was so upset that I didn't realize I had taken a piece of it with me to the car. I threw it straight in the garbage when I got home. How was I to know people like to steal the garbage?"

"Clyde and Noe were at your house the Friday before they went missing."

"Yes, I'm afraid they were. Clyde was helping me clean up the garden, and he brought Noe along. It was late. We didn't have a lot of daylight left, but he was upset. I let them pull weeds, and fed them pizza. I'm sure that he didn't tell his mama because I'm afraid June Darling doesn't like me very much."

"If you didn't have anything to do with the killings, why didn't you tell anybody that the boys were there?"

Edmée looked out at the water. "I'm not proud of it, but I knew it would make me a suspect. And then they would start looking into my past and Billy Ray...." She stopped.

"Would find out."

"Yes, he would find out everything."

"Why should I believe you?" Raven said.

"Because I tell you the truth. The boys came over, helped in the garden before I insisted they catch the bus back home."

"Clyde told his mother that he wouldn't be home until late Monday because he had another job," Raven said.

"How am I to know what other work they were doing?"

"So, Dr. Long and Karen were there? They lied for you?"

"My husband was not at home. As for Karen, we pay our help very well."

"You're telling me on Friday night, it was you, Karen, Clyde, Noe, and the junkman Ozy who stopped by trying to return the bear paw? If I ask Karen again, would she agree with that?"

"No," Edmée said. "I'm afraid that she wouldn't."

"Why is that?"

"Because my stupid cousin came over shortly after the boys left. She's been trying to make up to me. Sends me flowers, letters. Saying that she begs for my forgiveness one day and threatens to spill my secrets the next. She's not begging for forgiveness. She's just trying to get at my money. The place she's at now isn't doing so well."

When Edmée said that last piece about not doing so well, Raven's thoughts zeroed in on Stella Morning. What had she said about selling the blood of her slaughtered animals? She needed every penny she could get. That tall, rawboned woman in the all-weather work boots standing on her porch welcoming her and Stevenson in a lilting voice so she could tell them about her process. That same woman with the stark living room and a slaughterhouse in her backyard.

"Where is your cousin, Edmée?" Raven asked.

This time Edmée did put the gun down. She put both elbows on the table, cradled her face in her hands. "She should be in the jail, shouldn't she? For what she did to me? But no jail time. Her clients were too powerful. They helped make her a deal with the prosecutor. She got another farm by tricking my grandparents, and later taking my aunt to court. She lives far, but not far enough because she always comes to town for the torture."

Raven leaned forward. Edmée put her hand over the gun, but in a tired way that said all the fight had left her. Raven ignored the movement. She said softly to her friend, "What's her name?"

Edmée's answer was like a groan. "Stella. Stella Morning. Such a beautiful name for such a bitch."

"You mean the same Stella Morning who came to Noe's birthday party?"

"Who else would it be? Yes. That waste of flesh."

"But why bring her if you hated her? Why let her volunteer at Heron House?"

"Because she makes me do these things for her. She says if I don't, she will tell, and everyone in town will know what a whore I was. That's one of the reasons I drank so much that night, stayed away from her. Every time I saw her face, I wanted to vomit."

Raven jumped up from the table and started walking back through the alley. She barely heard Edmée's voice behind her asking about the confession, the arrest, wanting Raven to be the one to take her in. It was right there in her face the entire time. Stella Morning was the Sleeping Boy killer.

CHAPTER FORTY-EIGHT

Raven wasn't finished with what Edmée would have called 'the sneaking around', but she wasn't completely reckless. She called Stella and asked for an appointment to chat about the case. Raven told her that she had more questions about the process, piqued her interest by telling her that she needed to discuss a particular individual with her, something she couldn't do over the phone. Stella responded that she would be delighted to speak with her, but not that evening. She had a previous commitment that would take her away from the farm that night. They would have their chat in the morning, when, Stella said, she would have a nice pot of tea waiting for her. The heavens had finally smiled down in Raven's favor. No one would be at the farm that night but the sheep, and they wouldn't tell.

She drove straight to Stella's in what had now become a driving rain. She picked the lock to the farmhouse door in half the time it took her to pick Speck's. Alone and without the distraction of Stevenson breathing down her neck, Raven walked into the living room. She wondered how she had missed it. There was the sofa covered in pink tea-roses, the ladder-back chair and the pot-bellied stove. The magazines on the wooden coffee table were alphabetized by title.

But it was those boots that sealed the woman's guilt, there, drying in front of the stove, the same ones that Stella wore when she greeted Raven and Stevenson from the front porch days ago. Raven walked over to the boots, studied them carefully. They were Ariat, the same type of boot that left the print they found at the Memorial crime scene.

She strolled to the back of the house, where she assumed the bedrooms would be located, which indeed they were. Two of them. She cautiously called Noe's name. Nothing but a queen-sized bed covered with an old quilt, and a lone nightstand in the first one. A framed Ansel Adams print hung above the bed. The other was a guest room with only a twin bed and a nightstand with a lone lamp. She walked back to the living room and then to the kitchen. Empty except for dinner dishes dripping on the drain board.

She left by the back door to be welcomed by the sheep bleating in the rain. Raven ran her flashlight over them as they huddled together for comfort. In the abattoir all the doors had been rolled down over the once-open wall, and the place was dark and eerie. The doors weren't locked. Raven rolled them up and entered but didn't find dead boys hanging from the black chains in the ceiling. And aside from being a place for slaughtering animals, it was as clean as a newly buffed floor.

Outside the rain poured down. Raven was beginning to wonder if she had once again been killing precious time when she remembered something on the first visit. That old wooden trunk along the side of the house. Stevenson had almost fallen face first in the mud when he tripped over it. When she had asked Morning about it, she said she didn't use it but hadn't gotten around to removing it. Raven wondered why a woman as organized as Stella would let an old farm box linger.

Raven walked around the house until she found the box. There it was, beneath the kitchen window. Raven kicked the latch with her feet. There didn't appear to be a lock on it. She bent down, lifted the heavy lid. She thought she smelled something rotten before the rain drove it away. Running her flashlight inside, she bent to get a closer look.

As she inspected the box, she felt a blow to the back of her head. She tumbled into the box face first. She touched the back of her neck and came away with blood on her fingertips. She looked up. There stood Stella shining a flashlight down on Raven. "Nosey, nosey, pokey, pokey," she said. "I'd love to gut you right now. I wouldn't even stun you first. But it looks like I've got some cleanup to do. Stay there and be a good girl until I get back."

"Wait!" Raven said, trying to stand, but Morning kicked her with an Ariat boot that she must have put on when Raven was poking around in the abattoir. Raven fell onto her back. Morning slammed the lid shut. With all her might, Raven tried to keep her eyes open, but much stronger than her was the darkness clamoring to claim her.

CHAPTER FORTY-NINE

Raven didn't know how long she was out. When she was finally able to open her eyes, she was lying in a half-inch of water. The rain raged outside, the wind howled over the wetlands. Water streamed through the many holes on the lid covering the box. For a second Raven was relieved. Rotted wood signaled an easier escape. She pushed up on the lid with both hands. It stopped almost at once at the lock Stella must have put there.

"Be a good girl until I get back, my sweet behind," Raven breathed.

She kicked at the lid with her boots, this time with all the strength in her body. It wasn't enough. Whatever lock Stella had used – it held. Raven used both legs to push against the top of the box. With every movement her head exploded in protest. She hoped she wasn't hurt so bad that she couldn't go after Stella, who Raven was sure was now going after Noe. What's worse, she felt foolish. Stella probably had nowhere to go that night. She probably suspected that Raven knew something. Raven had let that dyed red-haired hellion trick her.

Raven abandoned attempts to kick the lid open. She booted the short end of the box while bracing her hands against the opposite end. Her effort only sent another blast of pain through her head. The box held her fast.

She was going to die here, she was sure of it. *That's right, Birdy Girl*, Floyd said. *Come on and see me now. I got more for you down here than you will ever have up there. Everything dies anyway. It ain't all your fault.*

At his words, a rage that Raven hadn't felt in a long time overtook her. It was a fire that started at her feet and flamed upward until it covered the top of her head. It wasn't at the world, at herself, or anybody else that she might blame for her predicament. It was at Floyd.

"How could you be such a worthless father even when you're dead? You give up. I'm not giving up crap."

She reached up with her hands, trying to push the lid up using the strength in her triceps. Nothing. The water lapped around her as she moved. She ran her fingers along the edge closest to the top of her head. She felt empty places around some of the nails. Not huge spaces, but they were there.

With some effort, she contorted her body until she could remove her knife from its ankle holder. She jabbed the blade along the edge where she thought she felt the largest breaches. She hacked straight down, turned the tip of the blade to dig when she came upon a nail, apologizing with a 'sorry, big fella' to the knife along the way. It took a while but finally she was able to split the box along one edge. She set the knife down and pushed again. Both the front and right side of the box creaked open. She hit and kicked until she had a big enough hole to crawl through.

When she finally got out, she sprinted for the rental car.

CHAPTER FIFTY

Raven knew she wasn't thinking right, especially after she tried to use her Android to call for help. The screen was not only busted because of the fight with Speck, the circuitry was now waterlogged. It was as useless as a brick. She threw it out the window.

She had no idea how long she was out, and didn't want to think about the lead time Stella may have had on her. It could've been ten minutes, fifteen, or, and with this thought her heart beat so fast it hurt, maybe an hour. *Please, not that long*, she hoped, no, prayed to a God that might not have his listening ears on for a cold-blooded killer, no matter how justified Raven thought Lamont Lovelle's death was.

Raven suspected that Stella was using the old farm for her kills. She wouldn't use the abattoir on her working farm. Not the woman with a sign in her slaughter house that read, 'The place where an animal dies is a sacred one'. Thin reasoning, she knew, but it was all that she had. For one horrific moment Raven knew she wouldn't be able to beat Stella to the farm. She needed a shortcut. In her desperation, she not only started to talk out loud to Floyd, she started to curse.

"Come on, you fucker," she said. "I drove with you through all these backroads helping you look for some evil to do, or for some place to hide. Tell me what shortcut to use to the farm at the end of Kingfisher Road."

But the usually chatty Floyd voice in her head was silent.

"Oh, you got your feelings hurt now?" she said. "Too bad."

As Floyd was apparently deciding whether or not to answer her, Raven racked her brain. Oh, what wouldn't she give for a memory like Edmée's. Raven knew if she drove all the way back to town to find help, Noe was dead. If she let Morning beat her there, Noe was dead.

"Tell me, old man!" Raven yelled.

Nothing. Raven knocked her head against the headrest. She was about to flip the car around toward town when a voice spoke up. It was sullen.

Well now, it said, *I'm guessing you could probably take the farm road right through the ole Sassafras place. It's a little windy, but that'll save you about fifteen or twenty minutes if you don't drive into the drink.*

"I need more than fifteen or twenty minutes," Raven said, not pleased.

We demanding, ain't we? Take the road through the old Sassafras farm, follow that around until you hit Peat Hollow, then turn left. That'll lead you straight to the farm on the south side. Nobody'll see you comin'. Me and you traveled that way plenty.

"Okay, okay," Raven breathed in relief, and then had to jerk the wheel hard when a Floyd voice thundered *HERE!* The car fishtailed. For a brief moment Raven did think she was going to end up in what Floyd called the drink, but the tires caught road and steadied. She was able to drive on.

When she reached the abandoned farm, hers was the only car she could see, but that didn't mean she was the only car there. She prayed that at least it meant that she had beat Morning. She parked the car, got out, and tried not to think about the rain plastering her hair to the sides of her face, driving her hoodie and jeans into her skin.

She didn't go to the house first because it was the logical thing to do. She did it because the hard, slanting rain like a hand at her back propelled her across the yard, and up the crumbling porch steps. Before she knew it, she was twisting the rusted knob and pushing the warped front door open.

Her flashlight revealed wallpaper splintering spider-like from mold-covered walls. Furniture sat disintegrating into the floor, including what was left of an ancient couch, an old-fashioned baby pram, and a wheelchair that had lost a wheel a long time ago. The floor was covered in drywall and wood driven from the ceiling by countless rainstorms. Something told Raven to go back. No way could Noe be in this disaster.

But he could be, sequestered in one of the back rooms shrinking like the abandoned furniture into nothingness, lonely and afraid while waiting for the grave.

She took a step, and then another, staying close to the edges, where the floor would be strongest. In the back, each room was the same, moldy walls, broken furniture, and parts of the ceiling on a destroyed floor.

She turned from the last empty room and made her way back to the living room. She should have searched the shed first. That was a mistake, but the bigger mistake was running straight across the living room floor, forgetting the need to be careful.

The rotted floor collapsed beneath her. She plunged waist-deep into filthy water. It wasn't long before she felt long wet ropes twisting all around her, slipping around her neck, between her legs, around her torso and over her face. She sputtered. The ropes bent and flexed as her body moved.

Whatever was in the water was alive.

Holding the flashlight high above her, she directed the beam at the teeming water. Snakes, what seemed to be thousands of them, twisting in and out of each other exploding in wet knots from holes in the floor.

Her scream was one of sheer primordial panic. Behind her tight eyes all she saw were heavy black bodies, the gaping pink mouths. She tried to pull herself up on what she thought was solid floor, but it crumbled down into the water. She fell onto her hands and knees, her entire face submerged. Snakes whipped through the water, climbed onto the frame under the house, wrapping their bodies around two-by-fours as if to get a better look at her. She stood, frantically shaking them off as she did so with all thought in her head erased.

Suddenly a strong hand grabbed her by the neck of her hoodie and pulled her out of the water. The hand dragged her across the floor, out of the house, back into the rain. Whoever this was no longer whispered or gestured. The voice roared. *Repent! Cleanse your soul!*

Now in the yard she scrambled away from him. She snatched the weapon out of her holster and flipped on her back. But there was nothing but the black air and silver needles of rain slamming down onto the muddied front yard. The rain was coming so hard that it hurt every bare spot on Raven it touched.

She sat up, tilted over to the side and vomited. She had no idea if she were bitten or not, didn't know if the snakes were poisonous. She wiped her mouth with the back of her hand. When her eyes focused again, she saw the shed standing there strong and solid. It had to be where Stella was keeping Noe. She took several, long, lung-filling breaths. When she felt steady she stood up and went to the shed.

No snakes threatened beyond the shed's narrow door. The floors were solid, strong-looking, the walls painted a stark white. It looked almost normal except for the blood spattering the walls, the chain hanging from the ceiling, the rusted galvanized steel bucket on the floor.

"Raven," cried a shaky voice. And again, "Raven. Wait! Don't!"

"Noe?" she cried, not heeding his warning.

He was naked, chained to a hook in the wall in a corner of the wide room. Within reaching distance was a bucket for his waste, and next to him empty to-go boxes from Chastain's.

She started toward him. He cried again with an urgency that made her stop. "Auntie!"

Raven turned. Beautiful Edmée Crowley, still in her now soaked white skirt, strode toward her with her long arm stretched straight out. At the end of it was the Smith & Wesson pointed straight at Raven's forehead. Before Raven's brain could register the surprise she felt, Edmée said, "Move, Raven."

Raven ducked and pivoted. Edmée shot, but missed Stella by what Floyd would have called a country mile. The bullet ricocheted around the cinder-block room before barreling through a high window. The recoil knocked Edmée off-balance, and Stella charged her at a dead run out into the rain and mud. Raven ran after them. Stella had managed to get on top of Edmée and was now raising a slaughter knife over her head.

"Get off her, you bitch."

Lowering her body, and squaring her shoulders, Raven smashed into Stella. They rolled over and over in the mud. Edmée was crawling around looking for the Smith & Wesson. She was cursing the entire time in French and then in Cajun French, her loud voice matching the volume of the rain.

Raven knew that she had gotten the best of Stella when she had her pinned face down in the mud. She had started to cuff her when she heard another voice. Looking up, she could see Stevenson's car, the lights on and the driver's-side door flung open.

"Let her go," he said, his face unsure, confused.

Her eyes never leaving his, she finished cuffing Morning and pulled her into a sitting position. Edmée had stopped looking for the weapon after she heard Stevenson's voice, but was still crawling aimlessly around in the mud. Raven helped her stand. Crying, Edmée slumped against an old well in the yard. She slid down until she was sitting, and even now, her legs were curled gracefully beneath her. Raven tried her best to wipe the mud from her face and eyes, told her to quiet when she started to apologize, to explain. From what Raven could tell, Edmée had thought about their meeting under the Texas Street Bridge and had come out to the old farm just to be sure that it was gone.

When Edmée was reasonably calm, Raven turned to Stevenson. Raven had never wanted to kill somebody so bad since Lovelle.

"You and Morning," Raven said. "You did this." She drew her weapon.

"No, Raven," Edmée said. "He had nothing to do with this. It was all her."

"It wasn't all me," Stella said, her teeth bloody, an evil grin on her face. "It was him this whole time. He made me do it."

Stevenson's eyes were wide with disbelief. "You think I had something to do with this? Are you crazy?"

"You knew about this place. You brought me out here," Raven said.

"I didn't bring you here!" Stevenson said. "I brought you over there." He pointed to the road where he had taken her picture, the place where all the deceit had begun.

"Don't listen to him," Stella said. "Arrest him. It was him!"

"Raven!" he said.

She didn't lower the weapon. *You can take that lying son-of-a-sumpthin' out right now, Birdy Girl.* Floyd spoke up in her head. *He made a darn fool out of you. Make 'em pay, like you made Lovelle pay. Think about them boys.*

"No, Raven, please," Edmée said. "She's lying!"

Come on, let's have some fun, Floyd whispered in her head.

Then she heard a voice that brought her back to sanity. It was Billy Ray. *No, Raven. No more killing.*

But like Floyd, the voice was in her head, because Billy Ray was nowhere near this ruin. He was at his cozy restaurant, or most likely in his bed. When she saw him she would ask him what right had he to tell her anything after he had abandoned her. He had changed. Maybe by pulling the trigger she wouldn't have to deal with the man he was about to become. Still, Lord help her, she would probably die trusting him. If she killed Stevenson, she didn't see him standing by her. Not this time. She would lose him for good.

She lowered her weapon, holstered it before walking slowly over to Stevenson. With her eyes on his, she kneed him as hard as she could in the groin. Unlike Speck, he dropped.

No one said anything for a few moments. There was only Stella's crazed laughter. Raven stared at Stevenson writhing in the mud, relished his suffering for only a second or two before going into the shed for Noe.

CHAPTER FIFTY-ONE

Raven wrapped Noe in a blanket Edmée had in her Mercedes. She then put them both in the backseat and turned on the heat before calling for an ambulance. Edmée sat beside Noe, still muddy from head to toe but crying happily with her arms around the found boy.

After they were safe, Raven felt her mind slowly begin to slide from its mooring. All she could think of were the snakes, which Edmée had assured her were just harmless water snakes. But she couldn't explain the man who pulled her from the house because Raven didn't tell her about him. His voice was beginning to fade, and the words that he had spoken no longer sounded as if they came from this side of the grave.

As for Stevenson, Raven learned that Rita called him, giving him the same news about the soil samples that she had given Raven. He was following a hunch. When he saw Raven's rental he thought it belonged to the killer. Just like a good little detective, he called for backup before going in. The wail of sirens now cutting through the pounding storm was because of him.

Doors slammed as uniformed officers poured from the police vehicles. Raven knew what Billy Ray would say to her if he were standing here with her now. As he should be, she thought bitterly. He would tell her that going back to Chief Sawyer would do worse than kill her; it would destroy her.

"But you're not here, are you?" Raven breathed to no one in particular. "So, you don't get a say."

As the EMTs gently helped Noe out of the Mercedes, Raven threw all thoughts of her old partner from her mind. She searched through the rain, looking for the mysterious man who pulled her from the snake-infested waters. She could have sworn that she saw a shadowy figure walking away toward the west where her father was born. She studied the figure of her tormentor and savior melting into the rain, moving further and further away from her. She wondered if he were the price she had to pay for the peace she thought she had obtained from killing Lovelle. She wondered if Floyd sent him up from hell.

The chief called her name. He sounded as if he owned her. She gave the man's retreating figure one more long look. Knowing she was walking back into a hell with Floyd or something worse waiting for her, she turned toward the chief, to the flickering red and white lights. Homicide wasn't finished with her. She had killed in cold blood, and now there was more work to do in order to make up for that sin. She could only do that if she returned to the chaos.

304 • FAYE SNOWDEN

CHAPTER FIFTY-TWO

"Still confused as to why Stella didn't just kill Noe," Billy Ray said.

It was a week later and Billy Ray and Raven were alone at the restaurant during the hour when the sun was still new and golden. They sat at a small table near the bar. Early morning light slanted through the tall windows and fell across their table. White tablecloths and sparkling silverware awaited customers who would soon turn the contemplative atmosphere into a boisterous, devil-may-care place of food and laughter. Raven hoped it would be enough to blot out the pain the town had experienced these last months, especially for her brother and nephew.

Noe was in the hospital, and Cameron, vowing to be a better father, hadn't left his side, not even to shower or eat. If it weren't for Raven bringing him food every day, or cajoling him to the hospital's cafeteria, he would have, as Raven's stepmother was fond of saying, dried up and blown away.

Noe was well enough to give a statement. He told them that Clyde had convinced Edmée to let him and Noe help with her garden on that Friday after school. Clyde lied to his mother because he knew June didn't approve of Edmée. He thought he would be able to convince Edmée to let them stay the weekend in the guest house. The boys had planned to leave for school from Edmée's place on Monday, and after school let out, catch opening night for that new movie, the one with serial killers and chainsaws that June had already told Clyde he couldn't see. That was why Clyde texted his Mom from Noe's phone that they would be late getting home on Monday.

"We had spent the entire lunch hour watching videos on my phone. I was already almost out of juice," Noe said in his statement. "And right

after Clyde texted his mom, my phone died." This explained why the
last ping to Noe's cell phone was at school on Friday afternoon.

Clyde failed to convince Edmée to let them stay. She kept saying it
wouldn't be appropriate to allow them to stay the weekend, especially
without talking to their parents. They were walking back to the bus stop
when Stella drove alongside them.

"She had stopped by when we were in the garden," Noe said. "But
Miss Edmée acted real weird and told her to leave."

Stella asked them if they wanted to make more money by helping
her around the farm during the weekend. Noe didn't want to go, but
Clyde, seeing dollar signs, talked him into it. "Come on, bro," Clyde
had said. "She's okay. We know her. Besides, more money for the
movies. We'll have enough to take girls."

During the drive out to the farm, Clyde sat in the backseat, talking
nonsense and telling lame jokes the entire time the wheels were on the
road. Noe thought that Clyde had been nervous, and that his friend
knew something wasn't quite right. He peppered Stella with questions,
made jokes about her sheep, bragged about how he couldn't wait to see
one of them 'cut'. Clyde was so nervous he didn't catch the vibe in the
car, missed Stella's one-word answers. He was laughing so hard at one
of his own stupid jokes that he didn't hear her whisper 'shut-up, shut-
up, shut-up'.

At the stoplight on the road leading out of Byrd's Landing, Stella
motioned for Clyde to come forward. When his head was between the
front seats, she drew a circle on his forehead with her index finger. He
laughed, started to pull back. But Stella smiled, and told him to stay still,
that everything would be okay. She had a surprise for him.

"She took this long black thing from her bag, and touched
it hard to Clyde's head. Here." Noe drew a circle on his own
forehead. "And then she pressed it down, hard. That's when all
hell broke loose."

Noe knew Clyde was hurt, but didn't know how. He jumped out of
the car only to have Stella drag him back.

"She had this long knife," Noe said. "Man, it looked so sharp. She kept it on me the entire time, said she would stick me like a pig if I gave her any more trouble."

When they reached the farm Stella forced Noe to remove Clyde from the car. But it was raining and muddy and Noe couldn't see through his tears. He kept tripping, kept dropping his best friend's dead weight in the mud.

After he wrestled Clyde's limp body into the shed, Stella made Noe strip. And then she made him watch. She chained Noe to the wall, cut Clyde's throat, hoisted him, and let his blood splatter into a rusted steel bucket.

Raven stopped the story; she swallowed. "That was rough," she said, looking out the window at the sunshine. "Listening to him, seeing his face while he told it."

"So that's why Clyde was dirty?"

"Yes, from Noe dropping him in the mud," Raven said. "Having to deal with Noe distracted and disoriented her. Plus, Clyde's kill was impulsive. I think she wanted that body away from her as soon as possible. So, she didn't wash him. Just wrapped him up and dumped him."

"Still, why not kill Noe and get it over with?" Billy Ray asked.

"Back-up," Raven said.

"So, I guess Noe isn't the only one making statements?"

Raven nodded. "You'd be right about that. Stella doesn't want the needle. She's singing like a bird. She wanted back in Edmée's life, her money, sure. But more than that, she wanted control over Edmée, and in some sick way, she wanted Edmée to love her again. Like Edmée did when she was little and didn't know any better. When Stella heard that Ronnie True had been killed, she immediately thought Edmée did it. So she carried on that revenge by making everyone involved in placing Edmée's son pay for their mistake."

"By taking it out on their sons," Billy Ray said.

"Or if they didn't have sons, their nephews or cousins. As close as she could get. When it was all done, she planned to go to Edmée and tell her what she had done. Stella thought Edmée would be glad."

"That's not just plain evil, that's crazy-evil," Billy Ray said. "But I wouldn't expect less from this town."

"So you've told me," Raven said.

"Still doesn't explain why Noe is still topside."

"Like I said, Clyde's murder shook Stella, made her doubt. What if Edmée wasn't thrilled that boys were being killed in her name? If Edmée threatened to go to the police, Noe was Stella's ace-in-the-hole to keep Edmée in line long enough to get out of town. She was going to use Noe to make Edmée give her running money as well if it came to that."

They sat in silence for a few moments longer. Billy Ray was drawing invisible patterns on the table with the tips of his fingers. Then he said, "Sorry I wasn't there with you that night."

"No worries," she said. "I handled it."

"But you shouldn't have had to do that by yourself."

She said nothing. She was hoping he would change the subject. As if reading her mind, he said, "Well, we sure know how to pick 'em."

"Please don't tell me that you were sleeping with Edmée. After everything I've been through, I don't know what I'd do if I thought I didn't know you as well as I thought I did."

Billy Ray grunted. "Your imagination is something else, Raven. You know there's no way I'm sleeping with a married woman. She was, no is, a friend."

"Have you been able to see her?"

"No. We did talk on the phone, though. I told her I was there for her, but she just cried and hung up. Have you seen her?"

"Yes," Raven said. "I've been by the house. She's out on bail, doing okay given the circumstances. She's tough. I think Long is talking the DA into manslaughter. If she's convicted, she'll do prison time, but at least it won't be for the rest of her life."

"Maybe she'll get off," Billy Ray said, rubbing the side of his face. "Sounds like she wasn't in her right mind when it happened."

They stared at each other for a few long moments. Raven finally agreed with a weak, "Maybe."

"You said Cameron was off the hook? Completely?"

"Looks that way," Raven said.

"But what in the hell was he doing with two of the same kind of blanket Stella was using for her kills?"

"Even with all this you still looking with a side-eye at Cameron?"

"I'm just wondering, Raven."

She didn't say anything for a few moments, then said, "Noe was wetting the bed after his mother died and he moved in with Cameron. Trauma, I guess. Cameron thought it'd be easier to have a couple of blankets and sheet sets on hand rather than wash them."

"That seems a silly thing to risk prison for," Billy Ray said.

"Cameron's not the most mature person I know. Besides, he figured Stevenson and Goldie wouldn't have believed him anyway. Thought it was a waste of breath."

"So Cameron being Cameron almost got his skinny ass sent to jail."

"I guess you can say that," Raven agreed.

"What's happening with Stevenson?" he asked her.

Her laugh was harsh. "I think the chief is going to keep him around a little bit. Still don't know if Breaker's coming back. Department could use Stevenson."

"And the Lamont Lovelle murder investigation? How you looking for that?"

"I'm not a suspect. I may have been in the state when Lovelle was killed, but they can't place me at the scene. Stevenson was rogue all the way. According to the chief, he's the only one in his department who likes me for Lovelle. Everybody else has moved on. Even Stevenson's boss."

"Moved on?"

"Yes, to other cases, maybe to victims a little bit higher on the morality scale than a serial killer. The case is officially cold."

"That's good for you."

She was about to answer, but he held his hand up. "I don't want to hear no more about it. You staying on at BLPD?"

"I don't have a choice."

"You have a choice with everything. The problem is you just keep insisting on making shitty ones."

"What am I supposed to do? Wait tables the rest of my life?"

"If you can make a living at it, and it makes you happy, why the hell not? Besides, I thought you wanted to be a teacher, do some good."

"That was a pipe dream, Billy Ray. I realize that now. The only good I can do is on the force."

"So you think."

"So I know."

He sat up, and leaned toward her. "You're going to be around so much killing that you'll get a taste for it more than you already have. How you going to protect yourself from that?"

She met his lean with one of her own. Staring him in his handsome eyes, she said, "By doing the very best that I can to set things right."

EPILOGUE

Detective Raven Burns and this tall-drink-of-water poop-bird by the name of Willie Lee Speck were standing with their hands stuck deep in their back pockets. They looked kind of useless at the moment. They stared at this white house that had a bunch of thick, dead vines twisting all over the sides and on top of it. It looked like them vines were trying to drag the entire house down into the underworld.

They weren't talking much. Her red Mustang was parked next to the van he used to take on jobs to clean up after the good citizens of Byrd's Landing finished beating each other or killing each other or simply having the nerve to die in their sleep so their beds become their cooling boards. There used to be this junkman who took to following the cleaning man around, but you don't see him much these days, especially since that Speck character don't work a lot of jobs no more.

Finally, Speck spoke. "We are two truly fucked-up human beans. You know that, Ray Ray?"

He said it just like that: *bean*, like the lentil. You'll have to excuse him because he's as crazy as an unmanned jackhammer.

All she said in return was, "You got that right."

"Sometimes it's hard for me to believe how bad my mind slipped. All those animals," he said, shaking all over. "Can't believe I did that."

"Some say I've done worse."

"What do you say?"

"I haven't decided that yet."

They stood not saying a thing for a while, staring at the house as if they were expecting it to talk to them.

Then he said, "Thanks for standing up for me at my hearing. All those nice things you said about me."

"I didn't mean any of it."

"Figured you didn't. You think by putting this house right all these crazy things will stop happening around town?"

"I don't think so, Willie Lee. But it's a beautiful place, and you and I have some making up to do."

"If we do it by the book like you want, it's going to cost a lot more."

"I'm ready for that."

"And it's going to be hard scraping what's left of your friend off the wall."

Now, it ain't for us to judge what she says next. It ain't right thinking or wrong thinking. It was just Raven thinking. What I call that get-along thinking when life has smacked you down so many times that you don't know how to get up.

"It's not going to be hard."

"What makes you think that?"

"Because no part of Oral is on those walls. He's not in some heaven, or even in the graveyard. That's not where the dead are."

"Where do you think they are?"

"In our hearts. The ones we want to keep with us, anyway." Like Jean, Raven thought, her stepmother.

Those words, sure as Monday follows Sunday, came out of her mouth. That fool Speck actually smiled. They walked up the steps ready to put death in a mop bucket like it was an easy thing to do.

But Raven knew that wasn't right. And it's hard to believe that even after all she had just gone through that she could look another human in the eye and lie.

Raven knows that the dead don't waste time setting up quarters in the heart. They like to set up their milk crates and their straight razors and newspaper stories about their killings in your head, so they can keep you company for the rest of your life. And it don't matter if you want them there or not. It's not 'til you join them in death that they'll finally let you alone.

FLAME TREE PRESS
FICTION WITHOUT FRONTIERS
Award-Winning Authors & Original Voices

Flame Tree Press is the trade fiction imprint of Flame Tree Publishing, focusing on excellent writing in horror and the supernatural, crime and mystery, science fiction and fantasy. Our aim is to explore beyond the boundaries of the everyday, with tales from both award-winning authors and original voices.

●

●

Join our mailing list for free short stories, new release details, news about our authors and special promotions:

flametreepress.com